Valentine's Day—a day of chocolates, flowers, and passionate love. Now indulge yourself with three novellas in Arabesque's first Valentine's Day collection. Share with Carla Fredd, Brenda Jackson, and Felicia Mason the pleasures of unexpected romance. . . .

A VALENTINE KISS

A Valentine Kiss

Carla Fredd
Brenda Jackson
Felicia Mason

BET Publications, LLC
http://www.bet.com
http://www.arabesquebooks.com

ARABESQUE BOOKS are published by

BET Publications, LLC
c/o BET BOOKS
One BET Plaza
1900 W Place NE
Washington, DC 20018-1211

Copyright © 2005 by BET Publications, LLC
"Matchmaker" copyright © 1996 by Carla Fredd
"Cupid's Bow" copyright © 1996 by Brenda Streater Jackson
"Made in Heaven" copyright © 1996 by Felicia Mason

All Kensington Titles, Imprints, and Distributed Lines are available at special quantity discounts for bulk purchases for sales promotions, premiums, fund-raising, and educational or institutional use. Special book excerpts or customized printings can also be created to fit specific needs. For details, write or phone the office of the Kensington special sales manager: Kensington Publishing Corp., 850 Third Avenue, New York, NY 10022, attn: Special Sales Department, Phone: 1-800-221-2647.

ISBN: 1-58314-469-2

First Mass-Market Printing: February 1996
First Hardcover Printing: January 2005

10 9 8 7 6 5 4 3 2 1

Printed in the United States of America

Contents

Matchmaker

Carla Fredd

Prologue

Summer 1995

"We don't want to scare them off, Lula." Marie Rodgers gave her best friend and new neighbor a glass of lemonade before sitting in a rocking chair. A hot summer breeze carrying the sweet smell of magnolias wafted across the front porch of her century-old house, the place they'd chosen to meet and plot.

"If we're going to get our grandchildren to marry, we have to make it seem like it was their idea," Marie continued, draping her tie-dyed cotton sundress across her legs.

"You're right," Lula Valentio agreed. "If my grandson thought I was interfering with his life, well, more than usual, he'd have a fit. I just want Justin to have the same kind of love that Ruddy and I shared. When I mention marriage, he says 'Been there. Done that.' " She rolled her eyes. "Justin can be so stubborn at times." Lula placed her glass on the wicker table next to her and picked up her favorite paper fan.

"Camille is no pushover either," Marie said with a bit of pride. "But she's just what Justin needs."

"And Justin is just what Camille needs," Lula added.

They rocked in silence, each lost in their separate dreams of seeing their grandchildren happily married. Lula giggled like a schoolgirl, breaking the silence.

"What's so funny?" Marie asked.

"Sparks are going to fly when they get together," Lula said.

"Hopefully there'll be enough sparks to give us *lots* of beautiful great-grandchildren. Goodness knows we've waited long enough," Marie replied with a hint of aggravation in her voice.

"Amen to that, sister," Lula said with conviction, then frowned. "How are we going to get Camille to Wainswright for any length of time? We both know Justin isn't going anywhere near Atlanta."

Marie sat up straight in her chair, staring at her friend in surprise. "Lula Valentio, are you getting old on me? When have we let a little thing like distance stop us?"

"Old! Who are you calling old." She waved her fan at Marie. "At least I haven't reached eighty."

"If you live to see tomorrow, you'll be eighty just like me." Marie rocked silently in her chair, then gave her friend a mischievous smile. "Don't worry about Camille. She'll be here before you know it."

"I know that look, Marie. What are you up to now?"

"Just a little matchmaking."

One

Winter 1996

"Oh, I feel good," Camille Johnson sang at the top of her lungs, ignoring the fact that she couldn't carry a note. Her voice and the gritty sound of the Godfather of Soul filled the interior of her brand-new convertible. Good was exactly how she felt. Last week she'd helped her little brother pack and move from Atlanta to Huntsville, Alabama, to start a new life, living on his own.

She was both happy and sad to see him go. Happy because he was excited to start his first real job as an engineer and sad because she would miss him. When their mother died in a car accident twelve years before, Camille became more than his big sister. At twenty, she became his substitute mother and full-time provider. Eric had never known what it was like to have a mother and a father. Their father was killed in the Vietnam War a few months after Eric was born. Keeping the family together became Camille's number-one priority even if it meant placing her dreams on hold to keep some semblance of family for her then-nine-year-old brother.

Now, at the age of thirty-two, she was about to start a new phase of her life, living alone as well.

" 'So good,' " she sang as she zipped along the highway, " 'I've got you.' " Her voice trailed off when she realized she'd zoomed past a police car parked in a small clearing in the dense pine forest that lined either side of the road.

"Oh, no," Camille wailed a few seconds later when she spotted flashing blue lights in her rearview mirror. She didn't need to look at the speedometer to know that she was traveling well beyond the fifty-five-mile-per-hour speed limit.

She had traveled down this lonely stretch of highway to her grandmother's home hundreds of times without ever seeing signs of the police. Now, the very day that she'd traded in her old, practical station wagon for a brand-new sports convertible, she'd speeded past the police.

Easing her car to a stop on the side of the road, she wondered if this was a sign of things to come. Maybe I'm kidding myself, she thought. Maybe I can't be the carefree, live-for-the-day person I once was. Memories of the years when the heavy weight of raising her younger brother rested solely on her shoulders raced through her mind. She brushed aside the doubts. She wasn't about to let anything—including her own doubts—stand in her way.

"I've waited a long time for this," she said with determination. "One little speeding ticket isn't going to stop me from fulfilling my dreams."

So much for dreams, she thought as she glanced in the rearview mirror once more as she waited for the police. For years she'd imagined herself racing down a long, winding road in a sporty new black convertible. She'd wear dark sunglasses to protect her eyes from the hot summer sun and a long red silk scarf tied glamorously around her head, its ends flowing behind her in a sensuous rhythm. But most of all she wouldn't have a care in the world. No pressure, no worries, no responsibilities—just the utter freedom to travel.

Reality brought her fantasy to an abrupt end. The highway wasn't a long, winding road. It was January instead of summer, and the only thing flowing was the air from the heater. However, she *did* have a brand-new black convertible. She was racing down the highway, and, more important, for the first time in twelve years she was free to travel anywhere without heavy responsibilities and worries. Her fantasy did *not* include the police.

She waited with a growing sense of dread as the police car came to a stop behind her. The man who stepped out of the car seemed as tall as the pine trees that lined the South Georgia highway, and he looked big enough to lift her car with her inside without straining himself. The heavy dark brown jacket emphasized his broad shoulders. He walked with a slow, easy stride. Confidence was in every step he took. He carried a pad that she was sure contained a speeding ticket with her name on it.

She rolled down her window. Immediately, the cold winter wind stung her cheeks. A chill settled inside her once-toasty car.

"What's your hurry, ma'am?" he asked when he reached her side. His strong, deep voice was as intimidating as his size.

Camille pursed her lips and looked at her reflection in the mirror lenses of the policeman's sunglasses.

"I'm s-sorry, Officer," she stuttered. "I didn't realize I was going above the speed limit."

The policeman stood silently beside her car for a moment. "Ma'am, I clocked you at ninety-five miles per hour in a fifty-five-mile-per-hour zone."

"Ninety-five," she gasped. "I couldn't have been going that fast."

"You're the only car on the road," he said without a hint of emotion. "May I see your license and registration please."

"Does this mean I'm gonna get a ticket," she asked, hoping he would give her a warning instead.

"Yes, ma'am."

"I was afraid you were gonna say that." With a sigh she reached across the seat to pick up her new designer purse that she'd purchased that morning. She pulled out her wallet, which was also new, and searched for her driver's license. She found her credit cards, library card, and voter registration card, but no driver's license.

She smiled tentatively at the waiting policeman. "I know it's in here," she said as she looked through her wallet again. Out of the corner of her eye she saw him cross his arms across his chest. A few moments later she stared in disbelief at the empty wallet. I'm going to go to jail, she thought with growing dismay. She'd taken everything out of her wallet and her driver's license wasn't there. "I can't find my driver's license," she mumbled, and slowly turned to face the policeman.

While she'd been looking in her wallet, he had removed his aviator-style sunglasses. For the first time, she got a full, unobstructed view of his face. She nearly forgot about the ticket and the possibility of going to jail, because she was looking at the most gorgeous man she'd ever seen in her life.

His wavy, ink-black hair was closely cut in a no-nonsense style. His brown bedroom eyes held secrets that she couldn't begin to comprehend. Smooth, velvety medium brown skin stretched over his high cheekbones and firm, square jaw. A neatly trimmed mustache framed full, chiseled lips, lips that were now moving.

Camille felt as if she'd been blindsided. She'd never reacted this way to anyone, not even to Darryl, and she had loved him.

"Ma'am. Ma'am."

"Yes," she said weakly, still dazed at the sight of him.

He unfolded his arms and began writing on the pad. "Is this your car?" There was a hint of impatience in his tone.

"Ye—" She cleared her throat. "Yes," she said firmly. "I bought it this morning."

"May I see your registration?"

Get a grip, she told herself. Camille could tell from his tone of voice that he didn't believe she had the registration. She leaned over, opening the glove compartment, then removed a stack of papers before returning to the upright position in the driver's seat.

"Here it is," she said, her voice full of relief.

She took a quick breath in surprise as she unfolded the registration papers and her driver's license and insurance card fell in her lap. "Here's my license and registration," she said, offering him both items.

She studied the giant of a man while he wrote on the pad. No man could be this good-looking, she thought while she searched his face to find anything to distract her from his devastating attractiveness. She didn't find a thing.

Her study of him came to an abrupt end when he held the pad out to her.

"Please sign by the X."

Her hand brushed against his, sending heat from her fingertips throughout her being. Instinctively, she jerked her hand away, sending the pad and pen to the ground.

"Oh, I'm sorry," she said, hoping that her face wasn't as red as it felt.

He reached down and picked up the pad and pen. "Why don't I hold it steady for you," he said, holding out the pen.

She signed the ticket and returned the pen to him. She listened as he explained the options: pay the fine or go to court. "You can go to the Howard County Sheriff's Department if you choose to pay the fine." He tore off the top copy of the ticket and gave it to her.

Camille took the ticket.

"Drive safely, ma'am."

Glancing at him, she said, "I will," before rolling up her window. She shifted her car into drive and entered the highway.

∼

Sheriff Justin Valentio watched the black sports car as it entered the road traveling at a much slower speed.

That is a *confused* woman, he muttered as he walked back to his patrol car. Beautiful but confused, he thought, remembering the curly, shoulder-length reddish-brown hair that framed her heart-shaped face. Deep brown eyes, café au lait skin, and full, kissable lips.

Kissable?

Where did that come from? Ms. Camille Johnson was from Atlanta, her license had said, and she had city girl written all over her. He and city girls didn't mix, and he had the divorce papers to prove it. Put her out of your mind, you'll never see her again, he thought. Besides, the woman had stared at him as if he were a piece of meat. In his younger days he would have been flattered by the attraction he'd seen in her eyes, but now, at the age of thirty-five, he wanted a woman who knew that there was more to him than his looks.

He was still thinking about Ms. Johnson when he entered the Wainswright City Hall. The three-story brick building housed the mayor's office, the jail, and the Sheriff's Department. Karl Valentio, his deputy and cousin, glanced up from the computer and gave him a brief nod when he walked in.

"Justin." Betty Gilmore, his clerk-cum-secretary-cum-gofer, waved him over to her desk before he could reach his office. At sixty-two, Betty looked like Mrs. Santa Claus, from her pure white hair, which was tied in a bun, to the small round glasses that were perched on her nose.

"Lula called three times looking for you," she said cheerfully.

"Did Grandma say what she wanted?" Justin hung his jacket on the coatrack.

"Justin," she admonished him, placing her hands on her hips. "You know I just write down the information. I try to stay out of other folks' business."

He fought to keep a straight face. Next to his grandmother, Betty was the biggest gossip in Wainswright.

"Is that why you kept asking her if she was *sure* she didn't want to leave a message," Karl drawled without ever looking up from the computer screen.

Justin smiled when Betty glared at Karl, her eyes narrowed with irritation.

"Were there any other messages, Betty?" he asked before she could respond, before the bantering between her and Karl could begin.

"Yes, there was," she said in a slow, syrupy voice. "Mrs. Jenkins wants you to come over and meet her granddaughter."

"Great," he said, his tone sarcastic.

"Hey," Karl interjected, "at least she's honest about trying to set you up with her granddaughter. You could have gone out to her house on a report of a suspicious person, only to find out that she was mistaken, and, oh, by the way, she wants you to meet her granddaughter."

"Thanks for the insight, Karl."

"Anytime I can be of help, just let me know."

"Do you want me to call Mrs. Jenkins to set up a meeting?" Betty smiled at him innocently, but her eyes were filled with mischief.

"No, Betty."

"Just trying to help," she replied.

Justin shook his head and went into his office. He was going to have to do something soon. First his grandmother had tried her hand at matchmaking. He'd quickly put an end to that—by asking her to stop, and when that didn't work, he refused to go to her house. Now it seemed that the women of Wainswright were taking up where his grandmother left off. Mrs. Jenkins was the fourth person that week who wanted him to meet a female member of the family. He didn't know what had started this ground swell of matchmaking, but he was about to put it to a stop.

Despite the current belief of certain women in his hometown, he'd not had trouble finding female companionship. Discretion was a must if privacy was to be maintained in Wainswright. He and the few women he'd dated in the past valued their privacy. He wasn't dating anyone now, and should he choose to ask a woman out, it would be because *he* wanted to, not because of well-meaning matchmaking relatives.

Justin walked to his desk, dropping the ticket pad on the wooden surface. A picture of the woman he'd pulled over for speeding flashed through his mind. He could clearly visualize her creamy brown face, her warm brown eyes and full lips. An unwelcome wave of desire flowed throughout his body.

"City girl," he muttered to himself, as if to deny his attraction to her. His mother and later his ex-wife had taught him that city girls didn't stay with country boys like him.

Two

Camille felt dazed as she continued her journey to her grandmother's home. Never had she responded to a man like she had today. She couldn't believe the man was *that* handsome and the sight of him had sent her heart pounding.

"I can't believe I stared at the man like an idiot," she muttered in disgust, tightening her grip on the steering wheel. Just remembering her actions caused heat to rush to her face.

"I hope I never see him again." But even as the thought crossed her mind, she knew it was a lie, because just the idea of seeing him again sent her heart racing. Determined to put the incident behind her, she turned on the radio and kept a careful eye on the speedometer.

Thirty minutes later she drove past the town square of Wainswright. City Hall, the general store, Joe's Gas Station, and Flack's Theater anchored the corners of the square with small shops in between. Driving two blocks down the road, she arrived at her grandmother's Victorian home. Before she could get out of the car, the front door opened and Marie Rodgers stepped onto the front porch.

Her grandmother wore the green and red jogging suit that she'd given to her on her birthday, along with a pristine pair of white running shoes. Her silver-gray hair streaked with caramel brown fanned around her shoulders. Camille felt a wealth of love bubble inside her heart.

With arms spread wide and a smile on her face, her grandmother walked down the stairs. "Come on over here and give your grandma a hug."

Camille stepped out of her car and ran across the yard, closing the distance between them, and embraced one of the most important people in her life. The scent of Chanel No. 5 brought back memories of the days when her mother was still alive and her grandmother would come to Atlanta to visit for the summer.

A cold blast of air swirled around them. Shivering, Camille stepped back and looked into the face of her grandmother, which was so much like her own.

"Let's get out of the cold," Camille said.

They walked to her car and made quick work of removing her bags.

"I like your new car, Camille. It suits you."

"That's because it looks like your old MG," Camille teased as they walked to the house.

The sweet smell of lilacs greeted Camille when she entered the house. Although she'd driven her brother there every summer, her job and college classes made it impossible for her to stay. Today was the beginning of a long-overdue visit.

"Do you want to stay in the guest bedroom or your old room?" Marie asked as she walked toward the stairs.

"My room," Camille said. "Shouldn't we lock the door first?"

"You're not in Atlanta anymore. But if it would make you feel better, go ahead and lock it."

Camille fastened the deadbolt and followed her grandmother upstairs. Her room was the back bedroom that she'd used every summer until she'd entered college.

It was a large bedroom, almost the width of the house, with odd nooks. The thing she liked most about the room was the private deck. As a teenager, she'd spent many summer nights on the deck, gazing at the stars and dreaming of France, England, and Germany, the countries that her grandmother had seen while stationed as a nurse in Europe during World War II. Camille had planned to travel to those countries and more, but her plans came to an end when her mother died.

"Let's look at you," her grandmother said after placing Camille's overnight bag on the feather bed.

Camille put one hand behind her head and the other on her hip, turning left, right, then left again in a pose reminiscent of movie stars of the 1940s.

"What do you zink, dahling," Camille asked with a mock French accent. They had played this game for as long as she could remember.

"Beautiful, of course," Marie replied, kissing the tips of her fingers. All traces of amusement faded from her expression. "I've missed you, child."

Camille relaxed her pose and closed the distance between them. She embraced her grandmother, then said with sincerity, "I've missed you too, Grandma."

They held each other tightly until the grandfather clock down the hall chimed the half hour.

Easing out of the embrace, her grandmother said, "Well, dinner isn't going to make itself. Let's go to the kitchen. You can make the corn bread."

The kitchen was just as she remembered. An old iron stove sat in the corner of the room. Blue and white gingham curtains dressed a large window above the white porcelain sink. A large, worn wooden island sat in the middle of the room, and to the right was the pantry that as a child she'd spent many hours exploring.

"This is just like old times, Grandma," Camille said as she measured and poured cornmeal in a large bowl.

Looking into the bowl, Marie said, "You better add about twice that amount."

"Why? We're not going to eat that much corn bread, are we?"

Marie gave her a puzzled look, then smiled in chagrin. "Oh, goodness, I forgot to tell you that Lula and her young grandson are coming over for dinner. I hope you don't mind them coming over the first night you're here, but I'd already invited them before I knew you were coming and I want you to see Lula again."

"That's all right." Camille poured more meal into the bowl. "I'd like to see Miss Lula again. Does she still wear those big hats to church?"

"Oh, you ought to see the new one she ordered. It looks like a black and white feather duster."

Camille walked to the pantry and removed two large cast iron skillets. "You didn't tell her that, did you?"

"Of course I did." She gave Camille a stern look. "She's been my friend for seventy years. If I can't tell her that her hat looks like a feather duster, then who can?"

"But . . ."

"I'm eighty years old. I can say what I darn well please."

"Yes, ma'am," she said, trying to hide her smile.

"Are you laughing at me, young lady?"

"No, Grandma."

Marie poured string beans into a casserole dish and placed it in the oven, then said, "Hmmm. Eric called me today."

"Oh," Camille said, surprised that her brother called.

"He didn't talk long. I think he's a little lonely," Marie said.

"I told him that he could stay with me until he found a job in Atlanta."

"You couldn't have stopped him from leaving. Eric's a grown man now. It's time for him to be on his own."

"I didn't try to stop him from leaving. I just feel like he moved out because he thinks I wanted him to leave."

"Of course you did," Marie said calmly.

"I didn't—" Camille denied.

Marie held up her hand, interrupting Camille. "I'm not saying that you wanted him out on the street, but deep down inside you wanted to have your own life. Parents have been facing this tug-of-war since the beginning of time. Be honest with yourself—aren't you happier now that you have just yourself to look after?"

Camille turned away, feeling a twinge of guilt. Was her grandmother right? Sure she felt a certain amount of freedom now that her brother had moved, but had she wanted him to leave?

She felt her grandmother's hand on her shoulder. "Don't beat yourself up about it. Eric wanted to leave. Now is the time for you to enjoy yourself. So, tell me, do you have a boyfriend yet?"

"Grandma!"

"Well, do you?"

"No. I don't have a boyfriend. I don't have time for a relationship now. I want to be responsible for me alone for a while."

"Who says that you can't do that and have a boyfriend?"

"Nobody, Grandma. I just want to enjoy living alone for a while."

"Okay, but it can get awfully lonely being by yourself."

"I won't be lonely. I've got too much I want to do. Like plan my trip to Paris," she said excitedly before launching into details about her travel plans.

∼

His grandmother was up to something, Justin thought. The mischievous gleam in her eye was a dead giveaway. Now all Justin had to do was figure out what it was. Cupping her elbow through the heavy wool coat, they walked side by side from her house to Mrs. Rodgers's house next door. Their breaths made puffs of smoke in the still, cold winter air. Getting information out of his grandmother had been nearly impossible in the past. Tonight was no exception.

"When did you decide to have dinner with Mrs. Rodgers?" he asked while adjusting his stride to match hers.

"For the last time, child," she said, coming to a stop in the middle of the sidewalk. "I told you she invited us to dinner last week. I just forgot to tell you."

"Hmmm."

"I'm eighty years old," she said, adjusting her pillbox hat. "I don't remember things like I used to."

"Only the things you want to remember," he muttered as they started walking again.

"What was that?" She gave him a sharp look.

"Nothing. Here, watch your step," he said when they reached the stairs leading to Mrs. Rodgers's brightly lit front porch.

"Are my feathers straight?" she asked when they reached the front door.

Justin studied her hat, its three long feathers pointed in three different directions. He wondered how anyone would know if her hat was on straight or not.

"It looks straight to me," he said, then rang the bell and waited.

"Lula?" The distinctive, husky voice of Mrs. Rodgers was muffled briefly by a thick maple door before it was thrown open.

"What are you doing ringing the bell?" she asked, giving them a puzzled look. "Why didn't you come on in?"

"Mrs. Rodgers," he said as he entered the foyer. "You should keep your doors locked."

"I've been living in this house for fifty years and I've never locked the door. Why should I start now? Here, let me take your coats." She paused and looked at Lula's hat, then said, "Nice hat, Lula."

Justin opened his mouth to speak, but the words died on his lips when he saw her. Camille Johnson. He remembered her name, her face, her kissable lips.

He didn't know what surprised him more, the fact that she was there or his reaction to seeing her again.

What was she doing here?

She'd changed out of the shapeless black clothing she'd worn that afternoon into an extremely short, form-fitting green dress that hugged her body like a glove.

A flicker of surprise, then recognition, flashed in her warm brown eyes.

"Lula, Justin." Mrs. Rodgers interrupted his lustful thoughts. "I'd like you to meet my granddaughter, Camille."

Her granddaughter. Justin looked from grandmother to granddaughter and wondered why he hadn't noticed the resemblance. Camille was the image of Mrs. Rodgers, only younger. The feelings he had for Mrs. Rodgers were of respect and love, grandmotherly feelings. He felt anything but grandmotherly toward Camille.

"Camille," Mrs. Rodgers continued her introductions. "You remember Mrs. Valentio, don't you? This is her grandson, Justin Valentio."

Justin took two short steps across the foyer, then held out his hand. "Nice to meet you," he said, his voice slightly huskier than usual.

She stared at him as if she were in a daze, and the silence stretched between them. Just as he was about to lower his hand, she jumped as if startled.

"Mr. Valentio," she said breathlessly, and gave him a quick handshake. Her hand felt soft, warm, and pampered in his grasp. The hands of a pampered city woman.

"Oh, call him Justin. We don't stand on ceremony here," Lula said with a wave of her hand.

"Justin," she said his name softly, not quite able to meet his gaze.

One thing he'd learned as a police officer was body language, and her body screamed nervousness. From her inability to make eye contact with him to the stiff way she held her shoulders, she acted uneasy and unsure of herself. As if she were trying to hide something. Uneasy people made him suspicious. He'd have to keep an eye on Camille.

"Come on back to the dining room while Camille and I put supper on the table," Mrs. Rodgers said.

Justin followed the women into the dining room that was as familiar as his own, with its twelve-foot ceiling, whitewashed plaster walls, and four huge windows.

"Do you need help?" he offered.

"No. Make yourself at home," Mrs. Rodgers said when they reached the dining room.

Justin saw the knowing look that his grandmother and Mrs. Rodgers shared. At that instant he knew exactly what his grandmother was up to . . . and he didn't like it. His grandmother was trying to set him up with Camille. Shock, then frustration, flowed through him as he helped her to her chair. He barely noticed when Camille and Mrs. Rodgers went into the kitchen.

It was one thing for a few of the older ladies in town to try their hands at matchmaking, Justin thought while clenching his jaw, but it was a whole other thing for his own grandmother to do it—*again*. He was going to put a stop to her plan now.

"Thank you, dear," she said as she settled in the chair. "You're such a good grandson."

Justin met her wide-eyed gaze. His eyes narrowed in suspicion at her innocent smile. Before he could speak to her, Camille walked into the room carrying a platter of carved roast beef and new potatoes.

He wondered if she was aware of their grandmothers' plans, and his eyes narrowed even more.

Then, as if she could read his thoughts, Camille looked at him. Her brown eyes widened like a doe caught in headlights. The platter banged loudly as she dropped it on the table. Dark brown gravy splattered on the crisp white tablecloth, and a lone new potato broke free of the platter and rolled across the table before coming to a stop at the edge of his plate.

Justin picked up the potato, placed it on his plate, and said, "This one must be mine."

"I'm s-so s-sorry," Camille said, trying to soak up the gravy with a napkin.

"Accidents happen," his grandmother said calmly, "no harm done but a little spill of gravy."

Justin could almost feel Camille's embarrassment. Her cheeks were red with heat and her hands shook slightly as she tried to wipe up the gravy. She didn't act as if she were in cahoots with his grandmother. Mrs. Jenkins's granddaughter hadn't bothered to hide her interest in him when he arrived to check out her grandmother's call about a prowler. On the other hand, Camille seemed as surprised to see him as he was to see her. She looked innocent, but he knew from experience that looks can be deceiving.

"What was that noise?" Mrs. Rodgers asked as she walked into the room holding a casserole dish.

"The platter," Justin said.

Mrs. Rodgers looked from the platter to her granddaughter's flushed cheeks. "Camille, why don't you bring in the string beans?"

Justin watched Camille gather up the soiled napkins and hurry out of the room. He was surprised by her reaction.

His ex-wife, Janet, would have had a tantrum. As the only child of wealthy parents, Janet was accustomed to having things her way. Mistakes, Janet felt, were things that other people made. If she had dropped the platter of food, she would have found a way to make someone else responsible for it.

He remembered one incident in particular when they'd taken one of her clients and his wife to dinner. Janet knocked over her water glass. Instead of muddling through the embarrassing moment, she'd found someone else to blame. She berated the waiter, insisting that he'd placed the glass too close to her plate, rather than admit that she'd made a mistake.

He'd been embarrassed by her handling of the incident, and he could tell that her client was also embarrassed. A few days later she told him that her client had requested another lawyer. He wasn't surprised.

Camille surprised him. He didn't like surprises.

Three

Why is it that I act like an airhead around that man? Camille wondered, leaning against the kitchen counter. She was acting worse than a teenager. A teenager had hormones as an excuse for acting weird. She didn't have an excuse.

When her grandmother said Mrs. Valentio was bringing her young grandson to dinner, she'd envisioned a schoolboy. Justin Valentio wasn't a schoolboy. He was a man in every sense of the word.

If she didn't know better, she would have thought her grandmother had deliberately deceived her. Shaking her head, Camille brushed the thought aside. Her grandmother was too up front and blunt with her opinions to do that.

Camille looked at the glass dish that was warming on the stove. It was the last dish to be served, and everyone was waiting for her to bring it into the dining room. She was tempted, really tempted, to stay in the kitchen and hide. But hiding went against her nature. Pushing herself away from the counter, she walked to the stove and removed the remaining casserole dish.

With her shoulders pushed back and her chin up, she walked toward the dining room. Nothing is going to keep me from enjoying this visit with my grandmother, Camille told herself. Not even the most handsome man she'd ever seen.

Her bravery lasted long enough for her to place the dish on the table without dropping it, and until she realized that her grandmother was sitting next to Lula. The only available chair was next to Justin. With a show of confidence that she didn't feel, Camille sat in the chair.

"Justin, would you say the grace," her grandmother asked.

Camille bowed her head.

"Thank you, Lord, for this food." His voice was strong and deep, provoking feelings within her that shouldn't happen while listening to grace. "Bless the hands that prepared it. In Jesus's name. Amen."

"Amen," she whispered.

Silence filled the room as they piled food on their plates.

"Camille," Mrs. Valentio said with a pleasant smile. "How long will you be in town?"

"I'll be here for three weeks, Mrs. Valentio."

"Call me Miss Lula. You used to call me that when you were a little girl. All the young kids call me that."

Camille smiled. It had been a while since anyone had called her a young kid.

"That's an awfully long vacation," Justin said softly. "Most out-of-towners get bored within a week."

Although his tone was cordial, Camille sensed that his words held a deeper meaning. Before she could form a reply, his grandmother intervened.

"Sugar, Camille isn't an out-of-towner," Miss Lula said. "She was born in this very house. When her parents moved to Atlanta, she would stay here in the summer."

Camille glanced from Miss Lula to Justin. Instantly, her mouth went dry as he subjected her to the full brunt of his gaze. She felt as if his hot brown glance had ignited a fire within her and its intense heat had sent her emotions reeling.

"My mistake," he said before returning his attention to his meal and releasing her from his spell.

With a silent sigh Camille took a sip of water, hoping to douse the flame of desire he had so carelessly kindled.

"I don't think I'll be bored after a week," Camille said when she'd regained her composure. "It's been a long time since I spent more than a couple of hours with Grandma. I've got a lot of time to make up before I travel to Paris." She smiled despite Justin's cynical smile.

"Justin lived in Atlanta. He was an Atlanta policeman for a while," her grandmother said when no one else at the table spoke.

Glancing briefly in his direction without really looking at him, a skill she'd developed from attending numerous staff meetings, she asked, "Oh, really, where did you live?"

"Buckhead."

"I love Buckhead," she said, surprised by his answer. "It's got great restaurants and shops. You can always count on something going on there."

"I didn't like Buckhead," he said.

"Oh." Lord, the man was prickly, she thought as silence reigned around the dinner table once more. For such a handsome man, Justin Valentio was distant and aloof. Seeing the concerned look that passed between her grandmother and Miss Lula, Camille broke the silence.

"Did I tell you that I have a new job, Grandma?"

"No, dear, you didn't. What are you doing now?" she asked.

"I'm a senior programming analyst. That means I make sure that the customized software for the company actually works."

"That's wonderful, Camille," Marie said.

"Congratulations," Miss Lula added, then said, "Justin was elected sheriff this year."

"Congratulations," Camille said.

"The Sheriff's Department has new uniforms this year. Justin looks so handsome in his. You should see him," Miss Lula said.

"I have," Camille replied.

"You two have met before?" Marie asked, puzzled. "Where?"

"On the highway. He gave me a ticket."

"Justin! You gave her a ticket? How could you do that?" Miss Lula gasped.

"She was speeding, Granny," Justin said defensively.

"Since you gave her the ticket, you can take it back," Miss Lula declared.

"I can't just take back a ticket."

"Of course you can," Miss Lula insisted.

"Since Wainswright is so small," Camille interrupted. "Maybe the Sheriff's Department doesn't have the equipment or expertise like a city the size of Atlanta does to do that kind of thing, Miss Lula."

Justin lay down his fork and glared at Camille. "Small doesn't mean ignorant, Camille. I could have your ticket removed from the records, but you broke the law, you got a ticket."

"I never said I didn't deserve the ticket," she said, surprised at the anger in his voice. "I didn't ask you to remove it from the records and I didn't say anyone was ignorant. I was only trying to be helpful."

"I don't need your help. I can explain the situation in great detail to my grandmother."

Heat rushed to her face as irritation swelled within her. This would be the last time she'd lift a finger to help him.

"Obviously, I've offended you, Sheriff. I apologize, and it won't happen again," she said. As a matter of fact, if I see you coming my way, I'll be sure to go in the opposite direction, she vowed silently.

The man was pricklier than a cactus. Camille made up her mind then and there to stay out of Sheriff Justin Valentio's way.

~

Marie waited until she was sure that Camille was settled for the night, before she made one telephone call.

Lula answered the phone on the first ring.

"Marie?"

"Of course it's Marie. Who else would call you at this time of night?"

"Well, dinner went over like a ton of bricks," Lula said, twisting the telephone cord around her finger.

"I know. We're going to have to be more aggressive," Marie replied.

"Aggressive. I like aggressive."

"You always did."

"I wasn't the one to run off and join the *navy* during the war."

"You're still mad about that, aren't you? It's been over fifty years since I joined the *army*. Get over it."

"Hmmm. I thought friends shared things."

"I do share things with you, Lula. We're going to share great-grandchildren if we can get Camille and Justin together."

"I've got an idea."

"Good, what is it?"

The two friends plotted the downfall of their respective grandchildren.

~

Justin turned his truck onto the gravel path that led to his house. When managing the farm had become too much for their grandmother to handle, he and Karl bought the fifteen-acre family farm, the Valentio Estate as the family fondly referred to it, from her. Making repairs on her new home delayed her move to town for months, but Justin wasted no time having his home built on his part of the farm.

As he drove down the bumpy road, he could see the light from Karl's house across the field. Karl had moved into his grandmother's old home about a month earlier. Neither he nor Karl were interested in farming, so they decided to lease the land to a local peanut farmer. Rounding the last curve, Justin felt his tension ease when his house came into view.

Although his house was the latest to be built in Wainswright, it was made to blend in structurally with the older homes in town—with a few modifications like cathedral ceilings instead of an attic. With a press of a button the garage door opened and he drove inside. He walked from the kitchen to his bedroom with only the light from the full moon shining through the skylights, something he wouldn't have done when he lived in Atlanta.

He wasn't obsessed with the past and the old ways of doing things as his ex had accused him. Computers, cellular phones, and fax machines were a part of his everyday life. He simply didn't believe in dumping the old because it was old. To him that would be like putting his grandmother in a nursing home because she was eighty.

Wainswright was old. Its people held on to an old-fashioned way of life. Neighbors helped neighbors, everyone knew everyone. Their way of life was nearly extinct in America today.

And he liked it the way it was.

When he'd lived in Atlanta, there was too much noise and the people moved too fast. He met people who thought because he came from a small town he was slow and backwoodsy. That's why he'd gotten so angry when Camille had made an off-the-cuff remark about his town.

He knew he'd acted like a jerk during dinner. His grandmother gave him a piece of her mind when he'd escorted her home. His grandmother was right, he'd treated Camille unfairly. But she'd struck a nerve with her comment about his "small" hometown. He had heard enough criticism about small towns to last him a lifetime.

Camille's remark wasn't the only reason he'd acted like a jerk. The sexual attraction he felt for her was strong. Stronger than the attraction he'd felt when he'd met his ex-wife for the first time. He didn't want to be attracted to Camille, yet he was, and very much so.

He had to stay away from her. It wasn't going to be easy with her living next door to his grandmother, but he was going to do it. The last thing he needed was another woman from the city in his life.

Huffing and puffing, Camille jogged down the street leading to her grandmother's house. For the past three days she'd risen at the crack of dawn and run for five miles.

Running hadn't gotten easier, as friends had told her it would. She felt just as tired now as she did when she began running a few years before. Running was the cheapest way to stay in shape, and she couldn't afford to join a club at the time.

I really need to run ten miles after all the food I've eaten, she thought.

Her grandmother made the best cream cheese pound cake. She watched her grandmother add butter, cream cheese, and six whole eggs to the cake mixture. She didn't want to *think* of the number of calories that she consumed with each bite.

The time she spent running also helped clear the erotic images left over from the dreams she'd been having lately. In her dreams Justin Valentio appeared in various roles. He appeared dressed in the flowing white robes of a sheikh, in the tight blue jeans of a cowboy, but the one role that made her take a cold shower in the middle of the night was one where he appeared wearing only a plain gold wedding band. A wedding band that matched the ring on her finger.

Dr. Ruth would have a field day analyzing my dreams, she thought. It just didn't make sense. Why was she dreaming of a man that she didn't particularly like and hadn't seen for three days?

Sure he was handsome. Okay, he was the finest brother she'd ever seen in her life, she admitted. But she wasn't so immature that his looks compensated for his rude behavior, was she? No, of course not, she told herself. All she had to do was continue to stay away from him and the dreams would come to an end. She hoped.

With smooth, continuous strides, she ran the last few yards to her grandmother's home.

As she began her cool-down stretches, she noticed a piece of paper attached to the front door.

"Somebody probably left a note for Grandma," she said. Completing a series of stretches, she went to the front door. A white sheet of paper, folded in half, with her name written on the front of it, was taped to the door. She recognized her grandmother's handwriting immediately. Removing the note, she began to read:

Camille, I have gone to visit a sick friend. I should be back before lunch. Just so you'd feel better, I locked the front and back doors. Love, Grandma.

Camille read the note again.

"But I don't have the key with me, Grandma." She moaned into the cool silence of the morning. Not only had her grandmother not said a thing about going out when she saw her that morning, but for the first time ever she'd locked her doors.

Shivering as the cold January wind whipped through her sweat suit, she twisted the doorknob, hoping that it would be unlocked. She'd hoped in vain. If it were summer, she would have found the situation funny. There was nothing funny about the chills she felt then.

Maybe the back door was unlocked, she thought. Camille went around the house to the back door. It was locked. She didn't even try to climb up the poles to reach the deck. The French doors that opened onto the deck were definitely locked. She knew because she'd made a point of locking them when she arrived the first night.

What was she going to do? She couldn't stay outside in the cold until her grandmother came back, especially since she was soaking wet from her run. What she needed was a locksmith and a telephone.

She looked at Miss Lula's house. Relieved to see a light shining through the front window, Camille walked over, then knocked on the door.

Miss Lula answered her door on the first ring, sporting a bright purple fedora.

"Camille? What are doing outside without a coat? Come on in here."

"I'm sorry to bother you, Miss Lula, but can I use your telephone? Grandma went to visit a friend, but she locked the doors. Now I can't get inside. I need to call a locksmith."

"She locked her doors? What made her do a thing like that? We hardly ever do that unless we're going out of town."

"It's my fault. I've been after her to keep her doors locked. Today she followed my advice."

"You sound like Justin with all that talk about locks. Wainswright isn't like Atlanta."

"I know, but bad things can happen anywhere."

"Honey, only thing bad that happens here is on Christmas Eve when Mr. Johnson gets drunk and goes caroling at two o'clock in the morning."

"I would still feel better if she kept her doors locked. Speaking of locks, is there a local locksmith around here?"

"Yes, but Sam won't be able to come for another hour. He takes his young'uns to school every day. He's such a good father. I'll leave a message on his answering machine for him to meet you here."

"Thank you."

Miss Lula picked up the telephone, then gestured to the back of the house, "There's coffee in the kitchen if you want some."

Camille entered the kitchen. It could have been her grandmother's kitchen. The same deep porcelain sink and iron stove anchored the room. It had a certain feel that said welcome to anyone who entered. She poured herself a cup of coffee. Even their coffeepots look the same, she thought. Leaning against the counter, she took a sip of coffee.

Miss Lula walked into the kitchen wearing a purple overcoat that matched her hat. "I'm on my way to Macon to do some shopping. I'd stay until Sam gets here, but I don't like driving in all that traffic. If I leave now, I'll miss it."

"You don't mind me staying here?"

"I don't mind. Now, I want you to stay here as long as you need to. Make yourself at home."

"I really appreciate this, Miss Lula."

"My pleasure, Camille," she said, as she put her purse over her shoulder. She paused when she reached the back door. "By the way, if Justin should drop by, tell him that the insulation is in the shed."

"Justin is coming by?"

"He said he was coming over this afternoon, but sometimes he comes by earlier. Bye, now."

Camille looked up at the ceiling and prayed. "Please, Lord. Let me be gone before he gets here." The last thing she wanted to do was explain why she was locked out of her grandmother's home.

An hour later she heard the sound of a car engine. Camille hurried to the living room window and opened the curtain. A full-size black pickup truck with tinted windows pulled into Lula's driveway.

"That's got to be Sam," she said, relieved that she would soon be able to take a hot shower.

She opened the front door as the driver stepped out of the truck.

Her prayer had been denied.

Justin Valentio stepped out of the truck.

Four

Justin slammed the door of his truck, reached in the back, and yanked his toolbox out of the cab. With his head down and a purposeful stride, he walked to his grandmother's home.

He'd spent his last hour on duty responding to a suspicious-person call, only to find himself invited for breakfast and being introduced to another single black female. Not that there was anything wrong with single black females. He honestly loved women. But he was tired of the little old ladies of Wainswright reporting fictitious crimes as a way to introduce him to their single relatives.

The problem he had was trying to reprimand women who were at least seventy years old and had no problem reminding him that they'd seen his bare butt covered with diaper rash. His authority as the sheriff had been sorely tested with each call to their homes. After dealing with them, he needed an aspirin, badly. The extra-strength pain reliever he'd taken earlier had barely begun to ease his headache. Hopefully, the physical tasks of laying insulation in his grandmother's ceiling and replacing the lock on the attic door would relieve the rest of the pain.

With Karl on duty, he didn't have to worry about another suspicious-person call. The old ladies of Wainswright were Karl's problem now.

Justin looked up in surprise when he heard the sound of someone opening the front door. He could have sworn that his grandmother said she was driving to Macon that morning.

He stopped in his tracks when Camille stepped outside. She looked touchable and soft in her worn gray sweatpants, plain white T-shirt, and scuffed jogging shoes. Wayward strands of hair framed her face, escaping the confines of her loosely braided pigtail.

Three days of avoiding her hadn't weakened the magnetism between them. He didn't like it.

"What are you doing here?" The words were out of his mouth before he could think. He watched as she straightened her shoulders, as if preparing for battle. Great going, Valentio. Antagonize her right off the bat.

"I'm waiting for the locksmith. Grandma went to visit a friend and locked her doors while I was jogging."

"Mrs. Rodgers locked her doors?" he asked in disbelief.

"Yes, she did. Unfortunately, my keys are inside. Miss Lula called the locksmith before she left to go shopping. She said I could wait here until he came. I thought you were he when you drove up."

Justin glanced at his watch. "He should be here soon."

"Good. I'll get out of your way." She turned and walked inside.

His gaze rested on her graceful form until she entered the house. He didn't expect that she would have been caught dead dressed that way to work out even if she were alone. Yet Camille managed to capture his attention in old gray sweats. Justin tightened his jaw, more determined than ever to ignore his attraction to Camille.

$\sim$

It had been thirty minutes since Justin arrived, and the locksmith was nowhere in sight. Camille nursed a cup of coffee while looking out the living room window. Had something delayed him? she wondered, and wished she'd asked Miss Lula to write down Sam's telephone number.

She'd called the operator to get the number, but there wasn't a locksmith located in Wainswright and she didn't know Sam's last name.

The way she figured it, she had two choices. She could continue to wait in her damp, smelly clothes until Sam showed up, or she could go upstairs and ask Justin to help her. The thought of a long, hot shower had her walking up two flights of stairs to the attic.

Rolls of insulation were stacked on the landing at the top of the stairs. Justin had to make two trips from the storage shed to the attic to bring all the insulation inside.

Madison Avenue couldn't have chosen a more perfect model than Justin in worn blue jeans. Muscles rippled as he strode across the backyard to the shed. His scuffed cowboy boots and buff Stetson created an aura of power and sensuality.

He was dressed almost exactly as she'd pictured him in her dreams with him starring as her cowboy lover.

She couldn't watch him make the second trip.

"The sooner I get this over with, the sooner I can get out of here," she muttered.

Weaving through the rolls of insulation, she reached the door leading to the attic. A ceramic clown leaned against the door, propping it open. His toolbox lay on the floor a few yards away. Through the open door she could see an old couch beneath a bare window. The pale morning sun spread light upon its faded green upholstery. A couple of foot lockers were stacked against the three finished walls, and boxes were scattered on the wooden floor.

Columns of two-by-fours divided the room in half. Layers of pink insulation were nestled among the wood columns. Justin was on his knees, rolling out the insulation. He'd removed his plaid flannel shirt. Dark, curly hair covered him from his broad shoulders down to his washboardlike stomach. Muscles rippled with strength as he worked.

I've *got* to get out of here, she thought.

"Justin," she said, stepping into the attic reluctantly.

He looked up briefly before continuing with his work. "Yeah."

"Sam hasn't shown up yet. I was wondering if you knew his telephone number."

"It's 555-4783."

"Thank you," she said, turning to leave.

"Camille, would you do something for me?"

"What is it?"

"Would you look in my toolbox and bring me the razor blades? Please?"

"Okay."

She retrieved the razor blades from his toolbox. When she reached the attic door, she nearly tripped over the ceramic clown leaning against it. Nudging the figurine aside, she entered the attic.

The door slammed shut when she'd walked halfway across the room.

Justin started violently. He turned in her direction. "What was that?" he demanded.

"Just the door," she replied, taken aback at his tone.

"Aw, hell!" He jumped to his feet and ran to the door.

"Wha-what's wrong?" she asked as he brushed past her.

He twisted and turned the ancient brass door handle for a moment before turning to her.

"We're locked in," he said bluntly.

"We're locked in?" she repeated slowly, as if she couldn't comprehend what he'd said. Her eyes widened in horror when the realization set in. She was locked inside the attic with Justin.

"Oh, no! It can't be locked," she said, joining him at the door. Frantically she twisted the handle, but the door remained stubbornly locked.

"Believe me, it's locked," he said in disgust.

"But—but, I've got to get out of here," she stammered. Her gaze dropped to his bare chest, then quickly moved to his face when he spoke.

"Neither one of us is getting out of here anytime soon. Last week Karl and I were locked in here for hours before Grandma came home from the store. That's why I had the door propped opened with that clown."

"I tripped over the clown when I went to get the razor blades," she gasped. "I moved it out of the way."

He stared at her. His lips parted in surprise.

"I didn't know," she said in her defense as heat rushed to her face.

His surprise gave way to resignation. "I know. I should have warned you about the door when I asked you to get the razor blades."

With that, he walked back to the spot where he'd stopped working, kneeled, then began rolling out the pink insulation.

She stared at him, stunned by his casual disregard of the situation. "Isn't there something we can do?" she asked.

"Yes, we can wait for somebody to come and let us out," he said while continuing to work.

"What about the windows? Can't we climb out one of them?"

"Sure you can climb out a window, but I won't recommend it. We're three stories above the ground, city girl."

Camille opened and closed her mouth several times before finally walking to the faded couch and sitting. With her elbows on her thighs and her forehead resting in her palms, she wondered what she did to deserve this. First her grandmother locks her outside, then she locks herself in the same room with the man who set her pulses racing with a vengeance. Jeez!

"Hey," Justin called.

She lowered an arm and glanced at him. Sunlight cast a golden glow around him, emphasizing his untamed sensuality. She swallowed as a tingling warmth set her pulses racing.

"It's not the end of the world," he said. "Grandma will come home sooner or later and let us out, if Sam doesn't get here first." He gave her an encouraging smile.

She responded with a tentative smile of her own, trying to ignore the accelerated beat of her heart.

"We'll be out of here in no time," he said cheerfully before he started working again.

Lord, I hope so, she thought. Leaning back against the couch, Camille closed her eyes and wondered how long was not long.

Time seemed to crawl by at a snail's pace. Justin had placed the remaining rolls of insulation on the attic floor. Her heart skipped a beat when he put on his shirt and joined her on the couch. Folding his arms, he stretched his long legs out in front of him, crossing them at the ankle.

A slightly tense silence surrounded them. She studied her running shoes, stubbornly refusing to look at him. Minutes later the silence was broken by his low, throaty laughter.

"What's so funny?" she asked.

"I can't believe that we're locked in the attic."

"You think this is funny?"

"Think about it. You get locked out twice in one day and I've got enough tools to take the door off the hinges, but the tools are on the other side of the door. The only reason I brought the tools was to install a new doorknob for *that* door."

Their gazes met, then they burst into laughter, breaking the tension between them.

"Come on," he said. "Let's look in the trunks. I'm sure there's a pack of cards stored away in one of them."

~

"I've got four aces and a king."

Camille groaned when Justin spread his cards on the floor. She tossed her cards aside as he raked the checkers they'd used as markers to his side. Her two checkers looked paltry compared to the stacks he had at his side.

"I think I'll forfeit the last game, Justin."

"You sure?" he asked, raising a single black brow. "There's still a chance for you to win."

"Uh-huh, slim to none."

He smiled at her remark.

She'd grown accustomed but not immune to his smile. In the hour and a half they'd spent playing cards, she'd learned that Justin was a patient man. He'd explained the rules of poker and gin rummy to her more than once, and sometimes reminded her of the rules without any sign of annoyance when she'd made a mistake.

The prickly, impatient man that she'd had dinner with the other night was gone. In his place was a man who made her laugh as he shared amusing anecdotes about his term as sheriff. Even as he revealed the humorous side to his job, his genuine concern for people was apparent in his voice.

When her stomach growled during their card game, he gave her the moon pie he had brought as a snack. Justin was a patient, funny, kind, and sexy man.

She liked him.

"Do you want to play something else?" The sound of his deep voice broke her thoughts.

"No. I'm not good at cards," she said. "And this floor is getting more uncomfortable by the minute."

He rose to his feet, then held out his hand to assist her. With gentle strength he helped her off the floor. She told herself to ignore the warmth that lingered at his touch.

Together they gathered the checkers and the deck of cards and returned them to the trunk. Justin picked up a board game, holding it up for her approval. Within minutes they were sitting on the couch, playing the game.

"Camille," he said as she completed the purchase of her second building on Fifth Avenue.

"Yes," she inquired while counting her money.

"I'm sorry for acting like a jerk at dinner," he said.

She was surprised by his apology. She studied his face. His dark brown eyes brimmed with honesty and sincerity.

Shyly, she looked down at the play money in her hands. "And I apologize for offending you. It wasn't intentional." Then she looked at him.

Their gaze met and held. Tension sprang between them. She recognized the attraction in his eyes. Holding her breath, she watched and waited in anticipation. Abruptly, he turned away. The muscles in his jaw clenched, then slowly relaxed. "Is it my turn?" he asked in a husky voice.

"Yes," she answered breathlessly.

He rolled the dice and moved his game piece around the board.

She was relieved that he'd turned away. Wasn't she? After all, she was there to visit her grandmother, not start something with Justin that would have to end when she went back to her home in a few weeks. But what wonderful weeks they would be!

Brushing the thought aside, she attempted to concentrate on the board game.

Justin Valentio was off limits, she told herself firmly.

Although she was glad that they'd cleared the air, she couldn't help but feel that she was traveling in muddy water where he was concerned.

~

Keep your mind on the game, Justin told himself as he moved his game piece on the board. For a brief moment he'd been tempted to close the distance between them and discover if her lips were as kissable as they looked. But the Atlanta sweatshirt she wore reminded him that she didn't belong in a small town like Wainswright.

"What do you plan to do when we get out of here?" he asked when it was her turn to roll the dice.

"Take a long hot shower, then wash and hang the laundry on the clothesline."

Justin raised a single brow. "Doesn't your grandmother have a dryer?"

"Yes. But she likes to have the clothes dried on the line."

"You're going to hang out the laundry?" he asked in surprise. "Do you know how?"

Camille tilted her head to the side. "I think so. Grandma explained it to me yesterday. It can't be that hard. What are you going to do when we get out of here?"

"Fix that door!"

Her soft laughter filled the room. Justin studied her smiling face for a few seconds before turning his attention back to the game. Camille confused and surprised him. His mother had wanted all the latest appliances. Now, this Atlanta girl really wanted to hang out clothes to dry when a dryer was handy? He needed to know more about this woman, he thought with a frown.

"So how long *were* you locked in the attic with Mrs. Rodgers's grand-daughter?" Karl asked, leaning against the door frame of Justin's office.

Justin shook his head, smiling. He wasn't surprised at Karl's question. However, he was surprised at the speed in which the story had been spread. Less than a day was fast by Wainswright's standards. "Did Grandma call you?"

"No," Karl replied. "I heard about it at the grocery store."

"The news is at Mrs. Neil's already?"

"Don't try to change the subject," Karl said as he pushed himself away from the door and folded his six-foot-eight-inch frame in a chair.

"Why are you so interested?" Justin asked.

"Because I'm nosy. I'm family. I want to know how long you had Mrs. Rodgers's fine granddaughter to yourself."

"I thought you said you hadn't met her yet?" He gave his cousin a suspicious look.

"I haven't, but everybody says she's pretty. Is she?"

An image of Camille in a sweatshirt and sweatpants, sitting on his grand-mother's faded sofa, flashed through his mind. Her red-brown hair pulled back in a careless ponytail, her face totally free of makeup, and her caramel-colored eyes shining in delight when she beat him at the board game they'd played.

"Yes, she's pretty," Justin said.

"Oh." Karl leered at him. "Locked in the attic with a pretty woman. You must have been disappointed when Sam showed up."

"No, we were *both* glad he got there when he did," he said firmly. "Like you and I were glad when Grandma came and got us out of the attic."

"So nothing went on with you two?"

Justin looked down at the report on his desk, unable to hold his cousin's piercing gaze. "She's a big-city girl, Karl. We have nothing in common."

"I don't think that matters. Attraction is attraction." Karl stood, walked to the door, then paused. "You know, you said you had nothing in common with her, not that you weren't attracted to her. Interesting," he said before walking out of the room.

Justin leaned back in his chair and closed his eyes. He should have known that he couldn't fool Karl. They knew each other too well. It'd been Karl who noticed the tension in his marriage, and Karl who was there for him when his divorce became final. But as close as they were, there was no way he was going to admit to Karl that he wanted Camille. He could barely accept it himself.

He didn't want to want her.

His mind knew it, understood it, and remembered his past mistake with his ex-wife.

"No matter how attractive she is," he muttered, "Camille Johnson is off limits."

Five

Camille stepped inside the heated Wainswright courthouse. With its one-hundred-year history, the building had an air of strength and rock steadiness.

It reminded her of Justin.

The guard tipped his hat and said good mornin' when she approached him for directions. Walking up a set of stairs and past the mayor's office, she came to a door with SHERIFF'S DEPARTMENT stenciled on its frosted glass. Pushing the handle, she stepped inside.

The biggest, darkest man she'd ever seen looked up from his computer when she entered. The Sheriff's Department patch was prominently displayed on the shoulder of his dark brown sweater. His shoulders seemed as broad as the desk he was sitting behind. She wouldn't want to be on this man's bad side. Yet his intimidating stature was at odds with the kindness she saw in his eyes.

"May I help you?" he asked with a voice that sounded like distant thunder.

"Yes, I'm here to pay a speeding ticket."

"You must be Mrs. Rodgers's granddaughter. I'm Deputy Sheriff Karl Valentio." He walked around the desk and held out his hand.

Her hand was swallowed in his, and she had to lean her head back to meet his gaze.

Valentio! Did he say Valentio?

"Are you related to Miss Lula?" she asked when he released her hand. She studied his deep brown, unsmiling face. It was a strong face, not nearly as good-looking as Justin's, but few men were as handsome as he.

"Yes. I'm her grandson," he said, walking around the desk to a wall of file cabinets. From his current location she could look him in his eye without straining her neck.

She turned around when the door opened behind her. An older woman wearing a red dress with a white collar stood in the door. She reminded Camille of the pictures she'd seen of Mrs. Santa Claus as a child, right down to the round gold wire-rimmed glasses.

"Camille Johnson. Lord, I haven't seen you since you were a little girl," the woman said with a cheery voice as she rushed to Camille's side. "I've been meaning to stop by to visit. How are you enjoying your stay in Wainswright? How long are you staying? How's your brother? Does he like his new job?"

Which question would she answer first? Camille wondered. And how did the woman ask so many questions without taking a breath?

"Betty, don't you think you should introduce yourself before you start pumping her for information," Karl added from across the room, his voice rumbling with dry amusement.

She waved her hand at him as if to brush him aside. "I'm Betty Gilmore. I taught Sunday school when you were small. You were in my class a few times."

"Nice to see you again, Mrs. Gilmore," Camille said.

"Have a seat," Mrs. Gilmore said, gesturing to one of the available chairs around the second desk, which Camille assumed was hers.

"Thanks, but I can't stay long. I came to pay my ticket before Grandma and I go to Macon."

"How long did you say you were staying?" Betty asked.

Camille was literally saved by the bell when Betty's telephone rang. With a grimace of annoyance, Betty answered the telephone.

Camille released the breath she hadn't realized she was holding. She wasn't accustomed to the frank questions she'd been asked while visiting. The people of Wainswright had no problem asking probing questions. In Atlanta, strangers just didn't walk up to someone, introduce themselves, and ask personal questions. She was still somewhat taken aback when it happened.

"Betty should have been a defense attorney or an investigative reporter. She can ask more questions at one time than anyone I know," Karl said when he'd reached her side.

Camille wrote a check for the speeding ticket and took her license.

"If you're going to be around next week, I'm having a birthday party at my house a week from Saturday. You're invited," Karl said.

Camille shook her head. "I don't want to intrude."

"Everyone in town is invited, so you won't intrude."

She smiled up at him, then said, "In that case, see you at the party."

Karl returned her smile with a smile of his own.

With narrowed eyes Justin watched Karl and Camille from the doorway of his office. He told himself there was no reason for him to feel jealous, but each second he watched them, he wanted to wipe that smile off Karl's face.

"Camille." His voice traveled in the office like a gunshot.

She jumped at the sound. He stood like an avenging angel, his brown eyes shining with anger. What is wrong with him?

"Good morning, Justin," she said.

"Morning," he said in a tight tone of voice. His icy gaze met and held hers for several moments.

"Is there something wrong?" she asked.

"No," he snapped.

With a puzzled frown she put her driver's license into her purse. She turned to Betty, who'd hung up the telephone. "Nice to meet you, Mrs. Gilmore." Turning to Karl, she said, "I'll see you soon."

Justin watched her walk out the door. Frowning, he turned to Karl. His cousin smiled, folded his massive arms across his chest, and asked, "Is there a problem, Justin?"

"No problem." He marched into his office and closed the door.

Karl and Betty shared an amused grin.

$\sim$

Justin definitely had a problem, and she'd just left. Camille was always on his mind. A picture of her would enter his mind at a moment's notice, creating havoc with his mind and body.

It didn't help matters when he saw her everywhere he went. If he went to the gas station, she was there, the same with the hardware store and church. Now his office wasn't immune. He was going to have to do something soon about this crazy attraction to her.

He winced when he remembered how he'd responded when he saw Camille and Karl smiling at each other. Karl was probably laughing at him at that very moment. But he had cared about one thing, it was her smile. If she was going to smile at a man, she should smile at him. Irrational as it was, he wanted her to smile only at him. He wanted her. Period.

He walked to his office window, opened the blinds, and looked down on the street below. He spotted Camille on the sidewalk. Her overcoat couldn't hide the sexy sway of her stride. He watched her until she walked out of sight.

It was time for him to get that city girl out of his system, he thought. Spending time with her should dampen his desire. With the problem solved, Justin returned to his desk. He would ask her out the next time he saw her.

Betty's voice came through the intercom, interrupting his thoughts. "Justin, Mrs. Parker says she saw somebody sneaking around her house. She wants you to come check it out."

Karl's unrestrained laughter filled Justin's office.

∼

I should have mailed in my fine, Camille thought as she walked out of the courthouse. What had made him angry though? The other times she'd seen him, he'd been cordial. And she'd seen Justin everywhere: at the gas station, Wednesday night Bible study, at the cleaner's. Every time she stepped out of the house, he seemed to be there. It wasn't coincidental.

Subtle, her grandmother was not.

Ever since she and Justin had been locked in Miss Lula's attic, her grandmother had been dropping hints as big as an elephant. With comments like "Justin is such a nice young man, and single too" or "Camille, if you want to go out on a date, don't feel that you have to stay home with me" or "Have you talked to Justin lately?" or, worse, "Look, isn't that Justin across the street. Yoo-hoo, Justin . . ."

She would have been amused by her grandmother's not so subtle hints if she weren't so attracted to the man. But his Dr. Jekyll-Mr. Hyde personality was wearing thin. With two weeks left of her vacation, she would make her grandmother understand that Justin was off limits. No more accidental meetings, no more broad hints. She would talk to her grandmother today on the drive to Macon. With that decision made, Camille threw back her shoulders and walked with determination to her grandmother's home.

∼

"Oh, darn," Marie Rodgers exclaimed.

"What is it, Grandma?" Camille asked, placing a sheet of cookies in the oven. They'd been baking since early that morning in preparation for Karl's birthday. She and her grandmother had picked up a gift for him while in Macon two days earlier, but her grandmother had informed her that she'd been bringing cookies and cupcakes to his birthday party for years.

"We're out of vanilla extract and I've got three batches of cookies to finish."

Two days before, she would have thought her grandmother was up to something, but since their talk, her grandmother had stopped dropping hints about Justin. "I'll go to the store and get some. How much to you need?" Camille offered as she removed her apron.

~

Marie smiled in satisfaction as she watched Camille drive away. She'd let her granddaughter think that she'd given up trying to get her and Justin together. For two days she'd held her tongue. Now was time for action.

She walked to the telephone and dialed a number. When the phone picked up on the other end, she said, "Camille is on her way." She nodded when the person on the other end responded, then hung up the phone.

Waiting a minute, she called Lula.

~

Armed with a grocery list, Camille entered the general store. The "store," as the Wainswright's citizens called it, was a combination grocery store, soda shop, and office supply. Walking down the aisles, she greeted the pastor's wife, Mrs. Combs. When she reached the spice section, she saw an older woman struggling to reach an item on the top shelf. Camille rushed over to help.

"Thank you, dear," the woman said when Camille placed the item into her basket. Despite her fragile appearance, her eyes sparkled with life.

Camille recognized her from church.

"You're Marie's grandchild, aren't you?" the woman asked, her voice trembled with age.

"Yes, ma'am. Do you need help with anything?"

Placing her wrinkled hand on Camille's arm, she shook her head. "No, my daughter should be around here somewhere. She helps me with the groceries."

The woman's eyes brightened, and she smiled at a point over Camille's shoulder. Turning to see why the woman was smiling, Camille expected to see the woman's daughter. Instead, she saw Justin.

Justin smiled in satisfaction when he saw Camille. He should have known something was up when his grandmother called to ask if he was going grocery shopping today. He always shopped on Thursdays. Rolling his cart down the aisle, he stopped when he reached the two women. "Good afternoon, Mrs. Parker, Camille."

"Hello," Camille said.

"Hello, Justin. I see my daughter waving. I'd better go." Mrs. Parker walked down the aisle, and soon Camille and Justin were alone.

"Fancy seeing you here," Justin said.

"Yeah, fancy that," she said dryly.

He raised a single brow in question. "What's wrong?"

"I think my grandmother and probably yours are trying to throw us together."

"Really?"

"Yes, really. I know this is a small town, but we shouldn't run into each other as much as we have." She frowned. "The day we met at the gas station, Grandma sent me there for propane. I'll bet your grandmother asked you to pick up something for her, right?"

He nodded yes.

"Grandma said she ran out of vanilla extract, and maybe she did, but I'll bet she knew you'd be here."

"I'm here every Thursday around this time."

"See what I mean? We've got to stop them."

"What do you think we should do about it?" he asked, his calm voice at odds with the shiver of unease he felt.

Giving him a speculative glance, she replied, "I think we should go out on one date to appease them. If they believe that we're seeing each other, then maybe they'll leave us alone. We could go out once, then tell them that we just didn't get along."

This was the opportunity he'd been waiting for. Justin looked at her, trying to control the smile that threatened to escape. With a grave tone he said, "I think you're right."

"You do?"

"Yes. Would you like to go out to dinner tomorrow?"

"Tomorrow?" she repeated.

"Yes, tomorrow."

"That's fine."

"Good. I'll pick you up around eight. Wear something casual."

"Okay," she said. "I'd better get this stuff to Grandma."

Justin watched her leave. When she walked around the corner, he released the smile he'd been restraining. If Camille had witnessed it, she would have known she was in deep trouble.

Whistling, Justin strolled down the aisle, his mind already envisioning himself out on a date with Camille. By the time dinner was over, he'd be over her. He wondered what she would make of Wainswright's best restaurant. There wasn't a place in Atlanta like it.

Justin smiled. Things were going to be fine.

~

Her grandmother watched her like a hawk. Camille kept her expression perfectly blank when she'd returned from the store. There was no way she was going to make it easy for her interfering relative. Casually, she placed the bag of groceries on the counter.

"That's everything you asked for," she said, picking up the apron she'd discarded earlier.

"Good." Marie stared at her intensely.

"So," Camille said brightly. "Do you want to continue with the cookies or start the cupcakes?"

"Let's finish the cookies," her grandmother said.

Camille nearly laughed at the disappointed look on her face. "I saw one of the ladies from church. I think Justin said her name was Mrs. Parker."

"Yes, Inez goes grocery shopping every Thursday."

"So does Justin," Camille added dryly.

"That's right," she said calmly, then added with surprise, "You don't think that I sent you to the store because Justin was there, do you?"

"Well . . ."

"Camille, two days ago you asked me to stop my matchmaking, and I respect your decision," she said firmly.

Camille noticed she didn't say she'd stopped matchmaking.

"Thank you, Grandma. I appreciate your faith in my judgment."

"When have I ever doubted your judgment? I might not agree with some of your decisions, but I never doubted *you*."

Camille felt a warmth of love overflow in her heart. For all of her interfering ways, her grandmother loved her. Camille went to her grandmother's side and gave her a hug and kissed her cheek.

They worked in silence, making more cookies and cupcakes than Camille dared to imagine. When they'd finished, Camille dropped into a chair and folded her arms on the kitchen table. "How did you do this before without help?"

"Who said I didn't have help? Lula and I would go to each other's houses and bake. Since you were here to help this time, Lula is baking cakes," Marie said as she sat down in the chair on the other side of the table.

"How many people will there be at Karl's birthday party?"

"Altogether I'd say about a hundred, but they won't show up at the same time. Justin is usually there all the time though."

"Oh, why?"

"Justin helps set up before the party and clean up afterward."

"Speaking of Justin," Camille said, then deliberately paused.

"Yes," her grandmother prompted.

"We're going out to dinner tomorrow."

Six

Justin was as nervous as a schoolboy going out on his first date. This wasn't a real date, he reminded himself as he drove into Mrs. Rodgers's driveway. They'd agreed to go on a "date" to get their respective grandmothers off their backs, and he needed to prove to himself that he, a country boy and she, a city girl, were like oil and water—they didn't mix.

His mouth went dry when Camille greeted him at the front door. He felt the familiar wave of desire that washed over him every time he saw her. She'd done something different with her hair. It was fuller, softer, sexier. His fingers longed to touch the loose brown curls.

Remember why you're here, Valentio.

Brushing aside his lustful thoughts, he let his gaze travel to her clothes.

The first thing he noticed was that her idea of casual and his were different. His new pair of Levis and flannel shirt clashed with her cuffed black wool pants, green pullover, and matching cardigan. Justin smiled with smug satisfaction. Yes, things were going just as planned.

"Hello," he said.

"Hello. Would you like to come in? Or do we need to leave now to make our reservations?" she asked shyly.

Reservations! She had no idea.

"No, I can come in," he replied, and stepped inside.

He was surprised to see *his* grandmother and Mrs. Rodgers smiling sweetly and innocently from their seats in the living room.

"Good evening, Grandma, Mrs. Rodgers."

"Hello," they replied in unison.

With her coat in hand, Camille walked to her grandmother and kissed her cheek. "See you later."

"Have a good time," Marie said smugly before grinning like a Cheshire cat.

The sweet smell of her perfume surrounded him as he helped her with her coat. With a final call of "good night" to their grandmothers, Justin and Camille walked out the door.

"Can you believe those two," she asked when he started the engine of his truck. "I'd have been so embarrassed if this were a real date."

His jaw tightened in irritation. She didn't have to sound so happy that this wasn't a real date. "They are obvious, but by tomorrow they won't bother us again."

"That's right. So where are we going to eat?"

Justin smiled. "At the best barbecue restaurant in the county."

～

"A gas station. We're eating at a gas station?" Camille asked in disbelief.

Three old-fashioned gas pumps stood like columns in front of the wood frame building. Halogen lights illuminated the parking lot, and a large billboard with the message WELCOME TO THE FILLING STATION. THE BEST BARBECUE IN THE STATE OF GEORGIA.

"It used to be a gas station, now it's a restaurant," he said, as he helped her cross the gravel parking lot.

The spicy aroma of meat cooking on the grill intensified when they entered the building.

Old gas signs and pumps were scattered throughout the large room.

Waitresses and waiters were dressed like gas pump attendants of the twenties. The wooden floor was covered with peanut hulls, which crackled under their feet.

Justin watched Camille's reaction as they walked to an empty bench. Her brown eyes were wide with curiosity.

Camille looked around the restaurant with a childlike smile. But his feelings weren't childlike when she removed her coat and cardigan, then leaned over the wooden table toward him, her lush breasts straining against her sweater.

"Hello, Justin. What will it be? Ribs or ribs?" their waitress/gas attendant asked.

He felt heat rush to his face and other parts of his body. "I think I'll have ribs and sweet tea."

"What about you, Miss Johnson?" the waitress asked, turning to Camille.

"I'll have the same thing," she said.

"You want the plate or platter?" the waitress inquired.

"Which one's bigger?"

"Platter," the waitress answered.

"Platter it is," Camille said.

"Uh . . . Camille," Justin said. "The platter is a big portion."

"That's good, because I'm hungry."

He was hungry, too, but he didn't think that the hunger he was thinking about was what she had in mind.

So far his plan wasn't working. She hadn't turned up her nose at the sight of the Filling Station, but then, they hadn't really started talking either. That would change.

Moments later their waitress returned with their food.

"Good Lord," Camille exclaimed as the waitress placed two large plates of food on the table.

"I told you it was big," Justin laughed.

Baby back ribs were piled high on the platters. Baskets of French fries, corn on the cob, and Brunswick stew rounded out the meal.

She picked up a rib dripping with sauce. "You didn't say it was enough to feed a family of four."

"Make sure you save room for the apple pie à la mode. It comes with the dinner," he added when she took a bite. Barbecue clung to her lips. He nearly groaned when her tongue moved across her lips. It was going to be a long night.

"That was really good," she said later that evening, wiping her fingers on a moist towelette. Her serving of pie, Brunswick stew, and half the ribs lay untouched on the table.

"You don't mind the simple atmosphere?"

"No. It gives the place character. The peanut shells on the floor are still a mystery to me."

"Atlanta has better restaurants. I'm sure you'd rather go to one of them," he said. It was the perfect opening for her to expound upon the fancy restaurants of Atlanta. The prices and the pretentious attitudes nearly made him ill. His ex-wife, however, would dine at a restaurant because it was the place to be, not because the food was good.

Camille pursed her lips thoughtfully. "Not really. I prefer to eat at the hole-in-the-wall places in my old neighborhood. They're inexpensive, they serve a lot of food, and my little brother, Eric, liked them. I had to raise Eric and put him through college, so I haven't had the chance to go to a lot of fancy restaurants."

"That had to be tough. Why didn't you move here? I'm sure Mrs. Rodgers would have helped to raise your brother, and it would have been easier for you."

"It would have been easy for me to rely on Grandma, but I didn't think it was fair to uproot my little brother from his school and his friends so soon after Mom died. And I had two years of college left. It just made sense to stay in Atlanta and finish college rather than move in with Grandma."

"Wainswright must seem like a step back in time compared to what you have at home."

Camille laughed. "I'm still getting used to people I don't know calling me by name, like our waitress. Everybody knows everybody in this town. It's very different. But then, you know about that, having lived in Atlanta."

He ignored her questioning gaze. He didn't want to talk about his life in Atlanta.

Looking at his watch, he said. "It's still early. Would you like to go dancing?"

～

The VFW held dances every Friday and Saturday night. The sound of country music filled the auditorium. Two lines of men and women twisted and turned in perfect form. It was perfect, Justin thought. Dancing without really touching.

Several people called out greetings as they slowly made their way to an empty table. When another song began, Justin held out his hand. "Would you like to dance?"

"Okay, but don't laugh. I haven't done this before."

He didn't remember when he'd enjoyed himself more. They danced for hours, stopping only when one of them wanted something to drink or when friends stopped by to introduce themselves. He'd received several nods of approval from both male and female friends after they'd talked with Camille.

She laughed at her mistakes while learning the Texas two-step, and she'd given up ever learning how to do the cotton-eyed Joe. The only uncomfortable moment happened toward the end of the night, when Camille clumsily threw everyone off step dancing the electric slide. When she was supposed to step forward, she stepped backward . . . her hips pressed into his thighs.

Desire raced through him, and from then on he was careful to dance beside her.

They were in the middle of the dance floor when the deejay invited everyone onto the dance floor for the last dance. The song played was a slow country ballad about love gone wrong. Up until then they'd sat out the slow songs. But when the lights were dimmed and couples around them embraced, Justin drew Camille into his arms.

It was a mistake.

He knew it the minute he'd wrapped his arms around her, bringing her body closer to his. She fit into his embrace as if they'd been dancing together for years instead of hours. The heady scent of her perfume went to his head like a strong, sweet wine. Her soft breasts pressed against his chest, and desire enveloped him as her thighs brushed against his. Justin felt his body harden. Camille stiffened in his arms, then relaxed, matching his slow, easy steps.

He felt as if the temperature in the room increased with each second the song played. The longer he held Camille in his arms, the more he wanted to explore the curve of her waist where his hand rested. Justin closed his eyes and gritted his teeth. He wanted her. Badly. But he wasn't going to do a damn thing about it. She was exactly what he didn't need. A city girl.

When was that damn song going to end? he wondered as desire raged through his body. When he thought he couldn't stand holding her in his arms a second longer, the song came to an end. He stepped quickly out of her embrace and without a word walked to their table.

∽

"I had a good time," Camille said as he helped her from his truck. Her grandmother's porch light shone brightly into the cool winter night.

"So did I," he said, surprising himself because he meant it.

"Even when I stepped on your toes?" she joked. She'd stepped on his toes more than once while he taught her the dance.

"I could have done without that part of the night," he said with amusement. "You didn't do so badly for someone who's never line-danced before. All you need is a little practice."

"I almost had the electric slide down tonight. See." Camille began dancing, performing the intricate steps on the front lawn. She was doing well until she made the turn, the point where she'd made mistakes all night long. She stepped into his arms.

The desire that he'd held at bay broke free. He lowered his head slowly, giving her a chance to deny the kiss. Her eyes closed.

And then he kissed her.

He spread soft, questing, nibbling kisses on her lips. Her arms circled around his neck, bringing her body closer to his. With one hand he caressed the nape of her neck. The other moved down her waist. His tongue teased and toyed until she parted her lips with a sigh.

He slipped his tongue between her lips, seeking and tasting the sweetness of her mouth. His heart raced, and heat spread throughout his body as their tongues mated in an intimate dance.

～

She was in trouble with a capital T. Lying in her bed, Camille stared at the ceiling. What possessed her to go out with him, knowing she was deeply attracted to the man? Sure, their grandmothers were throwing them in each other's path left and right. But to go out on a date with a man whose good looks had her dreaming sexy dreams about him was crazy.

Before, she could only dream of how it would feel to be in Justin's arms. Now she knew.

She knew the exact texture of his curly black hair. She experienced the touch of his lightly stubbled cheek against hers. She'd drank from his lips and had been intoxicated by his taste.

Justin was a dangerous man.

Thank goodness her grandmother hadn't waited up for her. If she'd seen her face after Justin's kiss, there would have been no way Camille could have told her that she and Justin hadn't gotten along. As it was, she hoped that she could get her emotions under control by the morning. Somehow she doubted that she would.

When Camille fell asleep that night, she dreamed of him.

His first mistake was asking her out. His second mistake was kissing her.

Justin drew those conclusions as he tuned out the choir of the First Baptist Church of Wainswright and concentrated on the curly brown lock of hair that had escaped Camille's French roll.

Camille had looked beautiful as she and Mrs. Rodgers walked down the aisle to the Rodgers family pew, which was directly in front of the Valentio family pew. Justin smiled when she sat in front of him, and the fragrance of her perfume brought to mind her kiss.

The very thought of that kiss made him shift in his seat.

His plan to get Camille out of his system had backfired with a vengeance. She enjoyed the food at the Filling Station and she had no problem listening and dancing to country music, things he'd been sure wouldn't have sat well with her city-girl ways. If anything, he'd found her more attractive now that he'd gone out with her. That was definitely not the objective of the evening.

He'd spent most of the night thinking about her, remembering how she looked on the dance floor. But most of all he remembered the way her body molded to his when they'd kissed. He could almost feel the softness of her lips and the taste of her.

Justin forced the thoughts aside when the pastor dismissed the congregation.

"That was a good service," Karl said with an unholy twinkle in his eye.

Justin muttered under his breath, embarrassed because he hadn't heard a single thing the pastor said, and he had a feeling Karl knew it. He stood up and his eyes met Camille's.

Camille felt her heart race when she met his dark brown gaze. Her lips tingled and heat rushed to her face as she remembered the passionate kiss they'd shared.

"Hi," she said, her voice breathless.

"Hi," he replied in a deep, sexy voice.

Embarrassed, she looked down at her hands. She couldn't think of a single thing to say to him that was proper in church. She wanted to ask him to kiss her again. She wanted to ask if he felt the same desire that she'd felt when they'd kissed. She wanted him to ask her out again.

"Camille." Her grandmother touched her arm. "I'm going to go with Lula to visit Inez. She's feeling poorly today. You're welcome to come with us, but there's no telling how long we'll stay. Or I can have someone drop you off at the house."

"I'll take you home," Karl offered.

"No," Justin interrupted. "I'll take her home."

Lula and Marie nodded their heads to each other.

The drive to her grandmother's house was made in silence. Justin seemed preoccupied, and she was nervous.

Should she be the nineties kind of woman and kiss him herself, or should she follow her instincts and go to the house alone. She was still debating with herself when he brought his truck to a stop in the driveway.

"Thanks for the ride," she said.

"Invite me in, Camille."

She looked into his eyes and saw hunger, desire, emotions that she was sure shone from her own gaze. In a low, husky voice she invited him in.

When they were inside, Justin helped her out of her coat, then shrugged off his own. She hung both coats on the rack in the foyer before turning to face him.

"Would you like something to drink?"

"No," he said, placing his hands on her shoulders, letting them glide down her arms, then placing her hands on his shoulders. "What I would like," he said softly, "is another kiss."

He tilted his head to the side and lowered his lips to hers. Camille felt a heady wave of desire wash upon her body. She slid her hands down his shoulders and around his back, luxuriating in the feel of him.

"Camille," he whispered when the kiss ended.

"What?" she asked, spreading kisses from his chiseled jaw, his cheek, before nibbling his lips.

"I thought . . ." He faltered when her tongue traced the seam of his lower lip.

"You thought . . ."

"To hell with what I thought," he said, and claimed her lips in another passionate kiss.

"Camille," he said a few minutes later.

"What." She kissed his cheek.

"We'd better stop."

She made a sound of protest and laid her head on his shoulder. She could hear the racing beat of his heart.

"Camille, would you like to go to the movies?"

Seven

On Monday they went to Flack's Theater, Wainswright's one and only movie house. They were one of five couples in attendance to see the romantic comedy's first run in town. Although the movie had been in Atlanta for weeks, Camille hadn't seen it. She and Justin were like teenagers out on a date.

They shared a large tub of buttered popcorn and held hands during the movie. He kissed her good night tenderly on her grandmother's front porch and asked if he could see her tomorrow.

On Tuesday he took her to a roller-skating rink in the next town. Neither of them had been on skates since their teens. They made fools of themselves, trying to hold hands and skate at the same time. Touching and holding on to each other in the most awkward places, they managed to skate a time or two around the rink without falling on the floor.

Later that evening he brought her to his house for dinner. It was the best chili cheese dog and potato chips she'd ever tasted.

On Wednesday they sat side by side in the Valentio family pew at Wednesday night Bible study. They received speculative glances from various members of the congregation. Their respective grandmothers beamed at the sight.

Sometime between the opening hymn and the beginning of the pastor's sermon, Camille realized she loved Justin. A heady sense of joy raced through her.

She was in love, totally and completely in love.

Not the infatuation that she'd felt with Darryl, whom she thought she'd loved, but real love. She turned her head to look at her love.

Justin.

She wanted to tell him then and there that she loved him. However, caution and fear kept her silent. Neither of them had spoken of the future. In a week she'd be driving back to her home in Atlanta and he'd still be there in Wainswright. He'd never indicated that he'd felt anything but desire and want toward her; neither had she, for that matter.

Looking at the hymnal in her hand, she decided to keep the knowledge of her love for him to herself. She had a week left with him. Maybe he could grow to love her as she had grown to love him.

On Thursday Justin worked the evening shift. He spent his dinner hour talking to her on the telephone.

When the telephone rang at nine o'clock Thursday night, Camille knew it was Justin. She answered it before the first ring ended.

"Hello."

"Hi, there," he replied in his soft, sexy voice.

"Are you making Wainswright a safer place to live?"

"You know it. Running in jaywalkers and giving traffic tickets is hard work."

She laughed. "I can relate to the traffic-ticket part."

"You're not mad because I gave you a ticket, are you?"

"No," she laughed. "You know, there's something I've been wanting to ask you."

"What?"

"How did you get the last name of Valentio?

"It was my father who gave me that last name."

"Oh, pul-leeze. How did you become a Valentio?"

"Okay. My great-grandmother went to Italy as a maid of a wealthy white family. While there she fell in love and married my great-grandfather Aldolfo Valentio. He died before she gave birth to their third son. She moved back with her children to her hometown, Wainswright, and now you have a black family with a very Italian last name." He smiled. "Speaking of families, have you talked to your brother?"

"I talked to him this evening. He loves his job," she said with a sigh.

"Sounds like you miss him."

"I do miss him. Last year I was looking forward to the time when my brother moved out. Even when you stopped me for speeding, I was thinking about my new condo, my new car, my new life without being responsible for his welfare. Now I'm not so sure I want to live alone. Funny, isn't it?" She twisted the phone cord in her fingers.

"No, just human nature. When I was in high school I couldn't wait to go to college in Atlanta. I wanted to get as far away from Wainswright as I could. After a few months I was ready to come home. People told me that I was just homesick and I would get over it. I never did. You don't miss what you have until it's gone."

"I guess you're right."

The line was silent. "Are you still going to Karl's birthday party?" he asked.

They continued to talk until his dinner hour had passed.

"I've got to go," he said reluctantly.

"Be safe."

"I will. Good night."

"Good night."

Camille stared at the telephone. She wondered how she was going to leave the man she loved next week.

～

"They talk to each other every day," Marie whispered into the telephone. Although Camille was upstairs and probably asleep, Marie was careful to keep her voice down.

"This is working out better than we'd hoped," Lula replied. "Hot darn! We could be great-grandmothers before the year is out."

"Don't go talking about great-grandchildren yet. Those two still have to get married first."

"Of course they'll get married," Lula huffed.

"Things are starting to heat up between them. If you know what I mean."

"I know what you mean. I haven't forgotten what it's like to be all hot and bothered."

"I haven't forgotten either," Marie replied. "I think Camille is beginning to fall in love. I'd hate her to be hurt."

"Justin could be hurt in this, too. Hopefully, he'll realize that he's in love before it's too late."

～

The party was in full swing when Camille and Marie arrived at Karl's home on Saturday night. Children chased one another around the room while their parents socialized or danced on the makeshift dance floor in the living room.

Karl spotted them from his position across the room and waved them over.

"Happy birthday, Karl," Camille said when she reached his side, giving him a cheerfully wrapped gift from her and her grandmother.

"Thank you," he said, ready to rip the paper off the box.

"Karl, give me that." A slender, petite woman walked up and held out her hand.

"Tamara, it's a party. Loosen up," he said, giving her the present. Then held out his hand to Camille. "Can I have this dance?"

Camille saw the flash of pain in the woman's eyes before Karl led her to the dance floor.

She loves Karl, Camille realized. She felt sympathy for Tamara for she knew what it felt like to love a man who didn't know the depths of your feelings.

As she danced with Karl, she scanned the room, trying to catch a glimpse of Justin.

"If Justin weren't my cousin, I'd be highly offended," Karl said jokingly. "Imagine, looking for one man while you dance with another."

Camille blushed. "Sorry."

"He went to the kitchen to bring out more punch. Don't worry, when he sees you, he'll be right over."

Her blush intensified.

Karl laughed. "I didn't mean to embarrass you, but it's true." His laughter faded. "Do you care about Justin?"

"Yes, I do."

"Then don't give up on him."

Before she could ask him what he meant, the song ended and another woman led Karl in a dance.

A hand touched her shoulder, and she knew it was Justin. Turning, she smiled.

Justin returned her smile. "I thought you'd never get here," he said.

"Me either," she sighed as she stepped into his arms. "I had to wait for

Grandma, or else I would have left with you when you picked up the cookies and cupcakes this morning."

"Good thing you didn't," he said, as they danced to the music. "I wouldn't have been any help to Karl if you'd come along."

"Are you saying that I distract you, Justin?"

"You do more than distract me, honey. And you know it," he whispered in her ear.

Camille felt desire into her very depths. When the song ended, he took her hand and walked to the table where all the presents were stacked.

Justin was rarely out of arm's reach all night. They danced, they ate, they sang "Happy Birthday" to Karl—together.

At ten-thirty that evening her grandmother left the party, as did parents with young children and other older citizens of Wainswright.

"I won't wait up for you," her grandmother whispered in her ear just before she left.

"Grandma!"

"What did she say?" Justin asked.

Camille blushed, then said, "Nothing. Let's dance."

The dance floor was filled with couples swaying to slow, jazzy tunes. Camille and Justin danced until the last of Karl's guests went home for the night.

The three of them made quick work of cleaning up the mess left behind, joking and laughing at the gag gifts Karl received. But all the while she worked, Camille felt tense, eager to be alone with Justin.

It was one-thirty in the morning before they left Karl's house.

"Do you want to go straight home?" he asked. The interior light of his truck cast a faint glow over them.

"No," she replied.

He drove her to his home. The garage door had barely shut before he took her in his arms and kissed her. His lips were firm and strong, his tongue hot and demanding.

"I've wanted to do that all night long," he murmured.

"I've wanted you to do that all night long," she whispered.

"Let's go inside." Hand in hand they entered his home.

The warm glow of the fire he'd started in the woodburning stove permeated the living room. Nestling beside him on the sofa, Camille lay her head on his broad shoulders, listening to the strong but steady beat of his heart.

"Did you have a good time tonight?" he asked, his thumb gently stroking her arm.

"I had a great time. Does Karl have a birthday party every year?"

"He has since he came back from Desert Storm. Something happened to him when he was in the Middle East. The war changed him and the party reminds him of his blessings."

"What happened?"

"It's hard to explain. Whatever it was, it made him lock part of himself away."

"Is that why he keeps Tamara at arm's length?" she asked, rubbing her hand over his heart.

His laughter was low, deep, and sexy. It wreaked havoc with her senses. "No. That's more out of habit. Tamara has been chasing Karl since high school."

"She loves him."

"Tamara?" he said in surprise. "I'll have to let Karl know." He looked into her eyes. "Definitely," he said, and pulled her deeper into his embrace. He kissed her forehead with a soft, butterfly-light kiss. Placing his hand under her chin, he tilted her head back and brushed his thumb across her lips.

A shudder went through his body when she gently bit the pad of his thumb, then stroked it with her tongue. Slowly, he leaned down and kissed her lips.

His kisses were hard, probing, and demanding, igniting burning flames within her. She responded by giving equally demanding kisses of her own.

Her hands slipped beneath his sweater, pulling the cotton T-shirt out of the waist of his jeans and caressed his warm, strong back. With a harsh groan Justin pushed her away from him.

"Justin . . ." she moaned in protest.

He pulled off his sweater and T-shirt in one graceful movement, giving her full view of his muscled chest. Camille leaned down, placing a tender kiss at the base of his throat. "Lord, you're beautiful," she whispered.

"Men aren't beautiful," he responded in a deep, throaty voice.

"You are," she breathed, rubbing her cheek lower against his chest. Her mouth nuzzled his small brown nipple before covering it with her lips and sucking.

Justin's jaw clenched and he sucked in his breath. Flames of desire burned a searing path from his chest to his manhood. Slowly, reluctantly, he placed his hands on her shoulders and pulled her from his body.

He breathed in and out with harsh, choppy breaths. "We'd better stop before this gets out of hand."

Camille took one of his hands from her shoulder and placed his palm between her breasts.

Through her wool sweater he felt the pounding beat of her heart amid the lush softness of her breasts. His desire burned higher.

"It . . . it's already out of hand," she said breathlessly.

"Camille. Sweetheart, are you sure?"

"I'm sure."

Together they rose from the sofa, and hand in hand they walked to his bedroom.

He swept her up in his arms before they reached his bedroom door. His expression was filled with tenderness as he walked across the room and lay her on his bed. His heart clenched, and a feeling of utter rightness came over him as he looked at her. His woman.

Sitting on the edge of the bed, he took off his shoes. He stood, then removed his jeans and underwear.

Camille caught her breath at the sight of him, muscled, huge, and completely male. Her love for him sprung forth in her heart.

"One of us"—he lay down on the bed beside her—"is overdressed."

She smiled a slow, sexy smile. "I need help with my clothes. Will you help me?"

"Tell me what you need," he murmured, fire in his gaze.

"Take off my sweater."

With more determination than skill he removed her sweater, revealing her sheer, white lacy bra.

Caressing her chin, he asked. "Do you need anything else?"

"My bra," she sighed.

Slowly, ever so slowly, he unclasped the front of her bra, peeling it away from her body, uncovering her soft brown breasts. Gently, he massaged her nipples with the tips of his fingers, groaning in satisfaction when she shuddered and her nipples hardened with desire.

Camille pressed his hands on her breasts. Looking deeply into his eyes, she guided his hand down her bare stomach to the waist of her jeans.

"Justin, take them off."

His hands made quick work of pulling her jeans and panties down her legs. He muttered a curse when he realized that they were hindered by her loafers. Quickly and deftly, he took off her shoes and removed the last of her clothes.

His glance raked boldly over her body. "You're beautiful," he said with a voice filled with passion.

When she reached out to touch him, he captured her hand, kissing her palm before pressing it against the mattress. "Not yet, honey." He turned and opened the drawer of his nightstand. Returning to her side, he held out the foil package and said, "I need help with this. Will you help me?"

Her hands were trembling when she took the foil package. When she finished, they were both shaking with desire.

Justin enticed her into his arms. Urgency and heat filled him as her hands caressed his body. Their lips and tongues mated in a rhythm that was as old as time. Her hips pressed against his in that same rhythm.

When he could stand it no more, he placed a pillow under her hips, then knelt between her thighs.

"Look at me, Camille."

Her gaze met his and he slowly entered her. He leaned forward, bracing his weight on his forearms. Taking deep ragged breaths, he resisted the urge to rush to completion.

She tightened her muscles from within.

He flinched, as if touched by lightning.

"Justin," she cried.

Slowly, tenderly, he began to move, taking them to a place of delight. A place of ecstasy.

Eight

Camille awoke to the feel of a hand caressing her hips.

Justin. Her love.

With her eyes still closed, she smiled and arched into his caress.

"Wake up, sleepyhead," he whispered in her ear.

"I'm awake," she replied with a slow, husky voice.

"Then why are your eyes closed?" He gently bit her earlobe. "Come on. Get out of bed."

She opened her eyes and looked at him.

He's so handsome, she thought. Dark stubble covered his chin and cheeks, giving him a rakish appeal. His eyes were soft, dark, and shining with desire.

Desire that she felt flowing lazily throughout her body.

"You're dressed," she exclaimed when she saw his shirt and jeans.

"Yes. I am," he said smugly.

She looked at him from under her lashes. "Can I convince you to get undressed?"

All traces of smugness vanished, and in its place appeared a deep hunger and yearning. "You could convince me of just about anything, sweetheart. But I'd hate to have our grandmothers walk in on us."

"What!" she screeched, and sat up in the bed.

He lifted his arm to look at his watch. "I figure your grandmother should be waking up and getting ready for church in about thirty minutes. Once she realizes that you didn't come home last night, it will take her another ten minutes to get my grandmother and come over here."

"Oh, my goodness." She scrabbled out of the bed, grabbing her clothes, which were scattered on the floor.

"The bathroom is right through those doors," he said, gesturing to a set of double doors.

He smiled lustfully, watching the sway of her bare bottom as she rushed through the doors.

Fifteen minutes later Camille tiptoed up the stairs of her grandmother's home.

∼

Justin studied Camille from his position on his living room sofa. The local newspaper he'd been reading lay in a rumpled heap beside him.

Camille lay on her stomach, a section of the newspaper on the floor in front of her. Her curly brown hair was tucked behind her ears. Her brows were drawn in a frown of concentration. She held a pencil in her hand and was poised to fill in the squares of the crossword puzzle.

Their plans for the evening had been disrupted by a five-car accident just outside of town. By the time the last ambulance had driven from the scene, it was too late for them to make their eight o'clock reservations at the restaurant in Macon.

When he called her with the news, she suggested they have dinner at his house and just hang out. She was waiting in his driveway when he came home. She'd listened to him rant and rave about the senseless accident caused by a drunk driver, then she hugged him until the tension and frustration went away.

Now he was restless. He couldn't believe that *she* wasn't bored out of her mind.

"You want to watch television?" he asked.

"No," she replied without looking away from the crossword puzzle.

He watched as she filled in a word, then asked, "You want to go to a movie?"

Laughing, she looked at him. "No. Are you tired of my company already?"

"No. I just don't want you to feel that we have to stay here. If you want to do something else, we can."

"I'm fine." She smiled and returned her attention to the paper.

Justin picked up the discarded newspaper at his side. He stared blindly at the page. His father often said his mother couldn't stand to stay at home. History had taught him that women like Camille weren't happy to have a quiet night at home.

"Are you sure you don't want to do something? I don't want you to be bored."

She put down the pencil and looked at him in confusion. "I'm not bored."

"Don't tell me you stayed at home doing the crossword puzzle in Atlanta," he said, skepticism dripping in his tone. "If you're traveling to Paris, I'm sure it's because the limelights of Atlanta bored you."

"I don't know where you got the idea that I go out all the time. Most nights I am at home. Until recently, I couldn't afford to go out. It's expensive paying two college tuitions. Paris is a vacation I've been planning for years."

"You had to go out and party sometime," Justin argued.

"Of course I went out, but not very often. I'm basically a homebody. I don't have to go out to have fun."

He saw the sincerity in her caramel-brown eyes. It surprised him. His mother had always begged his father to go to Atlanta for the weekend. She didn't have fun unless she was in the big city. He wondered if she would have fun here.

Camille rose from the floor and cuddled up beside him. "I'm exactly where I want to be tonight. I'm with you."

"I'm glad," he said softly, placing his arms around her shoulders.

"I know what we can do," she whispered. "It's not boring and you don't have to leave the house."

"What is it?"

She drew him toward her and began to show him.

~

Over the next few days they frolicked around Wainswright like teenagers in love. During the day Camille spent time with her grandmother, but the nights belonged to Justin.

~

Betty smiled at him when he came to work Tuesday morning. Justin's eyes narrowed in suspicion. Betty rarely smiled at anyone before eleven, and it was now nine o'clock.

He looked at Karl, who shrugged as if saying "I don't know."

"Good morning," he said cautiously.

"Morning," she replied, her smile brightening.

He walked across the room to his office and was surprised when she followed him. Betty had no qualms speaking her mind in front of Karl. That she'd followed him to his office *and* shut the door made him all the more suspicious.

"Justin," she blurted out in her best Mrs. Santa Claus tone. "You know I've got a cabin on my property."

He nodded, waiting for her to continue.

"You're welcome to use it," she added, looking over her glasses at him.

"Uh, thanks, Betty. I'll keep that in mind," he said in bewilderment.

"I don't like to get in anybody's business, but I just thought you and Camille would appreciate a nice, private spot to be alone." She walked out the door, leaving him staring at the empty space where she'd once stood.

At times, and this was one of them, he was surprised by the things she said. He wondered how she knew his relationship with Camille had become intimate. Betty had left Karl's party early, and she lived on the other side of town.

After Karl's party he thought they'd been discreet. He knew how quickly gossip traveled in town, and he didn't want Camille to be the subject of idle gossip. They'd made no secret of the fact that they were dating. But how did Betty know they were lovers?

He was still pondering the question when Karl walked in his office and closed the door.

"Justin," he said. "Macon has a lot of nice bed-and-breakfast places. I can give you the names of a few. I'm sure Camille would like them."

Camille was waiting for him when he came home that night. He'd given her a key to his house a few days before. It was something he'd never done until he'd met her. As he listened to her sing along with the artist on the radio, Justin realized how much he missed having someone waiting for him when he got home.

"You're not going to give up your day job, are you?" he asked as he stood in the doorway of his kitchen.

She closed the oven, then gave him a teasing frown. "Don't get smart with me, or it will be peanut butter and jelly sandwiches for you."

He walked across the room, put his arms around her, and kissed her lips gently. "Sorry."

"Well, I guess I'll let you have dinner," she said softly as she circled her arms around his waist.

"You didn't have to cook. I would have fixed something when I got here."

"I like cooking," she said, stepping out of his embrace. "Besides, this was the first time I've had the kitchen to myself since I've been here. Grandma acts like General Patton in her kitchen."

Justin laughed at her analogy. "Do you need help with anything?"

"No. I have it under control."

"Okay. I'm going to change out of this uniform. I'll be right back."

"Do you need help with anything?" she asked, then offered him a slow, flirty smile.

He smiled in return. "No. I have it under control," he said before walking to his bedroom.

When he returned, Camille had set the dining room table.

"We can eat anytime you're ready," she said.

"I'm ready now."

Dinner was excellent. She'd made penne pasta with chicken, salad, and brownies from scratch. Camille blushed as he praised her cooking skills. He couldn't believe that she, a big-city girl, cooked like this and enjoyed it.

He'd eaten his second brownie, when he remembered his conversation with Betty and Karl. He was reluctant to share this information with her, not because he didn't want her to know, but, rather, he felt as if he'd let her down by not protecting her from gossip.

"The whole town is talking about us," Justin said as he cleared the dishes from the dining room table.

"Really? What makes you think so?" she asked as she helped him clear the table.

"Betty offered us the use of her cabin." He paused, then mimicked Betty's voice. "So you can have a nice, private place alone with Camille."

She laughed. "That doesn't mean the whole town is talking about us, just Betty."

"Oh, yeah? Karl gave me a list of B and Bs in Macon, and Mrs. Parker stopped me on the street today to tell me about a hotel in the next town."

"Mrs. Parker," she gasped. "The sweet old lady I met at the store? That Mrs. Parker?"

He nodded. "That Mrs. Parker!"

She looked at him for a moment, speechless, then her eyes widened in horror. "My grandma."

Justin winced. "Yes. She's probably heard about us by now."

Camille placed her hands over her cheeks. "I'm so embarrassed."

"I'm sorry," he said, putting his arm around her shoulders. "I should have been more discreet."

"It's not your fault. Are you sure the whole town knows?"

"If Betty knows, then the town knows," he said.

Camille straightened her shoulders. "These are the nineties, not the fifties. Times have changed and Grandma will have to realize that."

"Change happens slowly in a small town."

She sighed. "I wish we were in Atlanta. We wouldn't have this problem there."

Justin stiffened at her words. She was already talking about leaving. Leaving his small town and leaving him.

$\sim$

Two nights later Camille drove down the road to Justin's home. He'd been right when he said the whole town knew about them. She'd received more knowing looks the past two days than she could remember. No one treated her differently than before, except for the looks, even her grandmother hadn't spoken to her about her relationship with Justin. She was embarrassed by the situation. "I'll get over it," she muttered when she reached his home.

Justin opened the front door before she could knock, gathering her in his arms, giving her a soul-stirring kiss.

"Hello, sweetheart." His voice was heavy with desire.

"Hi," she said softly, circling her arms around his waist and laying her cheek on his chest.

"How are things with your grandmother?" he asked.

"Okay, I guess. The first day we were both embarrassed, but today we seem to be back to normal. I've got to get used to people in town knowing my personal business."

"Is someone giving you problems?"

"No. I just didn't realize exactly how small Wainswright was and how everybody knows what goes on," she said.

Justin tightened his arms around her, and she felt her tension melt.

"Hungry?" he asked a few minutes later.

She gave him a sexy smile. "Very."

He laughed. "For food, Camille."

"That too," she said.

When they'd finished their meal, Justin insisted that she relax in the den.

She hadn't spent much time in that room. She walked to the entertainment center and turned on his radio. A local station played love songs. On the shelf above, she saw a cluster of pictures. Curious, she studied them.

A much younger Lula stood next to a man. She assumed it was Justin's grandfather. Another picture frame contained a photo of an infant. It was Justin's baby picture. The last picture was of a young woman in her twenties. From the style of her clothes, she guessed it was taken in the early sixties. Frowning, she wondered who this woman was.

"That's my mother," Justin said, leaning against the door.

"She's beautiful."

Pushing himself away from the door, he walked to her side. "Dad used to say he was the luckiest man alive to have married her," he said mockingly.

Her frown deepened at his tone. "Wasn't it true?"

"Oh, he was lucky all right. Lucky enough to marry a spoiled, rich, city girl who made his life hell. When she decided that she didn't want to play wife and mother, she left him high and dry with a two-year-old son to raise."

Camille ached at the pain and bitterness in his voice. She wanted to cry for the little boy within him who still felt abandoned by his mother. She placed her arms around his rigid frame.

"I'm sure she loved you, Justin."

"She didn't love anything but herself and her big city lifestyle. She didn't look back once she left us."

She held him tightly, laying her cheek against his chest until the stiffness left his body. As she held him, she wondered if she could heal the wounds made by two careless women, his mother and his ex-wife.

"I'm tired," he said, capturing her hands in his when she began to caress him.

"Do you want me to give you a massage?"

"No. Why don't you go home tonight? Call me when you get there."

Her heart clenched with pain. He was rejecting her.

"Are you sure? I can stay if you want," she said softly.

He shook his head. "I'm not good company for you now. Go home."

Dazed, Camille gathered her purse. He walked with her to her car. The January wind was as cold as the fear in her heart. Giving her a soft kiss, he said, "Drive safely."

As she drove down the dark country road, tears began to stream down her cheeks. She hurt. Wiping away the tears, she wondered if this was what she would feel when she left Wainswright.

Her grandmother looked up in surprise from the television when she walked in.

"You're in awfully early tonight."

"Justin was tired," she said listlessly.

Marie studied her. When she saw the traces of tears on Camille's face, she turned off the television with the remote control.

"Come sit down, child."

Camille sat next to her on the sofa.

"Did you two have a fight?" Marie asked.

"No, we didn't fight. He just sent me away, Grandma." The pain was evident in her voice.

Marie put her arms around Camille and held her. "I remember when Justin was about four years old and Lula bought him a puppy," her grandmother said. "He named him Spot. Justin loved that dog. He took the dog with him everywhere. One day Spot was gone. Justin looked everywhere for him, but the dog was nowhere to be found. Lula bought him another dog, but he had nothing to do with that dog and Lula ended up giving the dog away. You are like the second dog."

"Thanks a lot."

"Well, you are," her grandmother insisted. "Justin is afraid that you'll leave him, so he's pushing you away. Honey, he's had so many people and things that he's loved leave him that he's afraid to love."

Camille leaned her head on her grandmother's shoulders. "I love him so much."

"I know you do, child," she said, rubbing Camille's hair away from her face.

~

Justin watched her drive away until the red taillights faded into the darkness. Loneliness and pain engulfed him.

Get used to feeling like this, buddy.

His shoulders slumped forward and he walked into his empty house.

No matter how much he'd tried, he couldn't stop thinking about her. He'd wait by the phone for her call. An hour later, when the phone was still silent, he called her.

"Did I wake you?" he asked.

"No. I couldn't go to sleep." Her voice sounded melancholy.

"I couldn't sleep either," he said.

Silence stretched on the line. He wondered if he'd totally messed up with her.

"I shouldn't have sent you home. After you left, the house seemed so empty," he admitted. "I miss you."

"I miss you too."

The tension in his body eased and he leaned against the sofa in relief. "If I come by tonight, will you let me in?"

"I don't think that's a good idea. Grandma's asleep already."

"We can sit on the porch," he offered hopefully.

"It's the middle of winter! We'd freeze."

"Okay, I get the message. Good night, Camille."

"Good night, Justin."

He hung up the phone, disappointed that he couldn't see her again that night. At least she hadn't refused to see him at all.

~

The next day Camille started packing. She would be leaving in the morning to go home.

A month ago she would have been excited at the prospect of living on her own, but now the thought left her cold.

A month ago she hadn't met Justin.

She sat on the bed, sunlight shining through the French doors. It was such a beautiful day for her heart to be so heavy.

The phone rang. A few minutes later her grandmother said it was for her.

"Hello?"

"Camille."

The sound of his voice sent her pulses racing. "Yes?"

"Are you free for lunch today?"

"Yes."

"Good, then I'll pick you up around eleven-thirty."

He arrived at her grandmother's home at eleven-twenty. His dark brown sheriff's uniform reminded her of the day he gave her a speeding ticket. On that day she hadn't experienced the passion of his kiss or the intoxicating feel of his touch.

They made the drive to The Store in silence. She could tell from his expression that he had something on his mind. It was halfway during their meal that he spoke his mind.

"When do you leave?" he asked.

"Tomorrow morning," she replied. Tell me you'll miss me, she thought.

He nodded and took a bite of his ham sandwich.

She realized then that he wasn't going to invite her into his life. If she wanted to see him, she would have to make the move.

"Will you visit me in Atlanta?" she asked.

He sat perfectly still in his chair. "Do you want me to?"

"Yes," she said softly. Her heart pounded as she waited for his reply.

"When do you want me to come?"

She beamed. Throwing her arms around his neck, Camille kissed Justin in front of all the patrons of The Store.

What did she care, he'd given them a chance.

Nine

One week later

Justin felt trapped. He always felt this way when he drove in Atlanta traffic. At six o'clock on a Friday evening, traffic on the interstate was at a standstill, and it had been that way for the last hour.

His hands ached from gripping the steering wheel. He wouldn't have gone there if it weren't for Camille.

In the week since she'd left, he felt lonely. Lonelier than he'd ever felt in his life. Several times during the week he'd been tempted to take the day off and drive over to see her, but fear held him back. Fear that when she returned home, she wouldn't want a small-town country boy like him.

Thirty minutes later he pulled into the parking lot of her condominium complex. High-priced cars were lined in neat rows, like soldiers in formation. His pickup truck was definitely out of place.

The security guard checked his identification before releasing a magnetic lock and allowing Justin to enter the lobby. As a peace officer, he liked the security measures the building had to offer. As Camille's lover, he resented the measures because they reminded him that she could be the victim of crime.

He felt nervous as he stood in front of her door. Although he'd spoken to her on the telephone almost every night, he was still uncertain of himself. He wiped his palms against his pant leg, then rang the doorbell.

"Who is it?" Her muted voice flowed from the intercom.

"It's Justin."

He heard the sound of locks being opened and chains being removed, then the door swung open and Camille stood before him.

The smile on her face made the trip worthwhile.

His gaze moved hungrily over her face and body, drinking in the sight of her.

"I'm so glad you're here," she said.

"Me, too," he said. "I mean, I'm glad to be here." Feeling nervous, he put his hands in his pockets.

"Come in," she said, stepping aside.

Her home was decorated in a mixture of soothing blue and cream. He felt his tension ease the minute he entered the wide living/dining area. Unlike the on-the-edge modern furniture that his ex-wife had been so fond of, traditional pieces graced Camille's home.

He turned at the sound of the lock sliding in place. He didn't know who moved first, but seconds later they were in each other's arms.

"I've missed you," he whispered, running his finger through her hair.

"And I've missed you," she said, as she tightened her arms around his waist.

He tilted her head, lowered his, and began to kiss her. He kissed her eyes, her cheek, the tip of her nose, then finally her lips.

He nibbled and nipped until she parted her lips.

She tasted like heaven.

Justin moaned as her tongue advanced and retreated, sending sparks of desire through him. When the taste of her lips was no longer enough, he kissed her jaw and her neck.

Releasing the buttons on her blouse, he slipped it down and off. He brought up his hands, cupped her breasts, then kissed the full mounds. Through the lacy fabric of her bra he brushed his tongue over her nipple, then gently blew.

"Justin," she begged. Camille cupped his head, urging him to her. She threw back her head and moaned when his mouth closed over her.

She tugged impatiently at the tail of his shirt, pulling it out of his pants. Her eager hands caressed and stroked his back. She luxuriated in the feel of his hot skin.

His hands moved to her hips, caressing and stroking, bringing their bodies closer together. She arched her hips against him.

Her hands moved up his stomach, to his shoulders. Slowly, she pushed him away. His breath came in harsh gasps, his heart pounded.

"Camille?"

She gently took his hand and led him to her bedroom.

Later that night, in the darkened recess of her bedroom, Justin's stomach growled long, strong, and loud.

Nestled at his side in his arms, Camille rubbed her hand over his hard stomach. "You're not hungry, are you?"

He smiled and kissed the top of her head. "Just a little."

She stretched, pressing her body firmly against his. When she'd finished, she kissed his lips, then sat up. "So, what do you want to eat?"

Totally unselfconscious of her nakedness, she closed her eyes and stretched again.

The thought of food vanished from his mind as desire flamed anew. Leaning up on his arm, Justin closed his mouth over her nipple and sucked.

"Oh," she gasped in surprise.

His stomach growled . . . again.

Her shoulders shook with laughter. He released her from his hold and fell back into the pillows.

"Honey, I think we need to feed you," she said, her voice heavy with amusement and desire.

"You're right," he said. "What's open around here."

"Just about everything. Chinese, Mexican, pizza, the deli."

"I'll decide on the way there."

"On the way there? Honey, you're not moving from this bed. I'm having the food delivered."

The food arrived thirty minutes later. Dressed in gray sweats, Camille sat on the bed with her legs crossed, eating shrimp fried rice directly from the white cardboard carton. Soft music played gently on the radio. Justin relaxed against the pillows with the sheet pulled up to his waist. He waited until her mouth was full, then spoke.

"Good thing I was hungry," he said dryly. "I'd have hated to see *you* go without a meal."

Camille chewed her food and blushed. "I asked you if you wanted any?"

He chuckled. "I know, but I thought you were asking if I wanted some at that particular moment, not if I wanted some anytime tonight."

"Well, it's gone now," she said, putting aside the empty carton and picking up a new one. "Here, have an eggroll."

"Thank you," he said, taking the carton.

"You're not going to eat all of them, are you?" she teased.

"No," he said, his tone suddenly serious. "I'll share all that I have with you."

Later that night, as Justin slept, Camille lay in her bed, listening to the steady rhythm of his breathing. She was happy, frighteningly happy. When Justin arrived, he chased away seven days of loneliness.

She didn't want to think of the times when they would be apart longer periods of time. Telephone calls helped ease the loneliness, but she needed to be with the man she loved.

Rubbing her cheek against his chest, she wondered if he would be willing to share her world and her love.

$\sim$

The city was closing in on him. Justin sat in the passenger seat of Camille's car. He stared up at the towering skyline as she drove through the streets of downtown Atlanta.

"I'm sorry," she said. "I didn't realize the city was doing road construction this weekend."

"That's okay," he replied, but it wasn't okay. There were too many people and too much noise for his comfort. He leaned against the headrest and closed his eyes. For Camille, he would put up with it. For now.

They missed the first movie because of the traffic. With the next start of the movie two hours away, they decided to go to the mall across the street.

As they walked on the sidewalk, people rushed past him, stopping only when traffic forced them to. They were careful to not make eye contact with anyone else. Justin wondered cynically what they'd do if he spoke.

He didn't belong there. He belonged in Wainswright, where the people greeted you on the street. Where the people weren't stuffed like sardines on the sidewalks.

Camille took his hand and smiled at him. She was the one kind face in the sea of indifferent strangers.

They ate in a restaurant at the mall. Camille watched as other women looked at Justin. Some looked at him with appreciation for a handsome man, while others devoured him with their eyes.

He ignored the looks, but she could tell from the reddening of his cheeks that he was embarrassed.

"You're drawing a lot of attention," she teased.

He glared at her.

When their waitress walked over, the woman did a double take.

"Are you a model?" she asked.

"No. I'm the police," he said in his most stern voice.

The waitress quickly took their order and left.

"If all the policemen looked like you, crime would be rampant among women," Camille said dryly.

"Right," he said sarcastically.

"It would. Resisting arrest would be unheard of," she said. "On the other hand, groping, caressing, and kissing an officer would be a federal offense. I'd be in jail for years." She wiggled her brows at him, giving him a lustful look.

He laughed at her antics. "Are you planning to grope, caress, and kiss an officer?"

She leaned forward and stared into his eyes. "Every chance I get."

~

"Camille, could you slow down to at least seventy?" Justin asked tensely from the passenger seat. He'd seen several near accidents on I-285 since they'd left the movie theater. It was dark, and temporary construction barrels lined the highway, but the drivers, including Camille, traveled as if they were on a deserted two-lane road.

She drove her Miata with the speed and intensity of a race-car driver.

"I'm just keeping up with the flow of traffic. If I go any slower, the other cars will blow me off the road."

Justin held his breath as she drove up to the bumper of a slow-moving car before quickly changing lanes and going around the car. After that he decided he didn't need to see where they were going. He turned and watched Camille. Her face was aglow with excitement and determination. He realized she was totally enjoying herself. This is her element, he thought. The fast-paced big city was her world, and he was along for the ride.

～

Later that night Justin awoke as a wave of cold air flowed over him. Shivering, he turned toward the warmth at his side.

Camille.

She lay next to him, her arm resting on his stomach.

Happiness and satisfaction raced through him, and in that moment he knew he loved her.

He wondered when had he fallen in love with her.

Had he fallen in love with her at the Filling Station or at the skating rink, or even at church?

When he'd fallen in love with her didn't matter. What did matter was he'd fallen in love with another big-city girl, something that he'd sworn he'd never do again.

Easing out of her embrace, he got out of the bed. He watched her as she slept. She looked so beautiful, so right. She was so totally wrong for him. She was a big-city girl and he was a small-town boy.

There was no way he was moving back to Atlanta. He loved her so much that if he let her, she could talk him into staying for a while. But sooner or later he'd have to return to his home, where he belonged.

As much as he wanted to be with her, he couldn't ask her to give up her life and stay with him in Wainswright. She belonged in the city, where she could go to first-run movies, eat in nice restaurants, drive her car as if she were on a racetrack, and her neighbors wouldn't care if she took a lover to her bed.

He had to leave her there and his heart with her.

Justin walked to the bedroom window and looked out. The lights of the city shone and twinkled. He had to make a decision.

Would he end their relationship tomorrow when he went home, hoping to stem the pain that was sure to come, or would he spend his time with Camille, making as many memories as he could until it hurt too much to be with her.

When the sun peeked through her window, Justin made his decision. He put on his clothes, packed his bag, and waited for the woman he loved to awake, knowing that his heart would never be the same.

~

Camille reached for him in her sleep and awakened when she didn't find him.

"Justin," she called, shading her eyes against the early morning sun. She smiled when she saw him sitting in a chair across the room. "What are you doing up so early?"

"It's time for me to leave, city girl. It's time for me to go home," he said sadly.

She knew from the tone of his voice that he didn't mean leaving for today. He meant leaving her forever.

Sitting up in the bed, she gathered the sheet to her chest as if to hold back the pain. She couldn't just let him leave.

"I love you, Justin," she said.

He hung his head down, then said, "And I love you."

Camille got out of the bed and went to his side. "Then give us a chance."

He lifted his head and looked into her worried brown eyes. He wanted to give them a chance, but he couldn't. Deep in his heart he knew leaving now was for the best.

"I'm sorry."

Her heart shattered into pieces at his words. She watched him pick up his bag and walk out of her life. A single tear rolled down her cheek.

～

The next day Lula looked up as her back door opened and Marie walked in.

"What did she say?" she asked, pouring a cup of coffee for Marie.

"Nothing. She gave me some excuse about things just not working out for them," Marie replied with disgust. She removed her coat and took the cup of coffee, then sat at Lula's table.

Lula slammed her hand on the table. "Doggone it! What's wrong with those two? I thought everything was going fine when he went to see her in Atlanta."

"So did I," Marie added. "But something is obviously wrong, and Camille isn't talking."

"Justin is closed up tighter than a clam. You can look into his eyes and tell that he's hurting."

Marie nodded in understanding. "I could hear the pain in Camille's voice when I talked to her this morning. Do you think Justin's talked with Karl?" Marie asked hopefully.

"No, I've already asked him. He doesn't know what happened either."

The two friends sat silently at the table and wondered why their grandchildren couldn't see that they were perfect for each other.

Ten

Those first few days after he and Camille had broken up, he merely tried to cope. He went through the motions of everyday life, but his heart wasn't in it.

How could it be, when it was in Atlanta with Camille?

He tried to go on with his life as if nothing had changed, but from the speculative and sympathetic looks he'd received from people, he knew he hadn't succeeded.

Days passed, but the pain in his heart didn't. He couldn't get her out of his mind. Her presence was everywhere—at his house, at the Filling Station, even at his office. To help him bear the pain, he buried himself in his job. It didn't help.

It was five o'clock on Friday, and Justin was still in his office. His workday had officially ended at three, but he didn't see any reason to go home to an empty house. He rubbed his eyes and leaned back in his chair. Sleep had become elusive. His body craved rest, but his mind wouldn't let him relax.

"Justin," Karl said as he entered the office. "Why are you still here?"

He gestured to his desk. "I'm finishing some paperwork."

Karl looked at his cousin, noting the lines around his mouth and his bloodshot eyes, then said, "Camille must have really hurt you. What did she do?"

"She didn't do anything. It just didn't work out between us." Justin shuffled the papers on his desk.

"It didn't work out? Did she try to talk you into moving to Atlanta?" Karl asked, his voice laced with confusion.

"No."

"Oh, I see. She hated this town like your ex-wife did."

"No," Justin replied.

"I don't get it. What's the problem?"

"The problem is . . ." Justin's voice trailed off. What was the problem? She hadn't asked him to move to Atlanta. She hadn't asked him to change. All she'd asked for was a chance at love.

And he'd refused.

He'd rejected her love, and for what? He existed in his hometown, but he wasn't living.

Justin looked at his cousin and smiled. "There is no problem."

Karl smiled at him. "Well, it's about damn time."

～

Five days later Camille was miserable. Why couldn't Valentine's Day fall on the weekend? At least she would have been spared the pain of watching as roses and candy were delivered to her coworkers. On the day that people celebrated true love, she wanted to weep.

Her love wouldn't give their love a chance.

She wondered what he was doing. Did he miss her as much as she missed him? Had he gotten over her?

In the beginning her grandmother would mention Justin when she called. Lately she hadn't said a word about him. It was for the best, she thought. Pushing aside her thoughts, she concentrated on her work.

Thank goodness the day is over, she thought as she entered the lobby of the condominium. Today had been the longest day of her life. All she wanted was a hot bath and sleep.

A policeman approached as she walked through the lobby.

"Miss Camille Johnson," he said in a demanding voice.

"Yes," she said, staring at him in surprise and confusion.

"I have a warrant for your arrest." He thrust a piece of paper at her.

"I—I don't understand," she stammered. "There must be some mistake. I haven't done anything wrong."

The officer's face was grim and unyielding. "Your crimes are all listed in the warrant."

With trembling hands Camille opened the sheet of paper.

Camille Johnson is wanted for the theft of Justin Valentio's heart.

She gasped when she read the words.

She looked up. The officer walked out of the lobby and Justin stepped inside.

Fear, joy, happiness, and surprise tumbled within her as she looked at his face. She noticed the lines around his mouth as he walked toward her.

"Hello, Camille," he said, his voice thick and raspy.

She held out the paper. "What does this mean, Justin?"

"Can we talk upstairs?" he asked.

She nodded. They walked in silence to the elevator.

Did she dare let herself hope, she wondered as she opened the door of her home. He walked inside and gestured for her to have a seat.

"I love you, Camille," he said.

He'd said he loved her but that didn't stop him from leaving, she thought. "Do you, Justin? Do you really love me?"

He sat down beside her and took her hands in his. "I love you more than anything. Give me a chance to prove my love to you."

She lowered her chin to her chest.

He put his hand under her chin and looked into her eyes. "Marry me. I can't live without you in my life."

"Bu-but you don't want to live here."

"It doesn't matter where I live. I'll move here if you want me to. I don't care as long as I'm with you."

"No, I can't . . ."

He felt the blood leave his face, and he lowered his head in defeat.

". . . ask you to live here," she continued. "I'll move to Wainswright."

Slowly, he raised his head and looked at her. Her smile was soft, tender, and full of love.

"I love you, Justin, with all my heart."

He cupped her face, lowered his head, and kissed her.

Minutes later he held her in his arms. "You never said if you'd marry me," he murmured.

She kissed his chin. "Of course I'll marry you."

His arms tightened around her and her doorbell rang. Frowning in confusion, she walked to the door.

"Yes?"

"Delivery, ma'am."

Camille opened the door. A young man wearing a florist's uniform handed her a bouquet of red roses. "Sign here," he said when she'd taken the flowers. She signed her name and closed the door.

She opened the card. "To my city girl, with love, Justin." Before she could open her mouth to speak, her doorbell rang.

"Yes?"

"Delivery."

She looked at Justin. He smiled at her tenderly.

Another delivery man held out a box of candy. She took the candy and closed the door.

"I'd love a piece of candy," he said.

She joined him on the sofa and opened the box of chocolates. A single piece of candy was missing. In its place was an engagement ring.

"Somebody ate the best piece," he said in mock surprise.

Her breath caught in her throat.

He removed the ring and slid it on her finger. "Happy Valentine's Day, love."

One month later

The whole town packed into the First Baptist Church of Wainswright to witness the wedding of Justin and Camille. Camille had moved most of her things into their home last week. She'd negotiated with her employer and now she worked from home full-time.

Justin stood at the end of the aisle with Karl, his best man, at his side. He watched in amusement as his grandmother, wearing a hat that was the exact replica of his wedding cake, was led down the aisle and seated.

The music changed, the crowd stood, and his bride, escorted by her brother, walked down the aisle. His heart swelled with love at the sight of her. When she reached his side he took her hand, kissed it, then turned to make his vows.

He vowed to love her with all his heart. And he did for the rest of his life.

ABOUT THE AUTHOR

Carla Fredd lives in Atlanta, Georgia, and is an avid romance reader as well as the author of the bestselling FIRE AND ICE.

Cupid's Bow

Brenda Jackson

The poem *"My Love Is Yours"* was written by Brenda Jackson.

Prologue

This card is perfect. A satisfied smile covered sixteen-year-old Kimara Stafford's face. She had been standing for the longest time studying the vast display of Valentine's Day cards, trying to pick out the special one for Kyle Garwood, the son of her parents' best friends.

There was no doubt in her mind that she was truly in love with him. She thought of him every waking moment and constantly daydreamed over a picture she had of him. She never thought much of the fact that he was eight years older than she was. All she knew and cared about was that she truly loved him and had always loved him, but had kept her feelings a secret. Tonight, that would change.

"Haven't you picked out a card yet?"

Kimara turned around to her friend Sandy. She nodded, holding up the card. "I think this one is perfect." She opened the card and read the verses aloud. "See, it's just the card to give an older man. It's not mushy."

Sandy nodded in agreement. "When will you give it to him?"

Kimara smiled dreamily. "Tonight. He's flying in from D.C., where he's attending grad school at Howard. My parents and I are going to the Garwoods for dinner. Kyle's grandfather will be there too."

"It must be nice to have a crush on a twenty-four-year-old man."

"I don't have a crush on Kyle," Kimara murmured softly. "What I feel for him is true love—the real thing—and not some puppy-love or teenage hero-worship stuff." She grabbed Sandy's arm and pulled her toward the checkout counter. "Come on, let's go. I want to look my best when I see Kyle tonight."

Later that evening, after Kimara and her parents arrived at the Garwoods' home, Kyle walked in with a beautiful woman at his side. He introduced her to everyone as his fiancée, and went on to announce they would be getting married the following year on Valentine's Day.

Everyone was so busy congratulating the couple that no one noticed Kimara's stricken face, the tears gathering in her eyes, or the huge envelope she'd been holding being discreetly dropped in the wastebasket, just moments before she quietly slipped from the room.

No one noticed, except Kyle's grandfather.

One

Ten years later

"What stipulation!"

Kyle Garwood V's voice did nothing to hide the anger he felt as he towered over the man sitting behind the huge mahogany desk. "I think you had better explain just what you're talking about."

Mason Long straightened in his chair. "It was your grandfather's wishes that the terms of his will be followed. He has stipulated that in order for you to inherit the entire Garwood fortune, you must marry within sixty days of his death."

Kyle gave him a piercing glare, one known to stop men dead in their tracks. "If this is a joke, Mason, I'm not laughing."

Mason nervously patted the top of his head. "It's not a joke," he said with a wry grimace. "If you refuse to follow through with the conditions set forth, a hefty bulk of the Garwood fortune will be divided among your grandfather's favorite charities. The only companies you'll have exclusive control over are those left to you by your father."

Kyle turned away from the attorney and walked over to the window. Frustrated creases angled in toward the corners of his eyes. Leave it to his grandfather to pull one over on him, even at the end. Taking a deep breath, he let his gaze stare out the window at the view before him. Downtown

Atlanta, a metropolis of streets filled with honking cars, curious sounds, and huge glass skyscrapers. The city had been the home of the Garwoods for nearly one hundred years. The family had settled in Atlanta not long after the first Kyle Garwood began working as a young chemist alongside Booker T. Washington at Tuskegee Institute. While there, Garwood developed a formula that had basically revolutionalized the black hair industry. As a result, Garwood Hair Products were introduced and Garwood Industries founded. From there they had expanded into black cosmetics and later clothing and entertainment. There weren't too many money-making ventures Garwood Industries had not touched, making the Garwoods one of the wealthiest black families in America.

Kyle turned around. "Why did he do it?"

Mason leaned back in his chair. "Because he knew you would never marry by choice, so he decided to force you into it."

"He was right. I would never marry by choice," Kyle said, remembering the reason why. Nine years ago he'd been engaged to be married on Valentine's Day, but had called it off after finding his fiancée in bed with another man the day before the wedding. He swore after that that he would never be fool enough to trust his love to another woman again. And that was one vow he planned on keeping.

Mason leaned back as far as his comfortable chair permitted, and studied Kyle. He had been his grandfather's attorney for the past five years, and had been appalled over the conditions his client had ordered to be added to his will just months before his fatal heart attack. Kyle represented the fifth generation of Garwoods, and had a reputation for three things: good looks, being irresistible to women, and money. Not necessarily in that order, but when you were a Garwood, the order of things didn't matter. He stood well over six feet tall, had broad shoulders, and was considered by many to be extremely handsome. His sable eyes, short curly black hair, and velvety copper skin were the trademark of the Garwood men and were known to melt the heart of even the most resistant female. At the age of thirty-four, he had a reputation of being one of America's most eligible black bachelors.

"I won't marry, Mason."

"I think you should give it some consideration, Kyle. Just think of what you could stand to lose if you don't."

"I'm wealthy in my own right, I don't need my grandfather's money," Kyle snapped.

"That may be true, but there's never been anyone other than a Garwood in complete control of Garwood Industries. Are you willing to give up what's rightfully yours?"

Kyle turned back to the window, knowing the answer to Mason's question without really thinking about it. He breathed in deeply, trying to get his rising anger under control. He had vowed years before to never let his grandfather bully him into anything, especially marriage. However, he would not let the old man get the best of him. If he needed a wife to inherit what was rightfully his, then so be it. He would marry a woman to adhere to the conditions in the will. Then, within a reasonable time, the marriage would be dissolved. Of course he would make sure the woman received a nice settlement for her trouble.

A mocking grin touched his lips. He would contact his own attorney immediately. Afterward, he would contact Splendor Ray, the model he was currently seeing. Splendor wasn't wife material, but she would do for a quick marriage followed by an even quicker divorce. Quickies were her specialty.

"All right, Mason, I'll be married within the allotted time. The woman I plan to marry is presently out of the country and won't—"

"There are more conditions to the will," Mason cut it.

Kyle gave him a hard look. "What else is there?"

Mason straightened in his seat and plunged forward. "Your grandfather has chosen the woman for you to marry."

"He did what!"

Mason cleared his throat. "I said he's chosen the woman he wants you to marry, the woman he wants to continue the Garwood line. The conditions in his will not only stipulate that you must marry within sixty days of his death, but it names the woman he wants you to marry, and that the two of you must conceive a child within six months of your wedding night."

A look of disbelief and rage was evident in Kyle's features. Muscles twitched in his jaw and his hands tightened into fists at his sides. Of all the idiotic things he'd ever heard. The old coot had gone too far this time. Way too far. While alive, Kyle Garwood III had thrived on trying to run his grandson's life just as much as he'd thrived on running the family empire. The older man had had a reputation of being a corporate gambler, one willing to take a chance on just about anything, especially if he thought Garwood Industries would profit in the end. Kyle couldn't help wondering if his grandfather had been so desperate for him to settle down and produce an heir that he'd been willing to risk the entire family fortune on such a proposition—correction—stipulation? Kyle distractedly patted the top of his head, already knowing the answer to his question. Yes, his grandfather would take such a gamble. He would do just about anything to make sure his only grandchild had an heir to pass the company down to someday. Even if it meant forcing him into a loveless marriage. The idea was crazy, and Kyle had no intention of going along with anything so preposterous.

"I won't do it."

Mason shrugged at Kyle's outburst. "If you decide not to follow through with your grandfather's wishes, I'll have no choice but to enforce the terms of the will."

"I'll have it nullified and have my grandfather declared incompetent at the time it was written," Kyle threatened, his anger reaching the boiling point.

"That wouldn't be a good idea, Kyle," Mason cautioned. "Just think of what a move such as that will do to Garwood stock. Surely you don't want to jeopardize the current position of your own companies, and those of your father's that were given to you. Besides, no one will think your grandfather's request odd. He'd made it public numerous times that he wanted his only grandson to settle down, get married, and produce an heir. People will view this only as his last effort to make sure that you do so."

Kyle's gaze again found the view outside the window. A ray of sunshine shone in the midday sky and bathed the area with dazzling light. However, the situation for him appeared bleak.

"Who is she?" he asked in a curt tone. "Just who is this paragon who found such favor in his eyes?"

Mason cleared his throat. "I understand you've known her for quite a while. Your grandfather was extremely fond of her. She's a young lady by the name of Kimara Stafford."

Kyle turned to face Mason. A look of incredulity on his face. "Kimara Stafford! Chubs?"

The attorney's brows went up. "Yes, Kimara Stafford. However, I don't know anything about her ever being called Chubs."

Kyle's thoughts immediately fell on the woman his grandfather had chosen for him to marry and get pregnant. He couldn't help but remember the sweet but otherwise forgettable kid who used to follow him around. The Garwoods and Staffords were neighbors and the two families had been very close for nearly a hundred years. In fact, both his and Kimara's parents had been killed when a private plane his father was piloting had crashed enroute to the Garwood-Stafford retreat in the mountains of North Carolina, following a Morehouse vs. Howard football game in D.C.

Kyle had known Kimara Stafford from the day she was born, and the one thing he remembered above all else was that she loved to eat and as a result she'd had a weight problem. He would never forget how the overweight girl, who had been given the nickname Chubs, preferred remaining inside the house, shoving Twinkies and chocolate bars down her throat, to playing outside. He saw very little of her when he got older except for summers, when he came home from boarding schools. The last time he had seen her was at their parents' funerals eight years earlier. At the age of eighteen, she still had been the non-slim, non-trim Kim. He could just imagine how she looked now.

"I will not marry Kimara Stafford."

"I suggest you think about this before you make a decision."

"There's nothing to think about. Has she been told about my grandfather's ridiculous request?"

"Yes, I spoke with her yesterday after the funeral services."

Kyle frowned. He didn't recall seeing anyone who fitted Kimara Stafford's description at the funeral. "You didn't waste any time telling her, did you, Mason?" he sneered.

"I was merely carrying out your grandfather's orders. He requested that the terms of the will be explained to the two of you separately, as soon as possible, preferably with her first."

"And what was her reaction?"

"She handled the news better than I expected. She thought the world of your grandfather and felt that although she didn't agree with what he did, she understood why he did it."

"What do you mean, she understood? Are you implying that she wants to go along with my grandfather's stupid plan?"

"No, Kyle. I'm not implying anything. There are no added incentives for Miss Stafford to marry you. Inheriting Stafford Publishing upon her parents' death made her a wealthy lady in her own right. Also, your grandfather left her a sizable trust, among other things, with no conditions attached. I got the distinct impression that Miss Stafford doesn't want to marry you any more than you want to marry her."

Kyle let out a sigh of relief. However, Mason's words didn't sit too well with him. What did he mean that Kimara Stafford didn't want to marry him? Just who did she think she was anyway? Him not wanting to marry her was one thing, she not wanting to marry him was another.

"So the heiress of Stafford Publishing thinks she can afford to be picky?"

"And with good reason. Not long after her parents' death, under the recommendation of your grandfather she turned the running of Stafford Publishing over to a very capable CEO, who has done an outstanding job. The company is second in the nation behind Johnson Publishing. She worked at Stafford Publishing for a while after college, then decided to venture into other things. Miss Stafford is the co-owner of the Golden Flame Catering Services."

"A catering service? For some reason, that doesn't surprise me. She always had a fondness for food."

Mason raised his eyes toward the ceiling. "The Golden Flame is a very successful business here in Atlanta, Kyle. I might add that it's been the recipient of numerous cooking awards and rave reviews. Since you spend most of your time in New York, you're probably not aware of that."

"You're right," he replied coldly. "I'm not. And it sounds to me like Miss Stafford is an extremely busy woman. Too busy for a rebellious husband and a screaming baby. Since neither she nor I have any desire to marry or become parents, I'm positive our lawyers can come up with some suitable solution where we'll all be happy."

"Kyle, I don't think you fully understand," Mason spoke quickly. "Please feel free to consult your own attorney, but trust me, the will is airtight.

There's nothing anyone can do. Your grandfather made absolutely sure of that. If you're not married to Miss Stafford within sixty days, and if she's not pregnant within six months of your wedding night, I have no choice but to enforce the terms of the will."

Kyle's thoughts slumped into morose musings. "For heaven's sake, Mason, it's almost the twenty-first century. Arranged marriages played out years ago. Granddad's request is totally insane. Besides, what if she can't conceive? What if we aren't compatible?"

"Then you'll definitely encounter a problem your grandfather may not have taken under consideration," he responded mildly. "Let's just hope that's not the case. You have six months to find out."

Kyle shook his head in disbelief. His grandfather had it all figured out. First, he had to make sure there would be a wedding. Then to make sure it wasn't a marriage in name only just to satisfy the conditions of the will, he had further dictated that a child be conceived, which meant that the two of them would have to become intimate. Kyle rubbed his temple with his fingers as the enormity of the situation sank in. Being forced to admit he'd been outsmarted by the old man didn't sit too well with him.

"If I remember correctly, the Stafford estate was sold a few years ago. Do you have the address where Kimara Stafford is living now?"

Mason nodded as he reached into his desk drawer and took out a slip of paper. He handed it to Kyle. "She shares a house in Stone Mountain with the young woman who's her business partner."

Kyle gave Mason a hard, cold glare. "Don't look so smug. I still have no intention of marrying Kimara Stafford. Since she's as opposed to the idea of the marriage as I am, hopefully, together the two of us can come up with something. And I can guarantee you, it won't be a baby."

He turned and walked out of the office.

Two

Kyle spotted the street sign indicating Mackenzie Lane. It was located just off Broderick Road in an upscale neighborhood on the outskirts of Atlanta. It didn't take long for him to find the house sitting back off the road on a meticulously well-tended lawn. Oak and magnolia trees, whose tops swayed with the whisper of a warm breeze, flanked the stylish brick structure.

He parked his Lexus in the driveway, hesitating briefly before walking up the winding path to the front door. After ringing the doorbell several times with no response, he listened over the back drop of various noises for a sign that someone was home. He was just about to turn to leave, when his ears picked up an upbeat tune playing from a distance in the backyard. He followed brick steps leading around the back of the house.

The pungent smell of chlorine teased his nostrils and led him to an area surrounded by a privacy fence. The gate was slightly ajar, and without hesitating he opened it and went into the backyard. What he saw left him thunderstruck.

A woman dressed in skimpy shorts and an even skimpier bandeau top was on the patio, moving her body furiously to the rock music blaring out of a nearby CD player. Kyle stood hidden from her view in total awe at the sight of the curvaceous body whose chestnut-brown hair was piled atop her head in a ragged knot with wayward strands catching the midday breeze.

His gaze took her in from head to toe. She had a long, graceful neck that connected to a sleek back. That back merged with the gentle curve of a sexy behind. Her bare hips flared into long, straight thighs which were joined to a gorgeous pair of legs.

Kyle couldn't stop the rapid sensations of sexual hunger tearing through him as he watched her body bend, stretch, and strain to the music. He was suddenly at a loss at the intensity of his attraction to her.

In a daze he continued watching her, trying desperately not to make a sound and dismissing the thought that at the moment, he was no better than a peeping Tom. The back of her head was to him, but he had a hunch he wouldn't be disappointed with the face he couldn't see.

He was suddenly jolted senseless when she dropped her body forward to the ground, and with palms flat on the floor began walking on her hands, coming up on her toes.

He almost swallowed his tongue when he got a peek at her cocoa-colored face. He had been absolutely correct about her looks; she was gorgeous. She had a delectable mouth, full and inviting; high cheekbones; a delicate feminine chin; and thick, well-shaped brows.

His entire body burst into flames of desire. The more he watched her, the more he wanted to touch her to see if she was real or a figment of his imagination. Without realizing he was doing so, he began moving toward her, coming to a stop directly behind her.

The woman whose rump was in the air as she began her cooldown caught a movement out of the corner of her eye. A scream tore from her throat and she jumped to her feet, reacting in fear. Her sudden move made Kyle lose his balance and tumble over into the pool.

Kimara Stafford's eyes widened in shock at the sight of the drenched man in her pool. She was about to race off and barricade herself in the house, when she recognized him. She would know Kyle Garwood anywhere.

The years had been kind to him. Way too kind. He was still as handsome as sin. Even saturated with pool water he looked gorgeous. There was an inherent strength in his classically dark, handsome good looks, and she detested the fact that his features held a certain sensuality that was downright disturbing.

"How dare you sneak up on me!" she stormed. "Just who do you think you are, coming up behind me like that?"

Kyle pulled himself up over the edge of the pool and stood soaked to the bone in front of the seemingly hysterical woman. Her eyes, he mused, under normal circumstances, would be a dark brown. However, at the moment they were blazing with sparks of fire in them. "For Pete's sake, calm down! I can explain."

His eyes squeezed shut momentarily against the sting from the chlorine water. "I'm Kyle Garwood, and I was looking for your roommate, Kimara Stafford."

Kimara's lashes fluttered and rose in surprise. He thought she was Nicky? Did he not recognize her? Probably not. Her appearance had definitely changed over the years. "You're looking for Kimara? Do you make it a habit to sneak up on people?" she snapped.

Kyle willed his temper to stay in check. The woman was getting downright testy, and for no reason at all. "Look, lady, I didn't actually sneak up on you. I was about to make my presence known before you attacked me. As far as I'm concerned, you should be thankful I'm not a criminal with you bouncing around dressed like that with your gate unlocked."

"This is my backyard and it's private property. And I wasn't bouncing around. I was doing my aerobics. And furthermore, there's nothing wrong with the way I'm dressed."

Kyle frowned, wondering what was happening to him. Beautiful women were not uncommon to him. However, this one had him spellbound. His anger ignited at the thought that she hadn't had enough sense to be more cautious. What if another man had come upon her the way he had? Suddenly his anger became a shadow beneath the passion he felt snaking through his body.

He could not remember ever having been so affected by a woman. The intensity of it pulled at his insides. Her body was all feminine, all enticing, all womanly. It was a body that belonged to a woman ripe for love of the most fulfilling kind. In that instance he knew two things; making love to her would be all-consuming, all-fiery, and hot; and he wanted her like he had never wanted another woman before in his life. The thought that any woman could get under his skin like she was doing didn't sit well with him at all. In defiance of these strange feelings, he lashed out at her.

"If anything, I hope I scared some sense into you. Maybe next time you'll be more careful."

Kimara's anger escalated. She wanted him gone and off her property. "What do you want with Kimara?" she snapped.

Kyle glared at her. "It's personal."

She placed hands on her hips. "Too bad. She's not up to seeing anyone, so please leave."

"And who made you her spokeswoman? I came here to see Kimara, and I don't plan on leaving here until I do. Do you hear me?" Kyle said, raising his voice a little too loud for Kimara's taste.

"Yes, I can hear you, Mr. Garwood. So can everyone else in this neighborhood," she yelled back.

"Hey! What's going on? What's all the screaming about, and whose gorgeous car is that in the driveway?"

The two people turned around at the sound of the feminine voice. Kyle stared at the unusually tall, attractive woman who came from inside the house to join them. "I forgot my proposal for the Joyners' daughter's wedding and came back for it. It's a good thing I did. Sounds like World War Three out here," she said. "Is anything wrong, Kim?"

"Kim?" The name escaped Kyle's lips with a mixture of astonishment, disbelief, and surprise. He stood with his mouth gaped open in utter shock. A few seconds later he groaned and sucked in his breath as his eyes raked over the woman standing in front of him. There had to be some mistake. She looked nothing like the Kimara Stafford he remembered. "Chubs?"

"Don't call me that!" Kimara flared. "You've done enough damage for one day, so I suggest you leave. And do me a favor and don't come back, because we have nothing to say to each other." With those icy words, a fuming Kimara stormed into the house, slamming the door behind her.

The other woman cleared her throat as she approached the wet man. "I don't think we've met. I'm Nicole Britt, Kimara's roommate. But I prefer to be called Nicky. I already know who you are, Mr. Garwood. I've seen your picture several times in magazines and newspapers."

Kyle took the hand being offered to him in friendship as he gazed into tawny brown eyes that highlighted her almond-colored features. The woman who wore flat shoes stood equal to his six-foot-two-inch frame. "It's nice meeting you, Nicky, and please call me Kyle."

A smile touched Nicky's lips. "If you'll excuse me for saying so, Kyle, it seems like you've made quite a splash around here."

Three

Kyle took his gaze off the view outside the window and focused it on Mason Long. There was a purposeful intent in his eyes. "Are you sure she's going to show up?"

Mason's brows drew together in a frown. "My secretary contacted Miss Stafford earlier today and she agreed to meet with me." He leaned back in his chair. "Would you mind telling me what this is about, Kyle?"

Kyle rose from his seat and leaned casually against the closed door. He shrugged dismissively. "There's nothing to tell other than I've decided marriage may not be such a bad idea after all."

Mason sat there, blank-faced, amazed, and very confused. "Just a couple of days ago you were totally against the idea. In fact you said that you had no intention of marrying Kimara Stafford. What made you change your mind?"

Kyle stared at the man for a moment, his lips twitching at his obvious perplexity. He decided not to tell him it hadn't been that difficult to realize the advantages in marrying Kimara Stafford if he had to marry anyone; she wouldn't be after his money, since she had plenty of her own; she was well-bred and socially acceptable; marrying her would guarantee him complete control of Garwood Industries; and the idea of sharing a bed with her held a certain appeal. There was no way he would disclose those reasons to Mason.

"Let's just say I've had a change of heart. My grandfather was right. It's about time I settled down and produced some little Garwoods."

Mason looked at Kyle suspiciously, not easily fooled by his congenial manner and blithe acceptance of the situation. He had worked with Kyle's grandfather long enough to know that when the Garwoods were faced with something that couldn't be avoided, they had the uncanny ability to turn it to their advantage. It would be interesting to see what the younger man's game plan was.

He didn't have time to dwell on the thought any further, because at that precise moment his secretary's voice came across the intercom on his desk.

"Mr. Long, Miss Stafford is here."

"Please send her in, Mrs. Franklin." Mason stood and straightened his tie. Kyle, he noticed, had moved away from the door and stood across the room near the window.

The door opened and Kimara Stafford walked in. As far as Kyle was concerned, every other object in the room faded to oblivion the moment she entered. Her presence demanded his complete attention. She's everything dreams are made of, he thought, feasting his eyes on the woman who had haunted his thoughts ever since seeing her two days earlier. Her tailored linen business suit was a far cry from the skimpy outfit she'd been wearing. She strode into the office with the silky grace of an African queen and carried with her the scent of sweet magnolias.

His mind had drummed out Mason's greeting to Kimara until he noticed her surprised eyes on him. As he'd requested, she had not been told he would be there. He watched as her expression turned to one of displeasure.

"I believe the two of you know each other." Mason's words brought their attention to him.

Kyle came from his spot on the other side of the room to stand in front of her. "Yes. It's good seeing you again."

Kimara ignored Kyle's words and turned to Mason. "What's he doing here? What's this about?"

Mason cleared his throat. "I really don't know, but I'm sure Kyle will enlighten us, since he's the one who requested this meeting. Please have a seat, dear."

Kimara took the chair Mason offered and tried not to let her gaze take in the man standing not far away. His profile spoke of power and strength. His handsome face held some secret expression, and his lips were parted in a dazzling display of straight white teeth that framed a buttery smile. "What's this about, Kyle?"

Kyle took the seat across from hers. For several moments he only stared at her, not believing the transformation that took place over the years.

"I asked what this is about, Kyle," Kimara repeated.

Kyle noticed out of the corner of his eye that Mason had taken his seat and was undoubtedly waiting for his answer too. "I think it should be obvious why I asked you here, Kimara. I want to marry you."

At that moment Kyle expected a lot of things, but he hadn't counted on the clipped but dignified laugh that escaped her lips. "Was that supposed to be a proposal?" she asked, amused.

Kyle sat back in his chair, not seeing anything funny. "Yes."

A trace of a smile touched the corner of her lips. "In that case, my answer is no. How dare you assume I'll marry you." Her eyes then smoldered with resentment. "Mason, would you mind leaving us alone for a few minutes?"

"Not at all," the older man replied, quickly getting out of his chair. From his way of thinking, he didn't need to witness any disturbance that would make his ulcer flare up again, and he had a feeling if he stuck around, these two young people would cause just that. He hurriedly left the room.

Kimara stood and began pacing the room. Kyle remained seated, stretching his legs far out in front of him as he watched her.

"Why didn't you return my calls, Kimara?"

She stopped her pacing and turned to him. "I had nothing to say to you."

"I was calling to apologize."

Kimara raised a surprised brow.

"I want to apologize for frightening you that day," he said. "But I still think you should be more careful about keeping your gate locked."

Although she knew he was right, at the moment Kimara wasn't in a mood to agree with him. "I know why you arranged this meeting, Kyle, to discuss your grandfather's will. I want you to know up front that I have no intention of going through with what he wants." She leaned against Mason's desk, bracing her rear end on its edge.

Kyle was suddenly plagued with memories of that same rear end bouncing around while she was doing aerobics. That had been a breathtaking sight. "And I think we should go through with it."

Kimara gazed at him, anger reflecting in her eyes. "Why? So you can retain the Garwood millions?"

"No. So we can give my grandfather what he wanted most." Kyle knew his statement had hit home when he saw her reaction to it.

Kimara's eyes narrowed at Kyle. "When did you begin caring about giving your grandfather what he wanted? Poppa Garwood loved you and wanted to spend more time with you, but all you ever found time for besides the business was your numerous women."

"I made a mistake," Kyle said truthfully. He regretted not spending more time with his grandfather. He'd spent the last two nights at the Garwood estate finally realizing just how much he missed the old man's presence. At one time the two of them had been close. Things had changed after his parents' death, and to this day he never understood why.

"A mistake? To my way of thinking, you've made several of them," Kimara shot back.

Her words cut into Kyle. "Now, you wait just a minute. What gives you the right to judge me or my actions? I gave my grandfather plenty of chances.

I bent over backward several times to make amends, but he just wouldn't bend. I got tired of trying."

"Well, you shouldn't have. He needed you, Kyle. Your grandfather took our parents' death extremely hard. It was bad enough losing his own son, but then to lose my father, who was like a second son to him too. Just think what he'd been going through all these years. Do you know he blamed himself for the accident?"

Kyle was taken aback by her statement. "Why would he blame himself for that?"

"Because he was the one who talked them into chartering that small plane to fly to the retreat instead of taking a commercial flight."

"How do you know all of this?"

Kimara took a deep breath. "Because he eventually told me. I was there to listen when you weren't."

Kyle stood and slowly walked over to the window. "He could have told me what he was feeling. Why did he have to shut me out? He could have told me, and I would have understood."

Kimara looked everywhere but at Kyle. His pain was reaching out to her. She had urged Poppa Garwood numerous times to talk to Kyle about his misplaced guilt. But he had felt that doing so would drive an even deeper wedge between him and his grandson. "Yes, he could have talked to you. I even encouraged him to. But he chose not to tell you about the guilt he was carrying around. He didn't mean to shut you out of his life, he just didn't want to risk losing you too. He was a very proud man, Kyle, but he was also a good one. When I returned home after completing college, he gave me the strength to make a lot of decisions that needed to be made."

"And from what I understand, you also helped him. I thought the cigarettes and cigars would do him in long ago."

Kimara smiled. "I convinced him to stop smoking."

Kyle turned away from the window and came to stand before Kimara "I bet that hadn't been easy?"

Kim shrugged. "It was well worth the effort. He was the grandfather I never had. He was there so many times when I needed someone. I loved him and will miss him."

Kyle sighed deeply. "Even with all of our differences, I loved him too. He was the only family I had. I never wanted to disappoint him." With the words he'd just spoken, Kyle suddenly realized at that moment that he would do anything and everything to fulfill his grandfather's last wish—even marry. He owed him that much, and more. There was no longer any ulterior motives for him wanting to do so. He wouldn't do it for any advantages to himself, he would do it because he knew more than anything how much his grandfather wanted the Garwood line to continue. And unless he married and had a child, it would come to an end with him. "So, what do you want to do about the conditions of his will?"

"Nothing."

Kyle raised a brow. "Shouldn't we at least discuss them?" he asked.

"For what reason? I have no intentions of marrying you."

"I think you should at least think about it. When I first heard what Granddad wanted us to do, I was furious. He knew how I felt about ever getting married. However, now he's left me no choice."

"For the money."

"No, it has nothing to do with the money. I'm a pretty wealthy man without my grandfather's money. The only reason I'll even consider getting married is that now I realize just how much continuing the Garwood line meant to him for him to pull something like this. And whether you like it or not, you're the woman he wants to have the Garwood heir."

Kimara's eyes smoldered with anger. "I won't do it!"

"Hey, look, don't get angry with me. I didn't name you in the will, he did.

But I think you'll do just what he wants, Kimara. You'll do it for the same reason I'll do it. Even though we're madder than hell at him right now for doing what he did, we both loved him, and he knew it." Kyle drew in a deep breath. "Don't you see? Granddad went to his grave believing that he would get just what he wanted. And do you know why?"

Not waiting for Kimara to reply, Kyle continued. "Because he knew that the two of us would never deny him anything. He knew that no matter how we felt about each other or how crazy the plan was that he concocted, we would go through with it because we loved him. He died believing in our love for him."

The truth of Kyle's words rang in Kimara's ears. Deep down she knew he was right. She had spent enough time with Poppa Garwood to know how much continuing the Garwood line meant to him. And although his relationship with Kyle hadn't been at its best over the years, he'd known Kyle loved him.

"Think of Granddad, Kimara, and you'll realize there's only one thing for us to do."

"I need to think about this, Kyle, and I can't think straight now."

"Kimara . . ." he began. "Let's just—"

"No. I have to think this through. Give me a few days. I'll call you."

"Think of Granddad," Kyle repeated when she turned to leave.

After Kimara walked out of the office, closing the door behind her, Kyle drew in a ragged, nettled breath, angry with himself. The last thing he'd wanted was to show his vulnerability to any woman. He'd wanted to bottle up inside of him all the memories and pain of his strained relationship with his grandfather. He hadn't wanted to ever share them with anyone.

But he had shared them with Kimara.

And she had understood. No, he thought further to himself, she had more than understood. She had offered him an explanation for his grandfather's behavior the past eight years. Without realizing it, she'd made the ability to get through his grandfather's death easier for him. Somehow she'd known he was suffering and had shared his pain, mainly because they both felt the same loss. Kyle Garwood III had touched both their lives. Death was supposed to be final. Permanent. But somehow his grandfather had found a way to call the shots even from the grave.

Kyle leaned against the desk under the weight of both anger and grief. After a brief moment he shrugged his wide shoulders as if to ease the tension in them. Kimara had said she needed to think and that she would be contacting him.

There was nothing left for him to do now but wait for her call.

After leaving Mason's office, it didn't take Kimara long to drive the short distance to the building where the office of the Golden Flame Catering Service was located. She was determined for the time being to put Kyle out of her mind.

There were several messages on her desk when she arrived. All of them were regarding the Valentine's Day charity ball that the Golden Flame would be catering and her company, Stafford Publishing, would be sponsoring. With the holiday season now behind her, she needed to resume making plans for the ball that would be held next month.

This would be the third year that Stafford Publishing sponsored the event, with all the proceeds going to the United Negro College Fund. It was the only time she publicly took over her position as president of Stafford Publishing Company. This year she wanted to make the event more special than before. And to assure that goal, she had formed a special committee consisting of several members of Stafford Publishing's management team to work with her.

As in the past, a number of celebrities had agreed to participate, some of them coming from as far away as California. She'd already received firm commitments back from Halle and David, Luther, Spike, Whitney and Denzel, just to name a few. But still, there were others she hadn't gotten a response—like Sterling Hamilton. At present he was the number-one black actor in the country, and after the blockbuster success of his last four movies, he was also the latest heartthrob. She didn't want to think what a giant boost his presence would make at the affair.

This year's ball would be different in a number of ways, she thought. It would be the first time in three years that Poppa Garwood would not be her escort.

Kimara sat down in the chair at her desk and pensively glanced around the room. Her gaze focused on a painting on the wall. It was a piece of black art featuring a mother and child. Poppa Garwood had given it to her the day she opened her office.

Slowly, she pushed herself away from her desk, walked over to the window, and stood staring out. As much as she didn't want to, she couldn't help but think about Kyle. She'd seen him from a distance at the funeral service. Even then she'd wanted to go to him and put her arms around him to share his grief and his pain. She had watched him sit stiffly erect and withdrawn through the service, totally separated from the people around him.

The deep emotions she'd felt for him that day had touched her so deeply that for a while she had doubted her ability to get through the service. But somehow she'd found the strength to do so. And today, while closed in Mason's office with Kyle, she had not expected the feelings she had experienced as an impressionable sixteen-year-old to plague her again.

But they had.

Ten years ago suddenly seemed like yesterday. Each time she had met his eyes—those eyes that belonged to the man who had haunted her fantasies since childhood—she couldn't help but wonder if she had indeed gotten completely over him, as she had thought. There was no doubt in her mind that she was still attracted to him. Her body's strange reaction whenever she was near him was a surefire indication. There was no way she could ever think of him as just another man. To her he would always be more. Feelings for him had been instilled in her from an early age. They were feelings that should have lost most of their momentum over the years, but now upon seeing him again, those same feelings were trying to resurface—deep emotions that she didn't want to feel ever again. Unknowingly he had hurt her deeply before, and had basically ruined her for any other man. At sixteen she had gotten her heart broken. That was something she could not and would not forget. And knowing how she felt, the best thing to do would be to avoid Kyle at all cost. But deep down in her heart she knew she couldn't do that. Today he'd struck her where she was most vulnerable when he had said, "Think of Granddad."

She was indeed thinking about Poppa Garwood and the conditions he had placed in his will. She wanted to feel anger and resentment over his underhandedness and for being so manipulating, but couldn't. The reason she couldn't was that she knew that in Poppa Garwood's own special way, he'd sent out a clear message to her of just how much she meant to him, and just how much he thought of her to want her to bring his great-grandchild into the world.

She tossed her head, feeling she was fighting a losing battle in trying to make the most difficult decision of her life. She knew in her heart that she would willingly give to Poppa Garwood in death what he'd been denied in life. What Kyle had said was true. She could never deny Poppa Garwood anything. She couldn't let the complex and bewildering feelings she was experiencing for Kyle interfere with what she had to do. It wasn't about her or Kyle, but about fulfilling a special man's last dream. It was about giving him what he'd wanted most—future generations of Garwoods. It was the least she could do for the man who had always been there for her.

Kimara turned from the window and went back to her desk.

Four

The sound of soft music drifted through the restaurant. Kyle gazed over the candlelight to the woman sitting across the table from him. When Kimara had contacted him that morning requesting to meet with him, he had jumped at the opportunity to ask her out to dinner. At first she'd been reluctant, then had agreed.

Tonight he thought she looked even more beautiful than the other two recent times he'd seen her. The outfit she had on, a sleek sea-foam-colored silk dress, enhanced the lush curves of her body. And her creamy brown skin seemed to glow in the candlelight. Her silky head of layered chestnut hair brushed against her cheeks and touched her shoulders. Every single thing about her screamed sensuality. There was no doubt in Kyle's mind that any man who possessed a lick of sense would want to take her to bed and keep her there until he'd gotten his fill—which would never happen, because he would always want more. The thought of her giving birth to his child sent fierce stirrings of arousal through him. He wondered if she was presently involved with anyone. According to the information he'd been able to squeeze out of Mason as well as a few other reliable sources, although Kimara dated occasionally, there was no serious man in her life.

Kyle's fingers tightened around the long-stemmed glass he held in his hand. He'd promised himself before picking her up for dinner that he wouldn't let her beauty go to his head. He had let his guard down around her once, but wouldn't do so again.

Deep in thought, Kimara didn't pay any attention to the food before her. Instead, she was wondering what changes her decision would make in her life. What changes would it make in Kyle's? She put her fork down and looked up at him. To her discomfort, he had been watching her.

She cleared her throat. "I've decided to marry you, Kyle."

He continued to hold her gaze. "What made you change your mind?"

"I think you already know the answer to that. In fact, you stated it so eloquently in Mason's office. I could never deny Poppa Garwood anything. A great-grandchild is something he wanted, and it's now up to us to make sure he has one. I just hate that you didn't settle down and give him one before he died."

Kyle's gaze hardened. "My grandfather knew my position on marriage, and I wasn't about to go out and marry someone just to please him. My parents had a beautiful and meaningful marriage, and so did my grandparents. The one thing I apparently didn't inherit from the Garwood men was their ability to choose a good woman. My mother and grandmother were caring, devoted, trustworthy women. Instead, I fell in love with someone who had the morals of Jezebel."

"There are good women out there, Kyle. Maybe you weren't looking hard enough."

His eyes narrowed. "I haven't been looking at all because it was never my intent to marry. I don't want any woman getting foolish ideas about me being struck with an arrow from Cupid's bow, because it won't happen. I won't entrust my love with another woman again."

Kimara wondered if his words had been meant as a warning to her. "She really did a number on you, didn't she?"

He lifted a dark brow. "Who?"

"The woman you were engaged to marry."

His chuckle was chilling. "Let's just say that if anything, she taught me a very valuable lesson; only fools fall in love." He picked up his fork to resume eating. "I assume you do like children."

Kimara also picked up her fork, understanding completely that conversation pertaining to Kyle's engagement was over. "Yes, very much so. I've always intended to marry one day and have at least two or three. I'd just never given any thought to having one so soon."

Kyle nodded. "Are you familiar with the terms of my grandfather's will?"

"Yes, I met with Mason again today, and he went over them with me."

"Then you know Granddad was pretty specific about a number of things."

Kimara fingered the rim of her wineglass. "Yes."

"I'm to be married within sixty days of his death, and you're to be pregnant within six months of our wedding day. So the way I see it, six months is the longest we'll have to spend together, even less if you conceive right away. However, the will stipulated that we're to still be married the day the child is born."

Kimara's hands were trembling slightly when she picked up her wineglass to take a sip. The thought of sleeping with Kyle was too much to think about. "Kyle, have you given thought to another option we can use . . . for me to become pregnant? We'll still be married, but there wouldn't have to be any actual physical contact between us."

Kyle's brow rose. "I assume you're referring to artificial insemination?"

"Yes."

"A procedure like that is out of the question. I'd never agree to it. There's only one way I intend to get you pregnant, Kimara, and that's the old-fashioned way." He leaned back as far as his comfortable chair permitted and looked intently at her. "We need to have a clear understanding up front. If we decide to marry, we'll sleep together. Once you have conceived, I'll be out of your life. You'll be free to file for divorce right after the child is born, and I'll give you custody. Is that agreeable to you?"

"Yes," Kimara answered.

Kyle straightened back up in his seat. "By the way, how's your cycle? Is it pretty regular?"

Kimara nearly choked on her wine, totally embarrassed by the question Kyle asked. He had inquired about the workings of her body as comfortably as if he'd been inquiring about the weather. "You have no right to ask about a thing like that. It's none of your business."

Kyle smiled. "I disagree, under the circumstances. Since you've agreed to marry me, I want to do whatever I have to to stay within the allotted time. It will help matters if we could pinpoint a time of the month that you'll be able to conceive, unless, however, you want to play it by ear and make love each and every single night until we finally—"

"All right, Kyle, I see your point."

"I thought that you would."

Kimara sighed. "I have a good guess but I'll make an appointment to see my doctor this week to be accurate. I'm sure he'll be able to provide me with the information you're interested in."

"Good. I want you to contact me as soon as you get it. We should try to plan our wedding and honeymoon around it. If things go as planned, you might be able to get pregnant during the two weeks of our honeymoon."

"Two weeks?"

"Yes, have you forgotten that's another thing stipulated in my grandfather's will? Our honeymoon is supposed to last two weeks."

A frown covered Kimara's features. Unfortunately, she had forgotten. "In that case, I'd like to put off any plans of marriage and a honeymoon until after Valentine's Day."

A bemused look settled on Kyle's face. "Why?"

"Stafford Publishing is sponsoring a Valentine's Day charity ball, and I'm too involved in that to get away. Each year I'm doubly involved since the Golden Flame is also providing catering service. I'd rather be here during that time and not—"

"Someplace in my arms, making a baby," Kyle finished for her."

Kimara gave him a narrowed look. "I was going to say I'd rather be here than out of town during that time."

"Same thing." Kyle wiped his mouth with his napkin. "Valentine's Day is more than a month from now. I see no reason why we can't squeeze a wedding and a honeymoon in before then."

"Why the rush, Kyle?" she snapped.

Kyle met her gaze, and for the life of him he didn't have a reason to give her. He gave her the only reason he could think of. "We have only sixty days to marry, and a week of that has gone by already. If we wait until after Valentine's Day, that will leave only two weeks. I don't like being that close to any deadline."

"I'm sorry you feel that way, but I can't agree to anything before Valentine's Day, Kyle. I have too much to do."

"I'm sure you're very familiar with the word *delegate,* so pass on some of your duties to others. You have a partner at the Golden Flame, and I'm sure she's capable of handling things without you. As far as Stafford Publishing is concerned, everything's probably on schedule. How much trouble can one little valentine party be?"

"For your information, Mr. Garwood, this is not just one little valentine party. Some people consider it one of Atlanta's biggest social events of the year. Since it's been a while since you've made Atlanta your home, I really don't expect you to know that. All the proceeds for the ball will go to the United Negro College Fund. With the help of a number of celebrities, we're ensuring the college future for a number of well-deserving black students who wouldn't otherwise have a chance to go to college."

"You don't have to sell UNCF's merits to me, Kimara. Garwood Industries has been a strong supporter of it for a number of years. I believe in everything it represents. And even though I've never attended one of your Valentine's Day balls, I'm aware of them. I apologize if you thought I insinuated the affair wasn't important. I just don't know why you're making such a big deal of it this year. From what I understand, each year the event proves to be more successful than the year before. Why are you getting so bent out of shape about it this year?"

Kimara released a deep sigh. "This is the first year Poppa Garwood won't be here to give me guidance and support. Before he died he came up with an idea that I thought was wonderful and jumped on it. Now it seems like I may have bitten off more than I can chew."

"In what way?"

She placed her napkin next to her plate. "Each year the event is open only to celebrities, and anyone willing to purchase a three-hundred-dollar-per-couple ticket. And you're right, it's been highly successful because of the number of people who know the importance of UNCF. Eight months ago Poppa Garwood suggested that I make it a more people-reaching event, and invite fifty of the city's most promising high school students, those who would more than likely one day need UNCF. This would give them an opportunity to mingle with the celebrities. He felt this would broaden their hope for the future and provide further encouragement."

"That's not a bad idea, so what's the problem?"

Kimara smiled. "Some people really wouldn't think there is one. I'm the only one who isn't completely satisfied with the way things are going. The idea was well received in the community. A tuxedo shop has agreed to provide tuxes to the young men free of charge, and several gown shops in the area will dress the young ladies for the night. And a limousine service has volunteered to give free limo rides to the young honorees. The last thing we want is for any of the students to incur expenses for the event. Most of them couldn't afford to do so anyway."

Kimara took time to let the waiter place another bottle of chilled wine on their table before continuing. "The problem I'm having to deal with is the lack of response we've gotten from some of the celebrities. The same ones that usually come each year will be in attendance, but I was hoping that more of those who'd never attended before could put it on their schedule to come. The invitations were mailed out three months ago, and I haven't gotten a response from a number of them, and the ball is next month."

She took another sip of wine. "I've even sent follow-ups, but haven't heard anything. Although those who don't attend usually come through with a pretty nice donation to UNCF, I would like them to be there. I want the ball to be special for the students that are coming. For some, it will be the only opportunity they'll ever have to meet people they have admired, respected, and loved from a distance."

Kyle was silent for a minute. No wonder his grandfather thought a lot of her. She was a very caring person. He didn't know any woman who would take on such a task without an ulterior motive—like a chance to shine in the spotlight. All Kimara was concerned about was making sure the students she had invited would thoroughly enjoy themselves.

"Do you have a list of the names of the celebrities who have not yet responded?" Kyle found himself asking.

Kimara lifted a brow. "Yes, why?"

"I'd like a copy. I'm officially volunteering to be a part of your committee."

Kimara looked stunned. "What? I don't understand. Why?"

"Because I have every intention for us to marry before this blasted ball, and the way I see it, you won't agree to do so unless you feel certain a number of the people on that list are either coming or aren't. Either way, you'd like to know for sure, won't you?"

"Yes."

"Then that settles it. I don't know whose names are on your list, but I probably know a number of them, maybe even personally. Most celebrities leave the handling of their mail and invitations to their personal secretaries, who decide what functions they will or will not attend. I bet a lot of the people on that list aren't aware they were invited."

Kimara smiled brightly. "Thanks for any help you can give. I really appreciate it, and, Kyle?"

"Yes?"

"You aren't on that list. As usual, your response card was one of the first I received indicating you wouldn't be attending."

Kyle gave her a long stare with her comment. "I have personal reasons for not getting caught up with anything having to do with Valentine's Day," he replied curtly. "Are you ready to go?"

"Yes, I'm ready."

The conversation between them on the drive back to Kimara's home was primarily about the Valentine's Day ball, with her providing him with more details about it. Deep down, a part of him wished he could share her excitement, but he knew that he couldn't. Valentine's Day nine years ago was to be the happiest day of his life. Instead, it had been the most humiliating. Since then, he'd never thought much of the day. He believed that thanks to the greeting card industry, florists, and candy companies, the day was highly overrated. No one could convince him that the world was filled with that many lovesick people. Most men didn't give gifts on Valentine's Day as a token of their undying love, but gave them because it was expected. And like most men, he played the game, leaving the chore of ordering flowers for whatever woman he was involved with at the time to his secretary.

When Kyle stopped the car in front of Kimara's house, he picked up on her sudden eagerness to depart from his company. There was no doubt in his mind that he would not be invited inside for coffee.

He walked her to the door. She unlocked and slightly opened it before turning back to him again.

"Thanks for dinner, Kyle."

He nodded. "I'm leaving in the morning for New York. I'll call you in a few days."

"That's fine. Good night."

He stood in the doorway, making no move to leave. Instead, he leaned toward her and lightly touched her mouth with his.

Kyle's warm taste filled Kimara, and she closed her eyes when he deepened the kiss, pulling her closer against him. As if with a will of their own, her arms found their way around his neck as she eagerly accepted the intimate way his tongue mated with hers. How long had she fantasized about kissing him? When she'd been sixteen, that was all she had ever thought about—the day when Kyle would take her into his arms and kiss her, sending her mind and body spinning. And now, ten years later, he was doing just that. His kiss was everything romantic dreams were made of . . . and more.

Kyle slowly lifted his mouth away from hers, breathing deeply as he continued to hold her in his arms. "That kiss proves we'll be good together."

His words helped Kimara regain her composure and get a grip on her own ragged breathing. "Good night, Kyle." She said the words, then stepped into her house, quietly closing the door.

Kyle went to his car, but instead of starting it up and driving away, he sat in it for a moment. The kiss had been everything he'd known it would be.

Kimara's response to him had been genuine, not fake, and she had felt warm and soft in his arms. She had returned his passion with a fiery one of her own. He hardened at the memory of her leaning into his body as he tried kissing her senseless. There was no doubt in his mind that some of her lipstick now covered his own lips. For proof, he took his handkerchief and wiped his mouth, seeing the red-stained cloth in the dimly lit car.

He let out a deep sigh, feeling a kind of desire he hadn't experienced in years . . . if ever. And that, he thought worriedly, could present some problems later on. He had to keep his relationship with Kimara in perspective and not let her get under his skin. Their marriage was to be one of purpose, and nothing more.

His grip tightened on the steering wheel as his thoughts shifted to his grandfather. He found himself asking softly, in the quiet stillness of the car, "Granddad, what have you done?"

Five

The wedding took place a week and a half later. Kyle had made all of the arrangements and even made the plans for the honeymoon. The only thing he'd told Kimara was to pack plenty of warm clothes. The weather would be cold where they were going.

Kimara had been grateful Nicky had been out of town visiting her fiancé when she had gotten Kyle's call. She needed some time to think of how she would explain things to her friend.

Kyle had called her four days later, informing her that an old and trusted friend of both their families, Judge Nelson Williams, had consented to perform the private ceremony in his chambers late Monday evening. The courthouse would be closed that day in observance of Martin Luther King's birthday.

When Nicky had returned to town the day after Kyle's phone call, Kimara explained everything to her. Nicky, to her surprise, had not questioned her sanity and had readily agreed to act as a witness for the ceremony. She ended up doing a whole lot more than that and went out of her way to turn what Kimara had destined to be a dismal event into a joyful affair.

Nicky had taken it upon herself to arrange a small reception at their house after the wedding. She had also talked Kimara into going shopping for a wedding dress, and had seen to it that she had a small bouquet of flowers to hold during the ceremony.

Upon Kimara's arrival at the courthouse, she was very much aware of Kyle. The cliché of tall, dark, and handsome had been created just for him. He looked extremely handsome in his gray suit. He was standing talking to Mason, who was also a witness, and Judge Williams. At the sound of her footsteps, Kyle turned around and gave her an appreciative appraisal as an irresistible smile touched his lips. She was wearing an ivory-colored tea-length fitted lace dress with spaghetti straps, a shirred bodice, and a flounced skirt. Matching ivory-colored pumps of lace and satin adorned her feet, and her hair, decorated with magnolia blossoms and pearls, hung loose about her shoulders. He excused himself from the two men and came to face her, reaching his hand out to her.

Kimara nervously accepted the smile and the hand being offered. After telling her how beautiful she looked, he led her over to the other two men. "Judge Williams, I think we're about ready."

The warmth of Judge Williams's smile echoed in his voice. "I know both your parents would have been happy with this marriage," he told them.

"Not to mention your grandfather," Mason interjected as his smile spread with delight.

"Where's the young lady who's serving as your witness, Kimara?" Judge Williams asked.

"Nicky is on her way up. She needed to make a last-minute phone call to be sure everything is going according to schedule. She has a small reception planned immediately after the ceremony in our home," Kimara answered.

"It's not your home any longer, darling," Kyle said, giving her a smile that sent her pulses racing. "After today your home is with me."

"Yes, of course," Kimara replied, smiling smoothly, betraying nothing of her annoyance. She knew they were playacting for the benefit of Judge Williams. Mason already knew this was not a marriage based on love.

"Where will the two of you be staying after the honeymoon?" Mason Long asked.

"We'll be moving into the Garwood estate for a while," Kyle answered.

"And the honeymoon? Or is it a secret?" Judge Williams asked as a huge grin covered his face.

Kyle chuckled. "Now is as good a time as any to let Kimara know where we're going," he said. "We'll be spending our honeymoon at Special K."

Kimara's gaze flew wide open to Kyle's face. A look of total surprise and bewilderment covered her features. "Special K? But I thought your grandfather sold it right after our parents' death."

"On the contrary, Miss Stafford," Mason answered rather quickly. "Although he could not handle the thought of ever going there again, Mr. Garwood retained ownership of the mountain cabin. In fact, over the years he's made sure it's been kept up. The Garwood-Stafford retreat is waiting for a Garwood and a Stafford to bring it back to life again. I contacted the caretaker and he assured me everything has been prepared and is waiting your arrival."

Kimara absorbed Mason's words. She then turned to Kyle. "How long have you known about this?"

Kyle heard the quiver in her voice, and he understood. Special K held a lot of fond memories for the both of them. It had been the site of numerous Garwood-Stafford family picnics, special gatherings, and vacations.

"Mason told me about it a few days ago. I thought it would be nice to see the place again and spend some time there. I hope you don't mind."

"No, I don't mind. I'm just a little shocked. All these years I assumed your grandfather had sold it. I never asked him about it for fear of bringing up sad memories."

At that moment Nicky walked in and Judge Williams indicated it was time for the ceremony to begin.

The ceremony was brief. After Kyle placed the beautiful diamond ring on Kimara's finger, and the words were spoken declaring them husband and wife, Judge Williams gave him the go-ahead to kiss the bride. Instead of grazing her on the cheek like Kimara thought he'd do, Kyle pulled her to him and gave her a traditional kiss with all the trimmings.

It brought back memories of the kiss they'd shared the night he had taken her out to dinner. She was again taken aback by her immediate response to him. His lips moved softly but boldly over hers, making slow, circular motions before allowing his tongue to penetrate their depths. When Kimara's knees nearly buckled under her from the sensuous onslaught, he gave her the needed support by tightening his hold and drawing her closer as he continued to kiss her.

Kimara found herself thoroughly enjoying the intimate contact with the man who was now legally her husband. The unexpectedness of his kiss, along with the pure pleasure it was giving her, made her feel hot, tingly, and flushed. The feel of his lips on hers sent sparks of desire throughout her body. Kimara knew she was in trouble. Deep trouble. She became every bit as caught up in the kiss as Kyle. Later she would blame it on the sip of wine she'd taken before leaving home to calm her nerves. On the other hand, Kyle's lethal good looks weren't entirely guiltless either. They reluctantly pulled apart after Mason cleared his throat several times.

Nicky kissed her on the cheek and congratulated her. She then received hugs from both Mason and Judge Williams. Both men informed her they would be skipping the reception, but wished them the best.

A few minutes later Kimara found herself alone with Kyle as they got into an elevator to leave. Nicky had gone on ahead, to make sure everything was all set for the reception. Kimara stared straight ahead, trying hard not to concentrate on the man standing by her side.

"Are you sure you want to go to Special K, Kimara?" Kyle asked in a soft voice. "It's not too late for me to make other arrangements if going there will bother you."

She looked up at him. Her expression was tight with strain. "It really doesn't matter where we spend our honeymoon, Kyle. The purpose of us being there will be the same. Your goal is to get me pregnant, not to look upon our time together as some romantic interlude. Our marriage is a business arrangement, nothing more."

A faint light twinkled in the depths of Kyle's eye. "Are you having second thoughts about our agreement?"

"It would be too late if I were, wouldn't it?" Kimara replied in a resigned voice.

"Yes," Kyle answered, touching her cheek with a lone finger. "It would be, since you're now my wife."

The huskiness of Kyle's tone of voice, as well as his words, captivated Kimara, but she was determined not to let him get next to her. "For only six months," she snapped. "Even less than that if I get pregnant right away."

Before Kyle could respond to her statement, the elevator opened. They suddenly found themselves swamped by reporters.

"Blast it! Who tipped them off?" Kyle whispered in an agitated voice. He tried shielding her from the firing line of flashbulbs.

She smiled weakly. Anything Kyle did was news. It was rare to pick up a magazine or newspaper and not find him being featured in it.

"Is it true, Mr. Garwood, that you and Miss Stafford just got married?"

Kyle turned to Kimara and gave her a tender smile. An offer of apology for not making sure the news of their wedding was kept under wraps shone in his eyes. "Yes, Kimara and I just married. Now, if you will ex—"

"Why the secrecy?"

"Evidently it wasn't too much of a secret, since you found out," Kyle answered in a curt voice, ushering Kimara outside the building to his parked car.

Kimara noticed that Kyle had changed vehicles as he opened the door to a beautiful Mercedes. When they were in the flow of traffic, he reached over and took her hand in his and squeezed it. "I'm sorry for what happened back there."

"It wasn't your fault. Do you think they'll follow us?"

"I don't know. I hope not." He took a quick glance in his rearview mirror. "It doesn't appear that they are. To be on the safe side, do you want to skip the reception?"

"I can't do that. Nicky went to a lot of trouble. I don't want to disappoint her."

Kyle nodded as he swung the vehicle onto the interstate.

Kimara did little talking as they traveled, absently taking in the sights that she had seen numerous times before. She was glad when Kyle's car pulled into the driveway.

"I've made arrangements for us to fly out in three hours."

Kimara nodded. "I'll be ready." Deep down she knew she would never be ready for Kyle Garwood. The thought of spending the night with him was beginning to play havoc on her nerves.

A few minutes later she found herself smiling. The reception was everything Nicky had planned it to be. Their own company had catered the affair, and by the looks on everyone's faces, they had outdone themselves. The food was delicious. The only people in attendance were close friends of hers and Nicky. Kyle hadn't bothered to invite any of his friends or associates.

"Let's dance," he whispered in her ear after she had introduced him to various friends. Kimara moved into his arms as a slow, seductive melody by Boyz II Men filled the room. He pulled her closer to him. She pressed her cheek to rest against his hard chest as they slowly swayed to the music. The way he was holding her seemed to make every square inch of her body touch every square inch of his. She was so physically charged from the feel of him that she nearly forgot to breathe. He had rested his cheek against the top of her head, and their movements were so slow that at times it appeared neither of them was moving.

"You're a beautiful bride," Kyle murmured against her ear.

She smiled. "Thanks. And you're a handsome groom." She felt his arms tighten around her. Neither spoke again during the remainder of the dance.

"Nice party," Kyle said to Kimara an hour or so later, when they found themselves alone.

She nodded. "Yes, it is."

"Why don't we leave?" he said softly.

She felt a nervous flutter in the pit of her stomach. She began to panic. "Now?"

Kyle smiled that sensuous smile that came from him so easily. "Now is just as good a time as any. We've been here for a little more than a hour. I'm sure your friends will understand if we left a little early."

She took a deep breath. "Are we leaving for Special K tonight?"

"Yes. My plane is at the airport, waiting. Did my chauffeur come by earlier today for your luggage and all of your other belongings to take to the Garwood estate?"

"Yes. But I didn't send everything."

A spark of some indefinable emotion flashed in Kyle's eyes with her statement. "You didn't? Why not?"

Kimara's lips parted in surprise at his question. "Because in six months . . . maybe less . . . I'll be moving back."

A frown settled on Kyle's features. For some unexplainable reason, he didn't like her reminding him of that.

Six

Kyle studied the woman sitting across from him in his private jet. "Is it safe to assume you're no longer on the pill?"

Kimara lifted her head from sipping champagne and met Kyle's gaze with a smile of tightly held anger. Evidently he thought she was sexually active if he asked such a question. She decided not to waste her time telling him that she had never used any type of birth control. There was never a reason to do so. Unlike him, she didn't believe in engaging in casual affairs. Over the years, her mother's preaching of first you wed, then you bed had stuck with her. Instead of replying to Kyle's question, she decided to ask one of her own. "Can I assume you're sexually safe? One can't be too sure, especially since you have such an active sex life."

Kyle lifted a brow. "And just what do you know about my sex life?"

"Only what I read in the papers and magazines, like everyone else. If I remember correctly, according to one reporter, you're one of those rare men who honestly like women. You like them so much that you have the uncanny ability to work them into your busy schedule wherever you go. They are known as Kyle Garwood's women."

Kyle's jaw tightened. If she would have taken the time to read articles that printed more truth than hearsay, she would have learned that over the past year the wild life he'd been known for had lost most of its appeal. He had begun zeroing his time and energy less on the fast life, and the women that went along with it, and more on Garwood Industries' numerous corporations. In fact, he'd been finalizing a business deal in Paris when he'd received word of his grandfather's sudden heart attack, and not in some secluded French chateau with a woman, as one newspaper article had claimed. He didn't see the need to defend himself to her or anyone. What he'd done before their marriage did not concern her. However, he wasn't about to let the question of his infidelity hang between them.

"If what you say about 'my women' is to be believed, Kimara, as my wife, don't you feel threatened with my squalid reputation?"

Kimara shrugged, then gave a mirthless little laugh. "Me feel threatened? Not at all. Our relationship is strictly business. Your relationship with those women, I imagine, is purely pleasure. However, I do expect you to put your squalid reputation on hold for the brief period that you are married to me. As I said earlier, I assume that you're sexually safe, and while we're sharing a bed, I expect you to remain that way."

Kyle's gaze delved deeply into hers, his expression serious. "The only thing you'll get from me is a bundle of joy, hopefully, in about nine months from now. I give you the Garwood word of honor that as long as we are husband and wife, I'll make love only to you," he said in a deep, husky voice.

Kimara broke eye contact and placed her attention on the objects beyond the plane's window that glittered below in the darkened sky. She believed him. The same thing had occurred when they had held a joint meeting with their attorneys to draw up a prenuptial agreement. She and Kyle had sat there while the two attorneys bickered back and forth about what should or should not be included in the agreement. Each man was determined to protect his client's interest. She had met Kyle's gaze from across the table, and strange as it may seem, she had read his thoughts. *There had never been a question of trust between a Garwood and a Stafford before now.* Trust was one thing that had always existed between the two families. That trust had been passed on from generation to generation and had continued with their fathers, who had been the closest of friends. And now it appeared that the last remaining Garwood and Stafford were about to destroy that trust with a piece of paper. She had not been at all surprised when Kyle finally stood, bringing the conversation between the two bickering attorneys to a sudden halt. It was uncanny that her and Kyle's thoughts had been on the same wavelength. They'd both been thinking that although they hadn't seen each other in years, and were virtual strangers now, there would always be a certain degree of mutual trust between them on some things. And this was one of them. Without letting his gaze leave hers, he said, "There will not be a prenuptial agreement drawn up between me and Kimara. We don't need one." Kyle's attorney had looked at him as if he'd lost his mind, and her own attorney had swung his gaze to her, fully expecting her to disagree. Instead, she said, "I agree with Kyle." She knew that on that particular issue their decision was something no one other than another Garwood or Stafford would understand. Feeling Kyle's gaze on her, Kimara brought her wayward thoughts back to the present. "When will we be arriving at Special K?"

Kyle checked his watch. "We should land at the airport in less than thirty minutes. A chopper will be there to fly us to Special K, and we should arrive there before nine o'clock tonight."

She took a deep breath. She didn't want to think about the night that lay ahead. "It will be late."

"Yes, late for some things, but right on time for others," Kyle replied in a soft voice. He regretted his words when he saw just how jittery they made her.

"Look, Kimara, I know this has been a trying week for you as well as one hell of a day for the both of us," he said in a deep voice. "How about if we just relax a little and try getting reacquainted. Until I saw you again last week, I hadn't seen you since our parents' funeral eight years ago. What have you been doing over the years? What made you decide to start a catering service?"

Kimara took a deep breath, grateful for Kyle's thoughtfulness in trying to get her unruffled. She relaxed back in her seat. "I had been accepted at Howard before my parents' death, so I continued with those plans."

"I can't believe I didn't recognize you that day. You look different," he said.

Kimara smiled. "I took some nutrition classes in my sophomore year and learned how to eat all the right things and how to do without the others. Putting what I learned into practice as well as self-determination, I shed a lot of what my parents always referred to as baby fat." A smile touched her lips. "I painstakingly discovered it wasn't what you ate but how much of it that you ate. I also found out the importance of exercising."

"Your efforts are astounding, Kimara. You're beautiful," Kyle said in a husky voice.

Kimara's heart lurched at the thought that Kyle thought her beautiful. As a child, she had never thought her weight was a problem because no one around her acted like it was. Her parents had sheltered her and had gone out of their way to make her feel beautiful. It was only when she'd turned sixteen and had experienced her first broken heart did she take a good look at herself, and she began wondering if her weight had been one of the reasons Kyle had never noticed her.

"After graduation I left D.C. and came home to your grandfather," she continued. "He was the only family I had, and I think I arrived just in time. He was going through his own living hell not being able to accept our parents' death. I moved in with him for a while and went to work for Stafford Publishing Company."

"Doing what?"

A smile touched Kimara's lips. "A little bit of everything. I wanted to learn all there was to know about the publishing industry from the bottom up. But it became apparent that my presence was causing a lot of undue problems around the office. Some of the employees could not reconcile with the idea of the president of the corporation doing clerical duties or getting dirty by helping in the printing room. And I really wasn't happy working there. So after six months, I left."

Kyle laughed, a rich, deep, throaty sound. "I can see how your being there and doing those types of jobs could cause somewhat of a problem."

Kimara was suddenly filled with that warm feeling of two old friends chitchatting. "I knew I wanted to do something else with my life, but at the time I didn't have a clue as to what. By then Poppa Garwood had begun to get his life back in order, and one day he approached me with an idea. He had noticed how much I liked spending my time in his kitchen, working alongside his cook, trying out different recipes. He asked if I would be interested in going to New Orleans to study under the renowned Chef LaFranco DePetionne. It just so happened that one of his executives at Garwood Industries had a daughter who was also interested in going."

"Nicky?"

"Yes, Nicky. She and I hit it off immediately, packed our bags, and spent a year and a half at The DePetionne Cooking School. We both graduated with honors and returned to Atlanta ready to take on the world."

"And from what I understand, the two of you have done just that. According to Mason, the Golden Flame is doing exceptionally well."

Kim smiled proudly. "Yes, it is, but we can always use new business, so be sure to keep us in mind if you're ever in need of catering services."

Kyle smiled. "I will."

Kimara took another sip of champagne. "And how are you coming along with the list I gave you?"

He smiled. "I'd like you to know that my part in your Valentine's Day ball is completed. I've gotten a firm commitment or a decline from each and every person."

She smiled brightly. "You did? Oh, Kyle, that's wonderful."

"The ones that can't make it send their regrets. They will either be out of the country that night, or there was a conflict with some other event they were attending. This week my secretary will be sending your committee the names of those who will be coming to the ball."

"Thanks for all your help, Kyle. You accomplished in one week what I hadn't been able to do in three months. Do you know if Sterling Hamilton will be coming?"

Kyle shook his head. "No, he won't be able to attend. He'll be out of the country filming his latest movie. Why?"

"Of all the people on that list, he's the one I was hoping would come. A survey taken among the students indicated he's their favorite of all the celebrities, and the one person most of them wanted to meet."

Kyle leaned back in his seat. "I see."

"Oh, well, I guess nothing can ever really be perfect, can it?"

It was on the tip of Kyle's tongue to tell her that he was beginning to think she was, but he stopped himself. "Would you like some more champagne?"

"Yes, thank you."

He poured Kimara some more of the bubbly drink that had been a wedding gift from his flight crew. He wasn't sure how he was going to pose his next question, but all during her narrative of what had been going on in her life, she hadn't once mentioned an involvement with a man. A deep inner part of him wanted to ask her directly and not depend on the secondhand information he'd obtained.

"What about the guys who've been knocking the door down to get to you since I last saw you?"

To Kyle's relief, she didn't catch the underlying question lurking behind his inquiry. She gave him a cute little giggle. "There weren't many guys, and those who did come calling were screened thoroughly by Poppa Garwood, which made any serious relationships close to impossible. He frightened off any potential suitors. Too bad he wasn't in New Orleans when I met Adam Coffer."

His stomach lurched nervously. "Who's Adam Coffer?"

Creases lined Kimara's forehead as if giving his question considerable thought. It seemed like an eternity before she answered. "Adam lived in New Orleans and owned an engineering firm there. By the time our relationship ended, I had learned three valuable lessons in life."

Kyle shifted uneasily in his seat. "What were they?"

"First, a man who is skillful at conducting whirlwind courtships probably has had a lot of practice. Secondly, some relationships just aren't meant to be. Thirdly, the words 'I love you' don't roll as easily or quickly off the tongue of a sincere man as they will an insincere one."

Kyle looked down into the golden liquid swirling around in his glass. So she had been involved with someone. He felt a deep tightening in his chest. Why did the thought of her wrapped in some other man's arms cause his heart to ache? He lifted his eyes to meet hers, and was about to tell her he was glad things hadn't worked out for her and the other man, when the sound of his pilot's voice came through the intercom system, instructing them to fasten their seat belts for landing.

∼

It was past midnight when the newlyweds arrived at Special K.

When Kyle's jet landed at the airport, he discovered that due to miscommunication, the chopper was not there for them. It was an additional hour or so before they had gotten a rental car, and it took another hour to travel the dark, mountainous roads to the luxurious two-story cabin that was situated in the heart of the Carolina mountains.

By the time Kyle drove through the gates of Special K, he noticed his bride of six hours had passed out from a combination of exhaustion and champagne. She sat slumped down in her seat. He reached out to nudge her awake. "Kimara, we're here."

She opened one eye wearily and gazed up at him. "I want to sleep," she said drowsily.

"I know, and you will just as soon as I can get you inside." He got out of the car, went to the front door of the house, and unlocked it. Stepping over the threshold he flipped on the lights. Leaving the door ajar, he returned to the car and opened the passenger door. At the gentle touch he placed on her shoulder, Kimara turned trustingly and wrapped her arms around his neck. He kissed her cheek.

"Kimara?"

She opened both her sleep-filled eyes and peered up at him questioningly. "Hmm?"

"Welcome to Special K as my wife, and it's my honor to carry you over the threshold as Mrs. Kyle Harrison Garwood the Fifth." The phrase was a tradition that all Garwood men said to their wives the first time they brought them to Special K. Somehow Kyle felt sincere in saying it to Kimara.

"Thanks, Kyle," she mumbled, tightening her arms around his neck and closing her eyes once more.

With tenderness and long strides, he carried the sleeping woman inside the house, trying to remember the layout of the huge mountain cabin. He recalled two separate master bedrooms, one on the main floor, the Stafford suite, and one upstairs, the Garwood suite.

Making a quick decision, he made his way to the bedroom up the stairs.

With great effort he tried ignoring the warm breath on his cheek from Kimara's breathing. By the time he reached the Garwood suite, his body had become alive with want and desire.

Walking over to the king-size bed, he gently placed her down on the printed comforter. He glanced around the room. Dozens and dozens of red roses were everywhere, and filled the room with a sweet fragrance. He also noticed an ice bucket containing a bottle of champagne.

Remembering that he'd left the front door open, Kyle quickly left the room and went downstairs. When he returned minutes later, he stood in the doorway and watched Kimara asleep in the bed. Rubbing the back of his neck, he couldn't help but take a close look at her outfit.

Before leaving the reception, she had changed into a short split skirt and jacket. The outfit exposed her long, beautiful legs and wreaked havoc on his senses. He strode into the room, moving closer to the bed. Reluctantly, he bent over to begin the job of undressing his wife. With expert hands, it took no time at all to remove the top layer of clothing, leaving her body clad in white satin and lace. Somehow he managed to move the bed covering aside, place her beneath the top sheet, and flip the comforter over her. Stifling a groan, he took his eyes off the totally desirable woman and left the room to bring in their luggage.

It was close to an hour later before Kyle began removing his clothing and joined Kimara in bed. Knowing consummating their marriage tonight was out of the question, he pulled her into his arms, loving the feel of her hips and legs close to his. Her hand, soft and warm, absently came to rest on the soft, hairy cushion of his chest.

"Kyle?" Kimara said drowsily.

"Hmm?"

"Are we going to make a baby now?"

So exhausted, so sleepy, was Kimara, she didn't notice Kyle's hesitation before answering, nor did she fully comprehend the words spoken soft and tender from his lips. "You're too tired and sleepy tonight, sweetheart. The first time our bodies join, I want you to be wide awake to enjoy every minute."

Kyle cradled her closer to him. He looked down and studied her features—the long, sweeping lashes covering her eyes, her high cheekbones, her straight nose, high forehead, silky chestnut hair, and cocoa-colored complexion. He wondered what of her features their child would inherit. What of his?

Kimara shifted in sleep and her eyes opened. She stared at him for a moment, disoriented. A deep pulse leapt in Kyle's throat, and he struggled desperately for control and sanity. During that short moment while she looked at him through dark lashes half-lowered over drowsy eyes, it seemed like some kind of ethereal glow surrounded them, bonding them together. She closed her eyes again, breaking the spell, and Kyle slowly released his breath. A slightly confused frown creased his face as he pulled Kimara closer into his arms. He shook his head to clear it, wondering if he was somehow losing his mind. There seemed to be something magical about this place and the two of them together here. That thought was still on his mind when sleep finally overtook him.

Seven

The warmth of the morning sun glided its radiant beam into the bedroom, touching the bodies of the two people wrapped in each other's arms in the huge bed.

Consciousness slowly infiltrated Kimara's mind, and she gradually opened her eyes. She was snuggled next to Kyle, who was still asleep. His hand was resting on the curve of her hip, and her head was cradled against his shoulder and chin. She lay perfectly still for a moment as yesterday's memories came sailing through her mind.

Swallowing nervously, she fixed her eyes on the man lying next to her, who was holding her tight in a warm embrace. She couldn't remember a time when she hadn't known Kyle. A smile touched her lips when she remembered how at the age of six she had pledged her undying love for him. It was right after he had saved her puppy from drowning in the Staffords' swimming pool. From that day forward, he'd become her hero.

By the time she was twelve Kyle had entered college, and she saw less and less of him, but her feelings had only intensified over the years. By the time she was fourteen she was still operating under the strain of an enormous crush on him. At the age of sixteen her crush had transformed into love. It was that same year that she experienced her first heartbreak over his engagement.

In the following years, thanks to numerous publishers who loved to print news stories about the rich and famous, she had read with envy as Kyle wined and dined one gorgeous woman after another. She had long ago accepted that she was someone whom he would never be interested in.

She felt disappointment touch her with a tangible force. The only reason Kyle had married her was to fulfill his grandfather's wishes. She knew she was a far cry from the glamorous women he preferred. Luckily her heart was now inviolate to him.

A lump formed in Kimara's throat when she suddenly became aware of the state of her dress—or undress—which meant Kyle had removed most of her clothing the previous night. The last coherent memory she had of the night before was him carrying her over the threshold. She wondered what had happened after that? Certainly they had not made love. She would remember if they had. Wouldn't she?

Deciding it would be best not to be in the same bed with Kyle when he awakened, and to give herself time to try to remember exactly what did or did not happen in that bed, she tried easing out of his arms.

Kyle's hand resting on Kimara's hip tightened and his leg moved over hers. "Going someplace, sweetheart?"

Her gaze flew upward and the eye contact jolted her as an intense sensation erupted deep in the pit of her stomach. She lowered her eyes, suddenly feeling shy and uncertain. "Yes. It's morning."

Kyle's hold on her tightened even more. "I can see that," he replied huskily, pushing himself up on one elbow and looking down at her.

A warm feeling began to seep from Kimara's fingertips to her toes with Kyle's touch. "Kyle, I don't think we should—"

"You don't think we should what?" he asked, cuddling her closer to him. He nuzzled her face, then gently kissed her lips. "I think we should do whatever we feel like doing. After all, we're married."

She ignored the feel of the stubbly chin scraping her skin, but she could not ignore the feel of his kiss on her lips. Nor could she ignore the hair-covered leg over hers or the feel of the hard, masculine bulge that was resting against her side. A blush spread across her features. He didn't have on any clothes!

"Kyle, I think we should talk about this. I know the reason we married, but I don't think we should rush into anything. Shouldn't we get to know each other better?"

Kyle threw his head back and let out a great peal of laughter. "Get to know each other better? Baby, I've known you from the very beginning. Have you forgotten that I was here in this very house the night you were born? I was barely seven at the time. Our fathers tried their damnedest to talk your mother into going to the hospital, but she refused. My mother wasn't any help. She was encouraging your mom to be rebellious. Dr. Firestone arrived just in time. He was in this house less than five minutes before you were born."

Kimara couldn't help but smile at Kyle's recounting of the story she'd heard numerous times. According to her father, her mother had almost given him heart failure that night.

"Then there was the time I got into trouble when I was twelve for something that you did, Kimara."

She raised a brow. "And what did I do?"

A smile touched Kyle's lips. "You were around five years old at the time and had decided you wanted to play pirate by burying things. When I happened to come upon you on your knees, busy at work digging a hole in our backyard, I foolishly agreed to help you bury your treasure. How was I to know that little brown bag you were burying contained some of your mother's valuable jewelry?"

Kimara couldn't help laughing. She tried to ignore the slight ache in her head from her overindulgence in champagne the day before. "Oh, Kyle, I remember that! I did get you in trouble, didn't I? I really didn't mean to. It was just a game. I'll never forget the look of horror on my parents' faces when they found out a large chunk of the Staffords' gems were buried in a hole somewhere on the Garwood estate. It was a good thing you remembered where the spot was. I was too tired and sleepy after all that digging to even care."

Kyle's laugh was deep, warm, and rich. "Then there was the time that I jumped into that huge swimming pool to save that blasted puppy of yours and almost got my nose bit off in the process."

"He thought you were trying to hurt him."

"I was trying to save his hide."

Kimara tried to suppress a giggle. "He didn't know that. He was afraid."

"If you say so. But it didn't help matters when that same animal grew up to be an ungrateful mutt. He tried to bite me again when I dropped by to see you years later."

"He didn't remember you, and he was trying to protect me," she implored as a smile stole into her features.

"I guess in that case I can forgive him for the mix-up. But, as you can see, Kimara, we do know each other," Kyle said in a silky voice. "The only way we really don't know each other is intimately, but we'll remedy that soon, won't we?"

Before she could think of a reply, Kyle's mouth came down on hers. The unexpectedness of the kiss and the erotic feelings it evoked made her heart begin hammering in her chest. His tongue, silken and hot as a summer's night, flitted across her lips in a taunting play of feathery strokes. She found herself filled with a strange inner excitement. A shudder passed through her when Kyle deepened the kiss, allowing his tongue to penetrate the confines of her mouth, and at the same time he gathered her closer into his arms and held her snugly.

When his tongue came into contact with hers, a sensuous duel took place. Kimara's skin tingled with this intimate touch. When he finally released her, she relaxed, sinking into his cushioning embrace, totally in awe of the magnitude of the effect Kyle's kiss had on her. His breath was warm and moist against her face, and she could see the smoldering depths of his eyes and a light sheen of moisture on his lips.

Kimara blinked, then focused her gaze again on him. He stared back, his gaze beckoned her closer and closer. Suddenly she remembered that night, so long ago, when she was going to reveal to him the secret of her love. But only it hadn't worked out that way. He had chosen another. A pain surrounded her heart at the memory. She didn't want to fall under Kyle's spell ever again. Every time he kissed her she felt things she'd never felt before. Suddenly feeling a need to get away from him, she placed her hands on his chest, intending to push him away. But he didn't let her. He covered her hands with his.

"I'm not ready to let you go yet."

Kimara ignored the rich seductiveness in his voice. But she couldn't ignore the feel of his free hand as it slowly moved upward toward her inner thigh. "Stop it, Kyle. I have no intention of making love with you right now. The only thing I plan on doing is taking a shower and fixing breakfast."

Kyle frowned at the iciness in her voice and pulled both hands away. "And what about the kiss we just shared?"

"What about it? Our hormones were acting up, nothing more. We'll just have to work hard at keeping them under control, won't we? And what you said earlier isn't true. We *don't* know each other, at least not as adults. All we have between us are childhood memories, and they don't make a relationship."

Kyle looked exasperated. "Who's concerned about a relationship? We're not here to play a game of 'getting to know you.' We're here to—"

"I know why we're here. I allowed you to rush me into this marriage, but I won't be rushed into anything else, especially sleeping with you. I don't feel comfortable sharing a bed with a man I know nothing about other than what I read in the papers and magazines." She didn't add that she wasn't in a hurry to sleep with the man who had hurt her once, and if she didn't keep the upper hand, could possibly hurt her again.

"Please turn your back, Kyle."

He lifted a brow. "Turn my back? For what?"

"I need to get out of bed."

"What's stopping you?"

She took a deep breath. "I have no intention of parading in front of you half naked."

Kyle rolled his eyes upward, shaking his head. "Kimara, I undressed you last night. Besides, soon enough I'll know your body as well as I know my own. Why do you want to hide it?"

She shrugged. "I'll appreciate it if you'll just turn your back."

"What if I don't want to?" he said with a wicked smile.

Kimara's eyes reflected her anger. "You're impossible!"

"I'm sorry you think so. I just happen to love looking at you. You should have figured that out that day by your pool. However, since I feel like being a nice guy this morning, I'll be glad to get your robe for you. I put away some of your things last night."

The thought of him going through her luggage, especially through some of her intimate things, didn't sit well with Kimara, but she figured that now was not a good time to make waves. He might take back his offer to get her robe. "Thanks for being kind enough to get my robe, Kyle."

"Sure."

She regretted his act of kindness the minute he threw back the bedcovers. She had forgotten he didn't have on a stitch of clothing. A blush covered her face when he got out of bed and walked across the room to the closet completely naked. The man had no shame . . . but then, neither did she, she thought upon realizing she couldn't help but stare at his excellent physical shape. His lean tapered hips and legs were covered with fine hair. His stomach was firm and hard, and his shoulders and arms denoted supreme masculinity. His dark body stretched in a fine arch when he reached into the closet for her robe. Her throat went dry. She was speechless when he strode back over to the bed. She couldn't stop her eyes from moving all over him when he stood next to the bed with her robe in her hand.

"Anything else, sweetheart?" he asked, his voice hoarse, thick, and suggestive.

She somehow found her voice. "Yes, you can get your own robe and cover yourself," she retorted sharply. She was angry at herself for the desire she had begun to feel for him all over again.

Her words seemed to amuse him. A flash of humor crossed his features. "You may as well get used to seeing me this way. I feel most comfortable when I'm wearing hardly anything."

Kimara snatched the robe from his hands. To her supreme relief, he sauntered off in the direction of the bathroom, giving her a more than gracious view of the planes and angles of his physique, especially his captivating backside. She released a deep breath when she heard the sound of the shower. Quickly donning the robe, she took notice of her surroundings for the first time when she smelled the fragrance of flowers. A smile touched her lips when she saw the numerous arrangements of roses around the room and the bottle of champagne. Ignoring the feel of the cool wooden floor beneath her feet, she made her way over to the arrangement that held the card. Her hand trembled slightly when she recognized the sprawling bold writing on it. She silently read the message it contained. So intent was she in reading the card that she had not heard the sound of the shower stopping.

"Kimara? Who sent the flowers and champagne?"

She glanced up. Kyle was standing in the bathroom doorway wearing only a towel around his hips. For a moment she was mesmerized upon remembering she'd slept snuggled to that magnificent body. Reluctantly, she pulled her eyes from his torso and back to his face.

"You won't believe it when I tell you who sent them, Kyle."

He raised a brow and walked over to her. "Really? Who sent them?"

She handed him the card.

Kyle recognized the handwriting immediately. It was distinct, with a flair that belonged to only one man.

His grandfather.

Eight

Kyle read the card he held in his hand.

> *To the granddaughter of my heart*
> *and the grandson of my blood.*
> *Thanks for fulfilling an old man's*
> *last dream. The Garwood and Stafford legacy*
> *will continue thanks to the two of you.*
> *I love you both.*
>
> *Kyle Garwood III*

"Aren't the flowers beautiful?"

Kimara's question drew Kyle's gaze. She was unaware of the captivating picture she made standing next to the arrangement of roses. "Yes, they are. There wasn't any doubt in Granddad's mind we'd get married like he wanted," Kyle said, smiling, and silently admiring his grandfather's wisdom in choosing Kimara as the woman to continue the Garwood line. He was beginning to see that there was more to her than the beauty that shone on the outside. She possessed an inner beauty that most people lacked. She was a woman to be admired for her accomplishments. Having survived losing both parents, she'd made an alteration in her life that had boosted her self-esteem but hadn't rearranged her priorities. And now he kind of liked the idea of her giving birth to his child. The thought of her gorgeous body swelling with his baby made a feeling of fierce pride flow through him. There was no doubt in his mind that she would make a good mother. He'd never been around children much, but he had watched Kimara interact with a little girl who'd been with her parents at the airport. It had been easy to see she liked kids. He knew at that moment he no longer wanted to think of the child they would make together as the Garwood heir. He wanted the baby for its own sake and not for any purpose it would serve or how it figured in his grandfather's will.

"I guess it's like you said that day in Mason's office. He knew deep down we wouldn't deny his last wish. I wonder how the flowers and champagne got here."

Kimara's words broke into Kyle's thoughts. "I bet he left Mason explicit instructions what to do. He was the one who suggested that we come here for our honeymoon. I wonder what other surprises we should expect. I have a feeling Granddad thoroughly enjoyed planning all of this."

"Are you saying Poppa Garwood knew he was dying? But that's not possible. He had a sudden heart attack."

"Sudden but not unexpected. I paid a visit to John Stone, his doctor, last week. He went over his case with me. Granddad began experiencing chest pains a couple of months ago. John ran tests that showed he needed to undergo open heart surgery. From what John said, he explained to Granddad there was a chance he wouldn't survive the surgery, but without it he could have an attack and die at any time. Instead of having the surgery, he opted to spend his last days planning our wedding and assuring the birth of his great-grandchild."

Tears gathered in Kimara's eyes. "Oh, Kyle. I wish he would have told us. I wish he would have let us share those final days with him."

Kyle pulled her into his arms. "You knew my grandfather, Kimara. He was a proud man. He wouldn't have wanted our pity."

"But we wouldn't have pitied him. We would have given him our love."

"I know. But in his way of thinking, for us to carry out the terms of the will is all the love we could ever give him."

"But he isn't here to know that we actually did it."

Kyle smiled. "He knows. In his heart he knows. All of this proves that he knew it before he died. There was never any doubt in his mind what we would do. He took the biggest gamble of his life and won. He's probably up there, looking down on us, grinning from ear to ear and feeling mighty proud of himself."

"You're probably right," Kimara replied, smiling. She wiped her eyes and pulled away from Kyle, fighting the need to be held by him. "Now, if you'll excuse me, I want to take a shower before preparing breakfast."

"May I come and watch?" Kyle's grin was irresistibly devastating.

A confusing frown covered Kimara's features. "You want to watch me fix breakfast?"

"No. I want to watch you take a shower." Kyle's eyes settled on her mouth. He liked the full, generous shape of it and couldn't stop remembering the feel of it under his.

Kimara drew on every ounce of self-control she had as her gaze met his. His words were a seductive challenge, and the shifting lights in the depths of his eyes were magnetic. To cover the passionate fluttering that arose at the back of her neck, her stare drilled into him.

"I think we need to get a few things straight, Kyle. I won't be at your beck and call for the next two weeks."

A teasing glint appeared in Kyle's eyes. "I'm disappointed."

"Then I suggest you get over it." She couldn't help noticing the towel around Kyle's waist had slipped a little lower. Her eyes moved from the middle section of his body to his broad chest, then back to his waist, his thighs, legs, and toes. When she raised her eyes, she found he'd been watching her ogle him.

"I hope you like everything you see, and especially something you don't, Kimara, because in the next two weeks you won't know where your body ends and mine begins."

"Do you have to say such disgusting things?" Kimara snapped, tightening the robe firmly around her. She suddenly felt hot, and her heart began thumping erratically.

Kyle straightened his stance and took a few steps toward her. The look in his eyes was intent.

Biting her lower lip, Kimara took a step back. When Kyle stood directly in front of her, she felt as if her breath was cut off.

"My words aren't disgusting. They're the truth. And for a reason I don't fully understand right now, so I'll blame it on the magic of this place, I want you to have my baby, but not for my grandfather, for me. When we leave here two weeks from now, I want a part of me left inside you."

Heat flooded Kimara's cheeks. Her heart rate surged. She looked at him for a very long while, wondering why he was so eager for fatherhood all of a sudden. Could it be the magic of the place, as he had suggested? Did Special K have some kind of lure that was supposed to enchant and captivate them? Is that why Poppa Garwood wanted them to spend their honeymoon there? Kimara shook her head, stopping her imagination from getting the best of her. She was too much of a realist to believe in magic.

Kimara should have expected what happened next and reacted to avoid it. She couldn't resist when she suddenly found herself in Kyle's arms. He lowered his head and his lips brushed lightly over hers. The pure pleasure the kiss elicited made her knees weaken. His lips were gentle and moved softly yet boldly as his tongue explored the recesses of Kimara's mouth. His kiss was provocative, his touch gentle and persuasive. His arms encircled her, one hand in the small of her back, the other cupping her chin as he smothered her lips with demanding mastery.

So carried away by her own immediate response, all Kimara could do was to continue to press open lips to his as he kissed her devouringly. She was powerless to resist.

At last, reluctantly, they parted, but for a mere moment she had no desire to back out of his embrace. He brushed a gentle kiss across her forehead, pulling her back into his arms. She relaxed, sinking into his cushioning warmth and at the same time feeling a multitude of uncertainties in the pit of her stomach. She had to be realistic. This place held no magic for her and Kyle. The only thing it held was childhood memories. And the only thing she was to Kyle was another conquest. He would use her body for the sole purpose of fulfilling the terms of Poppa Garwood's will, and enjoy every minute of it. Afterward, he would toss her out of his life like an old pair of shoes. She knew this. His love life was everyday news, yet a few minutes earlier she'd pushed that knowledge aside and let her guard down. When he had touched and kissed her, all common sense had deserted her. He had the capability of sweeping her away on a tide of desire until she was aware of only him and the feelings he was able to ignite in her. She had to be strong and resist him.

Kimara knew eventually she'd have to give herself to him, but she was determined not to be taken in by him. He had broken her heart once, and she was determined never to give him the chance to do so again. With that thought foremost in her mind, she straightened her shoulders, lifted her chin, and met his gaze with narrowed eyes. "I'll never become one of Kyle Garwood's women," she said angrily.

Kyle watched as she quickly disappeared into the bathroom, slamming the door behind her.

~

Kyle had been downstairs for nearly an hour before Kimara came down to join him. He was sitting on one of the sofas, his head thrown back in deep thought. The words she had tossed at him were playing over and over in his mind. *I will never become one of Kyle Garwood's women.* What could he say or do to make her believe that she could never be grouped with the other women he'd been involved with before? He shook his head as if to clear his mind. He didn't like the way his thoughts were going. Why was he concerned about what she thought? Why did he even care?

He lifted his head when she entered the room. She had showered and changed into a pair of jeans and a T-shirt and looked absolutely great. "We need to finish our talk, Kimara."

She frowned, flopping down in the chair across from him. "What else is there to say?"

"We didn't discuss the baby."

"The baby? What about the baby?"

Kyle met her gaze. "That night I took you to dinner, I agreed to give you custody, but we never talked about my visitation rights."

"Visitation rights?"

"Yes. I want very frequent visitation rights."

Kimara was silent for a moment. She wondered just how frequent he meant. "I'm surprised you'd want them."

"And why wouldn't I?"

"Because you're a very busy man."

Kyle's eyes bored into hers. "I'll never be too busy for our child, always remember that. No matter how busy my father was, he always found time for me. I never came second to Garwood Industries. My mother and I were first in his life, and I plan to do the same for our child."

Kimara bit her lower lip. The same had been true for her father. He had never put Stafford Publishing before her mother and her. "Things are different. Our parents married for love, so they couldn't help but love us."

"Are you saying we can't love our child if we don't love each other?"

"Of course not, Kyle."

"Then what are you saying?"

"What I'm trying to say is that since we don't love each other, our child won't be part of a real family."

"That's a shame, isn't it?" Kyle stood. "Come on, let's go see what we can throw together in the kitchen. And later, I'd like us to take a walk around the place. It's been years since we were here."

Kimara stood and walked with him to the kitchen. Her mind was deep in thought over the comment Kyle had made about it being a shame their child wouldn't be part of a real family. What did he expect, when their marriage wasn't a real one?

"The kitchen is stocked with all sorts of goodies. Mason evidently wanted to make sure we didn't starve for the next two weeks."

Kyle's words brought Kimara's mind back to the present. She took a look around. The kitchen was massive. A sudden jolt of sadness touched her. The last time she'd been here, her mother and Kyle's had been busy planning dinner. She had been seventeen at the time.

"Kimara, how about if you fix the heavy stuff and leave the coffee, orange juice, and setting the table to me. My cooking skills can't hold a light to yours."

A few minutes later she wondered how such a spacious kitchen could suddenly become small. Kyle had insisted on offering his assistance to her after he had finished his tasks. It didn't help matters with the way he was dressed, in a pair of tight jeans and a plaid flannel shirt. No matter what position he held, whether it was reaching into the cabinets for the dishes, bending down looking in the refrigerator for the juice, or simply standing in a nonchalant way in front of the coffeemaker, he looked sexy.

Kimara couldn't stop her eyes from straying to his backside, his broad shoulders, his firm stomach, and his sinewy thighs. She found herself wiping perspiration from her forehead countless times while she was going about the simple task of cooking eggs, toast, and bacon. It was almost impossible to stop the hot and seedy thoughts that flowed through her mind.

To her way of thinking, it seemed that more than once he bumped into her deliberately or rubbed against her unnecessarily. More times than she could count, their eyes caught and held. He would give her a slow smile, then continue with what he was doing.

It was much later, while they were finally seated at the breakfast table, that Kimara make her announcement. "I've moved my things into the guest bedroom."

Kyle lifted a brow. "Why?"

"I enjoy my privacy."

He let out a deep, throaty laugh. "You didn't come here for privacy."

Kimara toyed with the food on her plate. "Yes, I know, and that's what I want to talk to you about."

Kyle looked at her curiously. "What?"

"As I told you this morning, I need time to get adjusted to the idea of our sharing a bed."

He leaned back in his chair. "Kimara, we shared a bed last night," he reminded her.

"I want a little time before we become . . . intimate."

Kyle frowned. As much as he wanted to make love to her, the last thing he wanted was a resistant woman in his bed. He looked at her with unreadable dark eyes as he stood. "All right, I'll give you the time you think you need. But, Kimara . . ."

"Yes?"

"You can't put off the inevitable forever." He lifted his glass that was half filled with orange juice. "I propose a toast. To the beginning of what I perceive as an enjoyable two weeks. May our stay at Special K be a very productive and creative one."

Nine

Kyle and Kimara took a long walk after breakfast. The crisp highland air of January felt good and filled their lungs as they covered the massive grounds of Special K. The natural beauty was timeless, with snow-capped mountains in the background, a vast array of pine trees, and numerous blooms of dogwood, azaleas, and mountain laurels.

At first they walked quietly side by side, breaking the silence only to recall fond childhood memories.

"Tell me about yourself," Kimara asked Kyle some time later when they reached the huge lake on the property.

"Didn't the newspapers and magazines tell you everything, or did they just zero in on my sex life?" Kyle asked teasingly, tossing a broken twig into the icy blue waters.

"Hmm," Kimara answered thoughtfully, a smile touching her lips. "I'm afraid they mostly zeroed in on your sex life, so you'll have to fill me in on the rest. There's a lot about you I don't know."

"Like what, for instance?"

"Personal things. Like your favorite color, your favorite music, what you think of the present state of the economy? Stuff like that."

"My favorite color is whatever color you're wearing. My favorite music is the one you were exercising to that day by the pool, and right now the state of the economy is the furthest thing from my mind."

Kimara couldn't help but laugh at Kyle's attempt to flirt with her. "Will you be serious and answer my questions."

"I am serious." He pulled her closer to his side as they continued walking. "But I take it you don't like my answers." At the shake of her head he said, "All right, my favorite color is blue. I like all kinds of music, but jazz is my favorite, and I think the state of the economy has been pretty good lately, but that's not uncommon during an election year."

Kimara nodded. She liked this side of Kyle. There was a certain playfulness about him. He seemed more relaxed than he had been during earlier times, and she was glad of that. It was important to her that they get to know each other better, if for no other reason than for the sake of the child they would one day share.

As they continued walking, he told her more about himself, things she hadn't known about like his special appointment by the President to be a part of a task force of businessmen concerned with the juvenile crime problem in this country. As far as she was concerned, the news media had really done him an injustice by letting their interest in his personal life be their main focus of concern. After listening to him, it was apparent she had not known him at all. Over the past year he'd spent most of his time working hard to keep the New York office of Garwood Industries on top. Now with Poppa Garwood's death, he'd be working even harder to keep Garwood Industries a Fortune 500 company. She couldn't help but admire him and all he had accomplished.

After their walk they returned to the cabin and had soup and sandwiches for lunch. During that time she told Kyle about the different charities she was involved with and how she wished she could do more. "I wish there were more money around for sickle-cell anemia research. If only everyone would contribute more. But most people don't feel connected because they themselves nor anyone they know has the disease."

There was a long pause of silence in the room, and Kimara looked up from her meal. Her gaze locked with Kyle's warm stare. She eyed him warily. "What's wrong?"

A lazy smile lighted his face. "I was just thinking about how devoted you are to so many causes. It's really remarkable."

She almost became lost in his smile. "There's nothing remarkable about it. Some people tend to forget where they came from. I'm not one of them."

Kyle chuckled. "It's funny that you of all people should feel that way. Especially when you're one of the few blacks that was actually born with a silver spoon in your mouth."

Kimara nodded. "And so are you. But that doesn't exempt us, or any other well-off person, from wanting to help others, those less fortunate."

"I agree."

After lunch they played cards well into the afternoon. Dinner was simple—grilled steaks, baked potatoes, and tossed salad.

That first day established a pattern of how they spent their time together for the next few days, getting to know each other better.

Kyle kept his promise about giving her more time. As a result, she felt more at ease around him. Although she was fully aware of his eyes on her constantly, he was the perfect gentleman. Only once had things gotten almost too heated for her; and that was on the fourth night. She had changed into a blue silk jump suit for dinner. He had been quiet during the meal, and it was only after they'd cleared the table and washed the dishes that he told her what was on his mind.

"Do me a favor," he said softly, leaning against the kitchen counter.

"What?" she whispered, not able to ignore the sensual heat in the depths of his dark eyes and the deep huskiness in his voice.

"Don't ever wear that outfit around me again unless you're prepared for me to take it off you."

A heat had settled in the pit of her stomach upon realizing he was dead serious. She nodded in understanding. She herself had had identical thoughts that morning when she had seen him dressed in body-hugging jeans, a pair of logger boots, and a hooded sweatshirt that placed emphasis on his muscles. Not knowing what else to say, she had assured him she wouldn't before quickly retiring for bed. She had a hard time sleeping that night, tossing and turning most of the time. It was only after she admitted something to herself was she finally able to find peace. She loved Kyle. She always had and always would. She had loved him as a young girl, and she still loved him as a woman.

～

"The last few days have been simply wonderful, Kyle," Kimara said, coming down the stairs after taking a shower.

Kyle stood leaning against the fireplace. He had taken his shower earlier and was dressed in a pair of slacks and a white shirt. He watched as Kimara descended the stairs. Her feet were bare, and as she walked, the front of her robe would open and show a glimpse of beautiful legs.

He was glad she had enjoyed their days together as much as he had. He had felt comfortable enough to talk to her about his future dreams for Garwood Industries, and she had listened. Without saying a word, she showed she understood everything he'd told her. He also found her to be highly intelligent, and sincere in everything she did, especially the charities she was involved with.

Today after lunch they had gone to his grandfather's bedroom and packed up his things. While there, they had come across numerous photo albums containing pictures taken during a number of family gatherings over the years. After dinner he had gone upstairs to take a shower, leaving Kimara reading a journal she'd come across earlier that day in his grandfather's bedroom. He couldn't help noticing she had the journal tucked under her arm now.

"I'm glad you've enjoyed our time together, and so have I. I thought it would be nice to have a picnic by the lake tomorrow, if you like."

She smiled, coming to stand before him. "That sounds great. I came down to say good night."

"It's still early."

"I know but I thought I'd go to bed and finish reading your grandfather's journal. Are you sure you don't mind me reading it?"

Kyle shrugged dismissively. "Why should I? You're a Garwood now, and there aren't any dark family secrets I'm worried about. Besides, I'm sure my grandfather would have wanted you to read it."

Kimara nodded. "Did you know he renamed this place the night I was born?"

Kyle lifted a dark brow. "No. I recall him renaming this place years ago, but don't remember exactly when he did it or why he did it. It used to be called Mountain Lakes."

"Well according to Poppa Garwood's journal, the night I was born he renamed it in honor of the two of us. He named it Special K for the first letter of our names. He wrote that we were very special to him and it was his desire that the two of us would unite the Garwoods and Staffords through marriage. Can you believe he was contemplating our marriage even then?"

"Yes, sweetheart, I can believe it."

Kyle's term of endearment was spoken in a low, throaty voice. Kimara could feel her body pulsing to it. "Well, good night, Kyle."

"Wait. I have something to give you." He reached up to the mantel and retrieved two small boxes wrapped in silver paper. He handed them to her. "These are my wedding gifts to you."

Kimara's face showed her surprise. "I wasn't expecting anything. It's not like we're really married."

He grinned. "According to Judge Williams, we are."

"You know what I mean."

"Yes, I know. Now open your presents."

Kimara's hands shook nervously as she unwrapped her gifts. A beautiful diamond necklace was in one box and matching diamond earrings in the other. "Oh, Kyle, they're beautiful, but I can't accept them."

"Yes, you can. I want you to have them."

She looked up at him. "Are you sure?"

"Yes."

"Thanks. Well, I guess I'll go on up to bed now. Good night." She turned to leave.

He reached out and touched her arm. "Don't you want a glass of the champagne Granddad gave us before going to bed? We haven't had a chance to open it yet."

Kimara turned back around. The mere touch of his hand sent a shiver through her. His masculine presence was driving away everything except her awareness of him. She was attuned to everything about him, especially his touch. And she was deeply moved by the gifts he'd given her. "I don't know if that's a good idea after what happened to me on our wedding day," she said. "I drank enough of the stuff to last a lifetime."

Kyle's hand left her arm and moved to her neck. "I'll make sure you stick to your limit. Besides, I think it's a wonderful way to end such a beautiful week."

Kimara didn't respond. She couldn't even think. As she gazed into his eyes, her throat constricted, and she tried forcing air past her lungs.

"Come, let's sit down in front of the fireplace." His hand was firm under her elbow as she lowered herself to the carpeted floor, tucking her robe underneath her.

Moments later Kyle joined her there. His gaze lowered to the neckline of her robe, where a section of her dark, creamy skin peeped through. She smelled good, he thought, inhaling her scent. It was a sweet smell of magnolias that was exclusively hers.

"Here we are," he said huskily, expertly opening the champagne bottle. The sound of its loud pop echoed in the room. He filled her glass and handed it to her. Their fingers brushed in the exchange, and the flame that began growing within the pit of Kimara's stomach matched the one glowing in the fireplace.

Kyle then filled his own glass and raised it to hers. "I want to propose a toast to Kyle Garwood the Third. A man with a dream, a vision, and a goal. A man determined to get the two of us together, and I appreciate his wisdom in doing so."

Kimara's breath caught sharply in her throat with Kyle's words. Her heart began hammering in her chest. Looking at each other over their glasses, they drank.

Kyle smacked his lips and reached over to retrieve the champagne bottle to refill their glasses. "I would like to propose another toast." He raised his glass to her. "To you, Kimara Stafford Garwood. My beautiful wife and the future mother of my child." He took a sip of his drink and a few seconds later, after she had regained her wits, Kimara took a sip of hers.

She tried desperately to fight the quiver surging through her veins, and the hot ache in her throat as she watched him. She wondered if she'd gotten tipsy from the champagne or from the love flowing through her entire body for him, because at that moment she wanted him to make love to her.

Kimara knew she would have to make the first move. He had promised to give her time, and he would keep his word. But she didn't need any more time. What she needed was him. She didn't have any experience with seducing a man, but was willing to give it her best shot.

"I think it's time for our honeymoon to begin, Kyle," she whispered, nervously setting both their glasses aside.

He stared at her for a moment before asking, "Are you sure?"

"Yes," she said softly, wrapping her arms around his neck. "I haven't been more sure of anything in my life. I want you."

Suddenly he pulled her fiercely into his arms. The kiss at first was surprisingly gentle, but then he began kissing her with a hunger that belied his outward calm. His kiss sent new spirals of ecstasy through her and sang through her veins. While kissing her, his hand tugged at the belt at her waist until it came undone. With that accomplished, he stopped kissing her long enough to push the robe from her shoulders and take in the transparent nightgown covering her body. He began planting featherlike kisses on her face, neck, and shoulders.

"Kyle . . . please."

And he intended to. He stood to remove his clothes.

Kimara looked up at him through dazed eyes and began shivering. She desperately wanted the one man who had been a part of her dreams for as long as she could remember; a man who could fill her with an abandonment she wasn't aware she was capable of until now and a man she loved with all of her heart.

Kyle breathed deeply as he gazed down at Kimara. His gaze first focused on the hardening nipples of her breasts, then moved to her flat stomach, long legs, and smooth ankles. The shapely beauty of her body taunted him, making him harder for her, making his need and want of her almost unbearable. "Do you know just how much I want you, sweetheart?" he whispered. "I want you more than I've ever wanted any woman in my entire life."

Kimara's body began trembling with his words. She reached up to him. "Make love to me, Kyle. Please love me."

Kyle rejoined her on the floor before the fireplace, quickly removing the thin gown from her body. He drew her into his arms and pressed his lips to her forehead.

She could feel his hardness pressing into the softness of her thigh as he gathered her to him. The touch of his hand on her knee sent shivers of delight through her. She buried her face against his neck. His hand began moving higher and came to settle on the inside of her thigh at the same time his mouth opened over her lips, urging them apart. She complied with his sensuous request. Their tongues began a mating dance of pleasure. When Kyle splayed his hand over the very core of her femininity, she cried out to the workings of his masterful hands.

"Oh, Kyle, please . . ." She reached out and touched him the way he was touching her. She bit her lower lip to stifle any outcry of pleasure. Kyle sensed her anguish and was determined to stop her torment, but not now. He was determined to lavish her with bittersweet pleasure.

When he thought neither of them could take the torture any longer, he moved his body over hers and lay directly atop her. "You're mine. All mine." He said the words as his fingers sank even deeper into the creamy softness of her thighs, being mindful not to hurt her but at the same time wanting to hold onto her tight.

Their lips met again just as Kyle entered her. His kiss couldn't deflect her gasp of pain, nor could it cover up her body's proof that no man had ever touched her before. A shiver of surprise, happiness, and pride swept through him at this revelation. Their mouths again met in a deep drugging kiss as he pressed deeper into her body.

Pure waves of pleasure tore into Kimara in knowing Kyle was embedded deep within her. She sucked in her breath sharply when he began to move.

Her head thrashed about and her legs tightened around him as his tongue made love to her mouth using the same rhythm his hard body was using on her.

"Kyle!"

"It's all right, darling. Just let go. I'm here with you all the way. We'll soar together."

Kimara let herself go. Kyle moaned his pleasure at her abandonment, following her over the edge and releasing more than enough life-giving substance into her body to begin the next generation of Garwoods.

Ten

Sometime during the night Kyle and Kimara made it up the stairs with the rest of the champagne. Desire—heavy and urgent—consumed Kyle, making him take her over and over again. He relished in the soft sounds of pleasure that escaped her throat, and the passion and need that drove both of them over the edge of madness.

Kimara was the first to wake the next morning. She opened her eyes as memories of the night before flooded her mind and brought a smile to her lips.

Kyle was sleeping, breathing deeply and evenly next to her. His leg was thrown over her hip, one of his hands cupped her behind possessively, and the fingers of his other hand were ensnarled in her hair. But what she noticed more than anything, as she snuggled deeper into his embrace, was that their bodies were still intimately joined. They had fallen asleep after making love with him inside her, and had remained connected throughout the night. The thought that during the night she had been a part of him brought a warm feeling to her body. That feeling wasn't lessened by the slight soreness in muscles she'd never used before.

Last night he had made her feel special with the gifts and the toast. Then later he had whispered words, intimate and passionate, as he made love to her. Before they had finally drifted off to sleep, he had whispered in a very satiated voice she was his very own Special K.

Ten years ago on a Valentine's Day night he had unknowingly broken her heart. What she suffered then would be peanuts to what she would suffer now when they parted. She knew just as sure as the sun shone bright in the sky that the day would come when he would say good-bye. And it would happen as soon as all the conditions in Poppa Garwood's will were met.

She expelled a deep breath. In spite of her future predicament, she felt contented. At least this time, unlike before, she would be left with more than just a broken heart. She would be left with a part of him to have with her always. Her stomach fluttered at the thought that there was a possibility at this very minute that deep inside her something wonderful and miraculous could be taking place. They had made love enough times over the past hours for conception to be possible.

Kyle stirred. Kimara raised her eyes to find him watching her. She was entranced by the passionate darkness of his eyes. He said nothing as he continued to watch her.

She became nervous, not sure of what to say. Kyle gave her a sudden arresting smile sparked with deep longing. Desire stronger than anything she'd ever experienced swept through her, and she knew he felt it too. His arms drew her closer. Her breath caught in her throat when she felt that hard part of him begin to swell deep inside her.

"I should have warned you," Kyle said huskily, placing a light kiss on her lips. "*It* has a tendency to grow on you."

Kimara smiled. "And I should have warned you that those nutrition classes I took at Howard didn't completely cure my ravenous appetite. It seems a certain part of me is rather greedy where you're concerned."

"That's all right, baby," Kyle said, lightly fingering a loose tendril of hair on her cheek. "I'll enjoy feeding that part of you anytime."

She grinned. "I'm glad to hear it. And as far as your problem goes, never let it be said I'm a person who believes in hindering growth."

Kyle chuckled. His features turned serious. "You should have told me, Kimara."

She knew what he was referring to. She shrugged. "You thought you already had me figured out. You assumed I was sexually active."

"Most young women are."

"Not everyone believes in sex before marriage. I don't."

"What about that Coffer guy? Is that why the two of you broke up?"

"Yes. Adam wanted a woman who was willing to put out, and that wasn't me. After our breakup, I had a chance to look back on our relationship and discovered I hadn't loved him at all."

Kyle trailed his fingers along her thigh. "Have you ever been in love?"

She leaned back in his arms and looked up at him, hesitating briefly before answering. "Yes. When I was sixteen I was secretly in love with this guy. He was a few years older than me and was away at college most of the time. He barely knew I was alive and didn't love me back. Thinking back on it, I wonder how I thought he could have loved me. I wasn't all that pretty, I wore braces, and I had a weight problem. But my parents, in their own special way, had made me feel beautiful in spite of those things." She paused before continuing. "Needless to say, the man of my dreams didn't think so. He fell in love with someone else and broke my heart."

Kyle frowned. "At sixteen you were just a kid. What makes you think you actually loved him and that it wasn't infatuation?"

"Believe me, Kyle. It was love. I truly loved him."

He said nothing as he continued to hold her. He couldn't help wondering about the guy she'd fallen in love with at sixteen, the one who had broken her heart. Had she gotten over him? Would she ever be able to love anyone else? After finding his fiancée in bed with another man, he'd sworn never to fall in love again. Had she made that same vow? He wasn't given a chance to dwell on his questions any longer, for at that precise moment Kimara shifted in bed. Her movement made them more aware of their connected bodies.

Passion, sudden and acute, flamed between them. Kyle captured her lips in a kiss that racked them both. "I want to make love to you again, but I don't want to hurt you."

"You won't hurt me, Kyle. I'm not in any pain, and the soreness will go away soon. You could never hurt me while you make love to me. Besides, I want you too."

Kyle moved, and without separating them he positioned himself over her. "I'm yours," he whispered just moments before his lips captured hers again.

~

Passionate. Romantic. Heated. Intimate. Steamy.

Those were the words Kimara used to described the days that followed in a mist of sensuality. The only damper was knowing they were numbered. She glowed from the hours of physical loving Kyle bestowed upon her, never in her wildest dreams believing that she could lose herself in desire. All it took was a look from him, a touch, a special smile, to make her want him. She basked in the physical satisfaction that was more than she dreamed possible. And she gloried in their newfound relationship. Each day they were getting closer and closer, becoming friends as well as lovers.

The two weeks of their honeymoon were almost over. Neither of them spoke of what was to happen after they returned to Atlanta. Kimara knew she would be moving into the Garwood estate. Kyle headed the office of Garwood Industries that was based in New York, which meant he would be out of town most of the time. Those thoughts were on her mind on the eve of their final day at Special K. It seemed they were both tense and on edge, and had been all day. Neither of them wanted their time at Special K to come to an end, but knew that it would.

"Are you still worried about how the Valentine's Day ball will turn out, Kimara?"

She looked up to find Kyle watching her as she sat in front of the fireplace, watching the flames. She'd been quiet since dinner, lost in her thoughts. But they hadn't been about the Valentine's Day ball, as he assumed. She hadn't given much thought to that since her arrival at Special K. Her thoughts had been on Kyle and their relationship. She could not remain married to a man who did not love her, and she wasn't fool enough to think she would ever have his love. He'd lost the ability to love any woman after the hurt he'd endured nine years before. All she wanted was the strength to get through the days they would share until she found out she'd conceived. Then he would be free to walk away, and there was no doubt in her mind that he would.

"Kimara?"

She watched as he came and sat next to her. "No, I'm not worried about the ball. Thanks to your help, I believe it'll turn out better than I could have ever hoped for. My mind was on something else."

Kyle pulled her closer in his arms. "Something else like what? Talk to me. Share your thoughts with me, baby."

Kimara breathed deeply. Over the past two weeks she'd found those two things easy to do—talk to him and share her thoughts with him. But this topic of conversation wouldn't be easy for her. She didn't speak for several heartbeats, then finally, "I was thinking about us," she admitted softly. "Where do we go from here?"

Kyle stared at her, running her question around in his mind. It was a question for which he had no answer. A part of him wanted to believe his attraction to her was purely physical, but deep down he knew that wasn't the case. The only thing he was completely sure about was that once they returned to Atlanta, he didn't want the special relationship they'd shared for the past two weeks to end. He didn't know if he would be able to handle it if she began withdrawing from him. But another part of him wasn't ready for anything permanent. Nine years of pain couldn't go away easily.

"I can't answer that, Kimara. But I'd like to offer a suggestion if I may," he said, taking her hand and locking it with his.

"What?"

"Let's take things one day at a time. When we get back to Atlanta, things will be different. We'll both be involved with our respective jobs, and you'll be busy with last-minute preparations for the ball. We won't have the complete privacy we had here, and every single minute of your day won't be centered on me, nor mine on you. Let's not get uptight about anything right now. Let's just take things one day at a time and see how they go, all right?"

"All right." She couldn't deny him anything, although deep down she knew she could be setting herself up for another heartbreak. "What time will we leave here tomorrow?"

"Around noon."

Kimara heard genuine regret in his voice. "So until then, our hours together are precious ones," she whispered, turning into his arms. "Let's use them wisely. Give me memories to last a lifetime, Kyle."

He pulled her to him and kissed her. His lips were warm and possessive as he covered hers.

That night Kimara sensed something different in the way Kyle made love to her. Although it was still mind-consuming and shattering, it was gentler than ever before. And when he held her, it was as if he didn't want to let her go.

As she lay in his arms after he'd drifted off to sleep, a feeling of joy bubbled deep within her and a warm inner glow flowed through her. She knew in her heart and soul that sometime during their two-week stay at Special K their child had been conceived. Special K had lived up to its name.

Eleven

"Welcome back, girlfriend."

Kimara and Nicky embraced warmly as they stood in the middle of Kimara's office. Nicky took a step back to assess her friend. "There's something different about you, some kind of special glow. I think marriage truly agrees with you, Kim."

Kimara smiled at Nicky's compliment. She refused to dwell on the fact that her marriage was rather unique. It wasn't a marriage in name only, it was a marriage in baby only. She had been back in Atlanta for two days and was already back at work. Kyle had gotten called away on business to his branch office in Virginia. He'd caught the plane that morning and wouldn't be returning for a couple of days.

She smiled deeply. "Thanks for thinking that marriage agrees with me, but considering the circumstances, I'd think you of all people would know better." Nicky was the only person she'd confided in about the conditions of Poppa Garwood's will.

"Circumstances have a way of changing over time," Nicky hinted, smiling.

Kimara chuckled. "Perhaps. But I'm not going to get my hopes up about anything, especially my marriage to Kyle."

"And the baby?"

Kimara's smile widened. She placed a hand on her stomach. "We did it."

Nicky's eyes widened. "You're pregnant? But how do you know so soon?"

"I won't know for sure for a couple of weeks," Kimara said softly. "But in my heart I know."

Nicky smiled, happy for her friend. "Where's Kyle?"

"He's out of town on business and won't be back until Friday night, which is just as well," Kimara said, smiling. "I have a lot of stuff to unpack and Kyle has a tendency to be a distraction." Kyle being a distraction was putting it mildly, she thought, thinking of yesterday and how it had taken her half a day to unpack her luggage, something that should have taken less than thirty minutes at most. They'd spent more time making love than unpacking. She couldn't help but wonder what Mrs. Glass, the housekeeper, thought of her and Kyle locked in their bedroom most of the day.

"Kim? Are you okay?"

Nicky's question intruded into Kimara's thoughts. "Yes, I'm fine. I was just thinking about something." She walked around to her desk and sat down. "How are the plans for the ball coming along? We have exactly two weeks left."

Nicky took the chair across from Kimara's desk. "Super. I have to give special thanks to Kyle. Did you see the names of the people he was able to get a firm commitment from? I don't know what strings he pulled or what IOUs he called in, but I for one am eternally grateful. So far the number attending is well over five hundred. That's the largest crowd we've ever had."

"What about the menu?"

"Everything's under control. I've hired extra help for the evening and the agency in charge of decorations has confirmed they'll be able to get all the red and white balloons you requested."

Kimara nodded. "And the music?"

"The Davenport Orchestra will alternate with a number of musical groups, performing all love songs."

Kimara smiled. "You're right, everything looks good on the Golden Flame's end. I have a meeting with the ball committee at Stafford Publishing this afternoon to see how things with them are going."

She tapped her pen on her desk. "Have we heard anything from Sterling Hamilton? I know Kyle mentioned he'd be out of the country and wouldn't be attending, but I keep hoping there's a slim chance his plans might change."

"No, sorry. It looks like Mr. Hamilton won't be making it. His personal secretary sent a letter expressing his regrets, along with a very generous contribution."

Kimara nodded.

"What about Kyle, Kim? Is he coming? Garwood Industries have always supported this event, and now with Mr. Garwood's death and Kyle taking his place, I think it will be even more important for members of the community to see that Garwood Industries will continue to be a strong supporter and leader in various causes. We need more and more of our black businesses getting involved in worthwhile organizations like the UNCF."

"I agree, Nicky, and I believe under Kyle's leadership Garwood Industries will continue to do so. However, I don't know if he'll be coming to the ball or not."

"Why wouldn't he? I'd think he would come as your escort."

"I doubt that Kyle would come even if I were to ask him to. So I won't even bother. Valentine's Day doesn't hold a lot of meaning for him. He was to be married on Valentine's Day nine years ago."

"I didn't know that. What happened?"

"He found out the day before the wedding that his fiancée was sleeping around. He actually caught her in the act."

"Gosh." Nicky shook her head. She couldn't imagine anyone sleeping around on Kyle Garwood. "That's awful. But that was nine years ago. Surely he's gotten over it by now?"

Kimara rose from her chair and moved toward the window. "Some people never get over a broken heart, Nicky." At sixteen she'd thought her whole world had fallen apart when Kyle had gotten engaged. She could just imagine the hurt he must have felt at the age of twenty-four and very much in love. She would never forget how happy he looked when he'd brought his fiancée home to meet his family. The wedding was to have been the social event of the season, and was to take place on Valentine's Day, a day that symbolized love and forever-afters. For Kyle it had turned into a day of humiliation when the newspapers and television had gotten wind of why the wedding was called off. The *National Tattler,* the country's leading tabloid, had been at its worst and Kyle had been made into a laughingstock. Kimara had been seventeen at the time and had known only bits and pieces of what was going on. She'd gotten the full details of what had happened a number of years later from Poppa Garwood.

She turned away from the window and forced a smile as she faced her friend and business partner. "Enough about Kyle and the Valentine's Day ball. How are things coming along for the Joyners' daughter's wedding?"

Kimara put her key into the lock and opened the door, stepping inside the huge house. She immediately felt a feeling of loneliness. When she'd lived there for a while with Poppa Garwood, the house was seldom completely empty. Poppa Garwood believed in having company, even at odd hours. It wasn't unusual for him to hold as many business meetings in his home as he did at the office.

Feeling the need to relax, Kimara went to the bedroom, kicked off her shoes, and began undressing. Moments later, dressed comfortably in a pair of jeans, sweatshirt, and sneakers, she went to the kitchen to fix herself something to eat.

After quietly dining alone on a pasta salad, she went into the study. She hadn't yet unpacked a box of items Poppa Garwood had instructed Mason to give her upon his death. Keeping busy would help prevent her from missing Kyle.

She was just about to open the box when the phone rang. Immediately picking it up, she recognized the voice on the other end. "Kyle! I'm so glad you called. I miss you. How are things going?" She was so glad to hear from him. He had phoned her twice at the office, and both times she'd been out and had missed his calls.

Kimara laughed ruefully when he began teasing her about being such a hard lady to catch up with. "My first day back was kind of hectic. Yes," she laughed, "I'm still delegating some of my duties for the ball." She pushed her hair away from her face. "Kyle, I was wondering if you'll be available to take me to the ball?" she asked quickly. She'd just done the very thing she'd told Nicky she wouldn't do, and that was to ask him to the ball.

"No, that's okay. I understand that you'll probably have a lot of paperwork to do that night. That's all right." She tried to keep the disappointment out of her voice. "Okay, I'll see you on Friday. Good-bye."

After hanging up the phone, Kimara tried to will her disappointment away. How long would he allow himself to suffer from a broken heart? Even she had recovered from hers and was willing to give love another try—with the same man, if that wasn't being a glutton for punishment. She wondered if Kyle would ever be able to love again. Would he ever be able to give his heart totally and completely?

Kimara didn't have a clue as to how to proceed with her relationship with him. Of the many things he'd talked with her about at Special K, his broken engagement hadn't been one of them.

Deciding to get started on the task she'd been about to do before Kyle called, she dropped to her knees in front of the box sitting on the floor. Opening it, she discovered a number of items Poppa Garwood had wanted her to have, like his wife's collection of autographed books of poetry from James Weldon Johnson, Paul Laurence Dunbar, and Langston Hughes. He'd also left the Garwood family Bible to her.

Kimara's breath caught when she came to an envelope that had turned slightly yellow with age. She knew without looking what was inside. It was the card she'd bought for Kyle ten years before. How had Poppa Garwood gotten it? She distinctly remembered throwing it away that night. Evidently he'd gotten it out of the trash and had kept it all these years. Why?

She opened the envelope, pulled out the card, and read aloud the verses inside. It was a card she'd thought perfect for Kyle ten years earlier, and she knew it was still perfect for him today.

My Love Is Yours

My love for you grows stronger daily
And blossoms in so many ways,
It gives me hope for all my tomorrows
And a reason to cherish today.

My love for you gives me the strength
To endure loneliness whenever we are apart.
It burns just like a glowing flame
Down deep inside my heart.

And for as long as I live
My love for you will last through all eternity,
For together as one in heart, body, and soul
You and I were truly meant to be.

Kimara replaced the card in the envelope as tears clouded her eyes. Although it was ten years late in coming, she would give the card to Kyle on Valentine's Day and tell him how much she loved him.

~

It was late Friday night when Kyle arrived home. The house was dark when he stepped inside the foyer.

He missed Kimara. This unexpected trip had seemed to drag on forever. The only thing he'd wanted was to return to Atlanta and to his wife.

His wife . . .

Just thinking that she would be there when he got home brought a feeling of anticipation to him that he'd never felt before. While away, he had caught himself thinking of her at some of the oddest times, like in the middle of an important board meeting or while attending a conference with his stockbroker.

He had caught himself recounting memories of things they had done together at Special K. It didn't take much to remember making love to her, their long talks, their morning walks, and their quiet dinners alone.

Kyle dropped his briefcase on the floor by a chair. Then he saw her. Kimara lay curled up on the sofa asleep. He was deeply touched that she had tried waiting up for him. And to top things off she was wearing the blue silk jump suit.

Bending, he gently lifted her into his arms to carry her to the bedroom. She snuggled closer to him, murmuring his name against his chest. Pulling back the covers, he placed her in the bed. A low growl of need rose in his throat. Would he ever stop wanting her? Aching with a fierce desire, he quickly removed all his clothes. Leaning down, he began waking her by lightly kissing her jaw and mouth while undressing her.

"Kyle," she murmured, reaching out and placing her arms around his neck, coming awake. "You're home. I missed you."

He slid in bed beside her, drawing her into his arms. "And I missed you too, baby. I missed you so much." He captured her mouth in a long, penetrating kiss, glorying in her response. He wanted the feel of her soft body beneath him, her silky legs and arms wrapped around him. He wanted to bury himself in her.

And he wanted her now.

Kyle took her immediately, joining his body with hers, the need to become a part of her fierce, elemental. He wanted her a moaning, writhing woman in his arms, wanting him. Only him.

And all through the night, Kyle got everything he wanted.

Before dawn the next morning, Kyle slipped from the bed, being careful not to awaken Kimara. Going into the master bathroom, he put on his robe, then left the bedroom, closing the door behind him.

In the family room he took a quick swallow of Scotch. He needed it to get his bearings and to clear his mind. But no matter how much he tried, he couldn't dismiss the truth. He had fallen in love with Kimara. And he had fallen hard. Entrusting his love to another woman was something he had vowed never to do. And to make matters worse, she had whispered that she loved him before drifting off to sleep in his arms.

He knew he had to put distance between them. Although he loved Kimara and there was a certain degree of mutual trust between them, it was not enough for him. He could trust her with some things, but not his heart. No woman would ever betray him again. His ex-fiancée had taught him a valuable lesson. He'd been hurt once and he refused to set himself up for that kind of pain again.

~

"I don't understand, Kyle. You just got back last night. Why are you leaving?"

Kyle stopped his packing. "I told you, Kimara. I need to get away. I'm going to New York for a while."

Their conversation was interrupted when Mrs. Glass informed Kyle the car that would take him to the airport was ready. "Thanks, I'll be right out."

"Here's the number where I can be reached if you need anything," he said, placing a business card in Kimara's hand. "I'm sorry things just didn't work out for us. But I still want to know if . . . if you're pregnant. I meant what I said about being a part of my child's life."

Kimara threw the card down on the bed. "I think I deserve more from you than that, Kyle. I want to know what's going on. Just last night you were warm and loving, and now this morning you're cold and distant. What's wrong, Kyle? Please talk to me."

For a moment Kyle simply stared at her. "There's nothing to talk about." He turned to leave, then stopped. "Call me if you need anything, Kimara. Take care of yourself. Good-bye." He walked out of the room, quietly closing the door behind him.

"Kyle," Kimara cried out softly, knowing he couldn't hear her. She closed her eyes as tears flowed down her cheeks.

Twelve

Kimara was grateful for the last-minute hustle and bustle in preparing for the Valentine's Day ball. Since Valentine's Day fell in the middle of the week, a decision was made to end the ball at eleven o'clock instead of midnight, to accommodate the students, who had to attend school the next day.

She did everything she could do to stay busy and fill the loneliness. But nothing she did eased the pain. Nicky knew she and Kyle had separated and had gone out of her way to be there for her friend. She invited Kimara over to dinner a couple of nights and even spent the night with her a few times so she wouldn't be alone in the huge house.

Although she tried not to think of Kyle, Kimara found herself doing so anyway, especially in the wee hours of the night, when she longed to be held by him and loved by him. She was hurt and angered by the way he'd left, without an explanation of what had driven him away. He hadn't even bothered to call.

Over the next ten days she'd come to accept that Kyle's fiancée's betrayal had made him into an unloving and hard man, and no one would ever be able to change that about him. He would never be capable of loving anyone. He would never let himself be completely vulnerable again.

She should have known better. How many times in the past nine years had she picked up a magazine or newspaper that had given an account of one of Kyle's affairs? None of the women he'd ever been involved with had been able to hold his interest long. What had made her think that she would be any different? After all, she'd been forced on him as a result of the terms of his grandfather's will. She should not have allowed her head to get filled with a lot of romantic notions of her, Kyle, and their child being a real family and living together happily ever after.

Kimara knew she would have to go on with her life without him, just her and the baby she now knew for certain she carried. The at-home pregnancy test had confirmed what she'd known all along. She would give birth to Kyle's child in the fall. She and her baby would make it without Kyle in their lives.

~

Kyle sat in his office, trying to study the documents his stockbroker had dropped off earlier. But he couldn't concentrate, and if he was completely honest with himself, he would admit his concentration level had been at an all-time low since leaving Kimara.

It had been ten days since he'd left her to come to New York. Ten days of pure hell. Nothing had gone right since then. His employees had sensed his foul mood and made it a point to stay out of his way. And when he left the office in the afternoons, the loneliness he felt for Kimara was like a sharp knife, always cutting inside him. He tossed in bed most of the night, not getting much sleep. And she was the first thing on his mind when he did wake up in the morning. No matter what he did, he couldn't quiet the feelings that always rolled around in him whenever he thought of her.

And he couldn't stop loving her.

His grandfather had pulled a fast one on him. He had set up the conditions of the will knowing that Kimara was the type of woman any man could love—the type of woman that he would love. She had all the characteristics of a Garwood woman—caring, devoted, and trustworthy.

Trustworthy. He knew without a doubt that she was worthy of his complete love and trust. With his grandfather's help, he had been shown the very thing he hadn't realized until then. It wasn't meant for him to marry nine years ago. Kimara was the woman intended for him to marry. She'd always been a part of his life, a part of his family. Without even trying, she had captured his heart and had made him want to love and trust again.

He made a vow then and there to keep her a part of his life, to always love her. The pain from his past no longer mattered. It wasn't important. He was determined that a bond of love as strong as the one his father had for his mother, and his grandfather had for his grandmother, be created between them.

But first he had to ask her forgiveness for what he'd done. He stiffened when he thought about how cold and distant he'd been to her the morning he'd left. She had been right when she'd told him she deserved more from him. What if she didn't want him anymore? What if she no longer loved him? What if she couldn't forgive him?

No! He would not let doubt rule his mind and his heart. He and Kimara were meant to be together, and that was final. After all, they had his grandfather's blessing, and everyone knew that Kyle Garwood III left nothing to chance.

～

The huge ballroom filled with people got completely quiet when the two men made their entrance. They were the last two people anyone expected to make an appearance tonight—Kyle Garwood V and Sterling Hamilton. Both men were handsomely dressed in black tuxes. Last year they had been named by *People* magazine as two of the fifty most beautiful people in the world, and it was quite obvious why. And there was no doubt in anyone's mind that they would make the list again this year.

After the brief moment of silence, buzzing of excited conversations swept through the ballroom. But Kyle paid no mind to the slight commotion he and his best friend were causing. His gaze was too busy sweeping the crowded ballroom that was decorated in traditional valentine colors of red and white. He was looking for his wife.

"I'm dying to meet her, Kyle," Sterling Hamilton said. "She must be one hell of a woman to get you all tied in knots. You've been a mass of nerves all day."

Kyle took a deep breath. "And with good reason. I've wronged her, Sterling."

"Then I guess you'd better be prepared to get on bended knees, bro."

Kyle shrugged broad shoulders that barely moved beneath his jacket. "I'll do whatever I have to."

"Is she worth it?"

Kyle met Sterling's gaze and clearly understood the question. He and Sterling had been close friends a number of years, and was one of the few people who knew how a woman had also hurt Sterling—his mother. Her desertion when Sterling was young had left him bitter and distrustful of women. Kyle hoped one day love would come into Sterling's life as it had his.

"Yes, Kimara's worth it and more. When you meet her, you'll see why."

"I can't wait," Sterling said, glancing around the room and taking notice of a small group of people headed their way. "Don't look now, but here comes the reporters. Once they start firing their questions, you'll never get away to find your wife in this crowd."

"Oh, I'll find her, but I don't have time to be delayed."

Sterling laughed. "Does that mean you're leaving me alone to fend for myself?"

Kyle patted Sterling consolingly on the back. "Only because you're so good at it. Thanks again for coming. I owe you one, buddy."

"And don't think for one minute that I won't be collecting. When your first child is born, I want to be its godfather."

Kyle laughed. "That's a deal. And whenever you do get married, I'd like to be best man at your wedding."

"Don't hold your breath for that one, friend. I'm never getting married."

"Watch out, Sterling. I said the same thing for years." Kyle grinned as he walked off in search of his wife.

～

Nicky was beaming. "I'm not going to ask how you managed to get Sterling Hamilton here tonight, but thanks."

Kyle nodded, glancing around the room. "Where's Kimara?"

Nicky couldn't help noticing the lines of strain and tension etched deeply into his dark features. They were a mirror to those she'd seen in Kim's face over the past few days. "She's in the back doing a last-minute check with our catering staff."

"Thanks." Kyle turned and had taken two steps, when Nicky called after him. "Kyle, good luck."

He nodded, knowing he would need all the luck he could get. He found Kimara where Nicky had said she would be, in the back near the kitchen. She was talking to a man he assumed was her head cook. His breath caught in his throat. Her profile was to him, and she looked beautiful dressed in a red velvet gown that had a white satin sash around her small waist. Her hair was pinned up on her head, and to his delight she was wearing the diamond necklace and earrings he'd given her as a wedding gift.

He ached to pull her into his arms, to kiss her and to tell her how much he loved her. But first he had to explain things to her. He hoped to God she would listen and then forgive him.

The man Kimara was talking to walked away, and she turned. Surprise flitted in her eyes when her gaze met his.

A sudden rush of air flooded her lungs when she saw the man standing a few feet away from her. She tried not to think about how handsome he looked dressed in a black tux, or the powerful magnetism he radiated. What she did focus her thoughts on was how much this man had hurt her. She remembered the last time she'd seen him, twelve days ago, and how he'd walked out on her. Those thoughts made her shiver in anger.

"What are you doing here, Kyle?"

Kimara watched as he came closer. She was too caught up in her hurt, pain, and resentment to see the tortured look of regret that lined his face and darkened his eyes.

"I had to come, baby. I couldn't stay away from you any longer. I—"

"Spare me. Your coming here was a mistake. You made everything clear the day you walked out on me."

"Kimara, please hear me out. Let's find a private place where we can talk. I need to explain things to you. I need to tell you that I—"

"You want to talk? Well, it's too late for that. I asked you to talk to me that morning you left, and you said we had nothing to talk about. So why should I listen to anything you have to say now? Please leave, Kyle. Just go and leave me alone. You've broken my heart twice, and I won't let you do it a third time."

She made a move to walk around him, but Kyle blocked her path. "Twice? What are you talking about? How could I have broken your heart twice?"

Not wanting to tell Kyle about the time she'd been a young girl madly in love with him ten years ago, she faced him, her hands balling into fists at her side, her body filled with rage.

At that moment Kyle made the mistake of reaching out for her. "Don't touch me," she screamed, snatching away from him. "Just leave me alone. I hate you for making me love you. I hate you." She suddenly turned on him, striking out at him, and in her pain she pounded his chest.

"You walked out on me," she wept brokenly. "You made me love you and then you walked out on me."

Kyle let Kimara release her fury on him, deserving everything he got. When he felt her body weaken with exhaustion, he picked her up in his arms and carried her into the back of the huge room. He was grateful no one had been around to witness the scene between them.

He continued walking with her in his arms, her body still shaking with wrenching sobs. He came to a small vacant room that had a table and a couple of chairs. With Kimara still nestled in his arms, he sat down.

Her crying tore at his heart; her pain cut through him. He held her with tears clouding his own eyes, remembering the two weeks they had spent together at Special K and how much they'd enjoyed being together. He knew deep down in his heart that he had begun loving her then. He never had meant to hurt her, but in trying to protect himself, he'd done just that. The realization that he was the cause of her tears tore at him, almost ripping him in two.

"I'm sorry, baby. Please forgive me. I never meant to hurt you," he whispered hoarsely, holding her closer in his arms, closer to his heart.

The raw ache in Kyle's voice and the slight trembling of his body cut through the wall of anguish and resentment Kimara felt. He was holding her tight, and his hands were moving gently up and down her back, comforting her and at the same time spreading warmth all through her.

Taking a deep calming breath, Kimara fought for self-control and pulled herself out of Kyle's arms and out of his lap. "I'm fine now, Kyle," she said quietly, refusing to look at him. "Please leave now."

"I'm not leaving until you hear me out, Kimara," he said, taking her hand.

She pulled her hand free from him. The last thing she needed was to be touched by him. Her voice was tight with bitterness when she said, "I did hear you out once. It was that night at Special K when you said we would take things one day at a time when we got back here in Atlanta. But you didn't mean to do that, did you? You had no intention of the two of us ever sharing anything beyond what was stipulated in Poppa Garwood's will. You made me fall in love with you, Kyle. I told you that I never wanted to be one of your women, and I meant it. But you made me one of them anyway."

Kyle's body became tense at the calm acceptance in her voice. "I love you, Kimara."

Kimara stared at him. "What did you say?"

"I said I love you. And you could never be one of my women because you are my only woman. You're the only woman who lay claim to my heart. Only you. Please believe that." His voice was hoarse and tight, as if the words were being wrenched from deep within him. "Please."

He took a step forward. "I made a mistake by turning my back on you and my love for you. I was too afraid of the possible pain. I didn't want to trust my love to you. But now I know that my trust for you is complete. You and I were meant to be together. Granddad knew it, and I'm grateful that he helped me to realize it."

Kyle's words began crumbling the wall Kimara had built around her heart. When he held his arms out to her, she stepped into them, winding her arms tightly around his neck.

He wrapped his arms around her. "I love you, Kimara," he whispered.

"I've missed you so much these past twelve days. Please take me back into your life, into your heart. Give me a chance to make everything up to you. Please give me the chance to love you forever."

"I can't believe you actually love me," Kimara whispered softly.

"Believe it, because I plan on living the rest of my life showing you just how much." He tightened his arms around her, his mouth closing hungrily over hers, wiping away hurt and pain, replacing both with promises of love everlasting.

Kimara kissed him back with all her heart, loving the way he was taking her mouth, removing her doubts, and soothing her fears. She had missed him desperately, and by the way he was kissing her, he had missed her too.

When he lifted his head some time later, he kept his arms wrapped around her. "I love you," he whispered again, as if saying the words over and over would erase any doubt from her mind. "I love you, baby."

"And I love you too, Kyle," she said, moving closer to his warmth.

He gave her a slow, sexy smile and touched her cheek. "Today is truly a special day. It's a day meant for love. True love. Our love. I'll never think ill of Valentine's Day again. I now realize that it wasn't meant for me to get married nine years ago. You and I were meant to be together. You are my soulmate."

Kyle pulled her to him again for another kiss, their passion for each other almost blazing out of control.

"Harrumph."

The clearing of someone's throat made Kyle and Kimara part. They turned around to find Nicky had entered the room.

"I hate to intrude, but I'd gotten kind of worried about the two of you. Is everything okay?"

Kimara smiled at her friend, appreciating her concern. "Yes, everything's fine. Kyle and I were just discussing the weather."

Nicky laughed. "And I bet the both of you came to the conclusion it was rather hot."

Kimara grinned. "Yeah, something like that. I guess I need to get back to the ball. I've been gone a long time."

"Yes, but everything's under control. The students are having the time of their lives. Did Kyle tell you whom he brought to the ball with him?"

Kimara lifted a brow. "No, I guess he didn't get the chance to," she said, smiling at Kyle. "Whom did you bring with you, Kyle?"

Nicky was so excited, she answered for him. "He brought Sterling Hamilton. Can you believe that?"

Kimara's mouth fell open. "Sterling Hamilton! Kyle? How did you manage that? I didn't know the two of you were friends."

Kyle laughed. "Sterling and I are very good friends. In fact, I promised him he would be our first child's godparent. That is, if it's all right with you."

Kimara grinned. "Yes, that's fine with me, but how did you do it? I thought he was out of the country, filming."

"He was, but I went and got him. My jet will be flying him back tomorrow. I knew how much you wanted him here."

Kimara lifted her hand and placed her fingers against Kyle's jaw. "Thanks, Kyle."

"The pleasure of making you happy is all mine. Besides, Sterling's dying to meet the woman who has captured my heart."

"I think I'll leave the two of you alone again," Nicky said. "Just don't forget there's a party in full swing on the other side of the building. Come join us."

"We'll be there in a minute," Kyle said, turning back to the woman in his arms. "On second thought, Nicky, make that five minutes," he said, moments before taking Kimara's mouth again.

Later that night Kimara lay in Kyle's arms in front of the fireplace. The ball had been a huge success and everyone, including herself, had thoroughly enjoyed Sterling Hamilton's presence. She thought he was a really neat guy.

She stirred in her husband's arms, moving closer to his warmth and thinking that he was an even neater guy. When she'd arrived home with him from the ball, she had discovered her foyer lined with dozens of red and white roses. The sight of them had been beautiful and breathtaking. He had explained that he'd called the florist himself and made arrangements to have the flowers delivered after she had left for the ball. Mrs. Glass had assured him that she would be there to receive them.

Kyle gave her a gift, a beautiful gold charm bracelet. The charm was a golden cupid with his bow. After placing the bracelet on her wrist, he whispered, "The arrow from Cupid's bow has hit its mark. It struck a permanent place in my heart." His words almost brought tears to her eyes. "And I promise to add another charm on Valentine's Day each year. Happy Valentine's Day, sweetheart," he said.

"And Happy Valentine's Day to you, Kyle. I have something for you too. In fact I have two things to give you."

He watched as she padded across the carpeted floor in bare feet to get something out of his grandfather's desk. She returned to him and dropped down by his side, handing an envelope to him.

"I bought this for you ten years ago."

Kyle frowned. "Ten years ago? I don't understand."

Kimara smiled. "When I was sixteen, I loved you even then."

Kyle sat up, remembering the story she'd told him about falling in love at sixteen and how the guy had broken her heart. "You mean I'm that guy you told me about—the one you loved secretly? The one who broke your heart?"

Kimara nodded.

He shook his head. "Now I understand why tonight you said I broke your heart twice." He pulled her to him. "Oh, baby, I'm so sorry. I didn't know."

"It's okay. We're together now, and that's all that matters to me."

Kyle removed the card from the envelope and silently read it. He smiled at her when he finished. "My love is yours too, sweetheart, and you're right. Together as one is where we were meant to be. Thanks for being the love of my life and the keeper of my heart. I love you."

"And I love you. Now for the other thing I have for you." She took his hand and placed it on her stomach. At his bemused expression she smiled and said, "Your baby is growing inside of me."

A huge smile covered Kyle's face. He swept Kimara into his embrace, tightening his arms around her. He kissed her temple as a mistiness clouded his eyes. "You have made me so very happy, and I love you so much."

He whispered the words just moments before lowering his lips to hers, sealing their lives together.

Epilogue

"Daddy! Daddy! It's snowing outside. Can we go out and play?"

Kyle smiled and put down the book he'd been reading when two-and-a-half year old Kyle Garwood VI raced across the room to him. He picked up his son in his arms. As always, a feeling of fierce pride and joy touched him whenever he held the child who had been conceived when he and Kimara had spent their honeymoon at Special K.

"Can we go outside, Daddy?"

Kyle's smile widened. "What about Kareem and Keshia? Do you think they'll want to come with us?"

Little Kyle shook his head. "They're too little, Daddy. They might get buried in the snow."

Kyle laughed. He had glanced out the window earlier and there wasn't that much snow on the ground. The twins were almost a year old and were just beginning to walk. "Come on, let's go find Mommy to see what she thinks about going outside."

He found Kimara in the nursery, on the floor, playing with the twins. His heart swelled with love each time he saw her. Nine months after their honeymoon she had given him a son. Then eighteen months later, she had given him twins, another son and a daughter. As he watched her at play with them, he noticed the gold charm bracelet on her wrist. It had been a gift from him on Valentine's Day three years before. Since then he'd kept his promise and had added another gold charm every Valentine's Day since then. Each charm represented a year of their life together and their pledge of undying love.

Kimara sensed his presence and looked up. She smiled. "Hi."

"Hi yourself. I see Kareem and Keshia have you busy," he said, walking toward her.

She stood, leaving the twins playing with their building blocks. "And as usual, I see you have your hands full with him," she said, smiling up at her oldest son, who was sitting high on Kyle's shoulders. He was the spitting image of his father.

Kyle grinned. "He wants to go outside and play in the snow. What do you think?"

Kimara's smile widened. "I think that's not a bad idea if all of us can come with you guys." She reached up and ran her hand softly against his jaw. "I also think you're a wonderful father and I love you."

"And I love you." Kyle placed little Kyle down and watched him race off to join his sister and brother on the floor. He pulled Kimara in his arms. "Thanks."

She looked up into his eyes. "For what?"

"For everything. For giving more meaning to my life, for being my friend and lover as well as my wife, for loving me." He leaned down and kissed her lips. "And thanks for them," he said, indicating their children. He pulled Kimara back in his arms. "We now have three Special Ks of our very own."

Kimara put her arms around Kyle's neck. "Speaking of Special K, I have an idea."

"What?"

"How about if we take some time off and go there for a couple of weeks. The kids will love it."

Kyle laughed. "You know what happens whenever we spend a long time at Special K, honey. You always come back pregnant."

A teasing smile covered Kimara's face. "I wonder why?"

He smiled down at her. "Must be the water there."

"Oh, I don't think it's anything that bizarre. There's a very simple explanation why I always get pregnant at Special K."

Kyle leaned down and kissed her. "Really, what is it?"

Kimara looked into his eyes. She saw the same love shining in his gaze that she knew was in hers. "It's magical," she told him in a voice filled with reverence. "And your grandfather intended for it to be that way. It's a very special place and it's ours."

"Yes, ours," Kyle agreed, kissing his wife thoroughly.

"Does that mean we're going, Kyle?" She mouthed the words against his moist lips.

He moved his hand to the center of her back, drawing her closer to him. "Yes, I suppose so," he said, his voice deep and husky.

Kimara smiled. "Does that also mean you're ready for another baby?"

"Yes," he said, smiling, while pressing a series of kisses around her mouth and nose.

"Good," she said, bringing his mouth to hers again. "I love a man who enjoys being creative."

ABOUT THE AUTHOR

Brenda Jackson lives with her family in the city where she was born—Jacksonville, Florida. She is the award-winning author of eight Arabesque novels, and has penned the reader favorite Madaris family stories, including ETERNALLY YOURS.

Made in Heaven

Felicia Mason

One

If she closed her eyes and took a deep breath, Val Sanders figured her nightmare would end.

It didn't work.

He still sat there. The words still flowed from his mouth, the food still shoveled in at warp speed. Val absently wondered if a projectile of the prime rib he consumed would land on her blouse. She'd just gotten the blouse out of the dry cleaners.

"So I told the supplier there was no way I was going to let an inferior product in one of my warehouses. I told him to reload his little trailer and hit the road. That move cost me a pretty penny. I don't mind telling you, Valerie, that he had close to one hundred thousand dollars worth of merchandise in that rig. But you know what? Turning that shipment away was the best thing that ever happened to me. I cleared three point five last year. I don't have any stockholders. I don't have any bad debts. After expenses and salaries to my people, it's all profit." He grinned at her. "I'm just looking for the right woman to share it with."

This joker thought he was making all the right moves. He didn't even get her name right. And what he probably hoped was a suave Billy Dee smile was more like a smirk, the effort spoiled by the bit of spinach stuck to his tooth. Val dabbed her mouth with the crisp linen napkin and hid the smile that threatened.

Val placed the napkin back in her lap and looked away for a moment, if only to get her quickly slipping composure together. She glanced at their dinner table in an attempt to identify the crumbs clinging to the right corner of his otherwise well-groomed mustache. Ah, the hard rolls.

Val didn't like mustaches.

"There's a matching Maserati in my garage and the vanity tags say HERS," he continued. "My Nubian queen will ride in style. All she has to do is say yes."

Not in this lifetime, Val thought.

She'd agreed to this date with Conroy T. Franklin IV. They'd been out once before. When he called about dinner, she'd said yes for one simple reason: She couldn't believe that any man could be as obnoxious as he had been on their first date. Maybe she'd had a bad case of the flu that night. Her recollection of the evening may have been flawed. What she discovered tonight, however, was that her memory had been kind to the man.

Conroy had launched into an agonizingly detailed description of his vacation to the Middle East. "I bathed in the Euphrates and recited that wonderful poem by Maya Angelou."

"Langston Hughes," Val corrected him.

Conroy looked annoyed at being interrupted. "I beg your pardon."

"Langston Hughes wrote the poem about bathing in the Euphrates River."

"Oh. Whatever. As I was saying . . ."

Val knew poetry, and this guy was no scholar. It irritated her that he didn't even bother to acknowledge his error. Then she wondered how many other women he'd regaled with this tale. If the man had done any bathing at all, it was in the bottle of cologne he'd doused himself with before coming to the restaurant.

My God. I'm going to be thirty next week and my life has been reduced to this, Val thought.

"My masseur comes to the house three times a week. You'd like the exercise room in my home. I custom-designed the twelve-hundred-square-foot center for my needs and work out with my personal trainer every day. Valerie, I think we have something going here. I'd like to see you again. You're a little on the heavy side, but my personal trainer can handle that. You're such a pretty woman. My personal trainer can get rid of those few unsightly extra pounds you carry. Have you ever been to Belize? It's a wonderful country."

That's it, Val thought. I'm outta here.

Pleading a headache, she ended the date. Conroy pulled the Maserati into the parking space and Val hopped out of the car before he could turn the engine off.

Val let herself into her condo. She kicked off the high-heeled pumps she wore and came to a conclusion. Thirty might be staring her in the face, but if all the available men were like Conroy T. Franklin—and it sure seemed like they were—Val preferred to be single until she drew her last breath.

Val misted her plants as she listened to the two messages on her answering machine. Who in the world would be calling on a Friday night?

"Valentine, darling, this is your mother. Your father and I are looking forward to next week. We have a surprise for you. Call me sometime tomorrow, sweetheart. Love you much."

Val groaned. Surprises from her parents didn't bode well. And the unwelcome reminder about her birthday didn't lift her spirits.

The second message started. "Hey, girl. It's Shelley. And Kalinda," another voice piped up. "How was the big date with Mr. Independent Successful Businessman?"

"Girl, I don't know why you're wasting your time with that one," Shelley said on the recording.

"Get to the real message, Shell. You're gonna run out of tape," Kalinda admonished.

Val grinned. Her two best friends were a trip.

"Oh, yeah. Val, have we got *the* birthday present for you. You have to get it early, though, to get ready for next week. We're gonna give it to you when we go out tomorrow. See you at noon. Bye, Val."

Kalinda echoed her farewell on the tape.

Val finished misting the plants and replaced the sprayer under the kitchen sink. She opened the pantry and stared at the calendar tacked inside the door. February 14 loomed out at her. Her mother had put a little red heart sticker on the date. Val frowned.

For years people told her that being born on Valentine's Day was romantic. Val didn't see anything romantic about it. Valentine's Day was a racket. Look what it had done to her parents. Quentin and Naomi Sanders had been married for twenty years when they decided to call it quits on their marriage. The two had remained friends, though, and never ceased regaling their only daughter with the story of how they met one day in a department store. The very next week, on Valentine's Day, Quentin Sanders proposed to Naomi. Love at first sight, they claimed. A couple of years later, when their baby girl was born two minutes after midnight on February 14, the two had just the name for the cute infant.

Val didn't believe in love at first sight. Her parents stayed together long enough to raise her in a two-parent household and then called it quits. The love they thought they'd had for each other had faded. But they still loved Valentine's Day. Val had been fed a steady and sickening diet of hearts and flowers and candy and frills. She hated Valentine's Day. Most of the time she let people assume her name was Valerie just so she wouldn't have to answer the inevitable questions.

Val popped a fine marker pen out of the holder next to the calendar. She drew a circle around the heart on February 14 and then drew a slash through the circle. Growing up, her parents always dressed her in frilly lace and pink outfits for her birthday parties. Val didn't own a single pink piece of clothing and was darn proud of the fact. She was a realist, not a romantic.

"Maybe I can go to bed on the thirteenth and wake up on the fifteenth."

If left to her own devices, turning thirty wouldn't be so bad. If her parents and best friends could temper their excitement about the milestone, it would be okay. Being single wasn't so bad either. It was far better than attaching herself to someone like Conroy Franklin just for the sake of being considered part of a couple.

Val closed the pantry door and turned off the kitchen light.

~

The next day Val met her girlfriends for lunch at Patrick Henry Mall.

"That grin of yours doesn't bode well for me," Val told Shelley as the two women hugged.

"I'm just glad I'm not going to be the only one who has faced down the big three-oh," Shelley said.

"Why don't you two old ladies come on. They're calling our name," Kalinda said.

"Your day is coming," Shelley answered. "August will be here before you know it and you, too, will have kissed twentysomething good-bye forever."

Laughing, the three women followed the hostess to their table in the restaurant.

"I'm ordering dessert first," Kalinda said. "I never have room for it at the end."

Shelley rolled her eyes and Val laughed. After placing their orders, Shelley got down to business.

"Okay, spill it, Miss Thing," she said. Holding her nose up in the air and talking in a nasal tone, she did a fairly decent imitation of Conroy. "Was the date with Mr. Maserati all that?"

"It was all that and more," Val said. "After a night out with Conroy T. Franklin the Fourth, I decided that being single has its merits. The only thing together about that brother is his car."

Val leaned forward and, mimicking Conroy, said, "And he has a matching one in his garage for his Nubian queen."

Val and Shelley burst into giggles. Kalinda frowned.

The women leaned back as the waiter placed their drink orders on the table.

"What's wrong with a man who wants to treat his woman like a queen?" Kalinda asked.

"Nothing," Shelley said. "I'm looking for one who has that in mind."

"Some men can pull off that type of line. Coming from Conroy, being a Nubian queen sounded like a contagious disease."

"Okay, okay. Well, can we assume that you won't be seeing this brother anymore?" Shelley asked.

"You have that right," Val said, taking a sip from her glass of iced tea.

"Well, we're glad to hear that. Right, Kalinda?"

Kalinda nodded and grinned at Val.

"There's that conspiratorial grin again. What are you two up to?"

"For your birthday we're giving you a match made in heaven."

Val groaned. "Oh, God. Not another blind date. The last time I went out with someone you two hooked me up with, I had to hire an interpreter to figure out what the man was talking about. He had enough gold on his fingers and teeth to finance a small country. And a six-hour master jam rap concert at the Coliseum is not my idea of an ideal first date."

"Come on, Val," Kalinda pleaded. "I thought you'd forgiven us that one small error in judgment."

"Yeah, Val," Shelley added. "Besides, you got even by recommending I go out with that car dealer. Do you know that man is still calling me, leaving messages saying he can put me in a late model today."

"That's what you get," Val said.

The women paused long enough for the waiter to place broccoli soup in front of Val and Shelley and a huge cookie, ice cream, and hot fudge concoction in front of Kalinda.

"That looks good," Shelley observed. "Maybe I'll have one of those too."

The waiter grinned. "And you, ma'am?"

Val eyed the treat. "I'll think about it."

Shelley picked up her spoon and swiped a bit of Kalinda's dessert.

"Hey, wait for your own!"

Shelley popped the spoonful of ice cream and whipped cream in her mouth. "Mmmm."

Val started on her soup. "There's a new exhibit at the Peninsula Fine Arts Center. Want to go there after lunch?"

"Stop trying to change the subject, birthday girl. We have an appointment after lunch."

"Look, I'm really not up to any big splashes for my birthday, okay? I'd just like it to come and go without a lot of fanfare."

"I don't know why you always have such a negative attitude about your birthday. I celebrate for a week," Kalinda said. "You're supposed to have fun for your birthday."

"Your birthday is in August. Not on Valentine's Day," Val pointed out. "You get to celebrate just your birthday. I have to have all that mushy Valentine's Day stuff attached to mine."

"Having a birthday on Valentine's Day is very romantic."

Val's snort of derision answered Kalinda's comment.

"We digress, ladies," Shelley said. "And, Val, rest easy. This isn't a big splash. This time we're gonna do it right. You're going to get a match made in heaven, and so are we. It's past time we stop wasting our time on these losers and the ones who are on ego trips."

"That's right," Kalinda said. "So we all have an appointment. And yours is our birthday present to you."

"An appointment with who?"

"Actually it's an appointment with what," Shelley said. "Have you ever heard of the dating service called A Match Made in Heaven?"

"Dating service! You two have really flipped. Sisters, we are not that desperate."

"It's not about being desperate," Shelley said. "It's about weeding out all the weirdos. This company does that. They hook you up with people who have things in common with you, people who are likely to be a match made in heaven rather than a disaster made in you know where. How many more Conroy T. Franklins do you want to go out with?"

The conversation ceased for a few minutes while the waiter brought their entrees and the women got serious about lunch.

"None," Val said, picking up the conversation. "That's exactly why I decided last night that I'd rather just be by myself."

Shelley rolled her eyes. "Um-hmm. That's because you had a bad date last night. I'm telling you, this company is our answer."

"It's gonna be fun," Kalinda promised.

Val shook her head. "I'd really prefer a potted plant, girls. Maybe a nice hibiscus."

~

But at three o'clock Val, Kalinda and Shelley sat in the receiving room at A Match Made in Heaven. Val wasn't sure how she'd let her friends talk her into this. While Shelley and Kalinda filled out the extensive questionnaire from the dating service, Val looked around the office.

She had to admit, the place was tastefully decorated in mauve and pale green. The chairs were deep, wide, and comfortable, the type that made you want to sit back and visit for a while. Muted track lighting added a touch of ambience even though outside it was a busy Saturday afternoon. Towering potted ficus trees and flowering plants scattered about provided a soothing sense of place and comfort. Gentle instrumental jazz piped in on hidden speakers rounded out the overall impression of top-notch quality.

Spoiling it all were the red hearts outlined in lace doily material tacked to the walls, the cupids with arrows drawn hanging from invisible pieces of string from the ceiling, and the eight-foot-long banner over the reception desk proclaiming in humongous letters HAPPY VALENTINE'S DAY.

The mental points Val gave A Match Made in Heaven for its tasteful decor turned to negative numbers with the overdose on the sappy Valentine's theme.

Kalinda had already remarked that she thought the decorations delightful. They had each been handed a brochure with Valentine's Day history and lore on it. Val had read the first one on the tradition of the Valentine's Day card and rolled her eyes. At home in a box somewhere she had a dozen or so books about the hearts-and-flowers day, from little cutesy minibooks to coffee-table-size tomes, all given to her over the years by well-meaning friends and acquaintances who thought it was unique and neat that her birthday was on Valentine's Day.

Now all she could do was wonder about the people who ran this operation. What kind of person made a living doing this? she wondered as she took in the people gathered in the room. Business was brisk. Men and women hunched over clear acrylic clipboards jotting down the intimate details of their social lives.

"Excuse me, sweetie. Could you hand me one of those pencils, please? I just broke the point off this one."

Val turned and smiled at the lady sitting in the chair next to her. She was seventy if she was a day, but the twinkle in the woman's eye and the sparkle of her smile let Val know this was no retiring golden-ager.

Val uncrossed her legs and reached for one of the finely sharpened pencils in the acrylic holder on the end table next to her. She plucked one from the bunch, then shook her head. "It figures," she mumbled, taking a look at the red pencil decorated with white stenciled hearts.

"Here you are, ma'am," Val said, handing the woman the pencil.

"Are you a first-timer?" the woman asked.

"I beg your pardon?"

"This your first time at A Match Made in Heaven?"

Val nodded.

The woman tucked her clipboard in her lap and turned to Val. "Oh, sweetie, you are going to have so much fun. You're a beauty, so you'll have no problem finding a match. My name's Ruth," she said, sticking her hand out in greeting. The fringe on her Ultrasuede jacket bounced along with Ruth.

Smiling, Val shook the woman's hand. "I'm Val. And, yes, it's my first time here," she said. And my last, she added to herself.

"Well, let me just tell you, Netanya and Eric, the people who run this place, they do wonderful work. They introduced me to my dear Alfred," Ruth said.

Val didn't miss Ruth's fond look and misty eyes at the mention of Alfred. Since it would be rude to ask what happened to Alfred, Val waited for an explanation.

"He died two years ago," Ruth said.

"Oh, I'm sorry . . ." Val began.

Ruth laughed. "Don't be sorry, sweetie. You didn't even know the man. Alfred was a saint. But after Alfred I met Wade. We dated for four months, and do you know what that man had the nerve to do?"

"What?"

"Left me for an older woman."

Val couldn't contain her look of surprise. Ruth laughed.

"That look of shock on your face is exactly how I felt when he told me he was dumping me. I'll be seventy-five on my next birthday." She leaned forward and whispered. "And since I have no intention of spending that birthday alone, if you know what I mean, I'm here for another match. If I'm lucky, I'll meet hubby number seven here."

Val's mouth dropped open. "You've been married six times?"

"Oh, sure, sweetie. I like being married. Met three of my husbands here."

A cloud of pink and white descended over Val and Ruth. "Hello," the woman greeted Val and Ruth.

"Mrs. Randall, so nice to see you again. Won't you come this way," the woman in the pink and white ruffles said.

Ruth clapped her hands in delight. "Wish me luck, Val," she said as she gathered her purse and questionnaire. "And don't you worry. There's a match made in heaven just waiting for you."

I don't think I'll meet him at a dating service, Val said to herself. She watched Ruth follow the pretty, petite woman into an office, then settled in her chair to look over the rest of the people in the reception area.

A man wearing plaid pants, white socks, and an ice-blue leisure suit jacket scratched his head and consulted his watch before scribbling an answer on his form. He tapped his pen on the acrylic, then turned the writing instrument upside down and peered at the tip. Val watched him trade the pen for one in the plastic pen holder inside his suit pocket.

"If this isn't straight out of central casting, I don't know what is," Val mumbled.

"You aren't writing, Val," Shelley said from where she sat next to Kalinda.

"I know you guys mean well and you want to have some fun. But this just isn't my cup of tea," Val explained.

"How would you know?" Kalinda pointed out. "You haven't even taken the first step." Kalinda held up her clipboard and questionnaire. "You better get busy. This is pretty detailed."

"Linda, Shell, you aren't listening to me."

"We're listening, Val," Kalinda said. "Every year about this time you get real weird. Well, this year we're here to make sure you enjoy your birthday."

"I do not get weird," Val said in her own defense.

The main door opened and a very tall, very attractive man walked into the reception area.

Val looked him over. Shelley looked him over. Kalinda looked him over. The man went to the desk to register, then took a clipboard and found a seat.

Val glanced at her friends. "Well, maybe this isn't such a bad idea after all."

Two

Eric Fitzgerald kicked his feet up on the credenza behind his desk and looked out the window and over the courtyard. He smiled. The cupid fountain in the courtyard had been his idea. It was a cold but clear winter day, so no water fell from the fountain and no people gathered on the stone benches strategically placed around the courtyard. But Eric liked what he saw out his window today.

At thirty-five years old, Eric had everything he wanted: good friends, a thriving company, and all the creature comforts a man could desire. He already claimed as his own the house, the cars, even the boat, although he rarely had time to take it out on the water.

For the past twelve years, ever since he opened the first A Match Made in Heaven office, he'd been nonstop focused on his company and the goals he'd set for himself after graduating from college. He'd built the matchmaking agency from a room with a fax machine and an extra telephone line in his apartment to five independent sites across Virginia.

And Netanya had been by his side through most of it. She'd come on board in the second year and brought fresh ideas and a feminine perspective to the agency. Together they'd made a lot of money and put together a lot of happy couples. He and Netanya, as special guests, had attended more weddings than he could remember. And according to the letters and photographs from clients and former clients, there were several little children named either Eric or Netanya, in honor of the people who brought their parents together.

It was Valentine season, one of the busiest and most profitable times of the year for A Match Made in Heaven. Business was booming at all five locations, but particularly in the headquarters site here in Newport News and in Alexandria. Opening the Alexandria office in northern Virginia had been a stroke of genius, Eric thought. With all the metropolitan Washington, D.C., area to pull from, A Match Made in Heaven was so successful there that he and Netanya had been considering moving the headquarters to Alexandria.

But Newport News was home. And life was perfect.

Eric dropped his legs and stood up. Shrugging out of the pinstripe suit jacket, he loosened his tie.

"So why does it feel like something's missing?" he asked his empty office.

Since no answer was forthcoming, Eric glanced at his watch. Netanya was filling in today, doing interviews. Mrs. Randall was back, according to the staff. The spritely old lady had been a client practically since Eric had opened the doors. With Mrs. Randall's track record of either burying or divorcing husbands she found through A Match Made in Heaven, Eric wasn't sure if she should be counted as a success story or a dismal failure on the agency's part. He smiled. At least Mrs. Randall was happy, he surmised.

"Too bad you can't say the same thing for yourself."

Wondering where that thought had come from, Eric sat down again and turned his attention back to the computer monitor and the end-of-week reports filed from his office managers at the sites across the state.

~

Netanya finished up with Mrs. Randall and assured the woman that the agency had a large pool of men who would be interested in an older woman. After the experience with Wade, Mrs. Randall had decided she was interested only in men who were in their sixties. "Or younger," the charming widow had emphatically stated.

She saw Mrs. Randall to the studio where she would make a videotape and audiotape introduction to prospective dates. Then Netanya returned to the reception area.

These days, the only contact she and Eric had with clients was during exceptionally busy periods or when a long-time patron like Mrs. Randall came in to the office. Netanya greeted a few people who were filling out their questionnaires, then watched as the three attractive women, obviously a group of friends, followed one of the counselors into an interview room.

The women, particularly the one who had been chatting with Mrs. Randall, intrigued Netanya. Mentally she began to flip through the files of eligible men she knew who might be suitable for the woman. Her bright smile, pretty brown complexion, and rounded figure were physical pluses. A match was already coming to mind. But she'd have to know more about the woman than what she looked like.

"I'll be in with Shelia," Netanya told the receptionist. Then she made her way across the reception area and knocked on the door before slipping into the interview room.

When the door opened, Val paused after introducing herself to the counselor. In walked the pink and white cloud. The woman was petite and feminine with delicate features. The pastel pink blouse with ruffles at the bodice and sleeves and the form-fitting skirt gave the woman an angelic look. She was the kind of woman men like Conroy T. Franklin tripped over themselves to get to.

"Oh, hi!" the counselor said. Then, turning to the group of three, "I'd like to introduce you to Netanya Gardner. She's co-owner of A Match Made in Heaven and is one of the best in the business."

"Hello," Netanya said, coming forward to greet each woman. "I'm so very glad you chose A Match Made in Heaven."

"I'm Shelley Ward and this is Kalinda Michaels," Shelley said.

"Hi, I'm Val Sanders," Val said, stepping forward and shaking Netanya's hand.

"Hello there. You were chatting with Mrs. Randall in the lobby. It's a pleasure to meet you. Is Val short for something?"

Val couldn't hide the slight grimace. But before she could speak up, Shelley cut in.

"Her name is Valentine. And coming here to find a love match is our birthday present to Val. She'll be thirty on Valentine's Day. Frankly, we are all fed up to here," she said, indicating her forehead, "with shallow, egotistical mama's boys. We three are looking for real men, men who know how to treat a lady." The swing of her head sent Shelley's long braids flying.

"Please, call me Val," Val told Netanya.

"Well, happy birthday a few days in advance. I hope we can make this a very special Valentine's Day for you. Why don't you all have a seat and Shelia will tell you a little about A Match Made in Heaven," Netanya said.

The dynamics of this group was interesting, Netanya thought as she studied the three while Shelia gave the introduction to the dating service. If first impressions were important, and Netanya knew they were, Shelley was the dynamo, in-your-face one, and Val, who obviously had a hangup either about her name or about turning thirty, was the conservative one. Netanya hadn't missed the small shudder and the grimace Val tried to conceal at Shelley's introduction of her. Kalinda, who had yet to say anything, was possibly the shy one in the group. But Netanya wanted to know more about Val.

Val listened to Shelia explain about databases and compatibility, about expanding one's horizons and meeting the challenges and expectations of the dating scene. She shook her head. Once Shelley got on a roll, there was no stopping her. This Netanya woman, the pink-and-white cloud, probably thought she was some desperate type, eager to get a man. That wasn't the case at all. Val had plenty of dates. The problem was in the quality of the men.

"We at A Match Made in Heaven cannot guarantee that you'll meet the partner of your dreams," the counselor said, "but we do guarantee that you will be introduced to a significant number of people who meet the qualifications you have, and, more important, people who will expand your social contacts. If, in the process, you meet your match made in heaven, we all win. You will have entered a terrific relationship and maybe, just maybe," she said, smiling, "we'll get to add you and your match to our display of Heavenly Couple Nuptials."

Kalinda laughed at the name. "What does that mean?"

The counselor indicated the back wall in the small room. "Heavenly Couple Nuptials are the weddings of our clients. Many people meet their lifemates through our introductions."

Val glanced at the photographs of smiling couples, then crossed her legs and sat back in her chair. "And how many of your couples actually stay together after these hasty introductions and nuptials?"

Netanya fielded the question. "Well, Val, like any marriage, whether the partners meet through a dating service, a personal ad, through friends, or by accident, each person has to work on the relationship. Relationships don't just happen. Some of our clients are repeat clients. Not everyone who comes through our doors is looking for a life partner. Some people just want to meet new people, to expand their social network."

"You haven't answered my question," Val pointed out. "What's the divorce rate among your clients?"

"I don't have exact figures, but I don't believe the rate is any greater than those who meet without the assistance of a service like this one."

Val didn't look convinced. "All day long I listen to couples who were once so in love, scream at each other, and divvy up their personal property as if each china plate and copper pot were the crown jewels."

"You're a divorce attorney?" Netanya asked.

"No," Shelley piped up. "She's a court reporter who has had the unfortunate assignment of being sent to divorce court. She listens to all this poison every day and then transfers all that negativity to her own relationships. Everybody is not like the couples you meet in court, Val."

"Thank you for that analysis, Dr. Ward," Val said. "If I recall correctly, you have a Ph.D. in political science, not in psychoanalysis."

Shelley and Kalinda laughed at Val's tone.

"Don't mind Val," Kalinda said. "She had a bad date last night, plus she gets weird like this around her birthday every year. We're used to it."

"I do not get weird. And some friends you two are."

Netanya decided it was time to separate the women. Sometimes a group of friends meeting together worked. Other times it didn't serve any of the prospective clients very well. This looked like it was shaping up to be one of those times. "What we'll do now is tell each of you how the process works and then you can take a tour of the facility. Shelia, if you would get Marie to work with Kalinda. Val, you can stay here with me. Shelley can go with you, Shelia."

When the room was cleared, Netanya began again with Val.

"Tell me why you're here."

"I'm here under duress, Ms. Gardner. Look, I'll be totally honest with you. This was not my idea. This is Shell and Kalinda's birthday present to me. We went to lunch this afternoon and they sprang this matchmaking thing on me. I'm here to humor them. I'm not looking for a partner, a relationship, or a match made in heaven. As a matter of fact, I decided just last night that being single has its merits."

Val got up and walked to the wall of wedding and couple photographs. "I don't believe in love at first sight. And I definitely don't believe that all these people met here and then lived happily ever after."

Netanya watched the woman named Val. She was tall, full-figured, articulate, and pretty. She was a young black professional woman—a highly sought after commodity with a great deal of the agency's male clients. Without consulting a single computer file, Netanya knew there was a long list of men who would jump at the chance to go out with Val. But Netanya had one man in mind.

"As I said before, not every person is looking for happily-ever-after. Some people just want happily-ever-now."

Val smiled, then walked back to her seat. "Now you're talking my language. Romance is a farce, but having fun, now, that's something that I like."

"What do you like to do?"

Val settled in her chair and crossed her legs. "Do you mean like on a date?"

"Not necessarily. Just in general," Netanya clarified.

"I love to garden. I've converted a section in my condo to something of an indoor garden and hothouse. I like to do volunteer work. I tutor children on Wednesdays and Saturdays in connection with a youth program and recreation center here in Newport News, and I love the water."

Netanya grinned. "So do I. I like to just soak up the sun. Are you a sunbathing-on-the-beach type, or are you into water sports?"

"Both. I can't wait for it to warm up enough to get back on the beaches."

"Val, let me tell you how we operate here at A Match Made in Heaven. If you decide that it's something you'd rather not participate in, I'll be happy to redeem your gift certificate."

Val nodded.

"We provide a number of introduction services. You can write what we call a quick sketch letter of introduction that along with your photograph is published in our monthly newsletter. That newsletter is distributed to clients at our five offices across the state."

"Where are your other offices?"

"Richmond, Roanoke, Virginia Beach, and Alexandria," Netanya answered. "Another way we have people from across the state communicate is on-line. If you have a computer with a modem at home, you choose who you'd like to contact or you can come here to the agency and log on. We also have videotape and audiotape introductions. Why don't I show you our studios now? And I'll get a copy of the newsletter for you."

Later that evening, as she dressed for an event she was attending, Val thought about Netanya Gardner and A Match Made in Heaven. Val, Shelley, and Kalinda had all ended up doing videotape introductions. Kalinda had also opted for the newsletter photograph. An on-site makeup artist had calmed Shelley's fears about shiny skin on the videotape.

Val shook her head. "You know this is crazy," she told her reflection. Then, deciding as long as Conroy Franklin wasn't in the agency's database of bachelors, maybe it might be fun. Netanya Gardner was right. There was no law that said you had to marry the people you were introduced to. Just have some fun. Looking at it that way didn't seem quite so unpalatable. And the Gardner woman got credit: She never made a single comment or joke about Val and Valentine's Day.

Val applied a touch of mascara to her eyelashes, then got her coat and headed to the community center for the reception.

The first person her gaze landed on as she did a quick scan of the room was Netanya Gardner. The matchmaker had traded her pink-and-white ruffles for a matching pale pink blazer and tank dress. In the dead of winter, the pink should have looked ridiculous. Not on Netanya. She carried it off very well. And the tall, brown-skinned man standing next to her seemed quite appreciative as he gazed down at the petite woman.

Two things immediately struck Val about the man: his thick eyebrows and his hands. She wondered what it would feel like to smooth those eyebrows. And those hands. One was wrapped around the drink glass he casually held. He had strong, big hands, the kind that molded and shaped a woman's body as they stroked and stoked physical fires. With a skill born from years of the subtle once-over, Val took in the rest of him. He had a lean but athletic build. About six feet tall, she guessed, maybe six one.

The banded collar of the white linen shirt he wore buttoned to his neck precluded the necessity of a tie. Val liked the casual, elegant look. As a matter of fact, she had to admit, she liked the whole package. A lot. This brother was together.

Her gaze was drawn again to those hands. She wished she could see his fingers. Over time, Val had come to the belief that the width, length, and form of a man's fingers was in direct proportion to . . .

"Val! How nice to see you here," Netanya said. The cheery woman touched the man's sleeve, and the two advanced the few steps needed to reach Val.

As she watched them approach, Val's gaze slowly traveled up the man's tall form until she met his own laughing eyes. He knew she'd been checking him out! Val flushed, then blushed.

Then she extended a hand to Netanya. "Hi, there. Long time no see," she kidded.

Instead of shaking her hand, Netanya pulled Val to her for a quick hug, as if the women were friends who hadn't seen each other in a while.

Netanya then turned to the man. "Val, I'd like you to meet Eric Fitzgerald. Eric and I are partners at A Match Made in Heaven. Eric, this is Val Sanders. She lives in the city."

Val extended one trembling hand to Eric. What was it about this man that made her so restless? For goodness' sake, she thought, he's not the most handsome man you've ever met. He was okay: nice build, nice hands. Then he smiled at her and Val was lost. That dazzling, perfect, fun-filled smile made her knees weak and her heart race.

"Hello," she got out, pleased that her vocal cords still worked. "How do you do?"

"How do *you* do?" he said, taking her hand.

But it wasn't a greeting, it was a caress. He held her hand far too long, then let his fingers trail over her palm as he released her.

Off in a distance somewhere, Val was aware that Netanya was talking, but she was one hundred percent focused on this man, this Eric Fitzgerald, who with a smile and a handshake had her wondering things that she shouldn't be wondering about a stranger. Like how those fingers would feel in her hair, on her breasts. And what *he* would feel like all over her.

Eric was enchanted. He was also quickly becoming aroused. It had been a while since a woman had given him such a deliciously thorough once-over. If the pretty color in her cheeks was any indication, she was embarrassed at having been caught at it. Eric smiled. The one thing he liked above all else was a substantial woman. This one had curves in all the right places. And she was incredibly beautiful.

Her skin was clear, the color of sweet toffee. Her curly hair was pinned up in the back. Eric wondered how long it fell when it was down. Would her hair be as soft as her skin looked?

The button-pearl earrings at her ears matched the buttons on the suit she wore. Eric let his gaze, as bold as hers had been, wander down the rest of her. The skirt stopped a couple of inches above her knees. Eric took a deep breath. He was a leg man, and this woman got a perfect score in that department. They went on forever. He wondered if she preferred stockings over pantyhose. He definitely had a preference. He smiled at the thought.

"Any friend of Netanya's is a friend of mine," he said.

Val swallowed. "Do you two volunteer here at the center?"

"I do," Netanya answered. "I've been working with the children for about three months now." With a playful elbow in his side, she nudged Eric. "I've been trying to get Eric here to volunteer some of his time. The young ones need positive male role models, particularly the boys."

"Are you a volunteer?" he asked Val.

"Yes," she said, wondering where the slightly breathless tone had come from. Get yourself together, Valentine, she scolded herself. "I work with the kids on Wednesday afternoons and Saturday mornings. I've been coming here for a couple of years."

"Netanya, you've finally convinced me," Eric said. But with eyes only for Val, he added, "I think I'll sign up for Wednesday afternoons and Saturday mornings."

They chatted for a few minutes until Val was called away by an acquaintance.

Since she didn't believe in love at first sight, Val could only conclude that her reaction to Eric Fitzgerald was a major case of lust at first sight. And lust, she knew, was easy enough to deal with: If you ignored it, it eventually went away. The only thing was, Val had a sinking feeling that this wasn't going to go away. Not when from across the room she could feel him watching her. And she responded, at least physically.

Now Val looked up, and sure enough Eric was staring at her. He smiled when their gazes locked, and Val put a hand out to the nearest support.

That support happened to be the back of the center director. The man turned around.

"Oh, Val. Let me introduce you to a couple of our other volunteers. Because you all come in at different times and on different days, you volunteers never get to meet each other."

Val let herself be pulled into the conversation. But her thoughts were across the room with Eric Fitzgerald. She'd only just met him, but she felt connected to him in a way that surprised, and, to some degree, annoyed her. She felt almost as if she'd known him, now and through time. The feeling was disconcerting at best, and at worst . . . Val positioned herself so she could see Eric Fitzgerald. Worst just didn't exist. The man was gorgeous.

Three

Eric watched Val Sanders watch him. She'd been peeping at him most of the last hour. She was good at it too, discreet. Had it been any other woman, Eric might not have noticed how thoroughly he was being scoped. But he'd been so busy eyeing her—he hadn't been as subtle—he had clued in to her quiet study of him. The reception was winding down and Eric knew he was running out of time.

Eric had always, *always* listened to the still, quiet voice inside himself. That voice, or intuition, as some people called it, had never failed him. But now there was no still and quiet knowing. The voice was shouting at him: She's the one! Val is the one!

He watched her turn to answer someone in the small group she was chatting with, and Eric went in search of Netanya.

"Excuse me, I'd like to steal a few moments with this pretty lady," he told the people Netanya talked with.

"Mr. Fitzgerald," a man lightheartedly complained, "you get to have her all the time. You're quite possessive, you know."

Eric laughed and Netanya took his arm. "I promise to return her to your company in just a few minutes."

He then proceeded to practically drag Netanya to a corner.

From across the room Val spotted the gorgeous Eric Fitzgerald whisk his dainty partner to a secluded spot. The two, huddled together, looked as if they couldn't wait to get in each other's arms. Val sighed. The good ones were always taken. But what she was seeing right now didn't reconcile with the messages she'd been getting from the man for the last hour. Maybe he just liked to prowl and Netanya Gardner looked the other way. Some couples had relationships like that.

She glanced at him one more time. Maybe he and his business partner were just that, business partners. Val had to admit that her reaction to Eric was purely physical. She didn't know anything about the man. She wondered how she could find out some basic information.

From where they stood, Eric scolded Netanya. "You've been holding out on me," he said.

Netanya bit into a small cracker topped with pâté. "Whatever do you mean, Eric?"

He grinned down at her. "You know exactly what I mean. Tell me all about her, Netanya. Is she single? Is she available?" Eric looked closely at his partner, then added, "She isn't—"

Netanya smiled and interrupted. "No, Eric, rest easy. I assume you're referring to Val."

"You have this matchmaker role down to a fine art. Who else would I be referring to? You blithely introduce me to exactly the type of woman you know I'm crazy about and then you both waltz off. I want to know why you've been hiding this particular girlfriend of yours."

"I haven't been hiding her."

"So, details, woman. I need details."

Netanya reached up and smoothed away a wrinkle in Eric's suit jacket. "She's single. Professional. Works partly out of her home. She's available, but I don't know if you're her type."

Eric frowned. "What do you mean, I'm not her type? I own my own business. I'm not wanted by the police or the DEA, and I'm not bad-looking."

Netanya laughed. "Actually, darling, you're great-looking. If I wasn't already committed, I'd give you a whirl."

Eric chuckled, then he leaned down and kissed Netanya on the cheek. "That's why I love you so much. You're so sassy. So, what you're telling me, in a very unhelpful way I might add, is that there's a green light here."

"Umm, you could put it that way."

"And you know what's best?" he added. "She's not one of those lonely hearts from the agency. As a friend of yours, I know she comes highly recommended. Thank God she isn't one of those desperate females who wants to find true love through one of our computer terminals."

Netanya sighed. "Eric, those so-called desperate females made you very rich."

"And I'm grateful to each and every one of them. I don't knock it. If it works for them, fine. It's just not my thing. Can you get home okay by yourself?"

"Eric, I got here by myself," Netanya pointed out. She looked around him. "If you're going to make a move, lover man, it better be soon. She's getting her coat."

Eric glanced over his shoulder. Val was standing in a short line at a makeshift coat check. "Uh, later, Netanya," he said absently as he headed in Val's direction.

For the most part contented and pleased with her work for the night, Netanya watched Eric head across the room. All she could hope right now is that it would work out. Between Eric's hangup and Val's reluctance to even talk with the A Match Made in Heaven counselors, sparks were bound to fly between the two.

But Netanya well knew Eric's physical preferences in women. He liked them well rounded with bright smiles and long, shapely legs. Val, in his book, probably scored an eleven on a scale of one to ten. But Netanya also knew he had a near phobia about desperate females who elected to find their love matches through agencies like the one they owned.

Netanya sighed. But then she smiled. It was Cupid's season. If Val and Eric were indeed a match made in heaven, Cupid's arrow would handle any little difficulties.

"The woman's name is Valentine, for goodness' sake. That has to count for something," Netanya mumbled as she rejoined the group she had been talking with.

Eric caught up with Val as the attendant handed her her coat. He took it from her arms and helped her into it.

Turning to thank the kind gentleman for his assistance, Val gasped when she saw Eric Fitzgerald. Her knees grew weak and her heart started to pound.

"Thank you," she murmured.

"You're welcome." Eric held her elbow as he handed his ticket to the attendant to retrieve his own overcoat. Then, draping it over his arm, he steered Val a few feet away.

"Pardon me if this seems a bit abrupt," he began. "Val, I know we only just met an hour or so ago, but I'd like to get to know you better. Would you go out to dinner with me? Tonight?"

He was so close that Val couldn't think straight, let alone breathe, so close that if she just turned her head a tad, their lips would meet. The musky citrus of his cologne wrapped around her senses. How could a man she'd just met make her feel so warm, so tingly, so ready . . . so fast?

"Mr. Fitzgerald, I don't think . . ."

Eric smiled and Val was lost. "Say yes, Val. I'm very hungry."

"Yes," she breathed.

In the next instant, his mouth covered hers.

She'd read about it. She'd heard about it. She'd even believed she'd experienced it a time or two. But in Eric Fitzgerald's arms, Val discovered the true meaning of the word passion. If she hadn't known for a fact that it was February, she would have bet good money that it was the Fourth of July, because fireworks and sparklers were going off all around her.

He deepened the kiss from one of exploratory inquisitiveness to an embrace that staked a claim. Eric pulled her closer and wrapped an arm under her coat. Val stepped into his arms and let the fullness of her body merge with the solid wall that was his. He lapped the sweet nectar from her mouth, and Val moaned her pleasure. Or had that come from him?

For an eternity they stood together. Eric traced the fine contour of her face with one large, well-defined hand. Val's gaze never left his as his arms slowly descended to brace hers. His head lowered again for another taste.

Then, appalled at her recklessness and remembering where she was, Val took a step back. This man was a stranger, someone she'd met a mere hour earlier. But Eric held her in a loose embrace.

"You're mine," he whispered.

Val's eyes widened. "Excuse me? What did you say?"

"All my life I've searched for you. All my life I've waited for you to arrive. Now that you have, I'll never let you go."

"Excuse me?"

Val shook free of his hands and wrapped her coat about her. "Look, I, Mr. Fitzgerald . . ."

"Call me Eric."

The sexy baritone of his voice washed over Val. There were several things she didn't believe in—love at first sight, wearing white shoes before Easter, and being hypnotized by someone's voice. Hypnotized or mesmerized, Val didn't know which it was, but one thing remained true: The instantaneous attraction she felt toward this man was like nothing she'd ever experienced.

Waves of longing washed over her. If the earth moved when he'd simply kissed her, what would it feel like if and when those hands, those gorgeous hands, touched her all over?

"There's a late-night café right across the street. Let's get a cup of coffee and a bite to eat," he suggested.

At the dubious and then cautious look in her eyes, he quickly added, "I'm not a criminal. I'm not a pervert. I have good credit. Netanya can vouch for my good character and name. I can't say that I've ever hauled a woman into my arms and kissed her practically moments after being introduced, but I'm told there's a first time for everything. I promise if you walk across the street with me, we'll start at the beginning. And I'll try not to kiss you again until I see you safely to your car."

Val smiled. Could he be feeling the same desperate sense of rightness that she felt? "That is the most compelling pickup speech I've heard in years," she told him. "Let's go get a cup of coffee before I change my mind and decide this is really not a good idea."

Val had been reckless before, but nothing like this. Throwing caution to the wind for now, she let Eric Fitzgerald lead her out the door and across the street.

At the waffle house they took a seat at the only available table, one with a wobbly leg and syrup stains on the green and white speckled top. A tired-looking waitress, her hair secured in a net and pulled back in a severe bun, wiped a damp towel over the Formica tabletop, then plopped two sets of paper-napkin-wrapped utensils on the table.

"Evenin' folks. My name's Jo. Can I get you some coffee?"

"I don't suppose you have espresso?" Val asked.

The waitress popped the gum tucked in her mouth and cocked a penciled-in eyebrow at Val. "The yuppie coffeehouse is three blocks over. But they're probably closing up about now. We got coffee, plain, Maxwell House."

"Well, I guess I'll take coffee. Plain. Maxwell House."

Eric managed to suppress a smile. "Make that two," he told the waitress. "And a couple of menus, please."

The waitress walked away, rolling her eyes.

"That wasn't very nice," he said.

"I know. She just looks so worn out. Make sure you leave her a big tip."

"Who said I was paying?"

"You started this little chase. I'm just along to see how you play it out." She glanced around them at the many customers in the brightly lit restaurant. "And I'm wondering what kind of impression you're trying to make on me."

Val wasn't about to tell him that she was more than a little curious about a man who was secure enough with himself that he'd make their first "date" at an all-night restaurant. Then she smiled. He was obviously a man who took advantage of opportunity. This place was right across the street from the center. He'd probably figured she wouldn't object to something so nearby.

Eric leaned back in his chair and regarded Val. The speculation in his eyes was unmistakable. "You intrigue me."

"You don't know me."

"I plan to," he countered.

It was Val's turn to lean back. She crossed her arms and stared him down.

"If you knew what that look did to me, you wouldn't do it," he said.

"Maybe I do know and I just want to see how you respond."

Eric let out a hoot of laughter. Then, smiling, he leaned both elbows on the table. "Where has Netanya been hiding you? It wasn't very nice of her to not introduce us earlier."

"It was early enough. Are you really going to volunteer time at the center, or was that just part of the pickup line?"

"What would you say if my answer was both?" he asked.

"I'd say *you* intrigue me."

Val's smile was coy as the waitress placed two cups minus saucers on the table and poured steaming java just below the brims. She left two menus on the edge of the table. Eric and Val both ignored them.

"Would you go out with me?"

"I am out with you," Val said. She briefly wondered why she was being so combative. But the moment just seemed to call for this easy, flirtatious banter. And when she admitted it to herself, the conversation was kind of fun. The sexual tension crackled between them.

Eric nodded his head, conceding the technical point. "I mean a date," he clarified.

"I know. And the answer is yes."

"Why?"

Val opened a small cream container and slowly poured the liquid in her coffee. She flipped open the napkin holding the flatware, pulled out the spoon, and stirred the coffee before looking Eric dead in the eye. "Because you have nice . . . hands."

They made a date for Sunday brunch the next day.

~

For the umpteenth time, Val wondered if she'd lost her mind. She was attracted to Eric Fitzgerald. That fact didn't concern her so much as the fact that when she was around him she responded in ways she'd never responded to a man before.

She knew his name, she knew he co-owned the matchmaking service. Beyond that she couldn't think of a single thing, other, of course, than his physical attributes, that made her feel so connected to him. Right now, though, she was starting to feel irritated. He was almost twenty minutes late.

As she waited for him to pick her up at her condo for brunch, she tried to decide if it was all a game to him. At the A Match Made in Heaven office, Netanya Gardner had said it would take about a week to process her application and begin the matching process. Yet, it hadn't taken a week, just a moment, for Netanya to introduce her to Eric.

Val's doorbell rang. She took one last glance in the full-length mirror in the hall. Satisfied that her makeup was flawless and that the russet-colored sweater set she wore complemented her figure, she went to and opened her front door.

The smile of greeting died on her lips.

It was Eric all right. And he was covered in . . . what was that smell? Motor oil? Gasoline?

She folded her arms and leaned back against the door. "You're late."

"I can explain," he said. "May I come in?"

Val didn't move. She eyed the pullover sweater and the vest he wore. Both pieces of clothing were speckled with spots. His shoes and the bottom of his trousers looked like he'd been stomping through a swamp. "I don't mean to be rude, but what is that stuff all over you?"

"It's a combination of oil, transmission fluid, and mud."

"My carpeting is white, Eric."

She watched him step out of his shoes and roll up the cuffs on his slacks. "I promise not to track on your carpet. I'd just like to wash my face and hands and then explain to you why I'm late and why I'm here looking like a mechanic who has had a bad day."

Val stepped aside and watched as Eric came in. She directed him to the bathroom and then went in search of a towel.

When she returned a moment later with a big fluffy towel, washcloth, and hand towel, she could hear water running. It sounded like the shower. Was the man taking a shower in her house? Of all the nerve!

Val knocked on the bathroom door. "Eric? I'm leaving a towel for you on the floor outside the door. I'll be in the living room."

A muffled "Uh-huh" and something that may have been "thanks" drifted out to her. With hands on hips, Val stared at the bathroom door for a moment, then went to the living room. She turned the television on but kept the sound muted so she could keep an ear out for Eric.

He'd left his shoes outside her front door. She went to retrieve them. But one look at the muddy demi-boots changed her mind. She got a brown paper bag from the kitchen and took some newspapers from the recycling stack. After spreading the bag on the kitchen floor, she got the boots. Careful to keep the newspaper under them, she took the short boots and put them on top of the bag.

"What were you doing? Hiking in the woods on your way over here?"

Suddenly curious about what he had been driving, Val went back to the door and looked out over the balcony to the parking lot below her condo unit. The only vehicle she didn't immediately recognize was the small Alfa Romeo parked next to her Corsica. That one must be Eric's.

Val shivered in the cold and quickly stepped back into her condo. She put the kettle on the stove for tea, then stood for a moment, listening to sounds from the bathroom.

"This better be good," she said.

A few minutes later Eric emerged.

Val looked up from where she sat on the sofa and caught her breath. He'd stripped down to a white undershirt that hugged his chest. Well-defined pecs rippled as he walked toward her. Val's gaze slowly wandered over him. He'd obviously tried to clean the cuffs of his trousers, because they were now wet almost to his knees. There was something deliciously wicked about his bare feet nestled in her white carpet.

Val lifted her gaze back to his.

"That should be a class-four felony," he said.

"What?"

"The way you do that with your eyes."

Val ignored the comment. "What happened to you?"

"Do you mean what's happening to me now or what happened to me on the way over here?"

Val flushed but didn't dare look anywhere but up, at his face. "Why don't you have a seat."

Eric sat at the opposite end of the sofa, and she noticed for the first time that he still held the small towel. She watched him rub it over his head.

"You washed your hair?" She couldn't control the incredulousness in her voice.

Eric nodded. "Val, I apologize. This is really not how I typically start a date. I was headed over here, when I saw a car pulled over at the side of Interstate 64. There were two little old ladies peering under the hood of their vehicle. I stopped to help them. I should have kept driving."

Val smiled. "What happened?"

"They were arguing over what was wrong with the car. It was a huge old tank of a thing, the kind of beast Detroit made in the heyday of automaking. One insisted it needed oil, the other said transmission fluid. When Miss Ethel tried to pour oil into a funnel, Miss Clara grabbed it, yelling that that hole was the carburetor, not the oil place. The next thing I know, they were tussling over the funnel and Mr. Eric wound up with oil all over him."

Val bit her lip to stifle a laugh. The kettle whistled. Val got up and went to the kitchen. She measured tea leaves into a strainer, then poured water into a small ceramic teakettle. "And the transmission fluid?"

Eric sighed. "Dripping from the container Miss Clara forgot she left on the bumper."

"So what was wrong with their car?"

Eric snorted, then got up and took a seat on a high stool at the breakfast bar. He watched Val open a small packet of cookies and place them on a tray that held the teakettle and cups.

"They were out of gas."

Val laughed out loud. She handed Eric a cookie. "Poor baby. That's what happens when you try to be a Good Samaritan."

"I called an auto service from my car phone and waited for a tow truck to bring them some gas."

Val looked over at his boots on the floor. "Is that mud?"

Eric sighed and shook his head. "Miss Ethel's hat wound up over the embankment. Gentleman that I am, I went to retrieve it. The hat, mind you, doesn't have a speck on it."

Val chuckled as she poured tea. "God'll bless you for being kind."

"I am sorry, Val. I would have called, but I didn't have your number." He glanced at his watch. "By the time I get home and get some clean clothes, we'll have missed brunch. Would you like to try for dinner?"

Val looked at Eric. He really seemed sincere, but this whole deal was just a tad weird. "I don't know. Maybe we should just—"

"Please don't say no," he quietly said. "I meant what I said last night about finally finding you. This feels right to me even though we don't know each other."

"Just dinner?"

"A whole date. We'll do it A Match Made in Heaven style."

"What does that mean?"

"Do you like adventure? Are you daring and willing to sort of let the chips fall where they may?"

Val eyed him. "That depends," she said cautiously.

"Nothing harmful. Just fun. We'll spin the wheel."

"We're going to play Wheel of Fortune on a date?"

Eric laughed, then bit into the cookie she'd given him. "Not quite. But something along the same lines. Tell you what. Why don't you come back to my place with me and we'll do it there."

"Excuse me?"

"That didn't come out quite right," Eric quickly amended. "Why don't you follow me to my house. I'll get changed and then I'll show you how we let clients spin the wheel when they can't decide what to do on a date."

"I don't think so, Eric."

"Why not?"

"It sounds hokey."

"We can always stay here and talk," he suggested.

"I'm hungry."

"Then let's go."

Val nodded to his head. "You can't go out with wet hair. You'll catch pneumonia. Let me get a hair dryer for you."

"It's not one of those bonnet ones, is it?"

Val laughed as she walked by him. "Now, that would be a sight to see. Come on back to the bathroom."

Eric grabbed another cookie and then followed Val.

She pointed him into the bathroom he'd used earlier and then ducked into her own bedroom. She emerged a minute later with a blow dryer.

Handing it to him, she said, "I don't believe I'm really about to say this, but take your pants off." When he looked at her with more than a cooperative and speculative smile, Val quickly added, "I'll toss them in the dryer for a few minutes and at least get the dampness out of the legs."

Val watched him grin. When he reached for his belt buckle, Val turned her back to him.

"Chicken," he taunted.

"Sometimes, if the shoe fits, you have to wear it," she responded.

Eric chuckled. Val closed her eyes and imagined what was being revealed when she heard the zipper on his slacks lower. The sound was very loud in the quiet apartment. A moment later she heard him step out of the slacks.

"You can turn around now," he said.

"I don't think so," she said. Val held a hand out over her shoulder to accept his pants. When she felt the garment in her hands, she sucked in her breath. "I'll, uh, put these in the dryer. It's behind the folding doors in the kitchen. I'll be, uh, in my office."

"Okay. And, Val . . . ?"

She jumped when his hands lightly clasped her shoulders. She hadn't heard him step forward. He leaned over her shoulder and placed a chaste kiss on her cheek. "Thank you for understanding."

Val stood rooted to the spot. She heard the bathroom door close and the hair dryer start and still she stood there. Then she turned and stared at the closed portal. "What have I gotten myself into?" she whispered.

She looked at the pants in her hands and her thoughts drifted to the physique the piece of clothing had just recently shielded. Val shook her head. "Lord, what a man."

An hour later Val was still asking herself what she'd gotten into by joining forces with Eric Fitzgerald. She sat at a table off Eric's kitchen and watched him pull several contraptions out of a sleek leather portfolio.

"Ready to spin the wheels?" he asked.

"This still sounds dumb to me."

"Where's your sense of adventure?"

Four

Eric watched her squirm. She opened her mouth to answer and then, obviously, edited what she was about to say.

"Tell me," he said softly.

Brown eyes framed by long lashes looked up at him. Eric closed the portfolio and left the materials on the table. He went to Val. Crouching on his knees so he could look her in the eyes, he took her hands. Slowly, he traced his large hands along the outside of her smooth, soft ones. His gaze, intense and masculine, never left hers as he lifted her hands and placed a kiss first on the backs and then in each of her palms. He felt the fine trembling in her and was encouraged.

Even as he leaned forward, she moved to meet him. He kissed her with a hunger that belied his outward coolness. When he felt Val open her mouth to him, Eric deepened the kiss. His hands left hers and cupped her neck, toying with the fine tendrils of her hair that had escaped her upswept style.

His whole body was filled with waiting. He'd been waiting for this woman, for this moment, all his life.

When Eric moved his mouth over hers, devouring her softness, Val moaned and wrapped her arms around his shoulders. She felt lighter than air, more joyous than she ever thought possible. She returned his kisses with restless abandon as shock waves rocked through her.

Somewhere in the recesses of her mind, Val knew that she'd never been kissed before, she'd never been held before. Not like this. Never like this. She'd never been loved the way Eric Fitzgerald was loving her with just his mouth. And his hands.

Eric shifted position and rose. Val went with him. They clung to each other. Dizzy with sudden longing, Val traced the contours of his chest. She felt his lips brush her brow and she pressed herself closer to him.

"I want you, Val."

His husky murmur was almost her undoing. But things were happening too fast. She felt too out of control. Val shook her head and stumbled back a step, out of his arms, out of harm's way.

Val, breathing just as heavily as Eric, tried to think. She tried to piece together what was happening to her. She stared at Eric, who was trying to catch his breath. Val knew within her heart that she was born to be with this man, this Eric Fitzgerald, whom she'd only just met.

But how could that be? she wondered. How could she feel so strongly, so sure about this?

Val trembled with the passion that flowed within her. It would be so easy to tumble in his arms and find the rapture that his mouth and his hands promised.

"Don't be afraid, Val," he whispered. "I won't hurt you."

"I know," she said. And she knew that to be true. Eric would never hurt her. That knowledge came from a place deep within her, a place she was afraid had more surprises waiting for her.

"Eric, we're . . . this is going too fast for me."

Gathering her in his arms, Eric hugged her close and tight. Then he kissed her on the tip of her nose and guided her to the chair she'd vacated.

Eric left her there and reached for the first wheels. He placed two of them in front of Val, then pulled a chair around so he sat close, so close that their knees touched.

"May I have some water, please," Val asked.

Eric simply smiled, then got up to get her a glass of spring water.

When he left, Val sank back in her chair and tried to sort through her feelings. This was lust, a maximum-strength dose of it, but lust nonetheless. She wanted Eric, wanted him like she'd never wanted any other man. She'd always wondered if she could be the type of woman who thought nothing of a one-night stand. Now she knew. With Eric she'd be willing, more than willing. That thought, coupled with his bold declaration, frightened her.

At the refrigerator, Eric held a glass to the ice maker and thought about Val Sanders. He knew without a trace of doubt that Val was his own match made in heaven. Eric accepted and readily admitted that he was a romantic at heart. In spite of, or maybe it was because of, the bottom-line realities of operating the type of business he ran, he was successful at what he did because he believed in the power of love, of fidelity, and of romance. He ran a business and his business was putting people together.

What worked for his clients was their belief and faith in his computers and videos and newsletters to find for them the perfect love match. For himself, Eric believed that soulmates found themselves by themselves. Sometimes it happened through a chance encounter, other times it happened by sheer coincidence. In his own case, he'd met his soulmate through his dear friend and partner, Netanya.

Eric grinned as he poured bottled water over the crushed ice. First thing in the morning he'd give Netanya a big, fat kiss on the lips for introducing him to her girlfriend.

"Eric, category two has 7-Eleven. We're supposed to eat food from a convenience store on a date?"

He laughed as he rejoined her at the table. "That's the whole point of this. It's something we use at the agency for first-timers who can't decide what to do on their date. Sometimes regulars will spin the wheels just to add a little variety to their dating life."

Eric reached for the other wheels. Each one was the size and shape of a pie plate. The outlined wedges contained the names of places or things. A spinner with a point on it was secured to the middle of each wheel.

"The rule," he said, "is that both parties have to agree to do whatever the wheel says."

Val eyed him dubiously and peered again at the red circle in her hand.

"That's category two. What to eat," Eric explained.

"Uh-huh. And it says pizza, Italian, Chinese, fast-food drive through, French restaurant, 7-Eleven," she added, glancing up at him for a moment, "hot dog vendor, TV dinners, grocery store samples. Grocery store samples! That's really trifling, you know."

Eric laughed. "It can be fun. You know you can make a meal out of those samples."

Val looked at him with a don't-even-think-about-it stare before consulting the wheel again. "She cooks," she continued, "he cooks, all-you-can-eat buffet, vending machines. You've *got* to be kidding?"

Val reached for the green wheel. Then, incredulous, "Wal-Mart is on here as an activity. Who goes on a date to Wal-Mart?"

Chuckling, Eric handed her the yellow wheel. "You'd be surprised. You're not game?"

"What if the clothes don't match the activity? What if, for example," she said, reaching for the green wheel and picking one of the items, "the activity is white-water rafting and the food is French restaurant? That doesn't match."

"So what? The idea is to have fun."

"People actually agree to this?"

"All the time."

Val picked up and read the entries on the blue category four wheel identified as the transportation. "We don't have carriages here or a subway system."

"Those modes of transportation are available in some of the cities where I have offices. You keep spinning until you land on an applicable one."

"You know what's missing from the activity wheel?"

"What?" he asked smiling, indulgent.

"Board games. Like Monopoly or Clue."

"I haven't played Monopoly in years," he said.

"Bet I could beat you," she taunted.

"Oh, yeah?"

"Well, Miss Real Estate Mogul. We'll just see about that."

Eric got up. A few minutes later he returned with a dusty, faded box. He grabbed a paper towel from a rack in the kitchen and wiped the dust from the box.

Val pushed the matchmaking date wheels out of the way.

"A buck says I beat you," he challenged.

Val shook her head. "Unh-unh. Let's make the stakes real ones. I win, I get to decide all of where we go on a date. You win, and we'll spin your little wheels and I'll eat dinner from a vending machine."

Eric grinned. "You're on. I'll be the banker."

As Val set up the board and he counted out the paper money, Eric smiled to himself. This was a win-win proposition. Even if he lost, he got to be with Val. Eric liked sure bets.

Eric was sitting in jail and Val had just bought a utility, when a loud rumbling and grumbling issued forth from Val's stomach. Her eyes widened. Clasping one hand over her mouth and the other over her stomach, Val closed her eyes. Her stomach growled again. This time louder.

"I bring you over here and then I proceed to starve you to death," Eric said.

"Oh, my God," Val moaned in mortification. "I could die of embarrassment."

"No need to be embarrassed. That's just your body's way of telling me I've been a very rude host." Eric reached for a cordless phone and dialed information for the number of a pizza shop.

"What do you like on your pizza?"

Val shook her head and refused to look at him. Eric chuckled and tugged at one of her hands until he could entwine his fingers with hers. "You should have told me you were hungry."

"I did. Back at my place."

Eric lifted one bushy eyebrow. "Ah, you did, didn't you? Oh, hi. One large with everything?" The question he directed to Val.

"No onions. No anchovies."

"One large, extra cheese with everything except onions and anchovies," he ordered. He gave his last name, address, and telephone number, then got up and went to the pantry. He came out and tossed a bag of popcorn in the microwave. A few minutes later he placed a bowl of the hot popcorn in the middle of the game board.

"I could die of mortification," Val said.

Eric plucked a couple of pieces from the bowl and, leaning forward, he held the popcorn to her. Val opened her mouth to capture the kernels. Eric either held his fingers there a moment too long, or, Val had to concede, maybe she took advantage of the opportunity in the moment. The playful gesture turned into something more serious. Val extended a hand to steady his wrist and capture his fingers. Eric traced the contours of her lips.

Staring into his eyes, Val knew she was lost. Forever.

"Val, you're playing with fire," he said.

The gentle warning was enough. If Eric felt half of what she did, he was right on the edge. Val wasn't willing just yet to push him or herself over into that next dimension. She let his fingers go.

Grabbing a handful of popcorn, she leaned back in her chair. She tossed a piece of the popcorn into her mouth. "It's your turn," she said. "Tell me how you got started in the matchmaking business."

Val watched Eric take a deep breath. His eyes lingered at her mouth. Val licked suddenly dry lips and looked on as Eric swallowed. He cleared his throat and shifted in his chair. Before answering, he grabbed a handful of popcorn and picked up the dice to roll his turn.

He tossed two fours and finally got out of jail.

"The idea for the company was born while I was in college," he began. "I needed some extra money, mostly just to have spending change and beer on the weekends. I saw an ad for an escort service in the student newspaper and answered it."

Val's mouth dropped open. "You were an escort?"

"Don't look so shocked," Eric said with a chuckle. "It was all quite legit, aboveboard—for the most part."

Val rolled her turn, landed on Free Parking, and pocketed the handful of cash. She grinned and winked at Eric as she counted out the money and added it to her substantial pile of paper currency.

"Are you the great-great-granddaughter of a robber baron?" Eric asked.

"I warned you. I'm good at this game. Roll your turn and tell me more about this escort business. What exactly did you do?"

"Well, I escorted women to and from social functions. Sometimes a little acting was involved."

"Meaning?"

"Sometimes I'd play the role of a husband or fiancé, sometimes a lady wanted me to pretend to be her boyfriend. I even got to play the role of sheikh once, that was for a masquerade ball. The fact that I'm fluent in a couple of languages increased my marketability. I made pretty good money for the two years I did it."

"Didn't you feel cheap or used?"

Eric shook his head. "There was nothing involved that made me feel that way. Now, granted, a couple of the older ladies were willing to pay extra for additional services rendered, so to speak."

Val glanced away and then looked at him. "And did you make a lot of *extra* money?"

"That wasn't my thing. I wasn't doing the job to get involved with anyone or to do anything that went against my principles. As it turned out, my initial reason for answering the ad proved to be less of a reason for continuing. I started because I wanted pocket money to hang out with the guys, take a girl out on a nice date. But most of the escort work ended up being on the weekends and I wound up not having time to do a lot of hanging out. I learned a lot about social situations and diplomacy while working as an escort."

Val reached for popcorn at the same time Eric did. Their hands collided in the bowl. Delicately choosing a popped kernel, Val held it out to Eric.

With a steady gaze that brooked no refusal and a gentle hand that held her true, Eric closed his lips around the popcorn and the tips of her fingers. White heat engulfed her. Val tried to ignore the flames of sensation that just his touch elicited. He licked the tip of one finger, then released her hand.

"Was the fine art of eating popcorn one of the things you learned?"

Eric smiled, male and predatory. "No. I'm learning those lessons right now."

The game forgotten for the moment, Val sat back. "What are you doing to me, Eric Fitzgerald?"

He leaned back, sizing her up. Val got the distinct impression that he imagined how she'd fit and feel in his bed. That's certainly the path her own errant thoughts kept wandering down.

"What do you think I'm doing?" he countered.

"If I had an answer, I wouldn't have asked."

"Then what are you thinking?"

"I was wondering if you were sizing me up and measuring me for the fit in your bed."

The candid response surprised Val. She hadn't planned on saying that. Not at all. But something about Eric made her feel that he would understand and not try to take advantage.

"Do you want my honest response to that most provocative image you just provided?"

Val folded her arms and bit her lip. "I don't know," she said honestly.

"I want you. I knew that the moment I set eyes on you in that community center last night. We're both adults and can do whatever we mutually choose to do. My desire is to get to know you. You're making it hard on me, pun intended, to keep my intentions noble."

"I'm not a tease."

"Netanya wouldn't have introduced me to you if you were."

"You two are very close." Val posed the question as a statement.

"We're like white on rice," he said. "Netanya is my girl. I don't know where I'd be today without her." Eric picked up the dice. "Whose turn was it?"

"I don't know. You go ahead."

Eric tossed the small squares and moved his piece forward on the board. "I got the idea to start a matchmaking company when I realized just how many people were out there looking for love, lots of times, as the song goes, in all the wrong places."

Val leaned her elbows on the table.

"I talked with some of my so-called dates from the escort business and re-ally got to know them. Some hired an escort just so they wouldn't have to go to a party or a wedding alone. Others just wanted a tall, good-looking—" His eyebrows flickered in a silent encouraging question.

Val giggled. "Fishing?"

Eric wisely held his tongue.

She nodded. "Yeah, good-looking," she conceded.

Amused and satisfied, he smiled and continued. "A tall, good-looking man draped on their arm. I had regulars and got to know them pretty well."

"When did you launch A Match Made in Heaven?"

"About a year after I graduated. I was working as a manager in a retail store, when I decided I wanted to be my own boss. I had a business degree and sat down to think of ways to actually apply it. The escort service sched-uler called out of the blue and asked if I wanted to reactivate myself on an on-call basis. I said no. That's when I started thinking about what some of those women had been telling me: that they just wanted a safe, reliable way to meet honest, decent men to go out with and have a good time. With no strings attached was frequently a caveat. The rest, as they say, is history."

Eric's doorbell rang. "That's the food," he said, rising from his chair.

A few minutes later he set the box on the table. A quick trip to the cabinets yielded plates, napkins, and soda. As they made headway into the pizza, Eric dabbed the corner of his mouth.

"So, tell me about you. I noticed the office you have at your place. It looks like a mail-order operation."

Val laughed. "Is that your way of saying I have a messy office?"

"No, no," he insisted. "Lots of boxes and whatnot, as if you do a lot of mailing."

"Actually, I do. I'm a court reporter."

"You work for a newspaper?"

Val shook her head. "The other court reporters. The ones you see typing into the little machines."

Eric nodded. "How'd you get started with that?"

Val laughed as she swiped a piece of pepperoni off a slice of pizza. "Bucking the trend and blazing new trails. I wanted to do something different from everybody else. My college degree was in literature and liberal arts with a focus on poetry, which left me eminently qualified to do nothing. I come from pretty traditional stock. My dad is a mail carrier and my mom is a teacher. That's about as hard-core middle America as you can get. Middle America didn't bother me so much as the lemmings-to-the-sea approach to a career."

She reached for a slice of pizza and bit into it. After a moment she continued. "Didn't want to be a teacher. Didn't like to write, so I nixed the journalism thing. Thought about being a librarian for about three months. That just wasn't me. So I took one of those job aptitude tests and ended up not liking the answers. I eventually heeded the call of the Peace Corps."

"Really? That's something I'd always thought about."

"I loved it. I built houses. One year I even taught school. Teaching in a third-world country is far different from teaching in American public schools."

"How'd you get from the Peace Corps to court reporting?" Eric got up and got more soft drinks and extra ice for their glasses.

She grinned. "Traffic violation. I got a ticket soon after I got back to the States. Driving on the wrong side of the road will do that."

His mouth twitched in amusement. "How much time did you do?"

"The judge was lenient. He made me pay a fine and ordered that I go to driving school. When I left the courtroom I wandered around the courthouse. People were jostling to get in one of the rooms. Television crews were setting up. I walked in and took a seat to see what all the excitement was about. Turns out it was a preliminary hearing for a big murder case. I was fascinated. Sat through the whole thing. From television shows, I knew what the woman up front was doing. I thought it might be neat to get to hear all of that testimony every day. Now, that, I figured, was a pretty cool job. I waited around and talked to her after it was over."

"And now you listen to the details of gory murders every day?"

Shaking her head, Val rolled her eyes. "I wish. My average day is very unpredictable. The big murder trials are few and far between in this area. For the last few weeks I've been wrapped up in some divorce cases. I tell you, people can get pretty ugly and very, very petty when they are screaming at each other across the table and divvying up their china."

Val shook her head again. "The worst ones are the couples who had the quickie weddings. Madly in love, they rush off to Vegas or Atlantic City and get married, and then six months or a year or two down the road I get to listen to them complain about who left dirty dishes in the sink or who didn't take out the garbage."

Eric listened to her and heard something that disturbed him. "You don't believe in romance?"

Five

Quietly and with an intensity Val didn't notice, Eric awaited her answer, her response important to him in ways he hadn't even contemplated until that moment. It had never occurred to him that he'd fall for a woman who didn't believe in romance the way he did. As for falling for Val, he accepted the fact that he was well on his way to being head over heels.

Eric had always believed that he'd recognize upon sight the woman meant to be his life partner. And he'd recognized Val as though they were soulmates through many lifetimes. The fact that he desired her only compounded the feeling of connectedness he had with her.

He watched her turn the question over. She opened her mouth to speak, then closed it. Big brown eyes looked at him over the table.

"That's a tough question," she finally said. "What do you mean by romance? What's your definition?"

Surprised at the question, it took Eric a few moments to get his thoughts together. He and Netanya had talked around this issue over the years, mostly in the context of the matchmaking agency. He'd never been forced to put into words his actual feelings.

"Let me start with what romance isn't," he said, closing the pizza box and pushing it out of the way. "Romance isn't sex and it isn't one-sided. I should clarify that. True romance isn't one-sided. Lots of times I've seen couples in relationships where she has to supply all the romance, or vice versa. Those relationships are seldom very healthy."

Val leaned her elbows on the table and propped her chin up in her hands. "What else isn't romance?"

"It's not something you can take for granted. Sometimes couples fall into the trap of believing that because they have simply endured—that they have lasted—that that's enough. They erroneously believe that endurance guarantees romance. Others think that because their relationship is new, romance is automatically a part of it. They confuse the physical urges with romanticism."

"So what is romance?" she asked.

Eric reached out a large hand and captured one of her smooth ones. "Romance is holding hands. Romance is sharing silence and not being uncomfortable with the space. Watching rain fall together. Playing Monopoly and eating pizza."

He watched her as he said the last and wasn't disappointed to see her small intake of breath. With his thumb, Eric began a slow, sensual caress of her hand.

"Expressions of romance take many forms. From the traditional flowers and candy that so many people will be receiving this Wednesday on Valentine's Day to the . . . what? Why such a face for Valentine's Day? Most people like Valentine's Day."

Val obviously hadn't done a very good job of concealing her negative reaction to her nemesis. "I'm not most people." She tried to pull away from his grasp, but Eric wouldn't let her hand go.

"Why don't you like Valentine's Day, Val?"

This time when she tugged, she defeated him. Val sat back and crossed both her arms and her legs.

"When Netanya introduced us, she very graciously overlooked my full first name. I'm Valentine Sanders. Val is my preference though."

Eric might have smiled at the revelation, except he sensed that to do so would be tantamount to stepping on a land mine. Val couldn't see that her name was perfect for her: light, sweet, and pretty. He instead asked what he hoped was a safe question.

"How did you come to be named Valentine?"

"You don't really want to know," she said with much maligned attitude.

Eric did smile that time. "Val, I *really* want to know."

She sighed. Then with a huff and an expression that clearly stated she'd rather be talking about something else, she looked at him. He seemed as if he really wanted to know.

"Those couples I was telling you about . . . the ones who do the quickie marriages because they are so in love. Well, my folks won the grand prize in the 'rushed and should have waited' category."

Eric moved the game board back into place and handed Val the dice. "What happened?"

She rolled the dice, moved her marker, and landed on a piece of property Eric owned that had been developed with a couple of houses. He grinned and held out his hand.

Val smiled in spite of herself. "I'm still going to beat you," she predicted.

"We'll see."

"My parents met on the escalator at a department store in Pittsburgh," she said, handing him the dice. "That store has long since been closed. But my mother was going up, my dad was going down. He says he took one look at her and knew she was the one."

Eric knew the feeling but kept his silence. He threw the gaming pieces but ignored them. He had eyes only for Val.

"My father tells the story of first trying to run up the down escalator to catch her, then elbowing his way to the bottom and dashing to the other side to go up and catch her."

"And what did he find at the top?" Eric asked.

Val grinned. "My mother, leaning over the side, looking at him and laughing. My father proposed the next week, on Valentine's Day. I was born a couple of years later. Unfortunately for me, it was on Valentine's Day."

Eric did smile then.

"If you laugh, I'll find something to throw at you."

"Valentine is a beautiful name for a beautiful woman."

Shy now for some reason, Val glanced up at him, then looked away. "Thank you," she murmured.

Eric got up. Before Val could determine his intention, he planted a quick, delicious kiss on her lips and sat down again.

"I just couldn't help myself," he said by way of explanation.

"Take your turn."

Val liked everything about Eric Fitzgerald, from the spontaneity exhibited in the kiss that she really and truly wanted more of, to the kindness he'd displayed to the two women who needed help with their car. She watched as he stretched an arm corded with strength across the board to move his game piece eleven spaces.

The word that came to mind to best describe him was grounded. Gorgeous ranked right up there too, Val thought, but grounded best fit the bill. He appeared comfortable but not pretentious with his success, settled in his approach toward life, and determined in his thrust-and-parry pursuit of her.

She ran hot and cold around him. Just when she got comfortable enough to let down her guard, Eric would turn up the heat a little more with a glance that lingered or a touch that spoke volumes, and Val would flush through and through.

"If you continue to stare at me like that," he said, "I can't promise that my intentions will remain honorable." The husky baritone of his voice promised unspeakable joy.

Val blushed from head to toe. He'd caught her again! Accepting the dice from him with no comment, she trembled when his fingers lingered as he passed her the small squares.

More than an hour later, Val sat back, astounded.

"I don't believe this. I *never* lose at Monopoly."

"Maybe you were distracted," he said with a sly smile.

"Umm-hmm. Or something like that."

Val glanced at her watch. "Oh, my God. You are not going to believe what time it is."

"It's after eight. I was sort of hoping you wouldn't notice, or that if you noticed, you wouldn't mind."

Big brown eyes stared into equally dark ones. "I didn't mind," she said quietly. "As a matter of fact, I enjoyed the time . . . and the company."

"Me too."

Val was the first to look away. "I—I have a ton of work to do. There's a transcript I want to work on tonight. I promised my client I'd deliver it by Wednesday. I want to be early. The client is new."

She helped him pack up the game board and pieces. As Val placed the top on the box, Eric reached for her hands. He pulled her to him, their bodies melding like two pieces of a puzzle.

Eric clasped his hands together at the small of her back. When he lowered his head, Val wrapped her arms around his neck and rolled her hips. Eric moaned.

The kiss held promise and commitment, tenderness and desire.

Eric came up for breath but didn't release her. He stayed her hips. "You owe me a date."

Val grinned. "So I do."

"Ready to spin the wheels?"

"You're serious, aren't you?"

"You established the stakes," he reminded her.

"So I did."

Val stepped out of his embrace and straightened her skirt and sweater. She hoped the sweater material was thick enough to conceal her body's desire for him. But Eric's gaze at her chest told her differently.

Eric swallowed, then reached for the A Match Made in Heaven date deciders. "This is going to be fun."

"Do I get to do the spinning?"

"Of course. I wouldn't want you somehow claiming that I'd rigged the outcome."

Val placed the yellow wheel on the flat surface of the tabletop. The little pointer would determine where she and Eric would meet on their date. "I rather like the idea of meeting at the library or a bookstore," she said, noting two of the choices on the circle.

Val held her middle finger with her thumb, then gave the spinner a flick. It rotated around the disk several times before eventually settling on POLICE STATION.

Val looked up at Eric, who tried to stifle a grin. "I don't believe this," she said.

The red wheel would determine what they'd eat. Without a word Eric placed it in her hands. Val cast her eyes up at him.

"If this lands on vending machine, all bets are off," she said. Val peered at the other selections. "I kind of like the 'he cooks' notion."

But that wasn't destined to be Val's fate. The spinner landed on FAST-FOOD DRIVE THROUGH. Val groaned and Eric laughed out loud as he handed her the green wheel that decided what activity they'd do on their date.

"There's still hope," Val said. She clenched her eyes shut as she flicked the little silver spinner.

Eric's bark of laughter let her know that they were in for something odd. Val was afraid to open her eyes.

"Just tell me," she said.

"This is going to be fun," he said. "I haven't done that in years."

Val peeped through one eyelid and read their fate. Then she couldn't help laughing out loud herself. The spinner squarely rested on ARCADE GAME ROOM. "I guess I'll get a roll of quarters from the bank tomorrow." She held out a hand. "Hand me the other two wheels. With my luck our transportation will be via skateboard."

Eric smiled. "No need. I'll drive and I pay," he said. "You just meet me at the cop shop."

"The good thing is the clothes will match. Casual sound good to you?"

Eric nodded as he stacked the wheels one on top of the other. "I'll meet you at the police station. It's on Washington Avenue. Say about six-thirty tomorrow night."

"It's a date. Where's an arcade?"

"How about the one at the mall?"

"I've passed by it. Can't say I've ever stopped in."

"This is going to be fun."

Val nodded. "I need to get home and get some work done. Will you see me to my car for now?"

"Of course."

Eric retrieved Val's coat and gloves, then walked her through the house and to his garage. He helped her into her car. Val started the engine and powered the windows down.

"Thanks for a fun afternoon," she said.

"I'll be counting the minutes until tomorrow night."

Eric leaned in the car window and kissed Val lightly on the lips. "Good night, sweet Valentine."

It wasn't until she pulled into her parking spot at her condo that something dawned on Val. The way Eric said Valentine made her name sound pretty, special. Pretty special. He'd called her sweet Valentine. Val smiled as she locked up her car and made her way to her unit. She'd have to see how Kalinda and Shelley fared in the matchmaking process.

"Okay. I admit," she said a few minutes later. Val and her girlfriends were on the telephone in a three-way conversation. "Maybe I was a bit hasty in my judgment about the dating service. Eric is nice, really, really nice."

"Eric? Who is Eric?" Shelley demanded.

"They set you up with a date in less than twenty-four hours," Kalinda said incredulously. "They told me it would take at least a week to get things rolling. What's wrong with me?"

"Who is Eric?"

"Kalinda, there's nothing wrong with you," Val said. "You need to stop putting yourself down. You're a beautiful black woman of power. There's a brother out there for you."

"I'm not restricting myself to just black men. And what power?" Kalinda asked. "I run a day care center."

"You're entrusted with the nurturing and development of children. They're our only hope for tomorrow."

Kalinda laughed. "Val, you always know how to put a spin on things."

"Excuse me, ladies," Shelley interjected. "I'm all for the empowerment thing. I just got my copy of the latest *Essence.* The only thing I want to know right now is: Who is Eric?"

"Yeah, Val. Who is this guy?"

Val slid her shoes off and kicked her feet up on the sofa. She settled back into the cushions and smiled. "Eric is tall and dark and handsome and funny and spontaneous," she said, and then, thinking about the two women he stopped to help, she added, "and he's generous and kind."

"Did you buy a puppy, Val?" Shelley asked. "Is that your birthday present to yourself?"

Kalinda laughed out loud. "I don't think a puppy would be giving her that dreamy-sounding voice."

"Did I mention sexy and funny? He has the most gorgeous hands. And a smile that makes me just say 'ummph, ummph, ummph.'."

"If memory serves me correctly, we were at that dating service office just yesterday," Shelley said. "And as Kalinda pointed out, they said it would take at least a week to get us all matched with potential dates. What's going on, Val?"

"Netanya Gardner introduced him to me last night. We're going out tomorrow." Val giggled, remembering how they'd set up the date. She'd lost at Monopoly. If she'd had her way, they would be going to dinner at her favorite restaurant in Williamsburg and then maybe catching a movie.

But, Val had to admit, fast food and an arcade had a certain amount of appeal, particularly if Eric shared in the adventure. The police station part was kind of weird, particularly since he knew where she lived and she knew where he lived. But meeting there would no doubt add to the fun. Val began a mental search through her closets for something to wear.

"I think she either hung up or fell asleep," Kalinda said dryly.

"Val! Wake up!" Shelley yelled.

Val frowned. "Good grief, Shell. I'm not asleep. I was just thinking about what to wear tomorrow."

"We still haven't heard how you met this man," Shelley said.

"I told you. Netanya Gardner, the woman in pink who that Shelia lady said owned the place, introduced us last night."

"You went back to the dating service office?" Kalinda asked.

"No. I saw her at the community center's reception for volunteers."

"I'm lost," Shelley announced.

"Me too," Kalinda said.

"Val, just start at the beginning. Start after we left A Match Made in Heaven."

Val scooted down into the sofa cushions some more, then crossed her legs at the ankles. "Okay. We left A Match Made in Heaven. Shell, you went to get your nails done. Kalinda, you went grocery shopping. I went home, then later that night went to a reception at the center where I volunteer. Netanya Gardner was there and she introduced me to Eric. He's tall, gorgeous, and her business partner."

Val decided to leave out the part about Eric kissing her at the coat check. That was just too, too close to share just then. She still had some sorting out to do in her head. The more she thought about it though, the more she realized she was going to come off sounding like a nut if she actually told her girlfriends that she and Eric had spent Saturday night at a waffle restaurant and Sunday afternoon at his house. After he'd taken a shower at hers!

"Uh," she said on the telephone.

"Well, what else?" Shelley asked.

"He asked me out," Val offered.

"Just like that he asked you out?" Kalinda questioned.

Val ran through the events in her head. He'd kissed her and she'd felt as if she'd been waiting for him all her life. They'd laughed and talked at the waffle place and then set a date for the next day. But it didn't quite turn out the way either of them would have expected. Instead of a pleasant brunch on a nice winter day, they'd ended up really getting to know each other over pizza and a board game. Eric's quiet intensity and smooth sensuality made her ache.

Desire flowed between them. There was no doubt about that. But Eric either sensed or knew that Val wasn't a one-night-stand type. With a tenderness and sensitivity that didn't threaten his masculinity, he'd let her know when she had pushed too far or when he was close to the edge. Instead of making him come across as weak, Val appreciated and respected his frankness. They had been candid with each other. No games, no child's play, just two adults connecting on a level that, quite honestly, Val wasn't used to. It made her feel vulnerable, but at the same time secure.

"Yeah," she finally answered Kalinda. "He asked me out just like that."

For a moment only silence came through the telephone lines. Val broke it.

"He's very special," she said quietly.

"Well, I hope that dating service introduces me to someone special," Kalinda said.

"I need to get some work done tonight or I'll be up all night tomorrow," Val told her girlfriends.

"Okay," Kalinda said. "Talk to you later."

"Take care," Shelley said.

Val disengaged the line and sat up. But before her feet hit the floor, the telephone rang. She smiled.

"Hello?"

"I heard a whole lot in that," Shelley said. "Mostly what you didn't say. What's the real deal, Val?"

Val smiled again. "I knew it was you."

"You don't just up and go out with someone like that, Val. I've known you too long."

"Shell, I don't know how to explain it. It's like I've always known him. Like I've always waited for him. He's special."

Shelley was silent for a moment. Then she added, "You be careful, you hear."

"I will."

"Do me a favor, will you. It'll make me rest easier. Call my office and leave a message on my voice mail letting me know where you're going to be. If this guy is some psycho, at least I'll be able to tell the police where you were supposed to be."

Val smiled. The safeguard was one she and Shelley had been using for years. "I'll do it, Shell. But he's not a psycho," she said, as she rang off with Shelley.

"I'm starting to think he's the one for me," she whispered, contemplating the thought even as she said it to the empty room.

Six

By the next morning Val had convinced herself that her reaction to Eric Fitzgerald had been born of pre-thirtieth-birthday stress, a disorder that to Val's way of thinking needed to be studied by professional counselors. With the big one just two days away, any new man in her life would take on the gallant qualities of Prince Charming riding a white stallion.

"Except you don't need to be rescued from anything," she said, shoving a pencil in her hair.

Val sat at her desk in her home office, transcribing material from the divorce commissioner's hearing. The couple, who in Val's estimation deserved each other, had been slinging mud faster than their attorneys could object. They had a lot of personal property to divide up. The only positive element Val had heard during the hours-long session was that the two didn't have any children. It was a blessing that kids didn't have to be privy to the poison.

The one good thing about her parents' divorce was that it had been amicable. As a matter of fact, Naomi and Quentin Sanders now saw more of each other than they saw of their daughter. As an only child already an adult when her parents split up, Val didn't have to go through a custody dispute.

She sat back in her chair and wondered if Eric Fitzgerald had ever been married. He struck her as the type of man who, once committed to a woman, would do everything in his power to ensure her and their happiness.

"Prince Charming is a fairy tale," she reminded herself. "Eric has some sort of fatal flaw. If you hold on long enough, you'll figure it out before you get in too deep."

That decided, Val turned her full attention to the day's work she had ahead of her. At twelve-thirty she stopped for lunch.

She'd just settled a bowl of tomato soup and a grilled cheese sandwich at the dinette table in the kitchen, when her doorbell rang. Not expecting any deliveries, she could only wonder who it might be as she made her way to the door and opened it.

"Delivery for Miss V. Sanders," said a voice behind a huge flower arrangement. There had to be two dozen pink roses in it.

"I'm V. Sanders," she said.

"If you could sign here, ma'am," the voice said. "I have a clipboard under my arm."

Val reached for the clipboard, scribbled her name on the sheet, and then accepted the flowers. "Let me get something for you," she told the delivery man.

"No need," the man said, already heading back down the walkway. "That's already been taken care of."

Val shrugged, called out "thank you," and then maneuvered the door shut with her foot.

Carrying the large arrangement to the breakfast bar, she settled the crystal vase on the countertop and plucked out the card.

She gazed at the flowers for a minute, then smiled and shook her head. "Daddy, you shouldn't have." Her father always sent flowers for her birthday, but he'd never been this extravagant.

Val pulled the card from the small white envelope. Her mouth dropped open.

Flowers are traditional and that's how I'd like to get to know you—the old-fashioned way. I'm looking forward to tonight.

Eric

The slow smile that creased Val's mouth couldn't be avoided. The man definitely knew how to push the right buttons. She leaned forward to inhale the light, fresh scent of the blooms. Val stepped away from the bar and looked around for the best place to showcase the arrangement. She moved an oversized volume of poetry from the coffee table, then transferred the flowers there.

Standing over the table, she gazed at the pretty pinks. For the first time in her life, Val discovered she liked something pink. Maybe Eric Fitzgerald was the antidote she needed to get over her aversion to Valentine's Day. The thought brought another unbidden smile as Val made her way back to her office.

The afternoon whizzed by despite the fact that Val got up every half hour to gaze at the roses. When she finally called it a day, she had to concede that she hadn't made a lot of progress since the arrival of the surprise Eric sent.

She showered and hot-curled her hair, then stood indecisively at her closet. They were going to eat food from a drive-through and play arcade games. The date didn't call for anything spectacular to wear, but Val wanted to look nice without being overdressed.

"Jeans really would be appropriate," she said, eyeing a neatly pressed pair. But she discarded that idea as too casual and reached for an ivory-colored tunic and slacks set. She added a pair of big, funky earrings and a matching necklace and liked the overall picture.

Pulling her hair back a bit, she clasped an ivory and black barrette at her nape. A touch of color at her cheeks and lips, and a spritz of a light, flirtatious cologne completed the ensemble.

Val glanced at the time. "You've never had a date that started at the police station."

But as Val put on her coat and headed out the door, she had to admit, she, too, was looking forward to the evening.

She didn't have any trouble finding the police department. The squad cars parked around the building provided a clue. A couple of them even had their lights flashing. Val parked her car in the back lot, but was hesitant to get out given all the commotion. A car that looked like Eric's finally convinced her to look for him.

She'd barely gotten three steps away from her vehicle, when two uniformed police officers approached her.

"Ma'am, are you Val Sanders?" one asked.

Val's eyes widened and she clutched her purse. Other than the driving infraction years before, she'd had not so much as even a parking ticket. To have police officers call her by name was more than disconcerting, it was downright scary.

"Yes. Why?"

"Would you come with us please, ma'am," the second officer asked.

Val took a step back. "Why? I haven't done anything wrong. I took the parking card and it's displayed in the front window," she said, indicating her windshield.

"Eric Fitzgerald is waiting for you inside the station," officer number one explained.

"Excuse me?"

"Eric Fitzgerald. You do know him, don't you? He asked that we be on the lookout for you."

All of a sudden Val was glad she'd left the message on Shelley's voice mail. *I knew he was too good to be true,* she thought to herself. Shelley wouldn't have to worry about calling the police, the men and women in blue had already captured Eric.

"Is he a criminal?" she asked the officers.

The two cops looked at each other. "Uh, not that we know of, ma'am. Is there something you'd like to tell us?"

For a moment Val looked confused. "Let's start at the beginning. My name's Val Sanders. What do you want from me?"

"Mr. Fitzgerald just captured a mugger. He's inside the station answering some questions," officer number two replied. "He was worried that you'd miss him and think he stood you up. He asked if we'd be on the lookout for you."

Val was more confused than ever. "Eric captured a mugger? Is he a cop?"

"Not unless he's a fed doing something undercover. Why don't you come this way," the officer said with more than an appreciative glance that lingered over Val. "I'm sure all your questions will be answered inside."

More than curious, Val walked with the two officers and went into the police station. It was the first time she'd been in a police station before. It didn't look anything like TV. It looked more like a regular office building.

After a short elevator ride, the officers led Val to a desk, where Eric sat holding a white cloth to his head and talking to a woman Val presumed to be another police officer.

Eric grinned and stood up when he spotted Val. The navy, tan, and olive striped vest he wore would have been a nice complement to the navy shirt and tan pants, except the vest had a big tear in it. Eric lowered his arm and Val gasped. His skin was scraped and bruised. The cloth had blood on it.

"What happened?"

"The good guys won," Eric replied.

An officer came forward and handed Eric some ointment and a gauze pad. "Couldn't find a Band-Aid, but this should do."

"Thanks," Eric said, accepting the items.

"Eric, what happened to you?"

The officer grinned and perched on the edge of the desk. "Mr. Fitzgerald here showed us up. Caught a mugger right around the police station."

"I had parked my car and was going to walk around the building just in case you parked on the other side. I heard a woman screaming, and then this guy came tearing past me."

"Mr. Fitzgerald pursued him. Wrestled the guy to the ground. But he managed to squiggle away. The idiot ran into the building across the street from here, hoping to get away."

Eric grinned and the cops started laughing.

Val looked from Eric to the officers. "What's so funny?"

"The building across the street is the city jail."

Val joined in the chuckles. Then she stepped forward and touched the area around the scrape on Eric's temple. "Should I take you to the hospital?"

Eric pulled her hand down and kissed her fingers. "No. I'm fine. I'll put some of this ointment on it. It's just a scrape."

"You're all done here, Mr. Fitzgerald," the desk officer told him. "You may be called as a witness when this goes to trial."

Eric nodded. He made a quick stop in the men's room, then joined Val at the elevator.

Val looked him over. He'd applied the ointment but forewent the bandage. "Looks like this used to be a nice vest," Val observed, eyeing the rip in the fabric.

"You know," he said as the elevator doors closed. "You're really rough on my clothes."

A few moments later the doors opened to Val's laughter. "You can't hold me responsible for the adventures you wander into."

"I seem to find these adventures only when I'm on my way to see you."

Val looked over her shoulder at him and smiled as Eric held the door for her. "Had we gone to a nice French-Oriental restaurant for this date, your clothes would be in one piece."

"True," Eric conceded. "But I wouldn't have had the opportunity to impress you with my heroic deed."

Val chuckled. "Touché. I am suitably impressed."

They walked the short distance to Eric's car. As he held the door open for her, Val asked, "Do we need to go to your place so you can get changed? And you know, you really should be wearing a coat. It's not summertime out here."

Eric closed her door and walked around to the driver's side. By the time he slipped into the seat next to her, he'd come out of the vest. "No need to change. The shirt is fine." He glanced at her, then with a devilish smile added, "You're not getting out of that fast food that easily."

Val snapped a finger. "Darn. I thought I had you."

Eric laughed. "And my coat is right here," he said, indicating some black leather. "It's not that cold."

Eric started the ignition. "Do you mind if we eat before we play. I'm starving."

"Fine with me," Val said. She patted the small handbag in her lap. "I'm armed with the antacids we'll need following this feast."

Chuckling, Eric paid the lot attendant and headed toward the interstate. Less than twenty minutes later he turned into a fast-food lot. Eric pulled into a parking space.

"No cheating, Eric. The wheel said drive-through."

Eric glanced at Val and grinned as he put the vehicle in reverse. "I thought you'd forgotten about that part."

"No such luck," she said in good humor. "I'm holding you to this spin-the-wheel thing."

A few minutes later they sat in the car, digging burgers and fries out of paper bags. Val took a sip of her vanilla shake while Eric tuned the radio to a cool jazz station.

Val fed him a French fry. "The roses were a wonderful surprise. Thank you."

"My pleasure, beautiful Valentine."

"Normally I bristle when people call me that."

"You bristle when men call you beautiful?"

A small smile tugged at the corner of her mouth. "I meant when people call me Valentine."

"Why?"

"Because of the whole Valentine's Day thing. Most of the time I just let people assume my name is Valerie. It saves on the explanations and the inevitable chuckles."

"I think it's very special that your birthday coincides with such a romantic holiday. You seem to me to be a very romantic woman."

Val shook her head. "Not a romantic bone in the body," she said. "You never did finish your definition of romance yesterday. Maybe you'll describe something that I might construe as romantic."

"You didn't think the flowers were romantic?" he quietly asked.

Val looked at him, then, inexplicably shy, she glanced away. "Well, actually yes. But, well . . ."

"You just want to give me a hard time?" he supplied.

Val's shoulders shook as she tried not to laugh. "Something like that."

"I'm glad you liked them."

They both seemed to run out of words. They ate in companionable silence for a few minutes while a sweet saxophone provided soothing background on the radio. Val reached a hand over to capture a bit of ketchup at the corner of Eric's mouth. She brought her finger back to her mouth and licked it.

Eric's hunger growing, he intently watched her. He placed his half-finished burger on the dash as he leaned toward Val. She met him halfway, staring at him with a longing that surprised him. His answering gaze was as soft as a caress and as hard as steel. A shiver ran through Val . . . and then the waiting was over.

Val gave herself up to Eric and into the kiss.

His lips, warm and sweet, danced a gentle melody along her senses. Val sighed into his embrace and felt Eric's large hand toy with the hair at her nape. She moaned his name and Eric deepened the kiss.

He was simply kissing her, yet Eric was content, at peace. Even as other parts of his body registered an urgency that demanded attention, Eric took his time, savoring, nibbling, loving Val in this simple way. Yes, he wanted her. He could admit that without shame. But more than sex, he wanted for-ever with Val.

She'd come into his life and in short order turned his world upside down. When he felt her hands in his hair, Eric slanted his mouth over hers, yet again deepening the kiss. His own mouth burned with a fire that he didn't want slaked.

An insistent and rude tone eventually brought them apart. "This has been a test of the emergency broadcast system," a radio announcer's voice said.

Val gave him a trembly smile, then touched a delicate finger to her lips. She halfway expected to feel a brand. "No one has ever kissed me like that," she said.

"Good."

"You make me want things."

"Val, you don't know the half of what you make me want."

Eric wanted forever. If he didn't think he'd scare her away, he'd propose right on the spot. For years he'd relied on the still, quiet voice in him for advice on everything from business moves to relationships. The voice was ringing in triumph now and had been practically from the moment he set eyes on her. He wanted her as his woman, as his life partner. But Val, by her own admission, had hangups about the type of relationship they were falling into headfirst. Eric figured he needed a plan to change her mind. The problem was, he didn't have a plan. He just had a throbbing and insistent need that was making it difficult for him to concentrate.

Val glanced out the window and tried to catch her breath. Things were moving so fast, yet it seemed as if her life, and particularly the last five minutes, had been in slow motion.

Eric started the engine and then ran a hand over his face. "What are we going to do, Val?"

She turned toward him and gave a small shrug. "I don't know," she said honestly.

Val finished off her milk shake and Eric ate the few remaining cold fries. Eric found a parking spot at the arcade, then went around and opened Val's door for her.

"You forgot your coat," she said.

Eric shook his head. "I need to cool down."

Val glanced away, but Eric captured her chin in his hand and turned her face toward him. He lowered his head and pressed his lips to hers.

"Don't be afraid of my desire, Val. We're not going to do anything until we're both ready."

Val nodded. But as they walked hand in hand into the arcade, Val wondered what more they could possibly need to be ready.

They entered the dark cave of the arcade and were immediately assailed by the striking, pinging, and ringing of the games. Val looked up at Eric and grinned. "I used to be a whiz at Pac-Man."

Eric nodded. "Let's just see how you fare in Mortal Kombat."

They spent the next two hours feeding quarters and tokens into machines. Then the trouble started.

It began with a few loud voices in the back of the arcade. The squabble became louder as more people went to check out the disturbance. The verbal altercation erupted into a physical one when someone threw a punch.

Eric assessed the situation and was leading Val to the door, when security guards arrived with a police officer. Eric and Val were detained at the door by a burly guard whose countenance didn't bode well for anyone who crossed him.

"Sir, we were just leaving," Eric said.

"Not so fast, buddy. Nobody leaves out of here until we get to the bottom of this."

"But we aren't involved," Eric said.

The guard smirked and pointedly stared at the bruise at Eric's temple. "That's what they all say, pal. Step aside and don't move too fast."

Eric flared up, but Val put a restraining hand at his chest. "He's just doing his job, Eric."

Val directed them to a place near the door but far removed from the hot spot in the arcade.

A few minutes later two guards escorted three youths from the arcade.

"Hey, what about this one?" the security guard called out while pointing to Eric.

"Now, wait just one minute here. I'm a law-abiding citizen."

"Eric, shhhh. You're going to make matters worse. Don't antagonize the man," Val said.

"I'm not antagonizing him. He's accusing me of being in a brawl."

"What's the problem over here, folks?" the police officer said, approaching Val and Eric with the security guard in tow.

The big guard nodded toward them. "They were trying to slip out when we got here."

"We weren't slipping anywhere," Eric protested. "We were leaving."

"Mr. Fitzgerald?" the officer asked.

Eric took a closer look at the cop in the dark arcade. "Oh, hi," Eric said when he recognized one of the police officers from the earlier fracas at the police station. "This seems to be our night for landing where the trouble is."

"We were playing right over there," Val said, pointing to a game a few feet away, "when the commotion broke out back there. What happened?"

The cop shook his head, then smiled at Val. "Couple of kids arguing over the high score. We'll take 'em downtown. Pardon me if this seems rude, but are you two out on a date or something?"

The cop's puzzled look made Val smile.

Eric, who hadn't missed the man's perusal of Val, frowned.

"Umm-hmm," Val answered. "Thought we'd try something different."

Eric wrapped an arm about Val's waist. "Are we free to go?" he asked the officer.

The cop took in Eric's possessive stance, then nodded and extended a hand to Eric. "Maybe we'll see you again before your date ends."

Eric shook hands with the man and steered Val toward the arcade's exit.

"That's my kind of woman," the cop observed to the security guard. "Too bad she's hanging out with such a cheapskate. What kind of man takes a woman to an arcade for a date?"

Val, who overheard the comment, looked back at the cop, smiled, and waved.

They walked around the mall's food court for a few minutes.

"You do know how to provide an action-packed evening," Val observed as the last security guards left the arcade.

They stopped at a frozen yogurt stand.

Eric cut a glance at her. "I don't want you to dump me because you think I'm dull."

"Not a chance of that happening," she said, smiling.

They ordered frozen yogurt in waffle cones and sat down to eat the treat. Later, when they finished, they walked hand in hand back to Eric's car.

"Where to now?" she asked.

"How about we pick up your car and then head to my place."

"To do what?" But Val took one look at Eric and knew what he had in mind.

"Show you my etchings?" he asked with a waggle of his eyebrows.

Delighted, Val laughed out loud. "Oh, you'll have to come up with something better than that."

Seven

But a moment later Val noticed how late it had gotten. By the time they picked up her car from the police station and Eric followed her home, it was after eleven.

They watched the end of the television news, then laughed through the monologue of a late-night talk show host.

"Can I get you a glass of wine?" Val asked during a commercial break.

Eric shook his head no. "I don't drink."

Curious, Val turned to look at him. "Why?"

After the question was out, she realized how rude it could be construed to be. Maybe he was an alcoholic. With that thought, Val realized she still searched for his fatal flaw. No man could be as perfect as Eric made himself seem.

Eric slipped an arm around her shoulders. Without thinking, Val nudged her shoes off and stretched out on the comfortable sofa, her head in Eric's lap.

Eric's arm surrounded her waist. He looked down at her and smiled. "Alcohol is an acquired taste. In college I did the beer thing because that's what college students do. As for the other stuff"—Eric shrugged—"I can take it or leave it. I never really got into it."

"What about your escort dates? Weren't you in social situations where you had to drink?"

"You're never in a situation where you have to do something that goes against your will. In each and every moment people have choices and make choices."

A slight grin from him had Val smiling. "What?"

"I think being a nondrinker boosted my marketability. The company and my 'dates' knew they didn't have to worry about me getting drunk and embarrassing them or wrapping their expensive cars around trees."

"So are you telling me you're a man without vices?"

Eric shook his head. "No," he said. "I have one vice that consumes me."

Val raised her eyebrows.

"You're it. My one and only vice," he said.

He felt more than saw Val smile. Eric liked the way they fit each other. They looked and felt like an old married couple, comfortable in their late-night snuggling while watching television.

Eric lowered his head to hers and kissed her. She tasted sweet and faintly of the yogurt they'd had at the mall. More than anything, he wanted to stay right where he was for the rest of his life. He marveled at the sense of grounding and rightness he felt with Val. They were meant to be together.

When the talk show came back on, Val turned to her side. Resting an elbow over his knee, she watched the program and settled into the soothing and warm feelings emanating from Eric's hands at her stomach and in her hair. With his palm flattened against her middle and his thumb doing an absentminded caress, Val's insides turned to mush.

Val purred and turned to face him. The movement caused his hand to brush over her breast. Val arched into the accidental caress.

"Eric?"

Eric took the tremor in her voice to be apprehension. He closed his eyes and held his breath for a moment to get himself under control. Val turned him on like no other woman. Yet she remained fearful.

Eric opened his eyes and gazed into the big brown ones that were so serenely compelling. Maybe he'd been mistaken. Had he misread passion and longing for fear? Without a word he ran a hand from her waist to her breast, lingering at the fullness of her bosom. When Val didn't object, he settled his hand over her and gently squeezed.

The plaintive moan could have come from either of them. Eric wasn't sure where it originated, but it echoed the need in him. Beneath his palm he felt her respond to his touch. Eric lost himself in the feel of her.

Val gloried in the gentle touch. Eric's slow hand didn't rush her. If anything, he moved too maddeningly slow. This man, in just a few short days, had found the key and unlocked her heart. She wanted to give herself to him, not as a capitulation to desire, but in celebration of the oneness she felt with him and for him.

She reached an unsteady left hand up and brought his head to her mouth. Her right hand covered his, and when he would have removed his hand from her breast, she stayed him, adding pressure that built not just there but through her body. She ached for the fulfillment she knew she'd find when they came together.

But now, right now, she wanted more of his hot mouth, more of the caresses that made her breasts expand and fill his hand. As they greedily kissed each other, she guided his hand from her bosom to her stomach. They lingered there for a moment, and then she guided their merged hands lower, and lower still.

The telephone rang.

Eric and Val jumped apart, Val sitting up with a quickness that made her head spin.

"What?" Eric asked.

Disoriented, it took them both a minute to realize what the interruption had been. Val's voice on her business answering machine echoed from the other room. "You have reached Sanders and Associates Court Reporting. Our office is closed now. Please leave a short message, your telephone number, and the best time for us to return your call."

Val sat on the edge of the sofa and smoothed her hair into place.

Eric took a couple of deep breaths and tried to dissipate the sensual fog he seemed to be surrounded in.

When the caller didn't leave a message, Val shook her head. "Probably a wrong number, someone trying to reach the pizza shop before it closes. My business number is 9851. A pizzeria that makes late deliveries is 8951."

"Val?"

She turned to him and was arrested by the quiet intensity and unmistakable masculine appreciation in his eyes.

"I think I'm going to leave. If I don't, I'll end up asking if I can stay."

Eric stood, not waiting to hear her answer to his unspoken question. He shrugged into his leather coat. Val met him at the door.

"May I see you tomorrow? And the next day, and the next, and the following day?"

Val's answering smile gave him hope. "And what about the day after that? Or will you have had an overdose of Val?"

He shook his head and gathered her in his arms. "Not likely. You give me the nourishment I crave."

"Hmmm," she purred. "I've never been an addiction before."

"I told you, you're my only vice."

Eric bent his head and captured her mouth for a leisurely kiss.

The kiss eventually turned into a fierce hug, the two clinging to each other, drawing warmth and comfort from the other's arms.

"May I see you tomorrow and on Val's day, your birthday?"

Val's smile was tender. "That, I believe, is the first time anyone has ever referred to it as my day as opposed to Valentine's Day the holiday."

Eric held her close and waited for her answer.

"Yes," she told him. "I'd like to spend tomorrow and then my birthday with you."

Eric nodded. "I'm glad. How about we catch a movie tomorrow night. There's a romantic comedy out that's gotten rave reviews."

"I like shoot-'em-up, action-adventure films."

Eric raised an eyebrow at that revelation. "Maybe we'll compromise and see two."

She smiled. "Are you going to guarantee the type of action adventure we had tonight? Chasing down bad guys, almost getting arrested?"

Eric gave her rear a playful swat. "My mother always told me to beware of sassy women."

Val gave him a liberal dose of sass as she swiveled her full hips in a lazy motion against his. Eric's eyes narrowed and darkened. He pulled her closer to him. Val felt the proof of his desire.

His voice was husky when he spoke again. "I'll pick you up here about six-thirty tomorrow."

She nodded and then stepped back a half-pace. But Eric clasped her to him for a hug. They stood together for several minutes just absorbing the tenderness of the moment. Then Eric pressed a gentle kiss to her cheek and let himself out the door.

Val closed the portal behind him, then leaned against it. Her smile was dreamy and her thoughts were with Eric. Eventually she turned off the television. Staring at the pink roses on the coffee table, she pulled one from the arrangement. She carried it with her to bed and dreamt sweet dreams of Eric Fitzgerald.

$\sim$

The next morning Val got a call from a counselor at A Match Made in Heaven. Her video had a glitch in it and they wanted her to come and have it reshot.

She thought it odd that they still wanted to have a video on record after introducing her to a perfect match, but Val shrugged the question off and made an appointment to go to the service's office that afternoon.

She finished the transcript she'd been working on and hand-delivered it to her client.

Eric spent the morning ignoring his own work and making plans for an extra-special and ultra-romantic birthday for Val. The fact that her birthday fell on Valentine's Day made it somewhat easier. But the challenge he gave himself was to ensure that the holiday remained underplayed and Val's birthday got the greater attention.

By noon everything was in place. Eric smiled, pleased with his work. The only thing that remained was to buy Val a gift. A two-carat diamond engagement ring proved to be the only thing he could think of. Eric stretched and smiled, then folded his arms behind his head. Last night it would have taken nothing to convince Val to let him stay. They would have made hot, sweet love. But he didn't want it that way. He wanted Val for not one evening, but every night and every day for the rest of their lives. He'd named his business appropriately, because Val was indeed a match for him who could only have been made and sent from heaven.

Val was everything he'd ever dreamed of finding in a woman. The other women he'd dated were nice, pretty, some even beautiful, but they never stirred his heart the way Val did. They never quite connected with that still voice inside him that he relied on. A small, wry smile curved his mouth. In truth, he hadn't spent a lot of time dating. For years now, he'd been completely focused on making his company a success. The hard work had paid off.

When he really thought about it though, Eric had to concede, he couldn't even recall the last time he'd had a real date. He went out a lot and did a considerable amount of socializing, but inevitably, just about every occasion was in some way connected with A Match Made in Heaven.

Val Sanders was his own match. He knew it just like he knew that the sun would rise and set the next day, just like he always knew that when he found the right woman—his life partner—he'd recognize her instantly.

Dropping his arms, Eric stood and then glanced at his watch. He knew he'd be just in time to catch the lunch hour and last-minute Valentine's Day shoppers, but he headed out in search of a birthday gift for Val. His first stop was indeed at a jeweler's.

Val had a one-thirty appointment in the studio at A Match Made in Heaven. But the more she thought about it, the more she realized it still wasn't something she wanted to do. Humoring Shelley and Kalinda had been one thing, actually committing to this ludicrous matching system was another— even if she'd met Eric as a result of it. There was no need to remake a video. Eric had obviously already seen the first one.

The way she figured it, whatever the problem happened to be with her videotape introduction was in actuality a message from on high telling her to cease and desist with the matchmaking thing. One, she'd already met Eric. And two, if Eric turned out *not* to be her so-called match made in heaven, she wasn't so desperate that she needed someone to find dates for her.

The agency office was just around the corner from the post office. Her mind made up, Val ran a few errands and picked up mail at her post office box. When she finally walked into the matchmaking office, it was to cancel her short affiliation with the service.

She was surprised to see the reception area just about empty. Compared to the bustling activity on Saturday, the place looked deserted. A man in a sport jacket and slacks filled out a questionnaire on a clipboard and a woman watched the same short introductory tape Val and her friends had viewed three days earlier. Val approached the receptionist's desk. She shook her head and tried to ignore the huge banner draped across the front.

Val placed her slim leather appointment book on the desktop. "I have a one-thirty appointment but I want to cancel it."

The receptionist consulted a roster of information and then pressed a discreet button on her console. "Miss Sanders?"

"Yes."

"Why don't you have a seat. Someone will be with you in just a moment."

"You don't understand. I don't need any assistance. I was here Saturday, but this just isn't my cup of tea. I don't want to participate."

Netanya Gardner came out and greeted Val. "Hi there, Val."

"Oh, hello, Ms. Gardner."

The receptionist looked at her roster. "Miss Sanders has a one-thirty appointment but she'd like to cancel her membership," she informed her boss.

Val noted with an inward roll of her eyes that Netanya Gardner was again decked out in pink. This time the woman's softly flowing cream-colored palazzo pants set and duster was accentuated with a pale pink blouse. The ruffled lapels of the duster had alternating layers of pink and cream. It was all disgusting, but it was gorgeous. Netanya pulled it off with a genteel charm. By comparison, Val, who was dressed in blue pinstripe corporate wear with pumps and pearls, felt positively unfeminine.

Netanya nodded to the receptionist, who turned back to her paperwork. She then led Val to a love seat in the reception area. The two women sat down.

"I had a good time at the center reception Saturday night," Netanya said.

"I did too. The kids are having a Valentine's Day party tomorrow afternoon, so that should be fun. Wednesday is one of my days to volunteer at the center."

Netanya nodded. "That's right. I remember you saying that. But what's this about ceasing your membership with A Match Made in Heaven? You've only just started."

Val smiled. "Thank you for introducing me to Eric. He's very nice." Val waved her hand to encompass the office. "This isn't for me though. I told you Saturday that my girlfriends signed me up for kicks. I, however, am just not interested."

"May I ask why?"

Netanya watched Val settle back in the sofa to contemplate the question. Out of the corner of her eye she saw Eric approaching the front door.

"Val, why don't we continue this in my office."

Val looked surprised but nodded her acquiescence and rose. Netanya tried not to panic. It wouldn't do for Eric to see Val talking to her like this. If she got Val to her private office, it would look as if a friend had stopped by to chat.

Netanya glanced back at the door as she steered Val down the hall. Eric had been detained, thank goodness, by someone on his way out of the building.

Netanya hustled Val into her office and then closed her door. Just as she expected, a few minutes later a triple knock sounded and Eric strolled in without waiting for her to respond.

Netanya looked up, feigning surprise. "Eric, look who's here? Val stopped by for a few minutes."

Eric grinned at Netanya, then smiled down at Val. "Hi, there."

"Hi, yourself," she said.

Netanya took in the private glances between the two and raised an eyebrow. It appeared that Eric had used the time since Saturday night getting to know Val. Netanya and Eric had not had their usual Monday morning confab because Netanya had been at the Richmond site. So she had not yet heard his impressions about Val. But judging from the way they gazed at each other, things went well.

"Why don't I go check on those numbers," Netanya said.

"Don't leave on my account. I need to be getting back to work anyway," Val said. "I just stopped by. I feel bad about canceling out on you, Netanya, but this—"

Netanya cut Val off with a wave of her hand. "I told you, don't worry about it." Netanya glanced at Eric. "I'm sure you have other plans."

Val rose. Netanya watched as Eric wrapped an arm about her waist.

"I'll walk you to your car," he offered.

Netanya waved as the couple left her office. "Whew. That was close," she said, sinking into her chair.

Eric, inordinately pleased at seeing Val, was glad he'd caught her. Tickled with the purchases he'd made, he couldn't wait to present the gifts to Val. But he had to wait, both to see the light in her eyes tomorrow and to see her later tonight, when they went to the movies. It also pleased him that Val broke an appointment with Netanya, probably some girls'-night-out plans they had, to be with him.

"I'm glad you stopped by the office," he told Val as they walked to her car. "You know, addicts have to have their fixes, and I was starting to experience withdrawal symptoms."

When Val stopped at her Corsica and turned to face him, a question in her eyes, Eric explained. He lowered his head and took a taste of what he needed.

"Maybe that'll be enough to see me through the afternoon," he said.

Val smiled. "Let me make sure you have enough." With that, she kissed him. Greedy, hungry, hot.

Eric hugged her close. "You're a sweet addiction, Valentine."

He helped her in the car, then closed her door. Val powered the window down. "See you in a few hours."

"I'll be counting the minutes," Eric said.

He stood in the parking lot, watching her car. The crisp air finally compelled him to go back inside.

Eric found Netanya at her desk. He came around her desk, pulled her up, and hugged her. "Netanya, Netanya. Where in the world were you hiding Val?"

Netanya hugged him back, then watched as Eric went around her desk and plopped in one of the deep, comfortable chairs. "I take it you're pleased."

Eric closed his eyes and shook his head. "That doesn't even begin to describe it. Val is everything I have ever hoped for and dreamed of in a woman."

He reached into his coat pocket and pulled a small jeweler's box from a bag. He opened the box and showed it to Netanya.

"Oh, my God! Eric, that's fabulous. It's for Val?"

Eric nodded.

"Eric, don't you think you're moving a bit too fast? I mean, you just met her. You two haven't really had a chance to get to know each other."

"We spent most of the weekend together."

A delicately arched eyebrow rose at that comment.

"Don't worry. I know she's one of your friends. I didn't do anything dishonorable. As a matter of fact, we spent the time laughing, talking, and getting to know each other."

"But still, Eric. It's just been a few days. That," she said, indicating the jeweler's box, "is a major commitment. How do you know it's right?"

Eric closed the box and tucked it back in the bag. His smile, tender and poignant, spoke volumes. "I know it right here," he said, placing a hand over his heart. "And I know it right here," he said, tapping a finger to his head.

"Speaking of which," Netanya said, indicating the fading scrape at his temple. "What happened to you?"

Eric laughed and told Netanya about the incident at the police station and then the arcade.

"If she still wants to see you after all that, it must be love."

"We're getting together tonight and tomorrow," he said.

"Tomorrow's her birthday, Eric."

He smiled. "I know."

"She doesn't care much for Valentine's Day."

"I know."

Netanya eyed his devilish grin. "What are you up to?"

"I'm celebrating Val's day in a big way this year."

"That a fact?"

"Umm-hmm. When I'm finished, Val will love the idea of her birthday and Valentine's Day falling together."

Netanya came around the desk and patted Eric on the back. "You just be good to her."

Eric nodded. Then he pulled Netanya into his lap. Wrapping his arms about her waist, he kissed her quickly on the lips. "Thank you," he said quietly. "Thank you for introducing me to Val. For recognizing and understanding through the years my desire to meet a real woman, not just some husband-seeker who comes to us with a desire to wave a magic wand over her, whisper a few incantations and produce Mr. Right. I've waited a long time to find Val. It was worth the wait."

Netanya disengaged herself from his embrace and stood up. "Eric, the men and women we counsel aren't all like some of the people you met back when you were an escort. I would have hoped that you understood that after all the years we've been doing this. Every woman who walks through our doors isn't hard up."

Eric's expression remained dubious.

"As a matter of fact," Netanya continued, "every one of them isn't even here willingly. Some come with friends just to see what we're about."

Eric stood up. "We've been through this before, Netanya. I don't have anything against those women. They just aren't for me. And I'm glad, truly glad, that Val isn't one of them."

Netanya couldn't meet his eye. She instead turned back to her desk and absently picked up a piece of paper. "What would you do if she were?"

Eric chuckled. "You always like to play what if? Well, as you know, that doesn't apply in this case, so the question is irrelevant." He glanced at his watch. "We have an appointment with that producer in about fifteen minutes."

Netanya bit her lip and turned back to him. She'd let the issue slide for now. But in actuality, it was out of her hands, and she knew it. Val and Eric's relationship would work or it wouldn't. But still she worried as their conversation turned to the upcoming meeting with a television producer interested in a cable-access Match Made in Heaven program.

Later that night Val and Eric sat in the theater, munching popcorn while waiting for the trailers to begin. People filed into the theater and found seats while Eric and Val talked.

Val had been thinking about the physical differences between herself and Netanya. Val was large but shapely. She knew her legs to be her best feature. Netanya, however—everything about her was coordinated loveliness. Did Eric really prefer that?

"Netanya is very pretty," Val observed.

Eric sat up and looked at her, his expression curious and for a moment puzzled. Then he sat back, thoughtful.

"I've always hated pink because my parents force-fed it to me growing up."

Eric relaxed and smiled. Val was talking about clothes. "That's her trademark. The pink. She's been wearing pink and combinations thereof just about as long as I've known her, and that's been a while. You should see her closets."

Val looked at Eric, her expression curious now. What would he know about her closets? Then she remembered how Eric and Netanya had huddled together at the reception Saturday night. The looks they'd shared then, and even earlier today at their office, had been tender. The kind only two people who shared a special bond would have.

"You two are very close," she said, posing the question as a statement.

"She means the world to me."

Eight

Val vowed not to ask him, but the question needed asking. Its answer could determine where, if anyplace at all, this romance, or whatever it was, with Eric was headed.

"Do you love her?" she asked quietly.

"In more ways than I'd ever be able to express."

Val would have asked him to try expressing a couple of those ways, but the houselights dimmed, signaling that the previews and the feature film were about to begin. By his own admission, Eric was a romantic. Netanya Gardner was romance and femininity personified to the nth degree. Like Eric, her business was romance. Val really wanted to dislike the woman, but she couldn't. Netanya, gentle, sweet soul that she was, had been friendly and helpful from the very first.

Val couldn't compete with the years-long commitment they had to each other. If Eric knew the intimate contents of the woman's closet, there had to be more to their relationship than friendship. They'd had years to cultivate their romance. And here Val was falling in love with the man.

Falling in love?

Val took in his chiseled profile, the one bushy eyebrow she could see from where she sat next to him, the smooth skin. She glanced down at the large, well-formed hands that had stroked her until she whimpered. Those physical things she appreciated, but she also liked his easy smile, his gentle but sometimes wicked humor, his love of fun, and the proud way he carried himself.

Falling in love? Yes, and with a man who loved another woman.

While Eric and the other people in the audience laughed at the highlights of a movie preview, Val felt positively glum.

But, she reasoned as the opening credits to the romantic comedy began, if Eric loved Netanya, why was he out with her? They have an open relationship, the voice of doubt quickly supplied.

She sighed. Seeing no use in fretting over the issue right then, Val decided to sit back and try to enjoy the film. She'd talk to him about it after the show.

In the darkened theater Eric's hand sought hers. He weaved his fingers through hers and gently squeezed her hand.

Maybe everything would be all right, Val thought. She then turned her full attention to the movie.

About two hours later they left the cinema laughing and chatting about the movie. By mutual agreement they'd decided to see two films, Eric's romantic comedy first, then Val's action-adventure. They had forty-five minutes to kill before the next showing and decided to grab a bite to eat at a rotisserie chicken restaurant adjacent to the theater.

Settled at their table, Val steeled herself to ask him about Netanya. But before she could articulate the question in her head and get it out of her mouth, Eric picked up their earlier conversation.

"I never did finish answering your question about my definition of romance," he said. Eric broke off a piece of a sweet corn muffin and contemplated Val. He smiled easily. "I've given it some thought."

"And?"

"And romance is what each person makes it. If two people madly in love think it's romantic to walk in the rain, wallow in the mud together, or rob a bank together, it's romance."

"Rob a bank? That's not romantic, that's criminal."

"But maybe the criminal couple considers it romantic."

Val was having trouble with the concept. "And what if the two people's notions of romance differ?"

Eric thought about that for a moment. "I don't know. Tell me your definition of romance."

She realized with a wry smile that she didn't have one. "I think I'm deficient in that department. I *know* I'm deficient in that department. For so long, Eric, I've been bombarded with the idea that my name and my birthday automatically signified I'd be a romantic. If anything, those assumptions helped reinforce the fact that I'm not."

She looked away shyly, then peeped at him. "It wasn't until yesterday that I realized how pretty pink roses are," she said quietly.

Eric picked up her hand and placed a kiss in her palm.

They ate for a few minutes. Then Eric wiped his mouth with a napkin. "How is it you're single?"

"I was wondering the same thing about you," she said.

"You first."

Val smiled. "I guess I'm one of those women who looked up one day and realized I'd forgotten something. After college I was so busy trying to find myself and my place in the world that I didn't even consider marriage. It wasn't until recently," she said, "that I began missing what I didn't have."

Eric gazed in her eyes. "Recently?"

Val simply nodded.

Eric shifted in his seat. "I've been so busy building up my business that I didn't even consider it. Until recently," he added. "I've always known I'd get married, have children. I just didn't write it on the goal sheets to check off along the way."

Val smiled. "How many kids do you want?"

Eric shrugged. "I never really thought about that either. I have this mental photograph of me, a wife, and children. There's no specific number, just more than one. What about you?"

"I'm an only child and I always missed not having brothers or sisters. So I've always favored a houseful, three, four, five. Whatever the market bears."

Eric smiled. "You'd be a terrific mom."

"How do you know?"

"Because you're a terrific lady."

Val smiled at the compliment.

"I like the idea of three, four, or five children," he said.

"Do you?"

Eric's expression was intent, masculine. She felt his gaze lower to her breasts, and Val wondered if he was thinking the same thought that crossed her mind. The notion of Eric's baby suckling at her breast didn't give her pause. It filled her with longing.

"We'd better head back to the theater," Eric said quietly.

Val nodded, rose, and took his hand.

∼

Later that night they stood in her doorway.

"Your shoot-'em-up film was good," he admitted.

"Told you."

"And what did you think of the romantic comedy?"

"It made me feel happy," she said. "I enjoyed tonight. Thank you."

"I'm glad. You should always be happy." Eric inserted her key into the lock and pushed the door open for her.

"I've agreed to spend my birthday with you. Where are we going?"

"It's a surprise. You can wait one more day."

Val gave him a saucy smile. "What about clothes? Do I need to spin a wheel to determine what to wear? Casual wear? Business attire?"

Eric laughed. "You'll get no clues from me. Dress special."

She eyed him speculatively. "What does that mean?"

Eric leaned over and kissed her on her cheek. "It means whatever you interpret special to mean."

"Hmm" was all she said.

Eric laughed. "I'll see you tomorrow."

"Eric," she said, taking his hand.

"Yes?"

Val leaned toward him. Capturing his chin in her soft hands, she kissed him slowly, tenderly on the lips. "Good night."

With that, she slipped in her door.

~

The one concession Val always made to her birthday was in taking the day off from work. She got up, dressed, and was about to start misting and watering her plants, when the doorbell rang.

She grinned.

When she opened the door, a floral delivery driver thrust a clipboard at her. "Happy Valentine's Day, ma'am."

Val signed the sheet and accepted the delivery. The package was covered in layers of dark green floral tissue. She brought it inside, placed it on the breakfast bar, and ripped the paper off.

"Oh!"

The elaborate flower arrangement consisted of an assortment of cut flowers, baby's breath, and greens. Val searched for the card. Eagerly, she opened the tiny envelope. She read the note and a puzzled frown marred her face.

The card simply read YOU. Val flipped it over, looking for more message. She then searched through the tissue paper and peered through the blooms, trying to find more information about the sender. She found nothing.

"What in the world does YOU mean?" she asked out loud. But the pretty flowers offered no response.

Val decided to leave the arrangement on the breakfast bar. She glanced at the note again, then placed it on the counter.

"YOU. Hmm."

Thinking about the card and the flowers, she completed watering the green plants and cutting back dead leaves. She'd just pulled out potting soil to transplant some cuttings, when her doorbell rang again.

"Hi, again," the floral driver said. Val signed the clipboard and accepted a small white box from him.

She had the box half open before she closed the door and got to the sofa. Tucked inside the box and protected by tissue paper was a mug with the words Pretty Woman scripted in calligraphy around the cup. A small assortment of herbal teas padded the box. Val found the card and opened it.

BRING

"What does BRING mean?" Val looked at the mug and the teas, then got up and carried the items and the small card to the breakfast bar.

"You bring. You bring what?"

Could the mystery packages be from Eric? Val couldn't quite imagine Shelley and Kalinda doing anything like this. She and her parents had a lunch appointment at twelve-thirty. Try as she might, she didn't believe her folks to be behind the presents. This just wasn't their style.

Val left the second card on the counter next to the first one. She turned on her stereo, then went back to puttering with her plants. An hour later, at eleven o'clock, the doorbell rang. Val glanced at the gifts on her counter, then went to the door.

This time she didn't recognize the delivery person.

"Miss Val Sanders?"

"Yes."

"Delivery for you. Sign here, please."

Val scrawled her name on the form, then accepted the vase full of daisies. The whimsical flowers made her smile.

The small white card, obviously the third in a series, read SUNSHINE,. Val looked at the comma after the word and tried to figure out the odd punctuation. With a delicate finger she gently touched the edge of a daisy, then placed the vase on the counter area near the sink. The card she carried to the breakfast bar. But before she could settle on a barstool, the doorbell rang.

Val laughed out loud. "This is great!"

The new arrangement had an obvious Valentine's Day theme. A balloon with HAPPY BIRTHDAY/HAPPY VALENTINE'S DAY on it was tucked into the display, as were red paper hearts.

Val placed the arrangement on an end table in the living room. She found herself unaccountably pleased to read not a solitary bold word on the card but a cheery birthday and Valentine's Day greeting from her folks. If Eric was indeed behind the earlier deliveries, he'd steered clear so far of the Valentine's Day theme. She liked that.

Half an hour later she was ironing the blouse she'd wear to the lunch appointment with her parents, when the doorbell rang yet again.

"You must have done something awfully special," the delivery driver said, as he handed her the clipboard.

Val laughed. "No. It's my birthday."

"No fooling. That's nice to have a birthday on Valentine's Day," he said as he traded the clipboard for a medium-size gold-colored box.

"This doesn't look like flowers," Val said, accepting the box.

The man shrugged. "They just pay me to do deliveries. I don't question the contents."

"Let me get you something for your trouble," Val said.

"Nosiree, ma'am. That's been taken care of. You have a good one. And happy birthday to you."

"Thank you." Val closed the door and went to the sofa.

Hidden inside the box were sinfully delicious Godiva chocolates. "Oh, Eric, you do know the way to a woman's heart," Val said as she selected a chocolate and bit into it.

The card read JOY.

"Okay, Val. The mystery sentence now reads: You bring sunshine, joy,. At least the punctuation makes a little more sense."

Val picked up the telephone and called Shelley. When she got her friend's answering machine, she remembered Shelley was at work. Valentine's Day wasn't a holiday that closed down the college where Shelley was on the faculty.

Val left a message. "Call me when you get in. You are not going to believe what Eric has been doing all morning."

Before Val left for lunch with her parents, she received two more deliveries. A golden pothos plant with a big yellow bow arrived with the card AND. And the word LAUGHTER accompanied a plush white teddy bear clutching a balloon that read "For your special day."

Since her cards now read YOU BRING SUNSHINE, JOY, AND LAUGHTER, Val couldn't determine if the message had ended. Just in case, she asked the parcel driver to hold any other deliveries that might come until she returned from her appointment.

She almost canceled out on her parents just to see what else might arrive at her condo. But she didn't.

"Darling," her mother said over dessert. "We have a wonderful surprise for you. Well, actually two," her mother said, glancing at Quentin and smiling.

"Turning thirty is a milestone," Quentin Sanders said. "And it should be treated like one."

"We wanted to get something for you that you'd always keep and remember."

"So we bought you memories," Quentin said.

Val's confusion was evident. "Memories?"

Naomi smiled as Quentin handed Val a gaily wrapped slim package. The balloons tied to the back of her chair bobbed as Val pushed the chair back a bit to open the package in her lap. It was awfully light.

She glanced up at her parents, then ripped through the wrapping. Val opened the lid of the box and peered at a thin layer of tissue. Pulling it back, she lifted an envelope from the box. A photograph of a to-die-for sunset scene off a beach was imprinted on the top of the envelope. Val glanced up at her parents, who beamed at her.

"Go ahead, darling. Open it," Naomi said.

Val opened the envelope. Her eyes widened and she clasped a hand over her mouth. "Oh, my God. Mom, Dad! Are you serious?"

Naomi grinned and shook her head. "Do you like it?"

"Like it? I love it!"

The envelope held airline tickets, destination: Hawaii.

"But how, why?" Val said, alternately looking at the tickets and at her beaming parents.

"Darling, we've been saving for this for you for years. Your father and I wanted your thirtieth birthday to be very, very special. We spent a beautiful week there before you were born. Hawaii is a place for beautiful memories. Happy birthday, darling."

Val's eyes got damp. She got up and hugged both her parents. "This is very, very nice. Thank you."

"We thought about someplace like Jamaica," Quentin said. "But these days, people go there for weekend getaways. We wanted you to be able to see someplace a little more exotic. The trip's for two, so take who you will with you."

"Oh, Dad. This is wonderful. Thank you both so much." Val dabbed her napkin at the corner of her eye.

Quentin glanced at Naomi. "We have another surprise for you."

Val took her seat and shook her head. "This is more than I ever would have imagined. You can't top this," she said, holding up the ticket envelope.

Naomi handed her another box. This one didn't have wrapping paper on it.

Val eyed her parents. "What is it?"

"Open it and see."

Val opened the box and lifted out a sheet of paper, a photocopy of some sort. Val read the paper.

"Oh, my God!" This time her exclamation drew the curious glances of people at nearby tables. "You two got married! I don't believe it. My parents got married."

Val was out of the chair in a flash and hugging her mother, then her father.

Naomi held out her left hand for Val to see. A stunning diamond anniversary ring was in the place where her wedding band used to be. Val hadn't even noticed.

"When? Where? How?" was all Val got out.

"Last night," Naomi said.

"This morning," Quentin said at the same time.

The couple looked at each other, then smiled and cuddled. Val went back to her chair. As they all sat, she reached a hand across the table to again look at her mother's ring. She never would have guessed that her parents were even thinking of getting back together. After years and years of living apart, living separate lives, why this and why now?

But as Val took in the beaming faces of her parents, she couldn't begrudge them their renewed happiness.

"We wanted to get married on Valentine's Day," Naomi said.

"So we did. Just a stroke after midnight," Quentin explained. Then, with eyes only for Naomi, he added, "I love your mother very, very much. Sometimes it takes being apart to realize just how deeply your love goes."

Val shook her head. "You two are really something. I mean, I know you got together from time to time. I just figured you remained friends. How did you manage to pull this off without me knowing?" she asked with a smile.

Naomi and Quentin shared a smile that only two lovers could understand. "Sometimes you're given a second chance to make things right," Naomi said.

"I don't think we ever stopped loving each other," Quentin added. "We just stopped communicating and let little issues become huge obstacles in our relationship."

Naomi patted her husband's hand. "But we know better now, right?"

In answer, Quentin leaned forward and kissed his wife on the cheek. "You're my sunshine and my stars."

Val's eyes widened as she thought about something. "You gave me your honeymoon. I can't take this," she said, offering her birthday present back to her mother.

"No, darling. Hawaii is yours. I meant it when I said we've been planning that for you for some time."

"But you need to go on a second honeymoon," Val protested.

"We are," Quentin said. "We're just postponing it a bit."

Naomi's smile was charming, girlish. "Your father's taking me to Paris in the spring."

Val's mouth dropped open. Then she clapped her hands delightedly. "I'm very, very happy for the two of you."

Just then a raucous group of waiters and waitresses descended on the table with a birthday cake and a loud off-key rendition of the birthday song.

～

When Val pulled into her parking spot at her condo a couple of hours later, she juggled balloons, the two small gift boxes, a box with birthday cake in it, and a birthday/Valentine's Day present from the kids at the community center. Their party had been fun.

Val made her way to her mailbox, opened it, and stuffed the handful of envelopes in her coat pocket. February 14 had dawned cool and clear. It had warmed up considerably through the day.

"Need a hand with any of that?"

Val looked over at her old friend the floral delivery guy. She laughed. "More flowers?" She made her way up the stairs with the driver following her.

"More something," he said. "I have a two o'clock delivery for you and this one, a three o'clock." It was well after three, almost four.

At her door, Val put the cake box down so she could get the key in the lock. She deposited everything on the dinette table and wrapped the streamers from the balloons over the back of a chair. She then signed for the two deliveries and thanked the driver.

The two o'clock turned out to be a lovely dish garden assortment of green plants. The card said TO. The word MY accompanied a hibiscus. Val spent a few moments deciding where to place the plants, then went to look at the collection of cards on the counter.

"You bring sunshine, joy, and laughter to my. What's the next word, Eric? I know this is all from you."

Val collected the teddy bear that she'd decided to call Joy and the mail from her coat pocket, then settled on the sofa. Birthday cards from friends and even a couple of clients constituted most of the mail. She laughed out loud as she read the gag cards from Shelley and Kalinda.

Val's gaze wandered over the pink roses Eric had sent and then at all the delightful deliveries that could have come only from him. She smiled.

"This turning-thirty business is all right." She got the boxes from her parents and looked at them. The Hawaii trip consisted of round-trip airfare for two and then seven nights at a resort hotel. Val shook her head. Her parents were really something else.

She conceded to herself that their remarriage might not have come as such a surprise to her if, like Eric, she viewed the world through the eyes of a romantic.

As a matter of fact, she rather liked Eric's notion of romance, it was, well . . . romantic. She carried Joy, the teddy bear, with her to her bedroom.

Eric had advised that she wear something special. Val rifled through her closet for a few moments, then her gaze fell on the perfect outfit. She pulled the red suit out and held it up to her. The suit, with its leopard-print cuffs and collar, was trim and elegant. The short skirt that fell to just above her knees would accent her legs. Val selected a high-heeled red sling and held the shoe up to the suit.

"Perfect."

She slipped the suit hanger over a hook on the door and then selected large gold earrings.

The doorbell rang.

She smiled and almost tripped over herself getting to the door. Then she stopped, ran back to her bedroom, and pulled a ten-dollar bill from her wallet.

"Package for you," the delivery guy intoned dryly. But he couldn't hide his smile.

Val signed for it, handed him the tip with a look that said "Don't even try to not accept," and accepted the box. This one had some weight to it.

"How many more are coming?" she asked.

The driver smiled, shrugged, then tipped his hat to Val and went back to his van.

Val placed the box on the coffee table, then dug in.

"Oh, Eric. It's lovely," she whispered as she pulled a delicate music box from the wrapping paper. She wound the back and opened the lid. The lilting, tender melody of "As Time Goes By" floated over her. Val swallowed hard but couldn't stop the tears that gathered at her eyes. The fundamental things in life did apply, and she finally knew what it was her parents had discovered so many years earlier on an escalator, the very thing they'd rediscovered in each other: love.

Val loved Eric Fitzgerald, heart and soul, mind and body. It didn't matter that they'd just recently met. It didn't matter that they had been introduced through a matchmaking service. What mattered was love. Is that what he had been trying to tell her?

Val rewound the music box and hummed along. "Well, I might disagree with the kiss part. A kiss from Eric is like no other."

She searched in the box and sure enough, a small white card had a single word on it. LIFE.

Val carried the card to the counter and read the complete message.

YOU BRING SUNSHINE, JOY, AND LAUGHTER TO MY LIFE.

She felt blissfully happy. The feeling intensified when it dawned on her that Eric had gone through a lot of trouble to make the day special for her. And there was more to come, the night lay ahead. Val hugged herself.

The day called for pampering. She gathered the music box up and took it to her bathroom. In her bedroom she pulled out hose and silky, sexy undergarments. Val drew a luxurious bubble bath and was just about to step into it, when the doorbell rang.

She slipped a caftan over her head and went to the door.

"You again," she told the driver.

The routine well in place now, she signed for the huge arrangement of red roses. Val carried the flowers straight to the bathroom and put the vase on the ledge of her big whirlpool tub. She wound the music box up, stepped out of the caftan, and slipped into the tub. Reaching up, she plucked the card from the roses, then settled back amid the mountain of bubbles. The card read: Happy Birthday, Val. He'd signed it Love, Eric.

Val smiled in contentment.

Life was good. Love was grand. And the future she and Eric might have would unfold as time went by.

Nine

When her doorbell rang again, Val knew she'd find Eric on her doorstep. She did. And he looked good enough to eat. The single-breasted smoke-gray suit made him look distinguished. The thin sage and periwinkle stripes in his shirt accented the tie at his neck. Clothes didn't make the man, but Eric sure made clothes look good. Val liked his style. And his smile.

"Good evening, gorgeous. And happy birthday."

"Hi. You look great."

Eric stepped in and snaked a hand around her waist. "You look absolutely divine. May I?"

"May you what?"

But Val recognized his intent as his head lowered to hers. When Eric finally got his fill, he smiled at her, the smile just as intimate as the kiss had been.

"I don't think I want to leave," Val murmured.

Eric's dark eyes flashed. Val was tempting him in ways she probably didn't even realize. She didn't know how partial he was to red. When she'd opened the door in that fire-engine-red suit, he wanted one thing: to see her out of it. He wondered if Val would be as wild and as sleek as the leopard at her collar and cuffs. He longed to pull the pins and combs out of her hair and run his hands through it.

But tonight, tonight was Val's night. He'd managed to control himself this long, he'd manage again. But there was one thing he couldn't resist—he had to hold her again.

Eric ran one large palm from her waist to her thigh. Her delicious ample curves made him break out in a fine sweat. He brought her hips flush with his. Val wrapped her arms around his waist.

"You are beautiful," he said against her lips.

He felt Val's smile at his mouth. "Thank you."

"I think we better leave now," he said. "Things are really starting to heat up."

"I think you're right."

Val reached for her small handbag and a winter wrap.

"Your chariot awaits, mademoiselle."

Eric turned off the lights and led her down the stairs.

A late-model sapphire limousine awaited them. The driver opened the door as Eric and Val approached.

"Eric! This is for me? I've never been in a limousine."

Eric handed her into the car. "Then tonight, sweet Valentine, is your night."

The driver closed the door behind them. They settled in, and Eric handed her a single red rose.

Val inhaled the heady scent. "This is beautiful. And thank you for all the surprises today. It's been fabulous."

Eric pressed a button and the gentle instrumental refrains of "As Time Goes By" filled the car's inner chamber.

Val turned to him with a trembly smile. "Oh, Eric. This is so romantic."

"You're not supposed to cry," he said, taking a handkerchief from his inside coat pocket and dabbing at her eyes.

"This has all been so beautiful. Thank you."

Eric gathered her in his arms. In his rich baritone he softly sang the words of the song to Val as they made their way to their dinner destination.

When they arrived in Williamsburg about half an hour later, Eric showed her into a restaurant. When Val recognized the building, she buried her head in his shoulder for a moment.

"This is my absolute favorite restaurant in the world. How did you know?"

Eric simply smiled as they were led to an intimate table for two.

Through seven courses they talked and laughed and shared with each other. When the last dishes were taken away, a waiter materialized with a bottle of champagne.

"I thought you didn't drink."

"This is a celebration. Every celebration should have a toast," he said.

Val smiled and picked up the delicate crystal flute. "Eric! Oh, my God."

Draped around Val's glass was a stunning diamond and gold link bracelet.

With hands that trembled, Val unclasped the bracelet. The diamonds shimmered in the candlelight. Eric took the jewelry and secured it to Val's arm.

"Happy birthday, Valentine."

She gulped hard, a hot tear trickling down her cheek. Eric wiped it away with the pad of a finger.

"Eric, you shouldn't have."

"You deserve this and more, Val. Tell me these tears are of joy and not something else."

Val managed a smile. "You do bring me joy, Eric. Thank you."

Eric poured the champagne. "A toast, then. To Valentine, an intelligent, beautiful woman who stirs my heart and fires my soul. Happy birthday."

Much later that night, Val realized something: Turning thirty had been downright spectacular. A gentleman Prince Charming to the very end, Eric had seen her home, kissed her good night, and left with the limousine.

Val drifted to sleep with the diamond bracelet still on her arm, Joy the teddy bear at her side, and a single red rose on her pillow.

⁓

When day dawned, Val fully expected the lovely fantasy to have been nothing more than an elaborate dream. Maybe she'd gotten her earlier wish to go to sleep on February thirteenth and awaken the fifteenth. But the cool fire at her wrist told her differently. Each double link in the bracelet joined the next with three diamonds. Val glanced at the cute stuffed teddy bear.

Val threw her legs over the bed and padded to the bathroom. If she'd needed any extra proof that Wednesday, the previous day, had been one to remember, there on the ledge of the whirlpool were both a huge arrangement of red roses and a pretty music box. Val wound the box and listened to the sentimental tune as she brushed her teeth and washed her face.

She lingered in the shower, then dressed, ate, and selected one of the flower arrangements to sit atop her desk as she went to work. When she turned to consult her appointment book, Val couldn't find the slim volume. After searching the desk, her purse, and even the car, she remembered. She'd left it at the receptionist's counter at A Match Made in Heaven.

Val called the service to ensure that the daybook was there. She then made as many calls as she could remember she had to before venturing out to greet the day and pick up her appointment book.

When Val arrived at the dating service office she was just in time to see Netanya Gardner stretching on tiptoe to remove the cupids dangling from the ceiling. Netanya sported pink stirrup pants and a pink baseball-type shirt. Val, who'd taken extra pains to look nice on the off chance of seeing Eric, felt positively matronly compared to Netanya. The long sleeves, long skirt, and relative shapelessness of the empire-style dress she wore made her wonder how high she'd score on the frumpiness scale. Netanya, on the other hand, looked as dainty and sweet as ever—even in casual wear.

Without reservation Eric admitted he loved this woman. Though the timing, the ambience, and the moment had been right, he'd spoken no love words to Val the previous evening. He'd been gentle, kind, loving, and abundantly generous with his gifts and his time, but not once did he mention anything lasting. Because his heart belonged to Netanya? Had she up and fallen in love with a man who was in love with another woman? Had his mission simply been the challenge to make Val believe in romance? If that were the case, Eric successfully completed the mission and earned bonus points along the way. He'd shown her in myriad ways over the past few days the many different ways romance could be expressed and enjoyed. But for him, had it all been simply an inventive challenge?

Val cleared her throat. "Ms. Gardner?"

Netanya turned around in mid-stretch. "Val, how nice to see you. I have your daybook. Just a sec."

Netanya captured the last cupid, then, with a hand from Val, she scrambled down from the top of the receptionist's counter.

"Thanks," she said, dusting her hands on her pants. "Come this way. It's in my office."

As Val followed Netanya, the other woman explained her attire. "Today's a half day for us, so I'm here trying to get some things done and some paperwork taken care of." Netanya walked into her office and motioned for Val to have a seat.

"The week right before Valentine's Day is one of, if not the busiest week we have. It's right up there with New Year's Eve. People don't want to be alone. We're always closed on Valentine's Day. Then we give the staff another half-day's rest before the second rush starts."

"What's the second rush?" Val asked.

Netanya gave a small smile. "The people who realized they were alone for Valentine's Day and decide that's not going to happen again. So they make appointments with us. We'll be pretty steady for the next two or three weeks, then it will ebb off and balance out."

"You've been doing this for a long time," Val observed.

Netanya nodded as she put the cupids in a box that held other Valentine's Day theme decorations, then sat at her desk. "Yes. Eric and I have been together eleven years. He'd been working by himself for about a year before I joined him."

"The two of you seem very . . . close," Val said.

Netanya smiled. "We are. Eric is terrific."

Netanya watched Val's face fall, and wondered what she'd said wrong. Val sat in the chair, her hands folded in her lap, looking dejected and to some degree defeated. It took Netanya a minute, and then she put two and two together.

"Val," she said softly.

When Val raised her eyes to meet Netanya's, Netanya placed a hand over Val's folded ones and squeezed. "Val, you don't understand."

Val nodded once. "I understand," she said. "You two have a very long history together, and it's quite obvious you love each other."

An indulgent answering smile was Netanya's first response. "Yes, you're right. I do love him, but I'm not in love with him. Val, I'm in a committed relationship."

Netanya opened a desk drawer and pulled out a heart-shaped pink and white ceramic photo frame. She handed the photograph to Val. "Yes, I love Eric. I love him as a dear friend and brother. My heart, though, belongs to someone else."

Val glanced down at the picture. Netanya and an equally attractive woman smiled at the camera. So obvious was the friendship between the two that they could have been sisters or best friends. Val looked up at Netanya.

"Do you understand?" Netanya quietly asked.

Val nodded. She looked at the picture again then at Netanya as she passed the photograph back to her.

Netanya placed the frame on the edge of the desk near them. "Eric and I met back in the days when I couldn't deal with issues that were important to my own well-being. I hired him as an escort one weekend to play out a little drama for my family. I've long since stopped the fiction, and my family has come to grips with who and what I am. Eric and I, we've been friends ever since. When he told me he'd started a matchmaking service, I offered him a few suggestions. Before long, we'd teamed up."

"So what this means . . ." Val started to say.

"Is I'm no threat to you," Netanya finished. "The only threat to you is if you don't hold on to Eric and never let him go. I knew soon after I met you that you were special. I wanted the two of you to meet."

Val nodded. "Thank you for being candid."

Netanya smiled as she slipped the photograph back into her desk. "Some things aren't generally known," she said.

The two women looked at each other. Val assessed all that she'd just been told. Val nodded. By unspoken agreement, a bond had been formed between the two.

"Well, I'd better go. I have to be at court this afternoon," Val said as she stood to leave.

Netanya extended her hand to Val. But Val ignored it and hugged Netanya. "Thank you."

Val swung the strap of her bag over her shoulder and moved toward the door.

"Hey, Val."

Val turned back to Netanya, who held a small leather volume.

"You forgot your appointment book."

Val shook her head, smiled, and accepted the book. "Thanks."

Netanya turned her attention back to the stack of papers on her desk.

Later that afternoon Eric breezed into her office. Netanya was gone for the day, but had left a message for him that he could find a draft of the company's new marketing and promotion plan on her desk. Eric spied the stack of papers, picked them up, and went to his own office to review the material.

But what he found tucked in the middle, in an innocent-looking little file folder, made him tinge the room blue with profanity. He punched Netanya's home number out on his telephone.

"You think this is funny, don't you?" he accused her when she answered. "Well, I don't care for your meddling, Netanya. I found Val's service folder on your desk. Did you set me up to prove some point?"

Eric listened to her response for a moment. "Yeah, you do that. I'll be here. I can't wait to hear how you're going to clean this up. And here I thought I was in love with Val."

Eric slammed the telephone down. He then dialed Val's number. Her voice on the answering machine made his gut clench. Eric left a terse message canceling the tentative plans they'd made to get together. He paused, then added the ultimate kissoff, "See you around."

Eric paced his office as he waited for Netanya to return.

"I should have known it was too good to be true. I should have known *she* was too good to be true," he railed.

Netanya had coached Val well, so well that Eric had never even suspected that it had all been a setup.

By the time Netanya arrived back at the office, Eric was so angry and worked up that she would swear she could see the steam pouring from his ears. But Netanya knew she could hold her own in a one-on-one with Eric. She just hoped he'd be able to see reason and not throw away the best thing that had ever happened to him.

"Eric?"

He turned away from the window view of the outside courtyard when he heard her. "Why'd you lie to me, Netanya?"

"I've never lied to you, Eric."

Eric paced the length of his office. "You said Val was one of your friends. I took you for your word, when all along she was just another lonely heart."

"I never told you that, Eric. You assumed she was a friend of mine. Sit down, you're making me nervous with all that pacing."

Eric glared at her, but he sat in the chair opposite Netanya's. "She's a client."

"No, she's not," Netanya said. "But even if she were, if you love her . . ." Netanya stared at him pointedly, but Eric looked away, refusing to answer the question. Netanya sighed. "If you love her, it shouldn't matter where or how you met."

"It matters to me," he said.

"Val Sanders walked through our doors last Saturday with two of her girlfriends. As a birthday present, the friends gave her a gift certificate for our services. I saw Val and immediately thought of you. I counseled her and she made it abundantly clear that she had no desire to participate."

Eric hopped up and grabbed a videotape from his desk. "Then what's this?" he asked. "People who don't want to participate leave. They say 'no thanks' and walk out the door. They don't make introduction videos."

Netanya sighed. "She did it to humor her friends, Eric. The entire package was a gift to her from her girlfriends. She went along with it for their sake. She came back a couple of days later to cancel."

"Umm-hmm," Eric said sarcastically. He remained unconvinced. "And how did you pull off the meeting at the reception Saturday night?"

"Eric, will you please get it through your head. This wasn't some sort of conspiracy. That meeting happened by accident, by providence."

"You two sure were chummy."

Netanya had the grace to flush. "I admit, Eric, I knew how you felt about women who use a dating service and I deliberately left that out of the introduction."

Eric nodded. "Right. You lied to me."

"I've never . . ."

Eric waved a hand. "We're splitting hairs here, Netanya, and you know it."

Netanya got up and came to stand at his side. With a hand on his shoulders she looked him in the eye. "Eric, you know I love you and want the best for you. I've never done anything to intentionally hurt you. I know how you feel about our clients. I'm sorry you hold that opinion, because you do them and yourself a disservice. Where Val is concerned, you told me just two days ago that she was the one. You ran out and bought the biggest diamond you could find. If you love her, I don't see how the facts surrounding how you met has anything to do with it."

She cupped his cheek with her small hand. "If you're going to throw away a perfect love for a reason like that, you're a foolish man and not the person I thought you were."

With that, Netanya took the tape from his hands and left his office.

∼

Much later Eric sat in his office. All of the agency's employees were long gone. It was dark outside and still Eric sat there, silently fuming. He'd searched for the videotape, but Netanya had apparently taken it with her.

Could she be telling the truth? He'd never known her to lie to him before.

He thought of Val's smile. Her delight in the gifts he'd given her. The fun they'd shared at the arcade and playing Monopoly at his house.

He picked up the telephone and called her. When he got the answering machine again, he slammed the receiver down and went home.

~

Friday night, Val wondered what had happened to Eric. The day before, she'd gotten an angry message from him on the machine. The message didn't really make sense, and in all honesty, it kind of ticked her off, particularly when the caller identification feature on her telephone indicated he'd called again, from work, but didn't leave a message. What was that all about?

She'd waited to hear from him, waited for an explanation. Tied up in a legal proceeding most of the day, she did not get the chance to call him at the A Match Made in Heaven office.

Val opened the telephone book but didn't find a residential listing for Fitzgerald, Eric. She flipped pages forward and wasn't surprised to find Gardner, Netanya also missing. She dialed information, asked for Eric's number, and got the computer operator's message that the number was unpublished.

"Figures. They probably live together." But she remembered the conversation with Netanya. Eric's business partner didn't pose a threat to her.

Val misted the plants that needed attention, then selected a piece of chocolate from the box Eric had sent for her birthday.

When her business line rang a few minutes later, she was surprised at how relieved she felt. But it wasn't Eric on the other end. It was Shelley.

"Hey," Val said without much enthusiasm.

"What's wrong with you?"

"Well, it's a Friday night and I'm home. I hadn't exactly expected to be, so I'm sort of at loose ends."

"Where's Eric?"

Val frowned. "That's a good question."

"Hmm."

"Why'd you call this number?" Val asked, curious that Shelley would dial her office number instead of her personal line.

"Oh! I was calling to leave a message of where I'll be."

"And where are you going?"

"Out. Remember that too-fine brother who walked into the A Match Made in Heaven office when we were there Saturday?"

"Yeah, the real tall, gorgeous guy. He looked like a model."

"That's the one and he is. A model, I mean."

"And?"

"And you're not going to believe this. But he works at the university. How I'd never seen him before, I'm still trying to figure out. But I was in the bookstore, when he walked in. He's an artist, girl, and he has work on display in a couple of galleries."

"You're kidding, right?"

"I speak the truth. We're going to Virginia Beach tonight to an opening of one of his friends who sculpts." Shelley gave Val the address of the gallery.

"I don't know where we're going after that. But no need to worry. He's genuine."

Val shook her head and smiled. "Well, you have fun. Hey, before you go, have you heard from Kalinda?"

"She's out on a date."

"With whom?"

"Val, this one you *really* are not going to believe."

Val sat on one of the barstools. "What? I'm sitting down. Tell me."

"You know how Kalinda wanted to take a photo for the dating service newsletter at A Match Made in Heaven?"

"Umm-hmm."

"Well, she and the photographer hit it off. He's a single dad and they started talking about day care centers. His kid is with a sitter and the two of them are off somewhere."

"I don't believe it."

"I told you you weren't gonna believe it. But it's true. Val, I need to dash because Michael will be here in about fifteen minutes. Are you going to be around tomorrow? I *do* want to hear all about your birthday. I'm eager to find out what Eric was doing that was so exciting."

Val smiled and fingered the flowers on the counter. "It was divine. But I'll talk to you later. Have fun tonight."

Val rang off with Shelley. She made a pot of tea, found a book to read, and settled on the sofa with the sound of the television muted. Val's gaze wandered over the pink roses Eric had sent early in the week.

"Looks like I'm the only one who actually met someone the official A Match Made in Heaven way."

Ten

Saturday morning Val was doing laundry when her doorbell rang. She opened the door to a somber-looking Eric.

"Hi. What's wrong?"

"May I come in?"

"Sure." Val, puzzled at his aloofness, stepped aside to allow him in. As he walked by and into the living area, she shook her head in appreciation of the lithe, athletic grace of his walk. She also liked the back view of the jeans he wore.

"Mercy. There ought to be a law," she mumbled as she fanned herself with her hand and shut the door.

"Pardon the mess. It's laundry day. Can I get you something?"

"I'm fine." Eric smiled, then patted the sofa cushion next to where he sat. He shrugged out of his leather bomber jacket and placed it on the other side of him.

Val joined him. She tucked one jean-clad leg underneath her and faced him. She couldn't believe that she'd fallen in love with this man, this gentle but fun-loving man who'd walked into her life a mere seven days before. She understood at last, really understood, the appeal of Las Vegas wedding chapels and justice-of-the-peace weddings. The mental image scene of her parents' whirlwind courtship played out in her mind over the years finally made sense. Love was like that.

Eric turned to her. With one arm on the sofa back, he let his fingers trail through the edges of Val's hair. He realized with a start that he finally got to see her with her hair down. It fell to her shoulders in a profusion of soft curls.

"I owe you an apology," he said.

"An apology? What for? Wednesday was perfect. As you can see," Val said, waving a hand to encompass the area, "I almost ran out of space for all the deliveries."

Eric smiled as his fingers moved from her hair to her mouth. He traced her lips.

"I love you, Val," he said.

"Eric, I love you too. I think from the moment I saw you in the community center, part of me knew that. The other part struggled with the fact that we'd only just met. And when you kissed me, well, part of me was outraged. The other part knew I'd come home."

"That's how I felt when I met you, Val. I'd come home. You're the woman I didn't know I was searching for. And I almost lost you."

"What do you mean, you almost lost me?"

Eric stood up. Val planted both feet on the floor and watched him pace the area in front of her.

"I apologize for the ugly message I left on your machine," he said. "I was angry at the time."

Val crossed her arms. "I wondered about that. For a moment it sounded like a brushoff to me."

Eric stopped moving and looked at her. "It was."

Val crossed her legs. She knew she probably looked militant, but there wasn't much help for it. After falling in love with the man, was she to find out now that he had a vile temper?

Eric came and sat on the edge of a chair. Val turned to him and their knees brushed. The contact sent an electric current through her. Val tried to ignore it and lowered her arms.

"Ever since I started A Match Made in Heaven," he said, "I've had what Netanya calls a near phobia about the women who come through our doors. As a single man operating a matchmaking agency, sometimes it looked odd for me to be without a mate. Netanya and I played to that because she, well she . . ."

"She told me," Val said.

For a moment Eric looked surprised. "Hmm" was all he said though. "Netanya and I on more than one occasion have played the role of the happy couple because it was prudent and necessary for the viability of our business. Sometimes it was also to get rid of overzealous women who believed I was their match made in heaven and men who took one look at Netanya and started revising their wills."

"She's a very pretty lady," Val said, this time acknowledging the fact with no lingering jealousy or self-doubting thoughts.

Eric nodded. "Pretty meddlesome. Maybe that's why she's such a good matchmaker. And she doesn't even use the computers."

"What do you mean?"

"She told me how you came to the agency."

Val grinned. "Talk about meddlesome. My girlfriends who set the whole thing up as a birthday gift for me can be the epitome of meddlesome. I told you how I felt about love at first sight. I couldn't quite buy into what you and Netanya do for a living. You are efficient though. I have to give you that."

When Eric looked confused, Val explained. "We three, Shelley, Kalinda, and I, had just been to your office Saturday afternoon. And then Saturday evening Netanya introduced us. I'd thought it was all a paper-and-computer thing, but I like the personal touch you used."

Eric shook his head. "That's what I'm trying to tell you. When we met last Saturday, that wasn't an official A Match Made in Heaven introduction. That was Netanya operating as a free agent. I thought you were a friend of hers and therefore safe to date."

"Safe to date?" Val eyed him. Something in his tone made her wary. Had she finally found his fatal flaw?

His mouth twisted wryly. "That's as good a way as any to put it. I have a policy against dating women who come through the agency. I've always felt they were, well, too clinging, too desperate."

Val was getting the picture. Clinging and desperate. Is that how he viewed her? So, this *was* a brushoff. He'd just come to deliver it in person instead of over the telephone. She folded her arms again. "I came through your company."

Eric nodded, then leaned forward and took her hands in his. "When I found your file on Netanya's desk, I went through the roof. I left that message on your machine and blessed Netanya out. But after I came crashing down, I realized something."

"What?"

Eric tried to press a kiss in her palm, but Val pulled away from him. He captured her hand again. "Hear me out, Val. I want you to know exactly where I'm coming from."

He began drawing little curlicues in her hand with his thumb. "I love you. I love you with all my heart and soul. If I let you go because of some stupid hangup I have, it would be like cutting off my arm or taking away my sight."

"Why should it matter how or where we met? I'm grateful for Netanya's meddling, if that's what it was," she said.

"That's what I'm trying to tell you," he said. "I thought about it most of last night and I came to the conclusion that the only thing that matters is that we found each other."

Val swallowed hard. "So where do we go from here?"

Eric smiled. He got up and walked around the coffee table to sit next to Val on the sofa. He reached into his jacket pocket and pulled out a small box.

"This has been burning a hole in my pocket since I bought it Tuesday. In a fit of misplaced anger, I almost returned it Thursday. Something held me back though. That something was your love."

Val swallowed the lump in her throat. "What is it?" she asked, indicating the box.

He handed it to her. Val looked at him, then took the top off the white box. Inside was a small velvet box. "Eric, what is this?"

"Open it and see."

Val dumped the smaller box into her hand and opened the lid. A huge diamond on a slim gold band sparkled at her.

"I love you, Valentine Sanders. Will you marry me?"

"Marry you? Oh, Eric. Oh, Eric." Val's eyes misted and she started to cry.

"You're not supposed to cry when I give you things. If you do that, I might have to sell A Match Made in Heaven and start up a handkerchief factory, because I plan to shower you with gifts and with love for the next fifty or sixty years. If you'll have me," he added quietly.

"I love you, Eric. Now, as for marrying you . . ." Val paused.

She tried to remember all the reasons she had been opposed to quickie marriages. Suddenly she wasn't so sure what her big conflict had been. Her brows drew together as she searched her memory. Obviously, all those couples she met during the course of her workdays had no clue what true love was about. And besides, the couples she came in contact with were probably a small percentage of all the people out there.

Could any man make any woman as happy as Eric made her? With Eric, Val felt as if they had invented love . . . and romance. Surely no one else ever felt this way, as if all the stars in heaven were looking down and smiling.

She wiped the tears in her eyes, then gently caressed the side of Eric's face. Oh, how she loved this man who brought sunshine and joy to her life, this man who taught her that romance wasn't a day or a thing but a way of life. She and Eric would have a lifetime to get to know each other.

"Yes, Eric. I'll marry you."

Eric let go a breath he didn't realize he'd been holding. "You sure do know how to scare a man. For a moment there I thought you were going to say no."

Val shook her head. "No way, mister. You're mine."

"And you'll be my forever Valentine."

Val smiled and wrapped her arms around his neck. They fell back onto her sofa. Eric folded her in his arms. The kiss held promise and forever.

Eric grinned and spoke against her lips. "Shall we spin a wheel to determine if we get married at a church or at a drive-through wedding chapel?"

In answer, Val laughed and smothered him with kisses.

ABOUT THE AUTHOR

Award-winning journalist Felicia Mason lives in Yorktown, Virginia, and is the author of the bestselling BODY AND SOUL